TEETERING

TEETERING

a novel by
J. Marshall Freeman

rabbitfish editions

Printed in Canada

ISBN# 978-0-9952856-0-6

Rabbitfish Editions
14 Yarmouth Road
Toronto, ON
CANADA M6G 1W6

rabbitfishhello@gmail.com

Cover and interior design by J. M. Freeman
jmarshallfreeman.com

First Printing

To Béla, who wanders with me in the Witch's woods,
and always remembers to bring the pebbles.

Contents

Acknowledgements

Teetering would not exist were it not for my wonderful friends and family, who offered so much of their valuable time to help me bring the book to completion.

Thanks to Brian Barfoot, Jojo Careon, and Tim Rutter, who read each section as it was completed and provided me with invaluable course corrections. Additional readers included Michael Wright, Stephen Coderre, Dale Rosenberg, and members of the Toronto Writers' Co-operative.

Matthew Cook, Martin Cohen, Béla Hegedus, Stanley Freeman, and JM read the final draft and pointed out a host of small problems that had escaped my eye. Béla was the king of line editing, with Stanley and Martin his able courtiers.

Bruce Small and David Demchuk offered moral support and marketing advice, Ana Shepard gave me feedback on aerial silks performance, and Derick Yap and a squadron of Facebook friends told me everything I was doing wrong and sometimes right in my cover design.

Many thanks to John Miller whose tireless work makes the Toronto Writers' Co-operative the kind of inspirational community it has become for so many writers, including myself.

And finally, much gratitude to JM, who helped me to understand that I had the right to tell this story.

Part I:

The Best City in the World

CHAPTER 1

You know what's kind of a shame? That the universe doesn't send you email or text or anything when something important is about to happen. The message might say, " Everything in your life is going to change in the next 24 hours," with a footnote that reads, "and everything you thought you knew turns out to be totally wrong." But maybe it wouldn't make a difference. Maybe if any of us got a message like that, we would say "Oh, it's just spam," and carry on as usual.

On a sunny Wednesday morning, early in May, Barnabas Bopwright woke to a sharp knock on his bedroom door and one of his mother's inspiring morning greetings: "You're going to be late for school again!"

This abrupt wake-up call dragged him from a dream, and as he sat up groggily, it was hard to shake its lingering after-images. Crowds were cheering him as he floated over the City in a balloon. He waved in humble gratitude, excited by the unaccustomed attention. His best friend, Deni was beside him in the wicker basket and she was deeply unimpressed.

"If they knew just how short you really were..." she said, not altogether without sympathy, but still, it hurt.

He climbed out of bed and began searching the mess on his floor for some clothes he could wear to school. His computer abruptly woke up and alerted him to an incoming VidChat message. He leaned over his desk and accepted the call. His half brother, Thelonius appeared onscreen.

"Did you get it? Tracking says you got it."

"Oh! Yeah, it's here." Barnabas picked up the strange device from the floor beside his bed. "I was trying to figure out how it works last night, but I fell asleep."

"They're new. Already really popular here." *Here* meant Japan, where Thelonius was teaching English. The brothers VidChatted often, and sometimes the computer screen seemed to Barnabas like a strange Alice in Wonderland mirror. Everything on the far side of the screen was familiar, but oddly different. For instance, Thelonius was now munching on something that looked like a pepperoni stick, but it was entirely possible that it was made, for example, of seaweed. Thelonius gestured with the mystery food stick at the device in Barnabas' hand and said, "It's called a *diaboriku*. Can you figure out what it does?"

"Di-a-bo-ri-ku," Barnabas repeated carefully. "Can you give me a hint?" He turned the device around in his hands: It was around the size of a baseball, surprisingly heavy, and made of some shiny blue plastic. On one side was a small glass circle, like a camera lens, and on the opposite side was a larger lens. The smooth blue surface, like a still sea, was studded with islands — three rubbery green buttons and one red one — that were clustered in a grouping that seemed purposeful but was utterly mysterious.

Thelonius, half a world away, smiled with smug amusement. "Read the instructions, Beaner!"

"They're in Japanese! And don't call me that." His phone buzzed with an incoming TxtChat message. "That's Deni. Hold on a sec." He picked up the phone from his nightstand and read the screen.

agirlnameddeni> **We have a real camera!!!!!**

Barnabas swiftly thumbed his reply:

barnabustamove> **Where from?**

agirlnameddeni> **Just get to school. Don't be late. I'm serious.**

He looked at the time and swore. "Thelonius!" he shouted. "Got to rocket. Talk to you tonight?"

They signed off and Barnabas pulled off the underwear and t-shirt he slept in, adding them to the compost of laundry on the floor. Wrapping a towel around his waist, he hurried down the hall to the bathroom.

Deni's text was good news; the special guest at that morning's school assembly was Arthur Tuppletaub, the Mayor of the City. As videographer for the Journalism Club, it was Barnabas' responsibility to make the footage look good. He was glad he wouldn't have to use his camera phone for this important shoot (and, anyway, he had forgotten to charge it overnight again).

Thirty minutes later, with breakfast in his stomach and his backpack fully loaded, Barnabas took the elevator down 35 stories from his family's apartment and stepped into the endless rolling boil of the City. No matter how often Barnabas joined the morning rush, he still felt an electric thrill to be part of it all.

It was the best city in the world, at least that's what its inhabitants said. But the claim was easy to justify. Just walking down the crowded sidewalks, you could feel the special buzz. This was the city of ideas, of innovation, and on every street corner, debates broke out about Sports! Arts! Politics! Barnabas loved the beautiful discordant symphony, whose orchestra was made up of cars, jackhammers, shouts of laughter, and shouts of rage. He loved the smell of hot chilli chestnuts that the vendors sold, and he loved the crowds, marching down the sidewalks, heads held high, carrying their steaming cups of KonaBoom coffee and looking up to see the sun glinting off majestic towers that kissed the sky.

Barnabas had lived in the City for all of his 15 years and five months. He had ridden the subway alone since he was 12, and he knew that whole underground labyrinth by heart. He could tell you to take the Green Line to the Manhammer Audio Dome. He knew which end of the platform to stand on if you took the Purple Line to the Jumble Market. And if you were going to River's Edge Park on a Sunday morning to see the best skaters on Earth perform their death-defying moves, he knew it was better to get off at Caramello Station and walk back through the marina than to do the obvious and exit at River's Edge Station. In short, Barnabas wasn't one of those fakes from the endless suburbs across the river who just came in on weekends to hang out at the obvious tourist spots. No, he was the real thing: a true child of the City. What better life could there be?

He walked three blocks and descended into Kiletko Station, where he took a southbound Red Line subway to Rebbertrue Station and followed the shuffling crowd up a short staircase, round a corner, and down an escalator to the Yellow Line.

The Yellow Line, which ran parallel with the river, was the first to have the flashy new subways trains because it was the line that most tourists used. The train cars were like sleek silver fish, each equipped with state-of-the-art 3D info screens, whose eye-watering graphics flashed a non-stop, high-speed stream of news and ads.

The recorded station announcements on the Yellow Line featured a different woman than the one who narrated the journey on the other four lines. She had a deeper voice that Barnabas' step-dad, Björn said was really sexy. To Barnabas' ears, she sounded sophisticated and sarcastic like she thought life was hilarious, like she could barely contain her slightly condescending amusement at this gig: "Deerlick Station is next. Deerlick." The second time she said it, she separated the words — "Deer–Lick" — as if she was saying "Did you all *hear* that? What does that even *mean*?" He rode the Yellow Line seven stops to its terminus, Admiral Crumhorn Station.

Barnabas thought Crumhorn was the best station in the whole system. He had even written a report on it for his History class. The station had been built for intercity rail traffic decades before the first subway tunnels existed. Sometimes when he walked through its cavernous spaces, Barnabas liked to imagine it was 100 years ago and he was Mayor Lawrence Glorvanious himself, dropping into the gentlemen's lounges, the elegant restaurants, or maybe checking in at the swanky hotel. All of these were now gone, but the majestic central hall remained, with its walls of honey-coloured stone. The columns, covered with carved figures of thinkers, artists, and manual labourers rose high into the air, holding aloft the great domed ceiling of stained glass. While everyone else marched along, noses down in their phones, Barnabas' eyes often turned upwards.

Maybe it was because he was looking up that he didn't see the kid coming. The collision was sudden and jarring, and Barnabas and the little human missile both found themselves on their butts on the hard floor. The kid was maybe 12, with unkempt, dirty blond hair and astonishingly wide eyes. He was wearing a pair of khaki coveralls that seemed overly generous for the bony body that stuck out at odd angles inside the garment.

"I'm sorry! I'm sorry!" the kid was shouting (louder than he needed to), running to help Barnabas up, and at the same, looking all around nervously.

Barnabas picked up his backpack, which had fallen off, and said, "It's fine. I'm okay."

The boy stared for another second as if waiting for Barnabas to say, "But, I'm calling the police anyway..." before he turned and began walking away quickly. Barnabas looked down and saw the kid had dropped a sheet of folded paper, printed in bright colours.

"Hey, buddy!" he called, and the boy spun around nervously. "You dropped something."

The boy actually said, "Eep!" like a startled cartoon monkey and scooped the paper up, holding it possessively to his chest. He opened his mouth as if to thank Barnabas, but then turned and ran off, vanishing quickly into the crowd. Barnabas snorted in astonishment.

"A northbound Green Line train has arrived on track 5," said a PA announcement that echoed across the vast hall. "All aboard."

Barnabas cursed under his breath. He should have been on that train, but it was too late to reach it now. Taking the next train would make him six minutes late for school. But today wasn't a bad day to be late; his homeroom teacher would just be taking attendance before leading the class to the assembly with Mayor Tuppletaub. Barnabas figured he could tell her that he was getting ready for his video duties.

The only real problem lay with Deni, who was going to interview the Mayor onstage. If her videographer didn't show up on time, she would be devastated. In his head, he could hear her say the word with high dramatic fervour: "DEVASTATED!" Still, six minutes late was okay, he reassured himself.

With a few minutes to kill before the next train, he pushed his way out of the thick, moving crowd and wandered over to peer in the window of the nostalgia store. For the past week, he had been eyeing a big blu-ray box set of digitally-restored private eye movies from the 1940s and '50s. His cinema studies teacher had introduced him to this stylish black-and-white world of tough guys and cool dames, and he loved them. But he knew he couldn't afford the set. Nor could he ask his mom to buy it for him like he would have in the past.

Everything had changed for their family a year ago when both his mom and his step-dad had lost their jobs, one after the other. Barnabas could tell they were worried even though they tried to keep the extent of their troubles a secret from him. Sneaking out of his darkened room after bed-time to spy on their hushed late-night conversations, he heard horrific cost-cutting proposals. They would move from the City, pulling him out of his small, private school and sending him to one of the giant suburban public schools where jock bullies roamed the halls, looking for short, quiet kids like him to squish like caterpillars.

"And what about after high school?" he heard his mother say to Björn during one of these late-night sessions, dropping her voice even lower. "How will we afford his university? He's not exactly scholarship material!" During those terrible months, his parents had kept fake smiles of reassurance on their faces, and Barnabas had pretended not to know anything.

After a few months of growing tension, his parents found new work, though neither of them was making as much as they had before. They sold the condo Barnabas had grown up in, and the three of them moved to a tiny apartment, where they were always tripping over each other and all their excess stuff. Barnabas had been able to stay in his school, (though Björn cringed every time he opened the latest tuition invoice). With his newly reduced allowance, Barnabas suddenly realized why people called the City an expensive place to live. Maybe he could get the box-set for his birthday.

But, in truth, things weren't so bad. His tiny room in the small apartment had an amazing view, and he liked their new neighbourhood, which was full of funky junk shops that sold vintage posters and old vinyl records, and weird little restaurants, where he ate amazing greasy food from around the world. Best of all, he hadn't had to leave his beloved City and his friends, especially Deni. He was kind of confused about Deni lately. Kids at school were teasing him, saying he was in love with her. Maybe they were right. The truth was, he didn't exactly know what love was supposed to feel like.

Sensing something like an itch in his ear, Barnabas snapped loose from his memories and turned around. There was a man moving towards him, still quite far away, but getting closer. The man and Barnabas locked eyes for a moment, and Barnabas quickly turned back to face the store window. *He's probably not looking at me,* Barnabas told himself, but when he glanced back, the man — closer than ever — was still staring as if Barnabas might be someone he knew… or someone he wanted to kill.

He was dressed in a worn khaki one-piece coverall — rather similar, Barnabas noted, to the one the kid had been wearing. There was a belt of tools at his waist and heavy boots on his feet, grey with dust. His shaved head glistened with a sheen of sweat, and as he passed the Koffee-Smile Bakery, his shiny scalp reflected its red neon sign which promised: "Hot and fresh, every day." Now the man was only about 10 seconds away, and Barnabas could see he was pretty old — maybe 40 or 50. Even so, he appeared powerful. His black eyes, piercing as a crow's, bore into Barnabas and seemed to pin him in place.

The man was saying something, and as he came closer, Barnabas could hear he was calling out, "Galt-Stomper?!" Barnabas didn't know what a Galt-Stomper was, but his heart started to beat faster, and he braced himself against a pillar. It felt like he had made an appointment with some terrible destiny, and the fateful day had finally arrived. But then the man stopped in his tracks and scowled. His black crow's eyes began searching elsewhere, and he turned and walked off. Barnabas understood the man had mistaken him for someone else.

Despite his relief, Barnabas had the perverse desire to follow him, like one of his movie private eyes, and figure out what this strange character was up to. But then the PA announced: "A northbound Green Line train is approaching on track 6." *So much for detective work,* he thought. If he ran, he could just reach his train. He was about to push his way back into the moving crowd when he heard a high, strained cry above the noise: "Mr. Glower! Mr. Glower, I'm here!"

Barnabas spotted the source of the alarmed voice: it was the kid in the matching coveralls! He was jumping straight up and down in the stream of commuters, appearing above their heads for a moment like a fish breaking the surface of the water, and then vanishing back under. He was waving the same paper document and calling out, "Mr. Glower! Help!" as if he couldn't break free of the pull of the crowd. Curiosity again overtook Barnabas, and he crouched behind a garbage bin as the big, bald man (whose name seemed to be "Glower") reached out a meaty hand to grab the gangly kid by his skinny arm and pull him free of the crowd.

Barnabas' phone vibrated aggressively in his front pants pocket, and he reached in awkwardly to grab it. There was a new TxtChat message from Deni: **"Cameras here. Where the hell ru?!!"**

He ignored this and looked up again. The boy was exuding a nonstop stream of punctuated babble: "... I didn't KNOW there'd be this, ohfatherglory, this MILLIONS of PEOPLE! ohmighty —"

"Be quiet, Galt-Stomper!" Glower barked at the boy. "We're not supposed to draw attention to ourselves, and here you are waving your arms and caterwauling like a howler monkey!" This kid must have been who Glower had mistaken him for. Really, they didn't look at all alike, other than their relative lack of height and generally messy hair.

Galt-Stomper, for his part, was too wound up to quiet down. "Sorry, sorry! And, look, I was following the map and, HERE, we're at Admiral Crumhorn, and we have to go all the way THERE to Minimus Junction and —"

"I know where we're going! Put that idiot map away," Glower growled, shaking the boy by the arm like he was trying to make apples drop off a tree. "You know it's a restricted document beyond the Frontier. Getting you a train pass cost me a lot of favours… and a lost day of collecting! Don't make me regret my decision."

Chastened, Galt-Stomper shut his mouth and hastily pushed the map into the back pocket of his coveralls. Glower dragged him over to the wall until they were standing right above Barnabas, who pulled himself deeper into the shadow of the garbage can. The kid was looking around everywhere like he'd never been in the City before. He was clearly afraid of both the crowds and the man holding his arm. The map was in Galt-Stomper's back pocket, but only just; it was mostly hanging out. *What did Glower mean it was a "restricted document?"* Barnabas wondered with burning curiosity, craning his neck to see if he could read anything on the folded paper.

Glower again grabbed Galt-Stomper by the arm and said, "I just need you to keep quiet and follow orders. Can you do that or not?"

"Yessir."

"Good. Let's go."

Barnabas felt a moment of dizzying panic; he was about to lose his chance to investigate the mysterious document! The pair lurched forward, vanishing into the crowd, and Barnabas found himself staring in shock at his own out-stretched hand. He was holding the map. For a frozen second, he just sat there, amazed at what he'd done. Then he jumped to his feet, waving the paper in the air and shouting, "Hey! You dropped your document!"

But they were already gone. And he had the mysterious map. Excitement overcame guilt as he crouched back down, unfolding the crumpled sheet halfway. To his grave disappointment, he saw that it was nothing but an ordinary subway map, the old paper kind from before everyone used the transit app. The different colour-coded subway lines were as familiar to him as his nose in the mirror.

His phone buzzed: **"BARNABAS?!!!!!!!!"**

He texted back: **"b ther in 5"**

"A northbound Green Line train has arrived on track 6. All aboard," said the PA and Barnabas cringed. It was too late to catch it. He was now at least 15 minutes late for school — not to mention a thief — and all for an ordinary subway map. He looked back down at it in disgust…

…and noticed something *odd*.

In the lower right hand corner was Admiral Crumhorn Station from where Yellow, Green and Purple lines shot out at different angles like limbs of a rainbow tree. He knew as well as he knew his own name, that this station was the final stop on the Yellow Line; but on this map, the line continued beyond the terminus, disappearing under the last unopened fold. And, although the line seemed to be a continuation of the Yellow Line, after Crumhorn the colour changed to blue. No, not blue. The line that emerged on the other side of his favourite station was *Aqua*. As he had learned in art class, Aqua was not blue or green. It was a mystical colour associated with the primordial sea, with the unknown.

With a sense of thrill and foreboding, he opened the last fold of the map, and there he saw another subway line, an Aqua Line that followed a strange, meandering path, first West, but then veering North to the edge of the city where the Tower District stood, and continuing… beyond.

The PA crackled once like it was clearing its throat before the announcement rang out: "A northbound Green Line train is approaching on track 5. Please make your way to track 5."

There was no more time to spend contemplating this mystery. Barnabas folded up the map, stuffed it in his bag and ran to meet his train.

CHAPTER 2

As soon as the Green Line train pulled from the station, Barnabas made his way to the very end of the car and squatted by the back window, while the other 200 people on board crowded as close to the doors as possible. Making sure he was unobserved, he took the subway map out of his bag. Just before he unfolded it, he had a moment's crazy panic that the new subway line wouldn't be there, that the whole thing was some strange hallucination. But no, there it was. Whereas all the other lines in the system ran relatively straight, the Aqua Line meandered drunkenly as if it couldn't quite make up its mind where it was headed. It even crossed under other lines , though there were no interchange stations. And the names of the Aqua Line stations were *madness!* Some were just numbers, although not in order. Others had names that implied much but said little: "Final Process," "Drum," "Lesser Holding," "Cracks," "Doomlock."

Other than the addition of a whole new line, the only other thing that marked this map as special was a perplexing motto in tiny font, down in one corner: "All Praise to Father Glory." A growing paranoia overtook Barnabas. He had the sense that he was holding something momentous, something dangerous, and that he'd better not be caught with it. His ride was nearly over, so he refolded the map and secured it in a zippered pocket deep in his bag. He tried hard to look nonchalant as he stood up. The train pulled into Blesskind Station, and he pushed his way through the crowd to exit.

He bolted up the stairs to street level, tightened the straps of his backpack and ran down the sidewalk, bursting through the doors of a mid-size office building and not slowing until his finger hit the "up" button beside the elevator doors with well-practiced precision.

The Junior Juggernauts School of Youthful Enthusiasm occupied the top four floors of the building, which also housed a P. R. firm, several lawyers' offices and two rival dating-app companies. There were just 127 students at the school, ranging in age from 12 to 18, but it was an exceptionally engaged group. After regular classes ended each day, almost all the students stayed for the extra-curricular activities. There were debates and model world governments, music-making of all types from medieval to hip-hop, gaming and game design, visual arts, theatre arts, and video production. Sports activities were rare, partly because the school's mission was, "to make the future brighter by igniting the creative spirit," and partly because a school in a narrow office building had no place for a field or gym.

The elevator door opened and Barnabas jumped out, almost colliding right then and there with Deni, who was practically quivering with fury.

"9:20!" she hissed through gritted teeth.

"9:16!" he insisted.

"You're trying to kill me," she responded helpfully and turned to the boy who stood to her right. "Calvin, camera!"

Cal Kabaway was new to the school, having recently moved to the City with his family from Dominica. It wasn't clear to Barnabas why anyone would bother showing up for the last two months of school instead of just starting in September, but the tall, shy boy with the black curls and cocoa skin had immediately become a person of note, and his good looks made most of the girls and a few of the boys swoon openly. Cal handed Barnabas the camera, already mounted on a sturdy tripod. It was indeed an enviable piece of gear — a ProVizaleer XV, midnight blue and shiny silver, styled more like a sports car than a video camera.

"Calvin is part of the Journalism Club now," Deni announced. Up to that point, she and Barnabas had been the only members, and he felt a little stab of jealousy. He wanted to say, *Why? Because he can afford a fancy camera?*

They were the only people in the reception area, and Barnabas could already hear an amplified voice coming from down the hall. Deni gestured for them to follow, and the three of them hurried to the auditorium (whose secret identity was the school lunchroom). As they walked, Cal explained the simple operating instructions to Barnabas in a slight accent that was annoyingly charming:

"Zoom is here. I have the white-balance set, and the image stabilizer on. Leave it in auto-focus. Once we start, don't bother pausing; I have a 128GB memory card in the slot. And whatever you do, don't drop it or my father will send me back home to work in the mines."

Barnabas looked Cal over. The haircut and clothes said "rich boy," so obviously the mines thing was a joke, but the serious expression meant that he wasn't fooling about the angry dad thing.

"I'll be careful," he assured him.

Standing outside the doors of the auditorium was a strange and intimidating man. He wasn't all that tall, but his heavily-muscled physique seemed ready to burst out of his tight, navy suit. He wore dark glasses, and his blond hair was styled in a bowl-cut that looked a little ridiculous — not that you would dare say that to his thick-jawed face. He had a name tag on his lapel that read: Klevver. Barnabas figured he was part of the Mayor's security.

"Who are you?" Klevver snarled as if they could be anything other than students. Barnabas felt kind of violated to have this man monitoring his comings and goings in his own school; at the same time, he was too intimidated to answer right away.

Deni, on the other hand, just threw her shoulders back and looked the man in the eye. "We're the Journalism Club. Will you please stand aside? We're late!"

Klevver looked like he was about to demand ID or handcuff them or something, but after a few tense seconds, he moved away from the doors. Deni pulled them open and waved the boys in.

The entire student body was already seated. A teacher near the door turned to them and brought a "shush" finger to her lips, but Deni had no time for authorities other than herself; she was in directing mode. She walked halfway down the centre aisle and showed Barnabas where to set up, whispering instructions to him about how to frame the image. In addition to providing the camera, Cal had brought a shotgun microphone, which he connected to the camera before moving to the edge of the stage, unspooling a long cable as he went.

Up on stage, the physics teacher, Mr. Shamblan was almost done with the morning announcements. On chairs at the back of the stage sat the Mayor alongside a sharply dressed, terribly serious woman who was whispering in his ear. She had to be some kind of advisor, Barnabas figured. Beside them, with her perpetually sunny expression was Mary Rolan-Gong, Principal of the school. She stood up and took the microphone from Mr. Shamblan.

"Hello, hello! So nice to see you all!" Ms. Rolan-Gong called out. "I've been away from the school for too long! But it was all on your behalf, believe me! When you see the guest teachers and speakers we've lined up, you will be running to sign up for another year!"

Barnabas wondered why she was saying this to the student body, but then he noticed that the front two rows were full of parents. It was tuition renewal time.

Ms. Rolan-Gong continued, "Before I introduce our very special guest, the Intermediate Choir has a special and pertinent performance for us all. This is a song that used to be a staple of civic gatherings, but has not been heard in many, many years. Please stand for the City's Anthem!"

The whole room got to its feet in bemused confusion as seven students in matching school sweatshirts moved confidently to the front along with the music teacher. Barnabas decided it was a good time to start shooting. With gusto and pep, the choir sang:

Hail to the future that has sprung from the land,
Hail to the roads built by spirit and hand,
A world where our children can prosper and play,
In this fair, golden city rising skyward today.

The loud applause was mixed with no small amount of sarcastic jeering — the song's sentiments were too hoary for the students' sophisticated ears — but Barnabas was glad to have another bit of the past brought back to life. Ms. Rolan-Gong gestured at some teachers in the audience, who shushed the students back into seated silence.

"And now," said the Principal, her enthusiasm climbing to yet another level, "It's my great honour to welcome to our school, His Honour, the Mayor of our city, Arthur Tuppletaub."

The Mayor's advisor was still whispering last minute instructions in his ear even as he stood up. He flashed the room his trademark smile, which opened up across his soft, child-like face like the ground opens during an earthquake. He was a strange creature: his unusually round head would have made more sense on a much heavier man instead of on the long, lanky body that was all angles and vectors. Maybe this mismatched arrangement made him top-heavy because he walked up to the mic stand at the front of the stage as if he were tumbling forward, grabbing at it like an inexperienced swimmer reaches gratefully for the edge of the pool.

"Hello!" he shouted over the applause. "Gosh, it's the leaders of tomorrow, all in one room! I'd better get on your good sides now."

Ms. Rolan-Gong, still holding her mic laughed brightly and made a little one-handed clap. She said, "Mr. Mayor, I know this is a busy time for you with the election just three weeks away. We're so grateful you could fit us into your schedule."

The Mayor nodded at her seriously. "No, no, I'm delighted to be here. It's important to help our youth understand the *awesome*, one-of-a-kind city they live in and get an idea just how complex it is to make it all work! So that it continues to be the best... just the *best* city in the whole world!"

He himself led the applause on this one. Barnabas panned around the room, capturing a bit of footage of the appreciative audience. Various students tried to ruin the shot by waving into the camera or pretending to pick their noses and eat it. He turned the lens back to the stage. He had never really thought of the Mayor as a real person before, just a media creature made up of video clips and sound-bites. But now Barnabas was the one making that footage. This electronic relationship with the Tuppletaub felt weirdly intimate.

Deni had moved up behind Barnabas, and she whispered in his ear with keen determination: "When I interview him, I'm totally going to get him off message. I want to startle him, so he says something that isn't scripted."

"Tell him you're the long-lost daughter he gave up for adoption."

"That's not funny," she said, but Barnabas thought she was probably giving the idea serious consideration.

The Mayor had started showing them an onscreen presentation, inserting himself into the history of the City that they all knew from civics class. He was saying: "And that is why my administration has worked so hard to maintain and build upon the visionary, uh, *vision* of Lawrence Glorvanious, whose vision of the City, almost 100 years ago, has made us the envy of the world!"

Deni whispered, "Code word: 'vision,'" and Barnabas had to control his laugh so he wouldn't shake the camera.

He whispered back, "Maybe that's what his advisor was telling him before: 'Say *vision* a lot.'"

A teacher turned around and whispered, "Sit down, Ms. Jiver," and Deni flounced back to her aisle seat as if it were her own idea. She pulled out her phone and started to go through her interview questions one last time.

The images in the presentation were familiar: Lawrence Glorvanious, Mayor of the City in the days before world wars and radio, looking dapper in his dark suit and top hat. He was smoking a cigar, and standing beside his architects and engineers (also in suits and top hats, also smoking) to examine the scale model of the new downtown that would be realized over his nearly two decades in office. This image was followed by a slide of Mayor Tuppletaub beside the same model in the municipal museum. Next was Glorvanious posing beside sweaty, muscled men who were digging the first subway tunnels with pick and shovel, and then a slide of Tuppletaub, talking "candidly" to patrons on a shiny Yellow Line car 100 years later.

There was a cool 3D animation Barnabas had never seen before about the growth of the Tower District, with the signature buildings rising up like blades of grass: The Jezebel, The Reaktion, Neverlander, Greatest Hiltz, Delphic Tower, and the Honey Pot. In the upper-right of the screen, a year-counter clocked forward through the 20th Century and into the new millennium. Inserted awkwardly into the middle of the animation was some video footage of Tuppletaub, entering Delphic Tower, where the City's mayors had lived since the middle of the last century.

The animation ended with a dramatic pull back to reveal the whole city with the river in the foreground and the towers standing in the back like the tall cousins in a family portrait. The sun glinted off the City's stadium, the Manhammer Audio Dome, sitting atop Gum Hill, and then began to set behind the skyline, creating dramatic silhouettes. The music was swelling, and up on stage, the Mayor was saying, "In good times and, uh, not-so-good times, it is the people of this great metropolis that have worked together to take what is already great and grow it into... into an even greaterer future!"

Even though Deni had taught him it was their duty as junior journalists to be sceptical about stuff like this, Barnabas couldn't help being moved by the presentation. He really did think he lived in the best and smartest city in the world. He remembered years ago when he and his mom had followed his dad around on tour for a few weeks — his real dad, in the days before the divorce, before Björn. Every city they visited seemed to be collapsing under the weight of urban decay and human despair, sinking slowly back into the earth. Meanwhile, his city seemed to stretch itself ever higher, buoyed by hope and civic pride. If he hadn't been the videographer, Barnabas would have joined in the loud applause and whoops of approval.

The Mayor leaned against his mic stand and shook his head as if he just couldn't believe how generous everyone was. Barnabas panned the camera around the room. He noticed that the parents at the front seemed less impressed than the kids.

"And now, Mr. Mayor," Ms. Rolan-Gong said brightly, "One of the City's up-and-coming reporters would like to ask you a few questions, if that's okay. Here's Deni Jiver from our Journalism Club!" Barnabas swung the camera around to follow Deni as she walked up the stairs onto the stage. He noticed for the first time how professionally she was dressed: her long honey-coloured hair was neatly clipped on top of her head, and she was wearing a slick jacket over a shiny shirt, her dark jeans tucked into black boots.

Despite being so well put-together, she looked kind of terrified, and Barnabas felt a twinge of sympathy for her. Would Deni really be able to catch the Mayor off-guard with her killer journalist questions? Things started badly; she seemed to be under the impression there were seven stairs instead of six, and she did an awkward half-stumble before she managed to mount the stage.

Soon, Deni and Mayor Tuppletaub were seated opposite each other on two chairs, each with a handheld mic. Barnabas framed them in a nice two-shot. Deni's first questions were pretty soft: why did the Mayor go into politics? What did he want to accomplish if he was re-elected? Her voice was low enough that someone at the back yelled, "Speak up!"

Deni seemed to find her confidence then. She cleared her throat and looked the Mayor in the eye. "It's a big and complicated city, Mayor Tuppletaub."

"It sure is!" he replied.

Deni continued, "And you have to deal with daily problems, political infighting, even among people you consider allies, serious divisions about how the City should move forward, not to mention a long, proud history you have to live up to. Do you ever have days when you just feel like the job is *too much for you?*"

Barnabas thought it was a great question; he zoomed the camera in tight on the Mayor's face, hoping to capture a moment of doubt. But the man smiled and nodded.

"Well, of course! And I'm sure you feel the same way sometimes," he said. "You have school, family, friends, and your future to worry about. I bet there are days when the problems seem so big, so many, you just don't want to get out of bed. Am I right?"

He flashed a smile in the general direction of the camera, and Barnabas realized that he was well aware of it, and just how he looked to its cold, probing eye.

"Sure," she said in response to the Mayor's counter-question, and Barnabas could tell she was trying to get back on top of the situation, not let her subject control the interview. "Of course there are days like that, but what I want to know —"

Mayor Tuppletaub interrupted, but with a smile that made it all seem okay. "Well, I have those days too, Deni. But you know what I remember then? That I'm not alone. Sure, I'm the Mayor, and people look to me for leadership, but I remind myself that I work with a brilliant team. And that the citizens of this city are with us, helping us to make all our lives better — day by day." He leaned forward as if he were letting Deni in on a great confidence. "So I get out bed because I know that if all those people are ready to do their part, I've got to do mine!"

Deni stared at him for a long second and then dropped her head to her phone's screen, scrolling up and down to find her next question. Barnabas' heart sank. The girl who might maybe he his girlfriend was in trouble. He thought, *Come on, Deni! Don't let him win!* But the Mayor took the opportunity to carry right on with his agenda:

"Did you know," he said, "That we're increasingly using steam power to cool buildings in addition to heating them? Trigeneration, it's called! Very environmental."

"What about subways?" Barnabas suddenly heard himself shout. Deni was so surprised, she dropped her phone with a loud clatter. Calvin swung the shotgun mic around to pick up Barnabas' voice, and then back around to the Mayor to record his answer. Barnabas felt every eye in the room on him. Deni's were the widest.

The Mayor blinked a few times, caught off guard. "Subways? Um, there aren't any plans for more … um, for development of any more —"

Barnabas' seemed to have lost control of his mouth: "There aren't any, like, unannounced projects? No, uh, *secret* subways? You know, that the public doesn't … use? Or know about?"

Mayor Tuppletaub's dimpled, jolly demeanour abruptly grew stony. He stared at Barnabas as if trying to see inside his head, trying to crack him like a walnut and expose the meat within. "No," he said, his voice a little husky. "There aren't any … secret subways."

Holding the mic against her chest, looking somewhere between furious and ready to cry, Deni shouted at him from the stage, "What are you talking about, Barnabas? *I'm* doing the interview!"

The Mayor recovered his poise and smiled indulgently at Deni as if he was sympathizing with her embarrassing situation. "No, it's fine. Good question, son! I'm afraid we don't work like that. New projects only go forward after rigorous environmental, economic, and logistical analysis." He laughed. "Heck, I wish I could suddenly stand up in a Council meeting and say, 'Tada! Here's a new subway!' or 'A new park, out of thin air!' I'd be the most popular mayor since Lawrence Glorvanious!"

Ms. Rolan-Gong, as pleased as ever, glided forward and took away Deni's microphone. "Well thank you, Ms. Jiver. And thank you *so much*, Mayor Arthur Tuppletaub for taking the time to come to our little school and be such a, gosh, inspiration for our students!"

As the students applauded, the Mayor looked out again with his beaming smile, but when his gaze fell on Barnabas, the smile faded and his expression grew dark and unreadable. The security man, Mr. Klevver, climbed the steps to the stage, and soon the Mayor was trying to point out the "subway boy" in the audience. But by then, Barnabas had ducked behind some taller students and was making for the exit. He knew he was supposed to stay and get some footage of Deni and the Mayor shaking hands, but he just wanted to get out of the auditorium before he got into some kind of awful trouble. The title of an old thriller popped into his head: "The Man Who Knew Too Much!"

CHAPTER 3

Barnabas loitered by his locker, reviewing the video footage, particularly the moment when the Mayor was staring daggers at him for mentioning the secret subway. From the tiny screen, Tuppletaub's anger shone out like the beam of a laser pointer. Barnabas cursed his impulsiveness. First he couldn't resist stealing the map of the Aqua Subway Line once he had heard it was a "forbidden document," and then he had actually had the nuclear-level foolishness to mention it to the actual Mayor of the City!

Barnabas decided he would show Deni the map. She was brilliant at coming up with plans to handle the adults in their lives — parents, teachers, random officials who held the keys to stuff she wanted. And this situation was definitely beyond Barnabas' ability to face on his own.

As the students and teachers shuffled noisily out of the auditorium, hurrying past him on their way back to class, he glanced furtively over his shoulder for any sign of the Mayor or the scary Mr. Klevver. But the only ones to seek him out were Deni and Cal, who appeared as the last of the students cleared the hall. Cal ran straight to his camera, checking it for scratches or fleas or whatever. Deni's approach was slower, and the whole way down the hall, she was giving Barnabas a cold, flat stare.

"If," she said as she closed the distance between them, "...you had any brilliant ideas for more interview questions, you could have shared them with me before we started."

"I know…"

"…instead of…"

"I know, sorry."

"…like a total… I mean, *secret subways?*"

Barnabas decided *not* to show Deni the map. She was already acting like the whole messed-up interview was his fault, and that wasn't fair! He told her "I was trying to help. You were looking a little… lost?"

Deni's face immediately changed from fearsome to pitiable. She fell back against the bank of lockers, and slowly slid down to the floor. "I know. I sucked." Her head dropped to her chest, and she sighed heavily.

Barnabas sat down beside her. "It's not that you sucked," he told her. "It's just the Mayor's a total pro at the interview thing. You should have seen how he worked the camera."

"I thought you looked very professional," Cal blurted out, standing above them. "And very pretty."

Barnabas stared up at him, annoyed. What was with Cal? Especially what was up with the way he was looking at Deni? Did he like her? Like her *like that?* Barnabas expected Deni to make some sarcastic reply to Cal's mush, but she just smiled at him gratefully. Barnabas watched their eyes locking, like they were sharing a super-special moment of mutual understanding. Barnabas' mouth dropped open, and he felt another stab of jealousy. Absurd as it was, the phrase "muscling in on his territory" occurred to him. After all, wasn't Deni kind of maybe *his* girlfriend? It was actually a conversation that had never happened.

He cringed at the memory of a cold day in November when he had asked her to go to a movie with him. Of course, this was nothing new — they had been going to movies together for years. But in his head, it was something different that day. When she met him in the lobby of her apartment, she didn't seem to notice how his pressed shirt was tucked tightly into his pants, and his hair was stiff with gel. Then she sniffed the air and looked at him queerly.

"Are you wearing *cologne?*" she asked with a laugh that felt like a long glass shard plunging into his stomach. "What is this, Barnabas?" she said with cold amusement, "A date?"

"No!" he shot back, annoyed. He untucked his shirt, messed up his hair and they went to the movie. But that was back when they had still been 14 and clueless. Now he was 15 and it was the end of the school year, and it all seemed like a long time ago. Yet still, nothing was definitive, not like with other couples who really were couples, who made out at parties and were rumoured to do even more. But her sudden interest in the new boy… It felt like a betrayal!

"We better get to class," Cal said, nervously checking the fancy watch he wore.

Deni, still a picture of misery, shook her head. "No, I got us permission notes. I said we needed to do technical thingies with our footage after the assembly. And thank God; I'm a wreck." She reached up a languid hand to Cal and he pulled her to her feet. She did a little awkward pirouette, and they both laughed. Barnabas didn't.

Barnabas decided he *would* show Deni the map. Maybe sharing this secret would get some of her attention turned back his way. "Listen," he said. "I have something in my locker. Something really, really cool."

Deni spun around and looked down at him, her eyes full of excitement. "No! I have something to show *you!*" Her depression apparently forgotten, she ran to open her locker, which was halfway down the hall. She carefully pulled a large, square paper bag from its depths.

"Check out what I found at the antiques market!" she said. In the bag was an old vinyl record album. Barnabas walked over to join her, Cal following him down the hall like an oversized shadow. The three of them examined the battered cardboard sleeve. "The Vinny Stinthouse Quintet, Live at the Blistered Lip," read the cover which, for no reason Barnabas could discern, showed a group of girls in bikinis, lounging by a swimming pool, holding tall, icy drinks with umbrellas in them. The faded colours of an old decade. The 1970s maybe?

She flipped the album over, and Barnabas already knew what he would find in the credits. "Tenor saxophone, Brownbag Bopwright." There were a lot of records like this he had seen over the years with his father playing on them. There had been a couple of incarnations of "The Bopwright Trio," but Barnabas' dad had told him he was happiest when he wasn't the main attraction. "I was born to be a sideman, man."

And yet, despite his lack of headline status, Brownbag Bopwright seemed to have fans all over the world; little pockets of passionate music lovers who all had favourite Brownbag solos and talked about his tone like they were connoisseurs describing a rare bottle of wine: "warm like old leather," "rich and purple," "sweet and heavy." Deni had learned her love of jazz from her mom, Amy who had been thrilled when she found out Barnabas was the son of the minor living legend.

Deni carefully extracted the album from his hands like he couldn't be trusted with something this precious, no matter how he was related. "I'll play it for you later, okay?"

"I don't really know anything about jazz," Barnabas mumbled. He found himself thinking of the last time he had seen his dad — a quick lunch at a little pizza joint back in March. It had been a spontaneous visit, exhilarating, but over so fast that Barnabas had spent the next week wondering if it had been a dream.

Cal called out cheerfully, "I want to hear it, Deni!" She ignored him and Barnabas gave him a withering look.

As she put away the precious record, Deni asked, "So, what did you want to show me?"

Barnabas' stomach felt a growing unease as he walked back to his locker. He knew Deni would be thrilled by the map. She would have all kinds of theories about what it meant, about some huge conspiracy that lay behind its existence. He knew that if he let her in on the secret, her fantasies of becoming a famous journalist would immediately kick into high gear. She would break the story to the world, making a name for herself at 15. He could imagine her being interviewed on the news, all poised and serious. He imagined her hosting a documentary that would introduce a million viewers to the mysteries of the underground world: "And now, we're arriving at the thrilling Doomlock Station!" she would say to the camera with breathless earnest. He felt himself burning with resentment as if all this had already happened. He thought, *Does she think she can just go running after Calvin AND take credit for* my *map?*

Barnabas decided *not* to show Deni the map.

At that moment, the doors of the auditorium creaked open, and they turned to see the Mayor's security man, Klevver, heading their way in his shiny, tight suit and dark glasses. Barnabas froze, feeling like guilt was written all over his face. But it was to Cal the man spoke:

"Hey, nice equipment! ProVizaleer! Very fancy. So, you're the school cameraman? The one who just shot the assembly? 'Cause I want to talk to you."

"That was *me*, not him," Barnabas said indignantly, and immediately wanted to slap himself. He needed to program his phone to send him hourly texts, reading "Think before you speak."

Klevver seemed delighted. "Excellent, thanks for the confession! I need to ask you a few simple questions."

The three kids looked at each other. Despite Klevver's friendly smile, they could all feel a fog of menace gathering around them. Maybe it was *because* of the smile. Barnabas reflexively backed away, until he was half inside his open locker, the corner of a textbook sticking into his back.

He had no idea what to say, and was relieved when Deni spoke up, though her voice lacked its usual bravado: "Actually, mister, we need to get back to class."

Klevver didn't bother to turn her way. He drew uncomfortably close to Barnabas, staring down the way a cat in a tree stares at a bird feeding below. "Yeah, you two run along. Me and the cameraman will just be a minute."

The auditorium doors flew open again, this time with a loud bang, and Ms. Rolan-Gong and the little army of parents emerged, talking loudly, laughing and gesticulating.

Klevver hissed, "Nuts!" With a decisive shove, he pushed Barnabas back into his locker and slammed the door. In the darkness, an avalanche of books and papers tumbled down on Barnabas' head. He heard his lock being clicked shut. Klevver whispered, "We'll talk later, little cameraman."

Barnabas was too shocked to move. A few seconds later, the laughing gang of parents swept past, and he heard:

"I'm supporting him because he can push my plan through Council! All those green obstructionists are costing me a fortune."

"Well, if Tuppletaub wants my name on the Youth Shelter, he owes me that zoning change."

"Seems fair."

"Oh, hello, Deni! I'll see you at Benjamin's birthday party next week, won't I? It's at the Marina Club!"

And then the buzzing swarm was gone.

Deni whispered, "Barnabas?"

"Let me out!" he shouted back.

"Well, what's your combination?!"

"37-14-47."

The door flew open, and he stumbled out of the locker, a cascade of books and papers following in his wake and spilling across the floor. He found Cal and Deni staring at him, looking confused.

"Why didn't you guys say something to the Principal?!" Barnabas demanded.

Cal shot back: "Why didn't you?"

Deni said, "Sorry, I wasn't sure what was the right thing to do. He-he rattled me! What is going on? Why does Klevver want to talk to you?"

Barnabas wanted to scream, *I found a map that could put us all in jail!* Now he was glad he hadn't shown it to them. In fact, he was going to get rid of it at the earliest opportunity. He shrugged, hoping this show of confusion would satisfy her. "Did you see where he went?"

Deni and Cal looked at each other. Cal said, "He just kind of… vanished. Do you think he'll come back?"

Deni said, "I doubt it; he's one of those idiots who likes to use his little sliver of power to push people around. I think the Rolan-Gong scared him off."

"Where was she taking those parents?" Barnabas asked her.

"Fundraising breakfast for the Mayor up on the 12th floor. Champagne, orange juice, and tax write-offs. Didn't you notice? Those were the richest parents in the school."

"No, I was locked in my locker."

"Oh, right. Hey, what was it you were going to show us anyway?"

Barnabas gritted his teeth. He was determined not to show them the map, but what excuse could he make now? He remembered he did have something of interest in his locker besides the map. He crouched and went through his bag. "Tada!" he said, popping up with the *diaboriku* in his outstretched hand. "My brother sent this to me. I have no idea what it does."

Cal asked, "Is it a camera maybe?"

Deni shook her head. "Why would anyone need a camera like this? It wouldn't be any better than our phones."

"Maybe," Barnabas said, "it's a kind of medical scanner."

Deni's rolled her eyes. "Ridiculous Theory-fest continues."

"No, you know," he insisted. "It could tell if your friend was a zombie. Or your mom had turned into an alien, or —"

"Stop, please!" she said as if in physical pain from all the stupidity. Barnabas was sick of humiliation; he decided he would make the *diaboriku* work. How hard could it be? Furrowing his brow, he tried various combinations of buttons: red, green1, green3, green2 — *nothing*. Red, green2, green1, green3 — *nothing!* Green1, red, green3, green2 — *nothing!!* A consistent, unenlightening *nothing*, over and over.

Deni plucked the *diaboriku* from his hands. "Let Cal try. He can figure anything out." The compliment clearly buoyed Cal's spirits, and he took the little sphere and began to pace up and down the hall, his fingers poking and prodding the big rubber buttons. Barnabas glared at his broad, muscular back.

Deni checked her phone for messages while Barnabas repacked his locker. He was up on his toes, attempting to force his physics text in among a thick pile of unyielding class handouts when he heard a gasp from Calvin, followed a scant second later by a high-pitched scream from Deni.

He spun around, a cascade of books tumbling painfully onto his head and shoulders, in time to see a monster rising up above them, huge, grotesque, and poised to attack.

CHAPTER 4

eni's scream was actually not all that useful. High as it was, it wasn't very loud. If, Barnabas figured, a scream was supposed to a) unnerve the predator attacking you and, b) alert other members of your tribe that you needed help, then Deni's was unequal to the task, and evolution would do away with her line. For example, it seemed to have no affect on the GIANT MONSTER!! that had appeared in the hall in front of them.

The creature was so large, its head almost hit the ceiling. Midnight blue with shiny silver streaks, it had a single cold, glistening eye, its pupil contracting and dilating as it turned its malevolent gaze on them. It stood on three legs, hissing and chirruping, each appendage tipped with a terrible, pointed claw. Barnabas dropped to the ground as the beast reared up on two of its legs and swung the third at him before gravity brought it back down again. Deni, backed herself into her locker, making more ineffectual noises.

Cal ran down the hall in the direction of the stairway, and the monster followed him. Deni screamed her pointless scream again, though it did seem to inspire Cal to make a U-turn. If he meant to save her, it wasn't working, because the monster had turned, too, and was bearing down on her. But as he ran after the creature, Cal managed to trip on his own feet, dropping the *diaboriku* ... and the monster vanished. The mysterious device rolled quietly across the floor, coming to a stop near Barnabas' feet.

Barnabas felt like reality had back-flipped in front of him. His heart was pounding and his armpits were drenched in sweat. The sound of three kids panting like dogs on a hot summer day was the only noise in the hall. He turned to see Deni sticking her head out her locker, her hair loose from its clip, staring at the spot where the creature had stood.

Cal's hand was shaking as he pointed at the fallen *diaboriku*. "Wh-what the hell is that thing?!!" Barnabas didn't understand what he meant at first… but then he did. Had the little sphere from the other side of the planet caused this creature to appear in their midst? Had it maybe opened a doorway into another universe?!

Barnabas picked it up cautiously. "I don't know!" he heard himself whine. "I thought it was just a toy!"

Deni extricated herself from her locker. "Words," she said. "There were words above its eye. 'Province' or something."

Barnabas noticed Cal's camera, standing serenely on its tripod, right where they had left it. Suddenly he understood. "ProVizaleer. That's what it said."

Cal wiped his sweaty brow with the back of his sleeve. "But that's the name of my camera…" He turned slowly and looked at the black camera with its shiny lens, standing on three-legs, just like the monster had. He looked back at the *diaboriku* in Barnabas' hand.

Deni walked over to him. "Do it again. Stand in the same place and push the same buttons." Barnabas handed Cal the device again, and he did as he had done. There was a simple, innocuous beep, and the monster returned, standing just down the hall, twitching and growling as before. However, now that they weren't terrified for their lives, they saw the creature for what it was: a vividly detailed, if somewhat distorted 3D projection. It looked solid, except where its limbs intersected lockers and furniture, and in those places, you could see that it was all a fake.

Barnabas said, "Oh my God, the *diaboriku* takes whatever you point it at and… and *monsterizes* it!"

Cal pushed the big red button, and the camera-monster vanished.

Deni grabbed Cal's arm. "Do another one. Do the fire extinguisher!" She pointed at the bright red canister hanging near the staircase. Cal crossed to it and punched in the sequence again. A great red robot was instantly looming above them — tall, cylindrical, waving its long, black, serrated appendage menacingly, terrible clangs emanating from its hissing insides. Barnabas now understood the two lenses. The small one read the source, and the big one projected the transformation.

Cal smiled and said, "That's pretty damn good! Well, the surround sound could use some work."

Annoyed, Barnabas grabbed the *diaboriku* back from him, and the robot vanished. "Now you're the expert! A minute ago you were crapping your shorts like the rest of us." He stuffed the device into his front pants pocket, where it only barely fit.

Deni checked the mirror in her locker, re-clipping her hair before closing the door with a bang. "I can take absolutely no more stress this morning!" she told them. "Barnabas, keep that thing out of sight before it causes more heart attacks. Let's go lock up the camera in the office; then I want a hot chocolate at KonaBoom."

Cal folded up the legs of the tripod and tucked the whole assemblage under his arm. "Will we make it back for third period?"

But Deni was already heading for the stairwell, and Cal hurried to catch up. Barnabas closed his locker and ran after them.

The auditorium and their lockers were on the ninth floor; the office was up on 12. As they climbed, Barnabas stayed a few steps back and watched Deni and Cal flirting with each other. Cal's relationship with her was already different than the way she acted around Barnabas. They were laughing together, bumping into each other not quite by accident, intimate in a way that made them look cooler, more grown up. Barnabas felt like Deni and Cal had climbed onto a bus whose destination sign read 'Mature' and driven away, leaving him standing at the bus stop in still-a-kid land.

They reached the 12th floor landing, and Cal and Deni turned right and headed down the hall to the office, but Barnabas decided not to follow. He leaned over the railing and looked down into the stairwell, letting himself get hypnotized by the repeating pattern of stairs and banisters that shrank as it receded, floor by floor. He imagined himself tumbling down into the abyss, like Alice down the rabbit hole.

Deni and Cal came back to the landing, and Cal looked relieved to be free of the burden of the camera. Deni said, "And now for my hot chocolate! Come on, Barnabas."

The last thing Barnabas wanted was to sit at a tiny café table and watch the two of them stare into each others' souls. "You go ahead" he said. "I'm gonna chill here."

She gave him a curious look, but then said, "Suit yourself," and she and Cal headed down the stairs. As they disappeared from view, he heard them sharing a little laugh, and he felt utterly abandoned. Deni could have insisted he come, couldn't she?

From down the left-hand hall, the sound of self-satisfied laughter wafted through the air like expensive perfume — the parents at their fund-raising party. Barnabas slipped down the hall and pressed his ear to the brightly-painted door. He couldn't hear anything specific, but he could imagine the rich adults in there, snacking on some fancy little platter of hors d'oeuvres, and twittering, "Oh, it's really too early in the day for a drink, but if you *insist!*"

He knew that Deni's Mom, Morgan — not the jazz-loving one, the other one — hosted a lot of fundraisers like this at their apartment. Deni hated them, but Barnabas' own mom would have killed to be there, making connections with powerful people. "Contacts are everything," she liked to tell him. "That's one of the reasons we send you to that school!" Barnabas resented this kind of pressure; he just wasn't the kind of person who could choose his friends based on their future usefulness.

Still, if he'd had a few friends around him, the security man, Klevver wouldn't have been able to sneak up on him, stealthy as a ninja. With the parents laughing uproariously on the other side of the door, Klevver dropped a meaty hand onto Barnabas' upper arm and said, "Come with me, please."

'Please,' Barnabas considered, was such a slippery word. It seemed to lose most of its meaning when it was combined with being basically dragged down the hall against your will by a man strong enough to snap you in two.

"Let me go of me!" Barnabas cried, then in an attempt to sound less like someone with something to hide: "I have to get to class."

"Easy, cameraman, just answer my questions and you're free to go. That's all the Mayor wants! Easy-peasy, right?"

Klevver maneuvered him backwards like they were dancing a tango until Barnabas found himself pinned in a corner between the concrete wall and the railing of the stairwell. Klevver was smiling that smile again — an wide grin that might make flowers spontaneously wilt — and Barnabas couldn't take his eyes off it. In the periphery of his vision, he saw the man's fist clenching and unclenching. Unlike the terror of the *diaboriku's* monsters, this menace of flesh and blood was real and dangerous.

"Okay, then," Klevver said, his tone a study in nonchalance. "As alluded to earlier, I have a little list of questions that His Honour, Mayor Tuppletaub, would like answered. You can do that, can't you?" Barnabas nodded, too nervous to speak. "Good boy," the man said, and cleared his throat. "Why did you ask the Mayor about secret subways?"

Barnabas shook his head and tried to speak. "I-I don't know… Just… needed to ask something. M-made it up."

Klevver's fist, in the corner of Barnabas' vision, clenched and stayed that way. The bodyguard started to chew, apparently on some gum that he had been storing in his cheek, like a hamster. "Have you ever been on a secret subway — that is if there was such a thing? Which there isn't, by the way."

Despite his terror, this odd non-question got Barnabas thinking. The Mayor and his cohorts were clearly hiding some crucial information, and Klevver was trying not to reveal it during the interrogation. With more confidence, Barnabas answered, "No! I was never on anything like that."

"Never," the man repeated incredulously.

"Nope."

The bodyguard chewed harder. It was kind of mesmerising to watch the cheeks working, the cords of tension twitching in his jaw. Even his brow got involved, furrowing with the effort of pulverizing the wad of gum. The term "rage-chew" popped into Barnabas' brain. If he was still alive later, he would do a search to see if he made it up or not.

Klevver continued: "Is one of your parents a…" He looked confused, chewing faster on his gum. His fist uncoiled, and he reached into the breast pocket of his jacket, pulling out a scrap of paper which he consulted. "Here we are. Is one of your parents or anyone in your family a deputized Guild Council Interlocutor?"

"Guild Council what?"

Klevver was wearing his sunglasses, but Barnabas could swear he saw the man's eyes narrow. "You heard me," he growled and leaned closer to Barnabas, taking hold of the front of his t-shirt in a grip that included some of the skin beneath.

"No seriously, I didn't hear."

"Guild. Council. In-ter-loc-u-tor!" Klevver answered with cold precision.

"I don't even know what that…" But he didn't get to finish the sentence. Like a construction crane, Klevver's arm lifted him into the air and swivelled him 90 degrees. Suddenly, he found himself up on the railing, the smooth plastic pressing into his back. And the weight of his head and shoulders was pulling him over, head-first into the stairwell. *This is DEATH!* he thought. *And I'm only 15!!* But he didn't fall; Klevver was holding him by the ankles.

Squirming, arms spiralling for some kind of equilibrium, Barnabas looked up from his inverted perspective and saw the security man leaning over the railing. His dark glasses were gone, his eyes insane blue marbles, and he was screaming, "Tell me! Tell me what you know, you little snot!" while Barnabas thrashed like a worm on a hook (which was probably not a smart thing to do when hanging over a 12-story drop). He felt something shift in the front pocket of his pants, and watched in shock as the *diaboriku* slipped loose and fell past his head. He swiped at the device, but too late; the toy hit the landing below and started bouncing — *bap, bap, bap* — down the stairs. There was no time to worry about it. Above him, the madman was red in the face, out of control. "You stinking little monkey! You slug! Who do you think you're trying to fool, you jacked-up little —"

"Klevver!" shouted a familiar voice. Barnabas, heart pounding, eyes blurred with tears, turned his upside-down head and saw upside-down Mayor Tuppletaub rushing up the stairs. "What the hell do you think you're doing, you idiot! There's an election in three weeks. I can't have my staff murdering children at a time like this!"

Klevver looked startled as if coming back to himself from a great distance. "Sorry..." he mumbled, like a shamed little boy. "I lost my temper again, didn't I?"

"Pull him up! Quickly, quickly," Tuppletaub hissed, and Barnabas was hauled over the smooth railing and deposited on his feet. His legs immediately gave out under him, and his butt hit the hard surface of the landing. The two men were right above him, but Barnabas was too stunned to even crawl into hiding.

Tuppletaub was still berating his security man: "What were you thinking?!"

Klevver whined back: "You said to get the information out of him; I didn't want to disappoint you!"

"Oh my God," answered the Mayor in disgust. "I'm surprised I didn't find you applying electro-shock to his eyelids!"

"That's actually really effective…"

"Shut up!" Mayor Tuppletaub reached down a hand to Barnabas, who took it rather gratefully. "Are you okay?" Tuppletaub asked.

"Yeah, okay… yes," Barnabas murmured, as he was pulled to his feet.

But as soon as he was standing, the Mayor poked a long, pointy finger into his chest and continued the interrogation. "Listen, boy! There are things you do not want to be involved in. How do you know about secret subways? What have you seen?!"

Though his head was still spinning and his heart pounding, Barnabas knew what to do: he had to make up a story and stick to it. "I-I was at Crumhorn Station and I overheard some, uh, I guess they were transit officials or something."

"Saying what exactly?"

"Nothing! Just like, 'You don't want to get caught using the *secret subway.*' Something like that."

The Mayor took a step back, staring him in the eye, trying to make him crack under the pressure. Barnabas held his gaze until Tuppletaub said, "And that's all they said?" Barnabas nodded. Then the Mayor grabbed him by both shoulders and moved close enough that Barnabas could smell the coffee on his breath. "Well, you just listen, little cameraman: there are *no* secret subways. Anyone who says there are gets in trouble. Big trouble. Sometimes they disappear and are *never heard of again.*" The broad, angry face filled Barnabas' field of vision and he felt a pathetic little moan escape his lips. "Have I made myself clear?" the Mayor asked.

"What is going on here?" said a concerned voice off to the side. It was a strange kind of concern — fluty and just on the edge of embarrassed laughter. Barnabas, Mayor Tuppletaub, and Mr. Klevver all turned their heads simultaneously to find Principal Rolan-Gong standing there.

Tuppletaub instantly let go of Barnabas' shoulders, and only then did Barnabas realize just how hard the man's fingers had been digging into his flesh. "Ah, Madam Principal!" the Mayor said, instantly jovial. "I was just reminding this young man about the importance of journalistic ethics."

"Oh, I see. But it seemed like you and your associate were —" She looked around in confusion, and Barnabas turned his head, too. Klevver had vanished again, like a thief in the night.

The Mayor shook his head as if it was all a sad misunderstanding. "I'm afraid this young man, Mr...?" he raised an eyebrow at the Principal.

"Bopwright," she answered.

"Mr. Bopwright needs to learn that being a journalist is no excuse for rudeness and impropriety. He was practically threatening me. It was almost amusing — as if I was hiding important state secrets!"

The Principal gasped. "Mr. Bopwright, I'm surprised at you! The Mayor is an honoured guest at our school." Barnabas felt his face burning red. Ms. Rolan-Gong turned to Tuppletaub. "I'm so sorry, Mr. Mayor. I think perhaps today's muckraking media is not the best example for our students to follow. All those paparazzi and leaked videos. *Intimate* videos! Perhaps we need to re-think the need for a journalism club."

Tuppletaub smiled and waved away her concern, "Oh, please, don't let it trouble you. I'm used to worse. You should look at the online comments whenever I give an interview. Complete lack of civility."

"Nonetheless, Mr. Bopwright, I will be informing your parents about your behaviour!"

Barnabas looked back at the adults in shock, unable to utter a word. For a second, he considered leading the Principal to his locker and showing her the secret subway map, trying to explain the whole crazy affair. But he was just a kid; no one would believe him, not when it was his word against the Mayor's! And if he did reveal the map, what would Tuppletaub do to him? Barnabas would disappear in the night, never to be heard from again, and the Mayor would say some sad words on television about another "troubled youth" and get away with it.

"Get to class, Mr. Bopwright!" The Principal snapped, before her voice again modulated from stern to gushing. "Your Honour, if you would please follow me; the parents are so anxious to meet with you!" She led the Mayor down the hall, giving Barnabas one more dirty look over her shoulder as she departed. He lowered himself to the ground again and dropped his head into his hands.

A growing cacophony of voices and footsteps rose up the stairwell; classes were changing from second to third period. Sitting in his history class for the next hour was the last thing Barnabas wanted to do. He felt run over, wrung out, closer to crying than he had in years. He rubbed at the sore skin on his chest and shoulders, and his ears seemed to ring with furious accusations of Klevver and the Mayor. Then fear slowly gave way to outrage — they had no right to treat him like that! To threaten him like that! But wasn't it his own damn fault? Why had he taken the map? Why had he asked the Mayor that damning question?

Barnabas decided it was best to return to class and try to put the whole incident behind him. He was just getting to his feet and straightening his clothes when he suddenly cried out loud: "The *diaboriku!*" In a second, he was running down the stairs, scanning every step and every dusty corner for the toy. The stairwell was still busy with the last of the students hurrying to third period. Some greeted him, but he had no time to answer. *Where is it?* he thought in panic. *Where?!*

And finally he spotted the little sphere, sitting placidly on the tenth floor landing, its big glass eye looking up at all the hubbub. With a warm burst of gratitude spreading through his chest, Barnabas sighed and headed for it. But just then, one last student ran past him and out onto the tenth floor. And as he passed, the heel of his shoe grazed the *diaboriku*. Almost languidly — like it was just crossing to the window to check the weather — it began to roll towards the stairs.

"No!" Barnabas screamed, but the toy didn't care. Casually, mischievously, it tipped off the edge and began bouncing downwards — *bap, bap, bap* — ricocheting off the wall of the next landing to continue its descent. Barnabas began to run in desperate pursuit, but the *diaboriku* rolled faster, and it was still accelerating. Flight after flight he ran, peering down into the stairwell, hoping to catch a glimpse of it. He stopped for a few seconds around the fifth floor, breathing hard, and in the echoes from below, he could hear the retreating *bam, bam, bam!* Barnabas started running again, taking the stairs two at a time, the palm of his hand rubbed raw on the plastic bannister.

He emerged into a short, utility hallway on the first floor where the recycling bins were stored. The *diaboriku* sat there against the emergency exit door. Hands braced on his knees, Barnabas tried to get his wind back. But at the very moment he straightened up, the heavy steel door opened to reveal Orlando, the building custodian, silhouetted by morning sunlight. With a lazy roll, the *diaboriku* passed between his feet and into the alley beyond.

"Barnabas?" Orlando said in surprise as the boy squeezed past him in the narrow door frame.

By the time he got clear of the door, Barnabas could see the *diaboriku* at the end of the alley, rolling between the feet of pedestrians on the sidewalk of Blesskind Boulevard. He ran to catch up, trying to keep his eye on the toy's path. He caught a glimpse of it, already surprisingly distant as it rolled into the street amid the heavy traffic, hurrying downhill, north towards the Tower District.

Barnabas ran half a block and jumped up on a concrete planter box. From this raised vantage, he scanned the dense and shifting landscape of people and cars, trying to find the proverbial needle in the haystack. But there was nothing! He swore and pushed his fingers through his sweaty hair, slowly succumbing to the desperate, guilty feeling growing inside him.

He played out an action movie in his head where he suddenly spotted the *diaboriku* on the road, about to be crushed by a giant truck. In his mind's eye, he ran heroically between the moving cars and dived forward to snatch it out of harm's way. Rolling clear and holding the toy up high in triumph, he would shout: *Thelonius! I didn't lose it! I'm not a loser!* But there was no last glimpse, no daring rescue; the *diaboriku* was gone. It might as well have fallen off the end of the Earth.

Barnabas had no idea how long he stood there, numbed by misery and regret, blinking back tears which could, in the end, not be denied. It might have been 15 minutes later — or maybe half an hour — when the man spoke.

"It seems you've lost something."

Barnabas looked down at him. Actually, given the man's height, Barnabas was barely looking down, even though he was up on the planter box, and the man was on the sidewalk. He wiped at his face in case there were still any tears there, and that was when he realized that the man was none other than Mr. Glower, the strange bald guy in the khaki coveralls from Crumhorn Station.

"Yes, lost something," Barnabas said, finding it hard to get his voice to work. "I lost my… uh… it's this round thing. Rolled down the street." His voice choked a bit as he added, "It's important."

"Mmm," replied Glower, nodding. He cracked his knuckles, and his black crow eyes studied Barnabas' face intently. The man didn't seem to remember him, much less blame him for the theft of the "restricted document."

A voice behind them made them both turn: "I know, I know! I've been trapped at this ridiculous school for hours!" It was the Mayor, exiting the school building, yelling into his phone. Barnabas jumped down from the planter box and ducked behind it, peeking around the side to see what

Tuppletaub was up to. A limo pulled up to the curb. Barnabas could see Klevver behind the wheel, the advisor seated in the back. The Mayor opened the back door but stayed out on the sidewalk while he finished his call.

"Well, wait till you see the donations I just got!" he crowed, one hand on the open car door. Then, almost as if he could feel Glower's eyes on him, he slowly turned his head. From his hiding place, Barnabas watched Glower give the Mayor a curt nod. Tuppletaub, startled, nodded back before almost throwing himself into the limo, leaving the door open. Glower walked toward the waiting car, but halfway there, he turned and looked down at the bit of Barnabas' face he could see behind the planter.

He said, "Sometimes things return to you. But usually, they are gone for good, and then you have to decide what to do with that terrible, burning hole in your heart. Some say you should learn to be content with your sorry lot. But there is another way. You can seek revenge for what was done to you. That's what life's really about: deciding which sort of man you are." Having delivered this dark sermon, Glower climbed into the limo, closing the door behind him. A moment later, the car was in motion, quickly disappearing around the corner.

CHAPTER 5

By the time Barnabas made his way back upstairs to school, it was lunch hour. He didn't want any company, so he ate in the stairwell. He went to his afternoon classes, but he couldn't really focus on anything. Over and over, he found himself replaying the events of the morning: Klevver hanging him over the edge of a 12-story drop, Mayor Tuppletaub threatening to make him vanish if he told anyone about the Aqua Line subway, Cal and Deni starring in their own personal rom-com. But worse than any of this was the loss of the *diaboriku*. How could he ever explain his carelessness to Thelonius?

After school, he just wanted to go home, but he had promised to edit video interviews for the Interactive Yearbook Club. When that was done, he stumbled to his locker with relief and began packing up his bag. He was on the verge of making a clean getaway when Deni found him.

"Hey," she said. "Come back to the video suite. We'll check your footage of me and the Mayor."

Deni still didn't know any of his troubles. Since he hadn't told her about the map, he didn't see how he could explain about Klevver and the Mayor. Also, since she didn't even know she might be his girlfriend, there was no way she knew he was jealous of Cal. Secrecy, he saw, could become a habit. Luckily, he had a legitimate excuse: "Sorry, I have to get home. My Mom sent me a text to remind me about family dinner tonight."

"Family dinner? I thought you guys never ate together. Your mom has all those late meetings and stuff."

Barnabas knew that Deni and her moms *always* ate together—late European-style dinners, where they discussed politics and art. He told her, "Mom read an article that said families who eat together raise more secure children. So she wants us to do it at least once a month." He closed his locker with a bang and turned to find her staring at him like he was a lab specimen.

"Are you depressed?" she asked.

"What? No!"

"'Cause you're acting depressed. Do you have a therapist? I used to see a *great* therapist!"

"No, and I'm not depressed." He started walking quickly towards the elevators, trying to get away from her, but she followed him with determination.

"You know what I would do if I was you and I was feeling depressed?"

"I'm not, but what?" He pumped at the elevator's down button, trying to bring it up to the ninth floor faster.

"I would pretend I was sick and then go visit your dad! You know, like follow him from gig to gig for a while!"

"I don't even know where he is. The tour dates on his website haven't been updated for two years."

"Well, maybe your mom can find him."

The elevator, mercifully, arrived then, and he dived inside without a word.

"I'll text you later!" she shouted as the doors closed in her face.

Rush hour was at its heaviest and most unforgiving. In the subway, Barnabas wrapped himself around a pole and let the crowd push him back and forth like seaweed in the tide. By the time he got back to his building, he realized he was looking forward to family dinner after all. On a day as bad as this one had been, he wanted to have his tribe around him for protection. He wanted a reminder that there was a home to come back to if tomorrow turned out just as grisly.

He could already picture the scene in their kitchen as he rode the elevator up to the 35th floor: his mom flustered and barking orders to his stepdad as timers beeped all over the kitchen, indicating that three of the eight dishes she was making needed attention. Since family dinner was such a rare occurrence, his mom had a tendency to overdo it. But when Barnabas walked in the door, there were no smells of exotic spices or toasting grains. In fact, his mom was at the door, struggling to get a chunky gold earring into place. She was wearing a work suit and her briefcase was on the floor.

"Oh, Barney-lamb!" she exclaimed, pulling out her phone to check an incoming text. "I'm glad I caught you before I left." As she read the message, she planted a quick kiss on the top of his head and said, "I picked up some microwave *pad thai* for you and Björn."

"But, mom, I thought it was family dinner night!"

She bit her lip. "I know, I know, but I've *just* been appointed to the board of a new charity." She frowned at her phone. "No, I did *not* promise that report for tomorrow morning," she muttered darkly at the text message before turning a no-nonsense boardroom smile in Barnabas's direction. "It's a *wonderful* new organization! We've all seen how *dreary* the lives of people in refugee camps can be. So we're raising money to send them *party kits!* Balloons, games, decorations for Hawaiian-themed prom nights…"

"But don't they mostly need, you know, food and medicine?"

His mother clucked her tongue at him and turned to her reflection in the hall mirror. She adjusted the jacket of her suit. "Do you always have to be so negative? If you want to get a start-up charity noticed, you have to *differentiate* yourself! Otherwise you'll never interest the donors." She looked back down at him. "Did I kiss you yet?"

"Yes," he said, struggling against resentment. His mother grabbed her keys from a plate by the door and then her briefcase. "Wait!" Barnabas called. "Mom, I wanted to discuss something that happened at school —"

She turned back to him, her face beaming with enthusiasm. "Oh yes! I got an email from your Principal. Don't worry about what she says — journalist ethics or whatever. You got the Mayor's attention! I bet if we play this right, we can parlay it into a summer internship at City Hall, or even a recommendation when you apply to university!"

"Unless they knock down our door tonight and arrest me," he moaned.

His mother clucked her tongue again as she opened the door. "Don't be melodramatic, Barney-lamb; it makes you seem needy. I'll be home late; don't wait up." She gave the door her usual, unnecessary slam, and the sound seemed to echo on into the silence that followed.

When Barnabas entered the living room, he found Björn with one of his indigenous musical instruments, turning it over and over, scrutinizing the horn and sinew that made up its body and strings. He gave his stepson a little smile that held the beginnings of an apology in it.

"Hey Björn," Barnabas said, trying to return the smile, but it felt like the corners of his mouth were held down by fishing weights.

"Sorry about dinner," Björn said. "But we'll have a good time. Just us men, right?"

"I'm going to go change. Meet you in the kitchen." Barnabas needed a minute to put on a better smile. He hated doing anything that made Björn sad. His stepfather had been an ethnomusicologist at the University, teaching about music from all around the world, until the department got downsized. A friend had finally landed him a job as a deejay at the fifth-highest-rated top-40 radio station in the city, and now he spent his mornings sounding out of his mind with enthusiasm for music he hated. Björn was really decent to him, and the last thing Barnabas wanted was to add to his worries. They ate their *pad thai*, talking about old movies — just about the only interest they shared — and after dinner, Barnabas headed off to his room, where he could finally feel safe from the world's assaults.

His bedroom was a tiny, perfect cube, three metres by three metres by three metres. All the necessities of life — from clothes to comic books, notebooks to army knives — lived in cubical containers on the floor-to-ceiling Sverbïlt shelving unit that was mounted on the west wall of the room

On the south wall, above his bed, were two posters. In one, a mountaineer stood atop some towering mountain in the Andes, alone, nobly contemplating his hard-earned view. The second poster featured old-time film director Stanley Kubrick with his long, scraggly hair and messy beard, looking through the lens of a huge pre-digital camera. Barnabas wasn't really planning to be a mountaineer, and being a movie director was only a vague romantic notion, but somehow both of these figures seemed like people he wanted to emulate: solitary and heroic.

Opposite his bed, against the north wall, was a Sverbïlt modular desk with built-in bookshelves whose collection ran from his most recent reading ("500 Strange Places You Must Visit in Your Life") to his earliest (a wordless children's book about a baby raccoon who chases a firefly through the woods and finds himself separated from his family.)

Barnabas crossed to the big windows on the east wall and looked out at the City, all golden highlights and dramatic shadows in the waning sunlight. He looked south to the treetops of River's Edge Park; he looked north and could see a bit of the Tower District. If it hadn't been for the condos across the street, he would have been able to see Gum Hill to the east, a steep-sided plateau on which sat the Manhammer Audio Dome, the City's great stadium. He loved this view; it made him feel like the City belonged to him. But tonight, he just felt exposed standing there as if malicious eyes, intent on revenge, were searching for him. He pulled the big drapes closed, and immediately felt safer.

Barnabas crossed to his desk and opened his laptop. It was time to get down to his homework, but he had a question he needed to ask first. He opened a TxtChat window, and clicked on the shortcut for his brother, Thelonius.

> *theloneliest>* **Hey, good morning**
> *barnabustamove>* **it's night here**
> *theloneliest>* **no kidding**

The app chimed and a VidChat window opened. "Hey, Beaner," Thelonius said, running his fingers through his messy black hair, eyes puffy with sleep.

"Aren't you getting ready for work?" Barnabas asked.

"It's my day off; the schedule keeps changing. Did you figure out how to use the *diaboriku*?" The authentic way he pronounced it sounded very cool to Barnabas. Thelonius' mother was Japanese; the only parent they shared was their dad, Brownbag Bopwright (whose real name was Harold). Barnabas sometimes spent long minutes staring at pictures of his 24 year-old half-brother (who the Japanese called "Teronisu") to see the ways they did and didn't look alike. For instance, their hair was the same thick, wavy mass, but where Barnabas' was chestnut brown, Thelonius' was black as liquorice. Sometimes, Barnabas would pretend that the picture was a version of himself from an alternate reality, one where he was born a samurai. (Deni called this fantasy racist.)

Barnabas wanted to tell Thelonius about the "monster attack" they had endured courtesy of the *diaboriku*, but he didn't want to also tell how he had lost it, so he just said, "Not yet. Still working on it." And before Thelonius could respond, he continued, "Listen, back when you were an Innervader, did you ever find a … um, another subway line? Like, one no one talks about?"

"No. I mean, there are a few ghost stations on the Purple Line," Thelonius replied as he stood to make coffee for himself. His apartment was so small, he could be anywhere in it except the bathroom and still be on camera. "And there's old City Hall Station down that separate loop. It's all in the mission logs on the website."

The Innervaders were a clandestine club of urban explorers, and as a teenager, Thelonius had been one of its youngest and most daring members. Barnabas vividly remembered the nights when his brother would sneak out of their room in the old condo to go on adventures with his friends. He would dress in black, like a super-criminal ninja, with coils of rope and different kinds of flashlights and crowbars. Any "No Entry!" sign was a defiant challenge to the Innervaders, a dare they had to take.

Barnabas had been a little kid of maybe eight or nine, unable to sleep for fear and excitement until his brother snuck back in hours later, sweaty and exhilarated, bearing treasures from his crusade: a chipped china plate from a shuttered hotel, a Bakelite knob from an old power station, or the "No Entry!" sign itself. Though Barnabas was sworn to secrecy, it was, of course, him who eventually, accidentally gave his brother away and brought an end to Thelonius' night-time exploits.

Thelonius raised an eyebrow at him and said, "I still know people in the club. If you want, I can hook you up on an infiltration. Just a small one to start…"

Barnabas drummed the desk nervously with a pen and looked away. "No, no thanks. Mom's says that if I ever got arrested doing it, I might not be able to get into a good university later."

His brother rolled his eyes. "She worries too much. You gotta learn to live a bit! But don't go down into the subway tunnels on your own. Too dangerous."

"I wouldn't do that!" he insisted.

Thelonius sipped his coffee and continued in a softer tone. "That's okay, Beaner, you don't have to do anything you're not comfortable with." Despite the kind tone, Barnabas felt like a loser. He would never be brave like his brother. He got through life by avoiding trouble, not by facing it head-on. But wasn't that the better path? Why invite trouble if you're not strong enough to handle it?

Thelonius had to sign off and get to work, and Barnabas just sat in his chair feeling alone, regretting now that he hadn't dared unburden himself about the Aqua Line and the Mayor's threat. He took a down a picture from the shelf above his desk and stared at it. It was a terrible image, gray and grainy, taken in the middle of the biggest drop on the Inferno Coaster at Seven Circles Amusement Park. The souvenir photo in its cheap cardboard frame featured him, Thelonius and their dad. No one really looked good in the picture; Brownbag was just a blur with a gaping scream of a mouth, and Thelonius looked like he was about to throw up. Only nine-year old Barnabas had a huge, unambiguous expression of joy on his face.

From the minute they'd arrived at the park, Barnabas had led them at a run from ride to ride, trying to cram as much into the day as it could possibly hold. Their dad's bags had already been packed before they started off that morning. He moved out that night, right after they got home.

Deni started sending increasingly worried texts as he worked through his math problems. (**"Are you suicidal? DON'T DO IT!"**), so he sent her calming replies with pictures of puppies until she left him alone. In truth, he didn't feel calm; more like worn out by worry. He managed to do a half-assed version of a book report for English, but by the time he was finished — even though it was barely 10 o'clock, even though his lights were still on — he fell onto his bed and was instantly asleep.

Barnabas' dreams were troubled ones. He dreamed that he was in the school cafeteria, pulling out the lunch container Björn had packed for him. It was huge; he wasn't even sure how it had fit into his backpack, and it took all his strength to pry off the stubborn lid. When he did, he was shocked to find what looked like a half-eaten baby dinosaur, cooked in some kind of thick, red sauce. One leg and a chunk from the side had already been eaten, but the rest was there, including the head. Where the eyes had been, there were two green olives. He wanted to show Deni and Cal this disgusting spectacle, but when he looked up, he saw he was eating alone in the cafeteria. Up on the stage, Mayor Tuppletaub was hollering knock-knock jokes into the microphone.

From the far end of the room came a familiar voice that made Barnabas' stomach clench in fear. It was Mr. Klevver, calling as he approached, "Knock-knock! Who's there? Greta! Greta who? *You're gonna re-greta day you met me!*"

Barnabas stood and ran from the cafeteria through the eerily deserted halls of the school and up the stairs. He didn't have to look back to know Klevver was gaining on him. *If I can reach the twelfth-floor office*, he thought, *Ms. Rolan-Gong will save me.* But then, even though Klevver had been behind him, he now stood at the top of the stairs, blocking Barnabas' path.

And the next thing he knew, Barnabas was tossed back over the railing into the bottomless stairwell. By some miracle, he was able to catch the railing with his outstretched hand, and he hung there with Klevver looming above him.

"Help!" Barnabas shouted. Looking around, he saw that the stairwell was now packed with familiar faces: all his classmates and teachers, his parents, Thelonius. Everyone was staring at him, but no one came to his rescue.

"Don't worry, dear!" his mother called. "If you fall, I'll start a charity for you!"

Klevver started shaking the railing, and Barnabas struggled to hang on. Soon, it wasn't just the railing shaking, but the walls and floors as well, and an ominous rumble grew ever louder.

"Mr. Klevver," Barnabas cried. "Stop! You'll bring down the whole building." And that's exactly what happened. The ceiling cracked, the floor gave way, and Barnabas was tumbling into the abyss, surrounded by all the contents of the school. Desks, whiteboards, wall maps, jars of paint, a hundred *papier maché* volcanoes from the grade nines, and a hundred aspirational collages from the grade twelves. And the students, staff, and family fell in chaos, disappearing into the void. *And all the King's horses, and all the King's men could never put Humpty together again...*

Barnabas awoke with a strangled cry, covered in sweat, heart pounding. He looked at the clock. It was just after midnight. On his desk was a plate with a lemon tart and a little note saying, "Good night, Barnie-lamb!" Even in his troubled, turbulent sleep, his mother had come and gone without waking him.

He picked up his backpack off the floor and, from deep in the zippered pocket, retrieved the subway map. Opening it on his desk, he again examined the meandering Aqua Line, racking his brain to make any sense of it. The document was dangerous, and as long as he held on to it, he and the people around him were in danger. He considered slipping out of the apartment and dropping the map down the disposal chute. Or maybe he should sneak into the kitchen and burn it in a pot. But the same reasons that made it dangerous also made it an irresistible object of desire, a treasure not to be given up lightly.

Barnabas locked his bedroom door. He pulled his desk chair over to the wall of shelves and removed a container from the top shelf, setting it carefully on the bed. Most people looking into this secret box of treasures would only see a mini-dumpster of useless garbage; but everything in the container held magic for Barnabas. A small, purple action figure which he used to imagine was sent to him personally from an alien civilization. A glittering, black rock given to him by Deni on a fifth grade canoe trip. A ticket stub from the concert he and his friends had seen at the Manhammer Audio Dome on his 15th birthday — Pulp Spirit with special guest Doc Salvage. It was the first show they'd been allowed to attend without adult supervision.

He dumped everything onto his bed and placed the map at the bottom of the box, before repacking and re-shelving it. He went to the bathroom and brushed his teeth, then returned to bed, willing himself back to sleep. He was almost there when he had a sudden flashback of Mayor Tuppletaub's face up close to his, hissing: *"What do you know about secret subways?!"*

He was instantly awake again, suffused with panic. Would the Mayor and Mr. Klevver be able to track him down? Of course! Ms. Rolan-Gong would tell them anything they asked! What if the police were about to burst through the apartment door and arrest him? But *no!* They wouldn't arrest him — if they did, they would have to admit their secrets. They would just grab him on his way to school, throw him into the back of a black van and carry him off to a secret, underground prison. He would be left to rot in some dungeon on the Aqua Line until he was an old man.

With these horrible thoughts running through his head, there was no point trying to sleep. He got out of bed and played video games until 2:30. Still wide awake, he went to his bookshelf and pulled down "500 Strange Places You Must Visit in Your Life." He sat on the floor with his back against his bed and read about haunted temples deep in the jungle, and regions in the sea where whales from every ocean congregate to sing songs that are heard nowhere else. As long as he stayed in these far-off lands where the fantastic was possible, Barnabas could forget about the dangers he faced. Finally, exhaustion overcame him, and he fell asleep on the floor, still holding the book. And that's how he woke up in the morning.

Daylight was throbbing from behind his drapes. Above him on the night stand, the alarm clock was beeping incessantly. He wasn't asleep exactly, but neither could he wake up enough to reach up and switch it off. His mother burst into the room, crossing over to his bedside to shut off the machine. "Seriously! It's enough to make a person in*sane!*" she said, before sweeping out of the room. She didn't seem to find it surprising that he'd been sleeping on the floor.

Barnabas started falling asleep again, but suddenly, out of the first layer of dreams, a black van, driven by Klevver, reared up like a raging bull. His eyes snapped open, and his heart started pounding so loudly in his chest, he was sure his mother would come back in to switch it off, complaining, "...enough to drive a person *mad!*" He went to the bathroom to shower, hurrying to make up for the ten minutes he had lost in his stupor.

Björn's radio show started right after the 9 o'clock news, so he was already long gone, but the lunch he had prepared for Barnabas (tuna, not baby dinosaur) was in the fridge. Barnabas made himself a bagel with peanut butter for breakfast and kept out of his mother's way. She was in her usual crazy morning state, thirstily slurping her coffee and furiously texting with well-toned thumbs. As she hurried to and fro, Barnabas, who couldn't stop yawning, tried to figure out if he could claim to be sick and ask to stay home. But their routine swept them both along, and he was too sleepy to break free of its momentum. Soon they were exchanging routine kisses, and he was out the door.

As he stepped out into the very ordinary sunny morning, the idea of the Mayor's henchmen in their black van seemed a little ludicrous. Still, he surveyed the street and sidewalk for anything unusual before he set off toward the subway. As he descended the steps into Kiletko Station, he decided to take a different route to school in case anyone — Mr. Klevver, for instance — was lying in wait along his usual path. Instead of taking the Yellow Line, he would get off the Red Line at Haverstall and ride a trolley across Blesskind Boulevard to school. Once he got there, he would make sure he was never alone. What could the Mayor do if he was always surrounded by friends?

He was grateful to find a seat for once, but it was a mistake to take it, since the train had barely left Kiletko station when he fell asleep, his chin resting on the backpack in his lap. He only realized his mistake when the train reached its terminus at Rebbertrue Station. He cursed his stupidity the whole walk to the eastbound Yellow Line platform. *It's okay*, he told himself. *If I keep my head down in the crowd, no one will spot me.*

He and a thousand co-commuters poured into the Yellow Line train when it arrived. By this time, he had thoroughly spooked himself. Without trying to look like he was looking, he checked out every face he passed, searching for signs that he'd been recognized. It was the oddest feeling — to be simultaneously so on edge and so tired. If only there had been a free seat.

He noticed something unusual: parked down at the end of the car was a tall red machine with big rubber wheels and several robotic arms. Its shape reminded Barnabas of some storybook grandmother: pleasingly plump, in a long skirt, arms folded across an ample bosom. The machine, which might have been built for anything from floor cleaning to helicopter repair, completely filled the gap between the wall and the empty operator's booth. Barnabas knew that there was a two-person bench behind the big machine. Could he get to it? He made his way through the dense crowd until he was standing beside the machine. All he had to do, he saw, was stand on the big rubber wheel and squeeze between the chassis and the wall — no problem for someone his size. At the next station, as the crowd re-shuffled to let people on and off the train, he made his move.

It was perfect, a cozy little cave. There was no leg room in front of the bench, but he turned sideways and brought his feet up onto the second seat. Not only was he comfortable, but when he scrunched down a bit, he was invisible to everyone in the car. Even the CCTV camera on the ceiling couldn't see him. Feeling safe and secure, he lowered his head onto the backpack in his lap and closed his heavy eyelids. *There's no place like home,* he told himself, and abruptly fell fast asleep in his little nook.

As Barnabas careened through the dark tunnels, his dreams were all pleasant ones.

CHAPTER 6

"The next station is Admiral Crumhorn," said the sexy Yellow Line announcement lady. Barnabas wondered what it would be like to be her son, to be woken in the morning by that captivating voice: "It's time to get up… Next stop: school!" He shifted his head into a more comfortable position and drifted off to sleep again.

"The station stop is Admiral Crumhorn," she said as the train braked, sending a deep, comforting vibration through the wall behind him. "This is the final stop on the Yellow Line. Transfers available for the Blue, Green, and Purple Lines. This train is now out of service. Please leave the train."

Barnabas' eyebrows knit in aggravation as hundreds of people exited onto the platform, each one, it seemed to him, trying to do it as noisily as possible. But then everything was blissfully still again. Barnabas felt like he could just go on sleeping forever.

Two more voices invaded his semi-consciousness. The distant one asked, "All clear?" and the near one — very near indeed from the sound of his voice — answered "All clear!" and then left the car.

"Please stand back from the closing doors," said the announcement lady, with breezy finality. "Doors are closing."

The door chimes sounded brightly, and Barnabas woke up with a gasp into utter, vivid consciousness. He sat up straight and looked over the top of the machine; he was the only person left on the train and he was about to be closed in. He grabbed his backpack and scrambled out of his hiding place, but as he cleared the wheel and headed for the door, the strap of his backpack caught on a corner of the machine, and he went crashing to the floor. With a pneumatic hiss and a definitive "thump," the subway doors closed.

"NO!" he screamed as the train began moving, not back the way it had come, but forward, into unknown territory. The safe, familiar platform of Admiral Crumhorn Station with its sky-blue wall tiles disappeared as the train entered the tunnel. The lights in the car dimmed to a sickly yellow, like yogurt gone bad.

Barnabas ran from end to end of the car and peered through the windows into the adjacent cars. He seemed to be the only one on the whole slowly-moving train. He tried to quell his panic and assess the situation calmly: he was somewhere he shouldn't be, and if he was caught, he might be in trouble. But the panic he felt was mixed with another emotion: excitement. He was on an adventure! He was an Innervader, after all!

The train arrived at another platform, although considering how slow they'd been moving, Barnabas figured they must still be within the mammoth structure of Admiral Crumhorn Station. There were people on the platform, and he instinctively ducked down and tried to decide his next move. He could wait for the doors to open and just march out confidently. He would just switch to the westbound platform and catch a train back to the normal world of the Yellow Line. "Sorry, I fell asleep," he'd say if anyone challenged him.

What do you know about secret subways?!!! Mayor Tuppletaub screamed in his head, and he suddenly lost his nerve. He retrieved his backpack and retreated to the hidden seats behind the big machine.

No sooner had he tucked himself back in when the subway began a series of shocking transformations. Loud motors growled, and metal scraped on metal as outside, large panels lowered over the big glass windows and the subway doors, leaving only narrow slits of thick, scratched glass to peer through. Inside, half of the seats began to fold themselves into the floor and various racks and hooks lowered from panels in the ceiling. The graceful lines of the Yellow Line trains all but vanished, and with shocking speed, the elegant vehicle turned into something resembling a long, heavy tank.

The digital screens with their colourful ads for movies and shampoo went black. The only panels that remained active were the ones that featured the

Yellow Line subway maps. On these, the pixels scrambled and reformed in blue. No, not blue… *Aqua*. They became Aqua Line maps, just the like the one hidden back in his bedroom.

The overhead lights flickered a few times and then came back on at full brightness. The newly reinforced doors with their tiny porthole windows scraped open. Barnabas' heart beat faster, and he lowered himself out of sight as people began to enter the subway. He listened to the mounting hubbub for a frightened minute before he noticed that if he raised his head just a bit, he had a clear view between two of the machine's folded appendages.

Tall. These new passengers were all very tall as if the population here on this side of Crumhorn consisted entirely of basketball players. Seven or eight of these giants — both men and women — entered the car. A few were in business clothes, carrying leather briefcases, but most were dressed in coveralls of various colours. They wore dented hardhats and muddy construction boots, and at their waists were wide web-belts full of unidentifiable tools. Some pushed large, wheeled machines, bristling with blades and hoses, or carts filled with bundles of piping and buckets full of bolts and widgets, coated blackly with oil.

They secured the machines and carts in place with lengths of woven strap that spooled down from the ceiling, and then sat and strapped themselves in with harnesses pulled from under the seats that circled their waists and criss-crossed their chests. Barnabas felt like he was watching preparations for a rocket launch!

Another gigantic fellow, this one caked in mud from his boots to his crusty mohawk was attempting to pull another strange machine into the car. As he twisted and turned it through the doorway, Barnabas could hear servos deep inside its battered metal chassis grind and complain.

"Denizen!" A voice yelled after him. "Halt!"

The giant with the mohawk, sweating from wrestling with the machine, turned as a uniformed woman (who was just as tall) entered the car from the platform with a no-nonsense air of authority. Her uniform was sleek, spotless, and aqua: a long jacket with padded shoulders, trousers that narrowed dramatically below the knee to fit snuggly into her shiny black boots, and a high peaked hat with a long black visor.

"Papers," she ordered and the man began digging through the pockets of his brown coveralls, causing cascades of dry clay to rain down on the floor of the subway. Without a word, he handed her a little stack of crumpled papers which she snapped from his fingers and examined with cold professionalism.

After 20 nervous seconds, she handed him back the papers, and he bent over to stuff them into a pocket down by his right knee. With him still bent double, she said, "I'll also need the transfer-allowance disputation contracts for your regalvinator."

"What what what?" The man replied, pulling himself upright. "No, that's not right! This unit is not in the mandate fleet anymore!" He slapped the top of the machine with the palm of his hand, and it gave a low whine of complaint. "It was released from Clouding's manifest last month, Officer, and Furrowing purchased it as an independent —"

The guard shook her head. "In that case your guild-node should have had the decommission plates installed and given you a copy of the transfer documents."

"No one told me that!" Everyone in the car was now watching the little drama, including Barnabas, who found he could peek through a small gap in his machine's chassis without exposing himself.

On the guard's belt was a dispenser with a tongue of paper hanging from its opening. She pulled out a strip of the shiny red paper and tore it off. Using the wall of the subway as a writing surface, she began filling in blanks on the paper. The man, looking more upset by the minute, tried to talk her out of whatever she was doing. At one point he seemed like he was going to grab the wrist of her writing hand; Barnabas watched everyone in the car lean forward, but then he dropped his hands meekly to his side.

The guard in aqua finished writing. She peeled a backing strip off the paper, and slapped it onto the machine like an angry, red bumper sticker. She touched the rim of her hat — an incongruously friendly gesture of farewell — and exited the train. The man with the mohawk looked like he'd just been run over by elephants.

"Jagged life," a giant in red coveralls said to him in a sympathetic voice.

"No one told me!" the man replied pathetically, shaking his head in disbelief. "Are they gonna throw me in Doomlock?"

"Who knows?" said a woman, also in coveralls (the ones in suits were pointedly ignoring him, suddenly very interested in documents they'd pulled from their briefcases). "Nothing to be done now. You better tie that down before we get underway."

Barnabas felt more nervous than ever. The word "Doomlock" echoed in his brain. He remembered it as one of the stops on the Aqua Line map. In fact, looking up at the display on the wall, he spotted the station, about halfway between Crumhorn and the serpentine line's terminus. Had he been right? Was there a dungeon in the world of the secret subway?!

A station announcement rang out (a male voice and stern): "The outbound Aqua Line train will depart in one minute. Please secure all burdens and make sure your personal safety harnesses are firmly attached." Barnabas stared at the open door nearest him. *I should get up,* he thought. *I should go through that open door before this goes too far.* He slid along the seat, ready to leave his hiding place, but as he stood on the big machine's rubber wheel and peered out through the open door, he saw the guard in aqua walking slowly, purposefully down the platform, her eyes searching every corner of her world for infractions. *Doomlock!* Barnabas returned to his hiding place.

The man with the mohawk had tied down his machine and strapped himself into his seat. He looked miserable, like he just wanted to run. Barnabas knew just how he felt. The door chimes rang like the bells of fate, but just as the doors began to close, one more person jumped through into the car — literally jumped — his knees raised almost to his chest. His landing was surprisingly elegant, and he slid across the floor on one knee, arms in the air as if to invite applause. And he *got* applause, not to mention grateful, amused laughs. Everyone in the car seemed excited to see him as he stood to his full height which, unlike everyone else on the train, was about the same as Barnabas'.

"Thank you, thank you," the little man said in a scratchy voice that filled the car. Veins stood out on his red nose, and age lines clustered around his sparkling eyes and mouth. He slicked back his stringy, greying hair with bony hands. "Glad I didn't miss the chance to be with you, folks!" He stood up and looked for an empty seat, spotting one halfway down the car. With exaggerated pleasure at its discovery, he began to walk to it, but immediately tripped, flipping a full turn in mid-air and landing on his ass. Laughter rang out. Even the miserable, muddy man in the mohawk couldn't prevent a little smile creeping across his face. Barnabas figured him for some kind of circus clown, though he wasn't sure why everyone on board recognized him if Barnabas didn't.

The lights dimmed again, and the train began to move. The clown hurried to sit and strap himself in. As the train left the station, Barnabas wondered about the need for all the security harnesses. As if answering his curiosity, the subway picked up speed and began to move downhill. The first curve was wide and easy, but the train was still accelerating, its angle of descent steepening. The clatter and bang of wheels on track grew louder as the subway picked up speed. The next curve raised up a screech at track level, and everything in the car rattled and jostled. The next sharp curve — this time in the opposite direction — caused a couple of oil-slick widgets to fly from one of the carts and rattle across the floor like a pair of dice.

Everyone on board seemed to take this violent passage in stride. Barnabas, for his part, had to brace himself against the wall and dig his heels into the smooth vinyl of the seat to keep from flying free like the widgets. The noise around him grew ever louder, and he gritted his teeth, hoping the ride would be over soon.

The train's rapid descent abruptly levelled out, and it burst into the next station. The lights in the car went back up to full brightness. The train had barely slowed as they approached, and now the driver was applying the brakes with such a heavy hand, the wheels squealed in protest against the rails and sparks flew up outside the windows. Barnabas was pressed back against the seats and then thrown violently forward into the side of the machine as the train stopped with a final jerk. He rubbed his temple where it had hit the hard metal chassis.

The door chimes sounded and the heavy doors scraped open. There was no station announcement, and when he raised his head to peek through the gap between the machine's arms, Barnabas saw nothing through the open doors but a dirty platform. There was no station name or ads on the concrete walls, no crowds of morning commuters — just a few men and women in coveralls getting off and few a getting on. Barnabas had planned to exit here, but now he wondered whether he should wait for something resembling a proper station. Still, he was only getting in deeper — literally deeper — the longer he stayed aboard. He steeled his resolve and slipped quietly out of his hiding place.

No one seemed to be paying attention to him. He pulled on his backpack and walked slowly for the nearest door. But before he got there, a terrifying beast entered through the door. Huge as it was, it must have been a dog, though it was taller than he was and moved with the coiled menace of a panther, sinuous muscles rippling beneath its matted blue-grey coat. There was a thick, studded leather collar circling the dog's powerful neck and a taut leash extended out to the platform.

The dog spotted Barnabas immediately, narrowing its eyes, showing teeth as long as a human finger, and growling. Barnabas hastily retreated to his hiding place. The man holding the leash entered the subway, and thankfully, he looked more than capable of controlling the beast. He must have been seven feet tall, barrel-chested, the biceps in his thick arms hard and round as two watermelons. He was followed by a woman with short, curly hair who was almost as tall as him and looked just as strong. She pushed a large cart full of tools ahead of her. Both of them were coated in dried clay that rendered their skin grey. Their hair was equally grey, and they left muddy footprints behind them.

As they strapped down their cart, the woman raised a hand in greeting to the guy with mohawk. "What's with the red ticket on your regalvinator, Derlik?" she asked him.

"Reg-slapped by an Aqua!" he called back.

The man in blue, grunting as he pulled a strap tight said, "That's utter sideways! Talk to your guild advocate as soon as you get home."

He and the woman plopped down in seats across from each other and secured their harnesses. The woman pulled a strange device off her tool belt — something between a drill and hand mixer — and examined it with disgust. "It's krumped!" she told the man, shaking the device to produce a rattling inside. She handed it to him and they began an animated discussion about different repair options.

Despite the fact that the people in the car couldn't see Barnabas, the massive dog seemed to know exactly where he was. It had lain down on the floor by the man's feet, creating an astonishingly large puddle of drool, but slowly it was shifting its body, twist by turn, to get closer to his hiding place. Barnabas looked longingly at the open door. He didn't know how long he had before the train left the station, but there was no way he could get past the beast who seemed eager for a chance to tear out his throat.

The chimes sounded and the doors slammed shut. Barnabas whimpered in frustration. The lights dimmed and the train jerked forward into the tunnel, resuming its roller-coaster descent, deeper and deeper into the earth. During one particularly tight turn, the dog slid halfway across the floor toward Barnabas, who saw, to his horror, that the man had relaxed his grip on the leash. Realizing it was free, the dog got carefully to its feet, its eyes shining hungrily. Its balance in the rocking train was impressive. Barnabas looked at the top of the machine in front of him and at the dog's strong legs. It sure looked to him like the beast could leap right over and get him if it chose to do so.

The two giants were arguing now, pulling tool after tool from their belts, and comparing them with emphatic gestures. Their voices were inaudible over the chatter and rattle of the speeding train. The dog's growl, too was all but drowned out, but Barnabas could see its throat quivering below the double collar. He couldn't even hear his own voice as he shouted, "Excuse me! Hey! Hold onto your dog!"

Just as the train levelled out and pulled into the next station, the dog tensed its back legs and made its leap. Up into the air it flew, its trajectory one that would easily clear the machine and land it on top of Barnabas. He screamed inaudibly, the sound lost under the identical scream of the braking wheels. The man looked up at that moment, tightened his huge fist around the leash, and the dog crashed back to the floor.

"Come on, Marigold!" he snarled at the dog, reeling her back in until the dog was at his side. "Stop fooling around. This is our stop." He began to undo his harness as the lights in the car brightened.

Barnabas made his decision. As soon as man, woman, and dog exited, he'd get off the train no matter what and get himself turned around. Whatever lay ahead was too dangerous, too strange for him. He wasn't an Innervader; his place was back in the familiar. *Sorry, Thelonius*, he thought. If he hurried, he might even make it to school by second period.

The train was standing in the station, but the doors remained closed. Barnabas peered through the slatted windows, and he could make out a sign that read: "Deadly Steam! Secure Q clamps before decompressing!" As if to illustrate this obscure injunction, a cloud of mist drifted across the window, hiding the sign. The air seemed to have grown warmer, more humid. The man and woman were on their feet now, removing the straps from their cart and moving to stand behind the closed doors. Marigold was panting from the heat, glassy-eyed, still throwing an occasional gut-churning growl in Barnabas' direction.

A light turned on above the doors, and they slid open. A blast of wet heat entered, and mud, dark and smelly, oozed into the subway car from the platform. The man took a flashlight from his belt and shone the beam, uselessly, into the steam outside. *What kind of disgusting subway station is this?* Barnabas wondered. Whatever it was, whatever he had to endure, Barnabas was determined to get off here. *As soon as these people...*

Before the giants could exit, the thick steam disgorged a trio of terrifying figures. They were even taller than the first two giants, and had to bend just to enter the car. They wore thick, green coveralls, heavy rubber boots, and three-fingered gloves. When they cleared the door and raised their heads, there were no faces, just helmets and masks of grey metal. At their necks, valves opened and closed with a sibilant hiss. Their eyes were invisible behind thick black lenses that protruded from the helmets like mushrooms growing on the trunk of the tree.

Worse, two of the helmeted figures (were they even human under those suits?) had enormous dogs of their own, straining on thick chains. These two beasts made Marigold seem like a lap dog, and as soon as they saw her, they barked ferociously, a sound that made Barnabas' head ring. The new dogs showed their teeth — polished triangles of razor-sharp metal.

Five giants and three animals squared off in the doorway, and no one moved. Muscles clenched, and hands moved to various tools on various tool belts. Barnabas wondered if there was going to be a fight. If so, it would be a terrible one. Everyone in the car was watching.

Marigold's owner spoke to the new arrivals, the strain apparent under his attempt to sound calm and in control: "Are you going to let us pass, siblings in Mercy?"

The helmeted figures did not move. Tension swirled around them all, like steam. The man with the mohawk called from his seat, "Come on, denizens! No one wants trouble here, right?"

The curly-headed woman with the krumped machine stood tall and said, "This is where we've been sent to work. If you have a problem with that, complain to your guild. In the meantime, let us pass!"

All three dogs began barking and pulled at their leads, their front legs lifting off the ground.

The woman gritted her teeth. "Gricklickers!" she muttered and then put a hand on her companion's shoulder. "It's not worth it. Come on. Come on!" She led him down the car to the next set of doors, but before they exited, she shouted, "Clouding doesn't run the Council! The Father didn't give the Valley to you alone!" They exited into the steam, Marigold pausing to give one last growl before her owner tugged her to his side.

The three helmeted people entered the car, moving to occupy the seats that the other giants had just abandoned. They reached up to pull latches at their throats. Three sharp hisses of released air, and they lifted off the helmets to reveal two men and a woman, with short-cropped, sweat-streaked hair and glistening faces. One man's face was deeply scarred, one of the eyes missing, the socket filled in by more scar tissue.

Barnabas thought they looked very pleased with themselves for making the others leave by the other doors. Right away, he knew them for what they were — bullies, confident in their cruelty, like so many he had met over the years, including Mr. Klevver. As the trio pulled their harnesses on, the little clown sauntered down the car to stand directly in front of them, hands on hips. Barnabas thought he looked like a rabbit standing up to a pride of lions.

"Ya know," the clown said, "You Clouders gotta learn to lighten up… Come on down to Tragidenko's and, you know, let off a bit of *steam!*" He did a little dance step and finished with a flourish. "Steam! S'a joke! Man, I waste my best material on the terminally humourless." He turned from side to side as it looking for a sympathetic audience, but this new performance seemed to make the other passengers nervous.

The faces of the "Clouders" darkened in anger. "The Father is sickened by your triviality, clown," said the one missing an eye. "Your weakness weakens us all."

The clown turned back to them. He touched his forehead and bowed slightly. "And the blessings of the Mother on you, denizen," he said.

Again he looked around as if for applause, and this time, he stopped and stared in Barnabas' direction. Barnabas thought, *He can't see me, can he?* But, sure enough, the clown looked him square in the eye and winked. Barnabas recoiled, pulling himself deeper into the shadows. The clown blithely turned and skipped away to the far end of the subway car. The two deadly dogs barked madly and strained at their leashes even as the door chimes sounded and the doors closed. The lights dimmed and the train continued its descent, shaking so hard now, it seemed poised to fly apart. With two dogs blocking his escape, Barnabas didn't see how he would ever get off the train.

The next station was even hotter, and sweat poured off Barnabas' forehead while the train sat there with the doors open. The floor was now filthy with mud, and the windows splattered and fogged. Giants got on and off, some with further unidentifiable machines that exuded smells like sour cabbage, or with carts bursting with scrap piping like a bowl of copper spaghetti.

Three stops later, the scary trio and their dogs finally exited, but by this time, Barnabas was paralyzed with uncertainty. The platforms seemed more like construction sites in Hell than subway stations. On some, guards in aqua patrolled; on others, there was no light — only the clang of heavy machinery and faint searchlights moving through the steam. Cramped and frightened in his little alcove, Barnabas didn't even consider braving these dark worlds.

As they skidded and sparked through the tunnel, travelling ever downwards, he thought back to the stolen map. Now he understood why there were no transfer stations where the other lines and the Aqua Line crossed... This subway had to be hundreds of meters below the regular ones. Barnabas wondered how deep in the earth they were. How long would the escalator have to be in these Aqua Line stations to get the passengers back to the surface? Or maybe these passengers never did go above ground! What if everything was different this far down? Who could he ask for help? A tear rolled down his cheek, joining the sweat from his brow.

The lights went out altogether just before they burst into the next station. When the train did finally shriek and jerk to a halt, the doors remained shut. They all sat in the darkness for many minutes, and the subway seemed to be hissing like a kettle coming off a hard boil. Barnabas heard his fellow passengers shifting, coughing nervously. Outside, there was the tap of boots on concrete, and the occasional *bang!*, like a metal door slamming. A voice called, "Secure to arrive!" and the doors slid open, though the lights did not turn on in the subway.

For once, the view through the open doors was not of mud and steam; all was polished surfaces of black and chrome, and the signs read: "Doomlock." Guards in Aqua stood at attention; some kind of supervisor walked along, inspecting their ranks, making ticks with a pen on a clipboard. A group of four guards, walking in formation, passed the nearby subway door. A minute later they returned, but this time they were surrounding a prisoner: a woman in shackles, her shoulders slumped in resignation. Barnabas held his breath, trying more than ever to remain utterly undetectable.

He could hear someone mumbling in the car, the voice growing in volume until he could make out the words: "Father Glory, hear your humble child. I am your strong right arm, and you are mine. Grant me the endurance of body and mind to build your Holy City!" It was the man with the mohawk, and he sounded terrified. His voice grew louder: "Mother Mercy, kiss the head of your humble child, and bring him close to your breast. Bless him with long life that he may spread your kindness to his fellow workers…"

A voice on the platform shouted, "Secure to depart!" and the doors slid closed. The subway moved forward with a drawn-out susurration, like a long-held breath finally released. Descending through the inky darkness faster than ever, the train screeched and rattled, kicking up sparks. Barnabas hid in his lair like a mouse in the forest hides when the pack of coyotes moves past. He felt like he had been away from the light for a year, like his normal life was somewhere far, far away. Crushed beneath the weight of rock above him, he gave up all hope of escaping his fate. He went where the tracks carried him, down into the belly of the beast.

From time to time, lights flashed in the tunnel around them. And in those momentary flashes, he could see the remaining occupants of the car, including the clown, sitting down at the end of the car. A short time later, the lights outside flashed again, and Barnabas saw that the clown was now sitting closer, halfway down the car, his big nose in striking profile. Darkness again for maybe ten seconds, then the train took a tight curve, and the sparks from the wheels were bright enough to see by. He looked at the last place the clown had been, but the seat was empty.

Darkness! The speeding train pounded out a rhythm with its wheels: *taka-taka-chang-chang, taka-chang-chang.* It was weirdly hypnotizing, and Barnabas found himself chanting along in a kind of delirium: "Taka-taka-chang-chang, taka-chang-chang."

The overhead lights in the car came on abruptly, blindingly bright. The clown was inside his hiding place, standing on the machine's rubber wheel and reaching out a bony hand toward him. Barnabas screamed as the clown pulled him out from behind the machine by his shirt-front, and in one smooth move, up onto a subway chair. The clown took the one beside him.

"No! No!" Barnabas shouted uselessly into the clatter and roar.

"Hey, shut it!" the little man yelled into his ear. He pulled a harness across Barnabas' chest and clicked it in place, doing the same for himself.

Barnabas shouted to the clown, "I didn't mean to be here! I fell asleep! I'm really sorry! Can I go home now?"

The clown's voice was a scratchy old vinyl record, his breath, a thousand cigars: "We'll worry about getting you home later. Now, you'll need to wear this." He pulled a red rubber ball out of his chequered jacket and stuck it unceremoniously on Barnabas' nose, pulling its elastic strap over his head. "Keep that on. And if anyone says anything to you ... *Anything* ... you answer 'raspberry soda,' got it?"

"What?!" He reached up to remove the red clown nose and the clown slapped his hand.

"Leave it! Okay, what's your name?"

"I'm Barnabas Bopwright ... *ow!*" This time, the clown had slapped the top of his head.

"What did I say you could say?"

"R-raspberry soda?"

"Good. And where do you live?"

"Raspberry soda."

"Perfect. Follow my orders and we might just keep you out of Doomlock."

The train suddenly levelled out. The brakes began their painful shriek. Through the mud-stained slit windows, Barnabas could see something resembling light. He gripped the pole in front of him as much to keep his mind from flying off into madness as to brace himself against the forces of deceleration.

They must have been going terribly fast, because it took the train more than a minute to stop. Finally when the shriek of the brakes couldn't be any louder, the train gave a final shudder and came to a decisive halt. It seemed to exhale deeply, like it too was relieved to reach the end of the ride. All was still for a moment, and then the doors opened.

Light streamed in. Not incandescent or fluorescent, not filtered through dirty yellow fixtures or glaring bluish from a bank of work lights. No, this was light like the first day of creation. This was sunshine.

INTERLUDE: MARCH, 1907

His Honour, Mayor Lawrence Glorvanious sat at his desk, which was massive as a football field. All around him rose towers of paper — a growing mass of architectural drawings, artistic renderings, memoranda, timetables, and official decrees. Collectively, they represented the new City that, like these paper towers, would soon climb heavenward. If he were steadfast and true of heart, in ten years time, he and his army of dreamers would turn this fat, somnolent town into one of the greatest metropolises on the continent.

It was a chilly, bright day in late March, and the Mayor was pouring over yet another set of plans, these ones for the new reservoir. With a freshly sharpened pencil, he made notations in his neat, decisive hand on the large sheets of paper. When he was done, he rolled up the plans and handed them to the assistant, who had been standing silently in front of the desk while His Honour worked.

Mayor Glorvanious wore black. The assistant wore black. The matters of this office were serious ones.

"Take these to the Chief Architect," the Mayor instructed. "Tell him I expect revisions by tomorrow evening."

"Very good, sir."

The room was cold, and the Mayor rubbed his hands together briskly to get some feeling back into them. "Is my son still waiting outside?" he asked.

"Sir, he is."

"Send him in."

Florian Glorvanious soon stood in front of his father. The Mayor assessed the boy. No, not a boy anymore — 18 years old and ready to take his part in the great enterprise. He was a serious lad and had always been obedient, yet Lawrence Glorvanious found himself unsettled by his son's eyes. They hinted at a restlessness that belied the young man's straight-backed discipline. Was the fire in those eyes a sign of great resolution and industry, or the blaze of incipient rebellion? The boy wore black, but his tie was crimson.

"Please sit, Florian. Take the chair by the fire if you're cold. The time has come for you to join me. Soon, we will begin construction of our great city, and I have an important role for you to play in the building of that dream."

Though his son paused before speaking, when he did speak, it was without apology: "Father, I'm afraid that isn't possible. Next month, I will enter the Seminary and begin my training as a minister."

"Are you still on about that? This romantic dream was amusing when you were 16, but..." He took a breath to control his temper. There was nothing to be gained by humiliating the boy. "Florian, this is the twentieth century. I'm afraid you must put aside idle fancy and help build the new world of commerce and progress. It is the era of steam, not of souls."

Florian's gaze did not waver, and his tone remained even. "I serve the Lord, Father," he said with quiet certainty.

The Mayor brought his hand down on his desk with a sound like a gunshot. "You serve me, boy!" He was shocked by how easily his son provoked him to rage. He stared into Florian's eyes again. They were green — his mother's eyes — but flecked with swirls of gold, like molten fury. The two Glorvaniouses glared at each other, and it was Florian who looked away first.

The Mayor's tone softened. "I'm sorry, son, but we are both of us in service to the demands of the future."

His son was silent, and the Mayor listened to that silence, trying to assess who was winning this battle of wills. Florian said, "And what does the future demand of me, Father?"

Lawrence Glorvanious cleared his throat. He knew every facet of the City to come, long before the architects and planners committed the details to paper. He knew how the streets of the mighty metropolis would be laid out, how the funds would be secured, what political enemies he must fight, and what powers take for himself to ensure success. And he knew what he needed from his son.

"The construction of the City will be a monumental work, akin to the building of the Temple in Jerusalem, to Noah's Ark, or the Tower of Babel." He thought himself very clever to invoke biblical images, but his son remained unnervingly still, taut as a bowstring. The Mayor continued: "But the work will not be over when the towers rise overhead. The true secret of our greatness will be the way the City continues to run, seamlessly and affordably decade after decade."

He put his elbows on his desk and leaned forward, caught up in the excitement of his own narrative. "Listen closely, my son, for this is the true inspiration of our plan: we will create a town outside the City, a town without a name, never to be drawn on any map. In this hidden town, the strongest men, keen and disciplined, will live with their families, and they will be the hidden engine of the City. We will give them shelter and bread, and give their life purpose. Generation after generation, unsung but loyal, will live and work there; they will be the secret of our success. And kept apart from the corruption of evil, foreign influences, they will remain loyal.

"Florian, It will be your job to assemble this group and instil in them a reverence for our cause. Then it will be you who leads them to their new home. You will be their Moses! Is this a task you feel you can take on? If you are not the man I think you are, if you balk at assuming this great responsibility, tell me now."

Florian seemed to relax. He sat back in his chair, closed his eyes, and brought his hands together in a gesture that might have been deliberation or might have been prayer. Now it was the Mayor who sat forward tensely. A full minute passed before his son opened his eyes and spoke: "Father, I accept your challenge."

Part II:

The Utter Flamtasmic

CHAPTER 7

The light streamed in through the subway doors, and Barnabas sat in his seat blinking, waiting for his eyes — and his brain — to adjust. Beside him, the clown unbuckled his harness and stood up. He pulled a cap out of his jacket pocket, soft tweed with a little crescent moon of a peak, and plonked it down on his head.

"Come on," he said. When Barnabas still didn't move, the clown reached up and unbuckled Barnabas' harness himself. He reached out a hand which Barnabas took automatically, and the clown pulled him to his feet. He turned the hand-hold into a handshake and said, "I'm Falstep. Falstep Fruntovuvver. Son of the late, great Onestep Fruntovuvver, Principal Clown of Tragidenko's Circus of Humanity!"

Barnabas, feeling dizzy and disoriented asked, "Who? You or your father?"

"Who what?"

"Is Principal Clown?"

"Both. Were and are. He were, I are." He reached up and straightened the clown nose on Barnabas' face. Falstep Fruntovuvver, Barnabas noted, didn't have one himself.

"Um, I'm Barnabas. Barnabas Bopwright. Where's your circus? And… where are we?"

"I'll answer questions later; let's go."

Hugging his backpack to his chest with both arms, Barnabas followed

Falstep out of the subway. They were outside, on an open-air platform with a concrete roof and no walls. Giants were all around them; some had just stepped off the train, others were there to meet them and help unload the machines and carts. Falstep was taking an energetic, meandering course along the platform, dodging around people and machines, occasionally hopping up and over benches and other obstacles. Barnabas, who was looking all around, trying in vain to orient himself, had to keep running to catch up.

The platform was in the middle of a huge, paved yard that seemed to be a loading dock. Big trucks manoeuvred around each other, and cranes and forklifts raised wooden crates, bundles of lumber, and piles of gravel into the trucks. The area was bounded by huge warehouses that stood with their doors open, accepting and dislodging yet more weighty miscellany. To the other side of the subway platform was a bustling food depot where every type of conveyance, from small hand-carts to large trucks, was being filled with boxes of vegetables, huge slabs of raw meat, and a thousand little paper bags of ingredients.

Barnabas and Falstep were now at the end of the platform, and the clown was shading his eyes with his bony hand and looking around. "Where the firksome inferno is he?" he muttered darkly as he pulled a half-smoked cigar out of the inside pocket of his jacket and lit it with a match. The movement was performed with a flourish like he was doing it for an audience. Maybe he did everything for an audience.

"Where's who?" Barnabas asked, because any answer to any question would be helpful at this point.

The air around the clown grew blue with cigar smoke. "Wickram! He's supposed to meet us. Damn unreliable kid..."

Barnabas stepped to the edge of the platform (getting himself upwind of the smoke) and looked around too, not that he knew what a Wickram would look like. His attention was caught by a huge statue in the corner of loading area. It was tall; almost as tall as the warehouses. Sculpted in white marble, veined with purple, it was shaped at its base like rolling steam, which rose to become a woman's robe. The woman wore a shawl made of intricately carved flowers. Her long hair flowed down on either side of her peaceful face, which smiled down on the bustling crowds. Her arms were outstretched as if offering the whole loading area a big hug.

But there was more to the statue — another figure above the benevolent lady, totem-pole style. It was a man with a stern face, his mouth set disapprovingly beneath a thick moustache, eyes aflame with judgment. His muscular arms were raised at 2 and 10 o'clock, and each ended in a clenched fist. Unlike the female figure, he paid the crowd below no attention; he was scanning the horizon as if looking out for invaders or new lands to conquer.

Barnabas tapped Falstep on the shoulder. "Who…? Those statues… Who are —"

"Father Glory and Mother Mercy," he said. "You'll see a lot of them." He tamped out his cigar on a concrete post and tucked it back into his jacket. "Wickram probably couldn't get into the main concourse at this hour. I guess he's in the parking lot. Let's go."

Falstep trotted down a set of steps into the chaos of the loading area, and Barnabas found himself running after him again. As they darted between moving trucks, he had to resist the urge to grab Falstep's hand like a little kid. They circled around a huge pile of chairs, tied together into a spiky tower of legs, and found themselves facing one of the guard's in aqua uniform.

"Dung," Falstep murmured as the guard noticed them. "Don't say nuthin', and if you gotta… *raspberry soda*, right?"

The guard approached them. "Denizen Falstep?" he asked.

Falstep pulled a small hand mirror out of his breast pocket and checked himself in it. "Yup! I appear to be me!" He adjusted his hat with a goofy grin on his face and put the mirror away.

The guard gave a little smile although he looked quickly around as if he were breaking a rule by doing it. "You just came off the train, denizen?"

"Yeah, a bit of circus business in the City." He reached again into his check jacket and pulled out a piece of paper with a red seal on it. "Transit permission, everything in order."

The guard waved it away. "That won't be necessary. We just had reports from a couple of passengers of a possible border penetration. Did you see anything, sir? Anyone?" The guard seemed to notice Barnabas for the first time. Barnabas wanted to appear calm and collected as he met the guard's eye, but he was pretty sure he was a picture of panic.

Falstep was saying, "No, nothing I can think of… some mook from Forming got reg-slapped. Didn't have all his doodads ship-shape —"

The guard interrupted. "Who is this with you?"

Falstep spun on his heel as if he had forgotten Barnabas was there. "This? This is a lump of useless that thinks he has what it takes to be a clown! Like it's something just anyone can aspire to!" He gave Barnabas a sharp whack on the head with his palm, and Barnabas winced.

"What's your name, young denizen?" the guard asked.

"R-raspberry soda."

Falstep rolled his eyes and muttered, "Here we go…"

The guard continued, "And is your residency registered through Pastoral Park?"

"Raspberry, uh, soda?"

Barnabas felt himself shaking, but Falstep pushed him aside. "Don't waste your time, officer. He's the kid of one of the stage hands. Only he's a bit…" Falstep whistled drunkenly and let his head loll around on his neck. "Can't even open curtains on cue. So what do they do? They give him to *me!* As if being skull-cracked means you're clown material!" He threw up his hands in frustration.

The guard seemed unsure what to do next, so he took the transit documents from Falstep after all and gave them a cursory glance. He handed them back to the clown. "Have a good day, denizen," he said. "I'm bringing my family to the circus in a few weeks. We got some of the first tickets for the new show."

"Great, Officer! I'll give the kiddies some special balloons!"

The guard turned and walked away, and Falstep let out a long, hissing breath. "Hoo-boy. You did good, kid. Let's get to the parking lot. The sooner we get you safely to Pastoral Park, the better."

Barnabas stumbled quickly after the clown, who was hurrying down a narrow path between two warehouses. He asked, "What would have happened if he…? Hold it, stop!" But Falstep didn't stop. They passed under an arch and found themselves in wide, paved area where trucks were idling. Beyond the lot, roads forked off in all directions, bringing trucks and vans to and from the depot. There was a railway track, too, and a unmarked trolley, crammed full of giants in coveralls, rattled along it slowly.

Barnabas was still shaking with adrenaline from their encounter with the guard, and he could feel his frustration growing. This Falstep character was dragging him off god-knew-where, and he was sick of not knowing what was up. While Falstep climbed up on a bench to search the parking lot for his friend, Barnabas pulled his phone out of his backpack. He noted that battery was down to 30%; he had forgotten to charge it again.

But that was the least of his problems: there was no signal. He held the phone in the air and walked in a small circle. Nothing. He asked Falstep, "Why can't I get a signal?"

Falstep ignored the question and said, "He's probably all the way at the back. Or he's totally late. Damn kid." He started walking quickly. Barnabas was sick of the clown assuming that he would follow him anywhere. But as the distance grew between them, he realized he had no choice but follow. Without the clown, and without cellular signal, he was lost in this strange place. He ran again to catch up.

"Listen," he said to Falstep as they continued to walk. "Thank you and everything. I know you're trying to keep me out of trouble, but I'm just going to get on the next train back to Admiral Crumhorn Station."

"Nope, none till next Tuesday. Tuesdays and Thursdays only."

Barnabas had never heard of a subway with a schedule like that, and his mouth just hung open a second or two before he said, "Well, I guess I'll call home and tell my stepdad to come and get me."

"From the City? How's he gonna do that?"

"He has a car. He doesn't use it much but…" Barnabas grabbed the clown's shoulder and pulled him to a halt. "Wait! What do you mean 'from the City'? The guard guy said something like that too."

"Huh? Where do you think you are?" Falstep asked, staring at Barnabas like he really *was* the addled-brained son of a frustrated stagehand. "You think you're still in the City?"

Barnabas was rattled. I mean, sure, they had travelled a long way, but it was still a City subway line. He said, "I'm not? But… but then how far away is it? Which way is the City?"

Falstep looked delighted, and not in a way that gave Barnabas any confidence. The clown slowly lifted one arm until he was pointing off to the right and up. Something was wrong. Something was weird. Barnabas turned slowly in the direction of the hand. He could see the subway tracks running out from behind the warehouses. They stretched through a landscape of scrubby plants and sparse trees and then disappeared through an arched portal into the base of a huge wall of rock and earth. Barnabas' eye moved slowly up the face of this mammoth cliff face, rough and unadorned but for a few little plants that struggled to hang on to narrow outcroppings. Higher and higher his gaze climbed until he had to tilt his body backwards to see.

And there, on the top of the wall, right up against the edge of the cliff was a long line of beautiful skyscrapers, glinting in the morning sun. Barnabas' mind, already bruised and confused by everything that had happened that morning, started to spin like a top. He knew those towers but they were the mirror image of the ones he knew. Then he realized he knew them from the *other side*. They were all the skyscrapers of the Tower District... but seen from behind. And there they stood, teetering on the edge of a giant cliff that shouldn't even exist.

"That's... that's impossible!" he stammered, and he could only just control the hysteria in his voice.

Falstep took off his hat and fanned himself. "It's quite a spectacle, all right. Especially if you've never seen it before. I admit, I'm so used to it, I sometimes go months without looking up."

Barnabas felt angry at this display of nonchalance. He whirled on his heel to face the raggedy clown. "Why didn't I know about this?! If the City was sitting on the edge of a cliff, wouldn't people be talking about it?"

"Oh, *people*!" Falstep replied as if that explained everything. "People believe whatever you tell them. Or don't tell them, in this case. Besides, they always think they have more important things to talk about. The price of smoked raisins, or how their favourite movie star waxes her armpits."

During this baffling speech, Barnabas had turned back to stare up at the towers. They were so high above him that the birds dancing around their peaks were tiny specs. And in the already spectacularly strange picture, he noticed yet more strangeness: "There are no windows! None of the buildings have windows on this side!"

The clown yawned loudly, his mouth wide enough to catch a grapefruit. "Wouldn't do to have them see the Valley. We don't even exist. None of this does." He extended an open palm and spun 360° on his heel. "Hey, there's Wickram! Come on!"

This time, Falstep didn't hurry. He sauntered like they had all the time in the world, relighting the cigar with lazy panache. Ahead of them, parked in the shade of an old oak tree was a sturdy, old-fashioned, four-wheeled cart. In the back was an open flat-bed surrounded by wooden rails, and up front was a driver's bench. Hitched to the cart were two, grey mules, chewing placidly on the weeds at their feet. A tall, gangly figure wearing dusty jeans and an embroidered denim shirt sat in the grass with his back against the tree. He had shoulder-length, straight black hair under a floppy hat, and both the hat and his long bangs hung low over his eyes.

Falstep banged on the back of the cart. "Hey, hey, fanfares and confetti, I'm back!"

The sleeper awoke, raising his head slowly. He was another tall giant, but Barnabas saw that he was a kid, too, about his age or a bit older with skin the colour of mocha.

The kid pushed back his hat although his hair still hung into his eyes. "Yeah, I could smell the fine aroma of burning stinkweed," he snapped back, but the smile on his face didn't match the harshness of his words. He stood to his full height, gave the mules a quick, affectionate pat and climbed up on the driver's bench, picking up the reins. Falstep climbed up from the other side and joined him.

The boy asked "What were you doing in the City? I didn't even know you went until Mom told me to come get you."

"Top secret! No one but my hairdresser knows for sure." Falstep turned around and said, "Hey, kid… What's your name? Platypus? Hop up in the back."

"It's Barnabas," Barnabas answered. He regarded the back of the cart dumbly until he saw the latch that allowed him to open the back like a gate. He climbed up clumsily, throwing his backpack ahead of him, and pulled the gate shut.

The kid up front was staring at him curiously, shaking his hair aside to reveal big brown eyes. "Whoa!" he said. "Where'd you find him?"

The clown puffed on his cigar and leaned back on the bench with great contentment. "He was hiding on the train."

"It was an accident," Barnabas said. "I fell asleep." He was sharing the back of the cart with several strange objects. There was a large face made of papier-mâché — half moon, half sun — that might have been a mask. Beside it were several dented cans of paint with hand-written labels, including: "Momo's darkest blue," "Faerie green," and "Don't Use This!" There was also an old acoustic guitar, its top covered in stickers, mostly with the names of different bands. Barnabas decided that the best place to sit was on a pile of red material, shot through with sequins.

"Yeah, sit anywhere. I'm Wickram. *Mother Mercy*, you live in the City? You are *so* lucky! Do you have the new DigiPlayah SmartMedia Centre?"

"Uh, no, but some of my friends do."

"I want one of those so bad!" Wickram continued. "There's nothing down here in the Valley except stones and dust and factories. Nice nose, by the way." He laughed and reached out to squeeze it. "Honk," he said.

Embarrassed, Barnabas quickly pulled the foam ball off his face and stuck it in his pocket. He had forgotten he was still wearing it.

Someone started shouting, "Hey! Hey!" until the three of them turned to look. It was another tall kid, with pasty, freckled skin and curly orange hair. "Hey, circus!" he shouted as he marched through the parking lot, lugging a big wooden crate. Barnabas saw Wickram's eyes narrow in anger.

"Coursing fitsker," Falstep murmured, but he didn't seem as annoyed as Wickram.

"Hey, circus!" the kid shouted again. "If you keep jugglin' your balls, you'll go blind!"

Wickram gritted his teeth and breathed hard through his nose, gripping the reins tightly, and looking anywhere but at the kid.

Falstep, casually picking some dirt out of his nails said, "You gonna let him get away with that?"

Like he had been waiting for the starting gun to fire, Wickram whipped around in his seat and screamed, "What tunnel wall did they scrape you off of, fungus-breath?!" He grinned at Barnabas, who had no idea what the insult even meant.

"Good work," Falstep said with a smile. "Now, can we hit the flippin' road?"

Wickram looked pleased with himself. He saluted. "Absolutely! *Yah*, mules! Let's go!" He gave the reins a shake, and the mules began walking at a leisurely pace. The cart jerked into motion, tipping Barnabas off the pile of material onto the floor of the cart.

"Did you get me something in the City?" The kid asked Falstep as he steered them out of the parking lot onto one of the roads.

"I was there on business."

"So?"

The clown gave a half-smile. "Well, let's just say you were on my mind —"

"I bet you got me a harmonica! Hey, Barn! Can I call you Barn?" He didn't wait for an answer. "Do you have those Grumpton Homing Shoes? The ones that point you to the KidLiquid treasure stations?"

"Uh, I did. But the OS was a mess. A bunch of little kids got lost in a bad part of town, so they shut down the network." They were clip-clopping down the middle of the road, the slowest vehicle in traffic. Big trucks had to swing out onto the shoulder to pass them. The great cliff was behind them, and Barnabas moved to the back of the cart to look up at the City. *His* city. It felt like it had just been stolen from him... the whole story of his life rewritten.

The tall boy continued to talk like the world was still normal: "I'm Wickram, by the way. Mice to neat you!" He gave a little wave. "But can you imagine? Homing shoes! That's exactly the kind of excellent balderdung you get in the City, am I right?" When Barnabas didn't answer, Wickram asked Falstep, "What's with him? He seems a little... off."

"Didn't know about the cliff. Or the Valley. Or nothing. He's having a total rube meltdown!"

Barnabas didn't like what he was seeing. "The cliff doesn't look very stable. What if a building falls off?"

"Hasn't happened yet," Wickram replied. "But all kinds of things fall off all the time. That's why we have the Tumbles. See that fence down at the base?" Barnabas squinted and saw a long chain-link fence extending in both directions as far as the eye could see, cordoning off the area at the base of the cliff. Wickram went on: "You wouldn't want to walk around in the Tumbles. Take a look!" He reached back and handed Barnabas a pair of binoculars.

With his view magnified, he could see what Wickram meant: every few seconds something was falling down into the valley. Mostly it was chunks of rock and clods of earth as the cliff face disintegrated piece by piece. But then he watched as three car tires went over edge, bouncing off outcroppings and tree roots on their way down. Moving his binoculars along the cliff face, he spotted a stuffed giraffe spinning end over end through space, like it had leaped over the edge in despair when some kid stopped loving it. Everything that hit the ground sent up a plume of dust from the dry ground inside the Tumbles. Some things — like a big green mailbox — were heavy enough that Barnabas thought he could hear the crash.

"Excellent, right?" Wickram said, turning around again. "There's only one guy brave enough to walk around in the Tumbles, and that's —"

Falstep turned around now. "Hey, Platypus! Sit your butt down before someone sees you." He gave Wickram a whack on the shoulder. "Where's your brains? We got to keep him secret until they organize some papers for him! We almost got busted by an Aqua at the depot already."

Barnabas sat down low with his back to the gate. It was just as well; looking at the City and the crumbling cliff it rested upon just made him want to start screaming. He regarded the backs of the clown and the tall boy and tried to figure out if he could trust them. They were going to a lot of trouble to keep him out of trouble. On the other hand, they were taking him farther away from the subway station, the only path he knew to get back home. He checked his phone again. No signal.

Falstep's head snapped to the side and he shot to his feet. All his movements reminded Barnabas of a cartoon character. "Oh, it's Maize's. I'm thirsty!" the clown said, tossing the stub of his cigar over his shoulder.

"Want me to stop?"

"Nope, I'll catch up!" and with cartoon abruptness, he leaped off the cart. Barnabas got up on his knees and watched the clown running towards a small concrete building with striped blue awnings that bore a sign reading "Maize's Tasties — Custom Drinkables."

Barnabas lowered his head again and crawled towards the front. "Wickram, is there anywhere here I can get a signal on my phone?"

"Is it the RoamFone Ultimate? With gigawave two-way GPS?"

"Um, not the Ultimate. Just the first gen."

"Still cool. Yeah, you can get signal from one place in the Commons, but it's kinda tricky."

"Can we try? It's important." He needed to phone Deni. And the only time he could do it was in the break between second and third periods when students were allowed to turn on their phones for a few minutes. He checked the time… he had 30 minutes.

"Your whisk is my demand, Barn!" Wickram said.

With a plan in place, Barnabas felt a bit better. His head was full of questions so he asked one: "What's going on down here? In the Valley, I mean? What's with all the trucks and the workers and whatever."

"This is how your City really works! Up there, you guys sit in your offices and then go shopping and stuff. But down here in the Valley, we do all the hard work. Been that way a long time."

Out of nowhere, Falstep jumped up onto the walls of the cart and climbed into the back beside a startled Barnabas. He was breathing a hard, his face beaded with sweat, and he was holding a brown-tinted bottle. He plopped down on his butt and popped out the cork. With the bottle at his lips, he tilted his head back, taking a more-than-generous swig of the liquid within. He wiped his mouth and smiled. "Mmm, I needed that! What are you telling the kid, Wickram?"

It was Barnabas who answered. "He was saying that the Valley does, uh, the work for the City? What work?" Falstep drank again from the jug, wincing a bit as the liquid went down his throat, and Barnabas asked him, "Can I have some?"

"Sorry, this brew ain't for kiddies. Wickram, give your buddy here something to drink, and I'll tell him a little bit about how the world really works." Wickram handed back an earthenware jug, and Barnabas pulled out the cork. The liquid inside fizzed, and he brought the jug to his nose to smell the contents. *Raspberries? Raspberry soda?* He drank. It was good.

"So here's the story kid," Falstep said, wiping his mouth. "This is what they don't teach you in school."

CHAPTER 8

"**C**erberus," Falstep said, licking his lips, rubbing his hands together. "I am going to tell you the tale of our lives. And of your life, though you never knew it before ..."

"It's 'Barnabas,'" Barnabas said quietly. "Not 'Cerberus.'"

Wickram looked back over his shoulder from the driver's bench and asked, with obvious excitement, "We gonna do the Guts and Glory Show?"

"You bet!"

"Flamtasmic! I know all the cues. Barn, hand me my guitar!" As he reached back to take the instrument, he gave Barnabas a wink. "By the way, Falstep, we're stopping for a minute in the Commons for Barn."

"Happy to," Falstep replied. He took another long drink from his jug before putting it down between his feet. He sat and breathed heavily in Barnabas' face, expelling a potent alcoholic cloud. The clown's eyes, Barnabas saw, had grown a little unfocussed.

"I bet you're happy," Wickram replied. "You do realize that none of the bars are open this early?" He hooked the mules' reins over his right foot and tuned his guitar. "Okay, get ready; here's the overture!"

Wickram began strumming the guitar with big sweeps of his long fingers and making trumpet noises with his mouth. He thumped a beat on the floorboards with one heel. Barnabas didn't play an instrument himself, but he had been raised around music, and he was impressed with what he heard; Wickram's voice was strong and his rhythm rock solid.

The overture built to grand finale although it got a bit confused as he slashed at his guitar strings and tried to sing three different musical parts simultaneously. He gave a final fanfare, ending with a drumroll on the top of the guitar and a fart noise. "Take it away, Professor!"

The haze seemed to instantly clear from Falstep's eyes as he began his oration: "The City was barely that. An overgrown town, struggling to find an identity in an age of industrialization. A way station between the important places where commerce flourished and ideas were nourished.

"But there were men of vision, oh yes, and they saw a brighter future, a chance to build a modern Rome on the shores of the mighty river."

The story wasn't as unfamiliar as Barnabas thought. He said, "Lawrence Glorvanious. I know; he was the one with the vision!"

Falstep gave him pitying look. "Oh, yes, we all know about the *great* Mayor. But what you City-folk don't know… You City-folk with your colour televisions and-and Nehru jackets —"

Wickram turned around and said, "He means 'drivecorders' and 'omni-float memory access.' He's old."

As if to belie this accusation, Falstep leaped to his feet in one smooth, athletic move. His arm reached out like he was addressing a much larger crowd somewhere beyond Barnabas' shoulder. "You City-folk don't know the true shaper of destiny, the genius, the god-mind made flesh: the one called Father Glory!"

Wickram began stomping a steady beat on the floorboard, playing a martial rhythm on the lowest strings of the guitar. Pulling the reins with his foot, he made the mules turn left onto another wide, paved road. Falstep stumbled, almost stepping on Barnabas, but quickly side-stepped back to his place like this little dance routine was part of the show.

He continued: "One day when the sky boiled in turmoil, when raging storms were closing in, Father Glory appeared in the great marketplace that stood across from City Hall. In a voice like thunder, he spoke to the hard-working men and women gathered before him. 'I need the strongest of you, the tallest, the bravest and most inspired. I will lead you to a life whose rewards are few, but whose glory will reverberate in your hearts, in the muscles of your arms and backs, in the power manifested by your will and your sweat.'

"Thunder sounded above, like the skies were saluting Him, and He raised two fists into the air, acknowledging their praise. 'You will be my children!' shouted Father Glory. 'You will be the true power behind the City that the fat men in their wool suits think *they* are building. You will build the City on earth and so raise the City in heaven!'"

Light glinted in Falstep's eyes like the reflection of the fire in Father Glory's words.

"Many followed the mighty Father, for they had listened with their hearts and found truth in His words. He led them into the verdant valley where vast groves of apple and pear stood, where Lake Lucid glistened coolly, offering to slake the thirst of the weary traveller."

"And just look what a dung pile the Valley is now," Wickram said with a snort. Without looking in his direction, Falstep pulled a walnut from his pocket and beaned the boy expertly in the back of the head.

"Ow!"

"And in the Valley, the children of Father Glory formed four great guilds!"

Wickram rapped out a drum roll on the bench and shouted: "COURSING!"

Falstep moved his outstretched arms up and down like waves. "Who brought water to the City!"

Another drum roll from Wickram, punctuated with knuckle raps and foot stomps. "CLOUDING!"

"Who drove steam from the earth to heat the houses and turn the engines!" Falstep shot his arms straight overhead, wiggling his fingers, a living geyser.

Another drum roll, followed by wide guitar arpeggios. "FURROW-ING!"

The clown stooped low, digging with an invisible spade. "Who delved in the earth to bring forth the raw materials that built the City."

The last drum roll, utilizing four limbs and all the percussive power in the guitar, was so outrageous, it finally startled the mules, who brayed and tried to pull the cart off the road. Wickram grabbed the reins and softened his tone, beguiling them: "Sorry, sorry, good mules..." He steadied their course before giving his final proclamation. "Annnnnnnnnnd FORMING!"

"Who shaped the girders that became the skeleton of the mighty metropolis. To this day, these four guilds, the true children of Father Glory, work tirelessly to... to keep the dream alive that..." The clown trailed off, although Wickram didn't notice and continued to *blat*, *thump* and *zing* the underscore for a while before he turned around to see what was up.

Falstep was looking off to the side, the tip of his tongue running over his upper lip thoughtfully. He said, "Hey, am I skull-cracked, or is that Ol' Man Klaktrap out by the coppersmith's shop?"

"You are skull-cracked, but yeah, it's him."

"I thought he was dead! Son of a fitsker owes me 200 farthings," he growled. "Go park outside the Commons. I'll meet you by the fountain."

Falstep leaped out of the moving cart again although less elegantly this time. Barnabas heard a thud and a curse. Peering over the edge, he saw Falstep pick himself up out of the dirt and head towards another store, this one bearing the sign, "Kettles and Fittings." The cart clattered along, leaving him behind. The area they were passing through was more densely populated with stores and brightly coloured, low-rise buildings. There was a row of custom tool shops and several shoe stores promising "The best work boots," and "We fit any foot."

Barnabas ducked back down. "What was that you were doing, anyway?" he asked Wickram. "A play or something?"

"It's a kids' show we perform sometimes, called 'The True and Revealed History.' But my mom calls it pure propaganda. It's better with the real band, of course. And the pyrotechnics! That Falstep. He cracks my skull utter! We didn't even get to the part about Mother Mercy. That has the nicest string part!" He hummed a plaintive tune as the mules slowed and grunted their way up the steepening road. Wickram encouraged them with little whistles and words of praise. From behind them came a loud honking and Barnabas turned to see a large truck, coated with mud and decorated with a hand-painted motto on the hood: "Mother Mercy, bring forth the waters of life to quench your children's thirst."

Wickram looked over his shoulder, annoyed. "Just dry your drawers, Gricklickers," he muttered. "Come on, mules..."

The truck revved its engine furiously and sped up as if it was going to ram them. Barnabas flinched, but the truck braked at the last minute. It made several more of these terrifying feints before suddenly pulling to the left to pass them, hopping the sidewalk and knocking over a table and chairs in front of a small restaurant.

As the truck passed them, worryingly close, a kid in the passenger seat leaned out and shouted at Wickram, "Get those sad-ass horses off the road and into the slaughterhouse where they belong!" It was, of course, the orange-haired kid from the parking lot. He brought both his hands up in front of his face and wiggled his extended fingers in what must have been a rude gesture, because Wickram's face, turned positively ochre.

"Drop into a sinkhole you mizzy slizpots!" he screamed up at the kid.

"And then you can pull the cart yourself, circus freak! You can crap on the road and eat your oats." The truck pulled back into the road ahead of them and vanished around the corner, leaving them in a cloud of dust.

"Gricklickers," Wickram shouted after them. He turned the mules and came to a stop on a small, concrete pad by the road. "Let's park here and walk."

As Wickram tied up the mules to a wrought iron fence, Barnabas checked the time on his phone again. He poked his head above the cart walls and said, "Um, are we almost there? The place where I can make my call?"

"Yeah, but we need Falstep," Wickram said, still tense and unsmiling from the confrontation. "Come on, we'll go up to the fountain." He put his guitar away in the back of the cart.

"But I thought I wasn't supposed to be seen." He opened the back gate and hopped down nervously, looking all around. "Should I put the nose back on?"

"Yeah, do that. It's firkin' hilarious!"

Barnabas wasn't sure if this was just a taunt, but he put the foam ball back on his face anyway. Wickram dropped a big, reassuring hand on Barnabas' shoulder and said, "Yeah, that's good. But don't worry too much. The Aquas don't usually bug folk on the Commons. It's kind of an unspoken rule. And besides, a knee-high like you wearing a clown nose? You totally look like part of our troupe."

"Okay. What was that about with the guy in the truck?" he asked.

"Oh, forget him. Stupid kid from the Coursing Guild. Some people don't get what we do in the circus. Like, they think we're weak because we don't come to dinner with dirty faces." He seemed to be cheering up, which made Barnabas relax a little. "Clouding Guilders won't even come to our shows. They say we demean the sanctity of the Valley! Gricklickers."

"Falstep had a fight on the train with some scary people he called 'Clouders.' Are those the same guys?"

"Ha! Yeah. Good thing he didn't get his plaid ass kicked."

They followed the curving street until they found themselves in a cobbled public square. The Commons wasn't all that large, but it was the prettiest place Barnabas had seen so far in the Valley. The buildings were painted with murals, and planter boxes, bursting with spring flowers, were everywhere. Most people there that morning were just passing through purposefully, but a few older folks sat on rough-hewn wooden benches, chatting or reading. The shortest person Barnabas saw had to be 2 meters tall.

The only place on the Commons that seemed busy was the largest of the structures: a big covered market, kind of like the farmer's market his parents went to on Saturdays. At the other end of the Commons stood a stage with a bright red band shell. Dozens of folded wooden chairs were stacked up against its side. Clustered around the stage were various kiosks offering different kinds of food (a sign promising "Raccoon fritters" caught Barnabas' attention) and games of chance ("2 for 5, or 8 for 13. Everyone's a winner. Skull-cracked play free!"), but most of these booths were closed up.

They arrived at the large fountain in the centre of the square and sat down on its stone edge.

Wickram dipped his fingers in the water and said, "They only turn the fountain on when there's more people around. You should see the Commons on the weekend, or on summer evenings. Sometimes it's so crowded, you can barely move." He gave a little shudder. "I hate crowds. Unless I'm on stage in front of them."

"Is this where I can make my call? It's almost time." He checked his phone, but he still had no signal.

"No, not down here. You have to climb the radio tower." He pointed to a slender structure that was strapped to the side of the market building. The market was two-storeys tall; the radio tower itself must have been four or five.

Barnabas' eyes bugged out. "You're kidding."

"No, you can definitely get a signal up there. Just hang on tight; it might get windy." Wickram didn't seem to think this plan was in any way unusual or, for that matter, potentially lethal.

Barnabas, his mouth suddenly dry, said, "Am I allowed to do that? Just climb the poll?"

"No, no, no. No way. Commons or not, the Aquas won't ignore that! That's why me and 'Step are gonna create a little diversion for you. That is if he ever gets… Aha!"

Falstep was strutting across the Commons with big long strides, his arm around the waist of the guy who owed him money. They were both sporting wide, satisfied grins, and their path was noticeably meandering. They parted ways with a big hug, and Falstep staggered on alone. The clown seemed to know everyone he passed, or maybe it was that they knew him. He shook hands or kissed them, and made low, extravagant bows, his head almost hitting the cobblestones. A pretty woman with brown braids gave him a dried sunflower. He smiled and flirted and stuck the flower in the buttonhole of his lapel, like an oversized boutonniere, before finishing his casual walk to the fountain.

Wickram's arms were crossed over his chest, but there was a pleased smirk on his face. "Feeling no pain, Mr. Principal Clown?"

"Two days in the City, kid! Do you have any idea how stressful that is?" His words were a little slurred. He pulled a fresh cigar from his pocket and bit off the end, spitting it into the water. He lit the cigar with a match and puffed with satisfaction.

Barnabas pulled out his phone and saw they were running out of time. Second period would let out in a five minutes. "Wickram! We have to hurry!"

Wickram put an arm around the clown's shoulder and turned him in Barnabas' direction. "Barn here needs a little distraction. How long you figure, Barn? Ten minutes?"

Barnabas ran his eye up the tower. Could he even climb that thing? "Yeah. Ten minutes should do it."

Wickram put of a gentle, cajoling voice, and leaned in close to Falstep, saying, "We could put on a little show for all your fans. I think there's still some juggling clubs under the stage from last fall. Might even be some drums and cymbals there."

Falstep didn't seem enthused at the prospect. "Let's just get back to the Park. I'm feelin' kind of blown out…"

Wickram pivoted the clown the other way. "That pretty lady who gave you the flower… she's standing right there. Wouldn't you like to impress her?"

This seemed to be the right thing to say. Falstep tamped out his cigar on the side of the fountain and put it in his pocket. He dipped his fingers in water and ran them through his hair. He gave the boys a big smile with a lot of teeth, waggled his hands and said, "Showtime! Wick, you introduce me and pass the hat. We might as well pocket a few farthings for our trouble."

Wickram gave the clown a noisy kiss on top of his damp head. "Excellent! Okay, Barn, get over near the market. I'm gonna make a lot of noise to start the show. When you hear that, you climb." The tall boy glanced up at the tower and his expression grew doubtful. "I guess really you should have a safety harness. Or a net under you…" Then his face brightened. "But oh well! No stakes, no prizes, right?"

The plan seemed less and less sound the closer Barnabas got to the market building. Standing at its base, the tower looked insanely tall. It was triangular in cross-section and made up of welded metal struts. A ladder of narrow rungs, just wide enough for one foot, ran up one of the three sides.

A few seconds later, a pounding drum and a cymbal crash sounded behind him. Barnabas turned and saw Wickram on the stage surrounded by various percussion instruments and a collection of juggling clubs, lined up like bowling pins.

"Denizens! Ladies and Gentlemen of the Valley," he called out into the Commons, his voice carrying impressively. Everyone in the square as well as the shoppers in the market turned their heads. "May I introduce the greatest entertainer of his generation, the man who has kept you laughing for years…"

Barnabas turned his back on the square, gave one last nervous look up the tower and then put a foot on the first rung. As he climbed, one careful step after another, he looked to his right and saw the still-incomprehensible sight of the great cliff, and sitting on top of it, the City — his home. A big white shape was tumbling down cliff. *That's a refrigerator,* he thought. It raised a huge cloud of dust as it hit the ground in the "Tumbles" beyond the chain-link fence.

When he was level with the roof of the market building, Barnabas ran out of rungs. After a moment's confusion, he saw that they continued on another face of the triangular tower. He carefully shifted around and began to climb again. Now he was ascending without the security of the building beside him. Not only was he more exposed to any eyes that might look up, but he was beginning to feel the effects of the wind. It wasn't enough to unbalance him, but he couldn't stop himself from imagining a big gust that would hurl him off the tower to crash on the cobblestones below. To stop such grim thoughts, he made himself look around at his surroundings as he ascended rung by run. A view of the Valley was unfolding beneath him. Some of it was desolate and hideous: open-pit mines that scarred the landscape like pock marks; huge factories that belched smoke into the sky. There were heavy trucks grinding their way along the grid of roads, and fat pipelines that criss-crossed the floor of the Valley.

Barnabas saw neighbourhoods of low-rise apartments, clusters of concrete block buildings with roofs of galvanized steel. There were also a few buildings that looked like churches, with stained-glass windows and bell towers. One large church of dark brick, with a grey, slate roof rose solemnly in the middle of one of these neighbourhoods. Barnabas recognized the statue on the front of the tower. It was the double figure of the gentle, long-haired woman and the fierce, moustached-man. *That's Father Glory*, he figured. *And so the woman must be Mother Mercy.*

Meanwhile, on the stage in the square below him, Falstep already had three batons in the air, and Wickram was tossing him the fourth and then fifth. As he attempted to deal with these, Falstep careened up and down the stage, always on the verge of falling off or dropping everything. Wickram punctuated every move with a cymbal crash. The crowd around them was growing, and laughter rose from the square like a vapour.

Looking down like this was making Barnabas dizzy, and when he reached for the next rung and found himself grabbing at air, he almost lost his balance. Sticking out one foot to recalibrate himself, he pulled himself in close to the tower, hugging it for dear life as his heart pounded. He stayed there for ten seconds before shifting to the third side of the tower where the rungs continued. Time was running out. He had to keep climbing.

This new direction finally provided him a with a beautiful view. A hill rose out of the landscape, much like Gumhill rose above the City. And just as the Manhammer Audio Dome sat on Gumhill, on this hill's plateau, there was a huge tent, painted brightly in an intricate design of red and yellow. The tent was surrounded by a soothing swath of green — meadows and groves that thickened as the plateau approached the great cliff, until they formed a dense forest.

He climbed the last section of the tower quickly, despite the rising wind, and soon reached the top rungs of the ladder. Just above his head was a small box of radio equipment and a transmitter dish, not much bigger than a dinner plate. He looked down to see that Falstep had left the stage and was performing on the cobblestones, his act more slapstick and acrobatic than ever. The plan was working; no one was looking up at Barnabas. Now it was his turn to act.

Letting go one hand from the ladder, he shrugged his backpack off his left shoulder, and swung it around to his front. Supporting the bag on his raised knee, he felt around inside until he found his phone. He checked the screen and almost cried out in joy: *Signal! Sweet signal!* There were only two minutes left until third period. He pushed the FastCommand button and called out loudly, "Dial Deni, speaker on!"

Barnabas dropped the phone into his shirt pocket and grabbed hold of the ladder again. He waited impatiently for her to answer as the wind rose and the tower began to sway in a nauseating waltz. *Come on, come on!* he thought.

"Barnabas!" Deni screamed from his shirtfront. "Where are you!"

He had forgotten to prepare a useful lie. "Um, I'm sick. Stomach thing. Did any teachers say anything? Did they wonder where I was?"

"Ms. Acrostik, but I said the same thing — that you were probably sick. They'll phone your home at lunch to check, you know."

"I know. Of course I know." His mind was trying to formulate a plan, but the wind seemed to be blowing the ideas away before they could take root.

"And if no one answers, they'll call your mom's cell." Deni paused, and her voice grew low with concern. "But your mom won't know where you are, will she?"

"Right," he answered quietly, looking down at the square below where Falstep was standing on his head, apparently singing opera.

"Are you okay? Seriously. Are you?"

"Yes," he said tentatively, then with more certainty: "Yes. I have it under control. But I need you to help me out. I'm not going to be at school... for a while."

"How long a while?"

He remembered what Falstep had said about the train schedule. "I'll be back next Tuesday," he told her. Would he be able to stay with Wickram and Falstep until then? He would have to worry about the details later.

"Next week..." she breathed, and Barnabas could hear the excitement in her voice. Deni knew him well enough to know something unusual, and maybe amazing, was happening. Her voice changed abruptly to serious-business mode. "Okay, so we need to cover this on two fronts. First, I'll phone the office and pretend I'm your mom. I'll tell the school you're off sick with a bacterial infection in your stomach. That takes a few days to clear up and makes you too weak to do stuff."

Barnabas' left foot starting cramping. He shifted his weight to the other leg and stuck the cramping one out into space, shaking it vigorously.

Deni continued: "Next, I'll let your mother know you're staying at my place for the week. I'll tell her we need to work on the video footage of the Mayor. And also that Mom Morgan will be giving us valuable political insight."

Despite the fact that he was hanging off a wobbling tower, hanging precariously above a painful, cobblestone death, Barnabas smiled. He knew Deni would be able to make all these crazy schemes work. "You're a genius, Den! And then I'll be back at school next Tuesday, and no one will ever find out. You totally saved me."

She asked the question in a voice so calculatingly casual, she almost sounded bored: "And… when did he get in touch with you?"

"Who?" There was something happening down by the stage. Wickram appeared to be shouting at someone in the audience.

"Barnabas!" Deni shouted from his shirt front, no longer pretending to be cool. "I know what's going on. You don't have to pretend."

Barnabas saw someone push through the crowd to stand in front of the stage; it was the orange-headed kid! "Deni, I think I better hang up… something's about to go wrong here."

She ignored his distress. "It's your father, isn't it! I mean your *real* father. He came and took you away this morning, right?"

"No!" He watched in horror as Wickram pulled the cymbal off the drum kit and brought it down on the kid's head. In response, the kid grabbed Wickram by the leg and dragged him right off the stage. The two were suddenly fighting on the ground, arms and fists flying. The crowd watching Falstep turned away from the clown to watch the boys going at it. And just as this was happening, Barnabas saw three Aqua guards entering the Commons from the far corner, opposite the stage. The crowd stood between them and Wickram, but it wouldn't take them long to figure out something was wrong. "Deni, I have to hang up!"

"DON'T YOU DARE!" She snapped at him in sudden fury. "If I'm going to help you, the least you can do is be straight with me!" As quickly as he dared, he put his second arm through the backpack strap and began to climb down.

Deni's voice ached with reverence. "Oh my God, Brownbag Bopwright… I grew up listening to his Village Vanguard bootlegs. Mom Amy used to play me 'Midnight Sun' as a lullaby. The way he could arpeggiate a diminished chord…" she moaned like it actually hurt to contemplate something that beautiful.

Barnabas wished he could make himself invisible. If any of the guards happened to look up, he was screwed. "Look, Deni, I can't talk. I… *He's* waiting for me. In a big vintage Cadillac!"

"Oh wow, you're *SO lucky!* Where is he taking you? New York? New Orleans? Paris? Is he going to bring you down to some waterfront dive where the jazz is so pure, you could light it like kerosene?!" Her voice started to break up as he descended out of signal range.

"Something like that…" The fight continued, though some adults were trying to break it up. From what he could see, it looked like Wickram and the boy were pretty evenly matched. But he wasn't sure that Wickram even knew the guards were approaching. "HEY!" he shouted, but then realized this was a bad idea and shut up.

"What's wrong?!"

"Uh, they just called our flight… Final boarding!"

"Go! Go! I'll cover for you here, don't worry about a thing. *Barnabas, listen!* This is *incredibly* important!"

He stopped where he was so she wouldn't be cut off. "What?"

With solemn gravity, she told him: "When you're on an epic journey, remember to enjoy the ride."

"BYE!" he shouted and climbed down the tower as fast he could. The call was cut off as he descended out of signal range, and he felt a little ache, like a safety line to the only life he knew had been severed by the scissors of fate.

CHAPTER 9

Down from the swaying radio tower at last, Barnabas ran as fast as he could across the Commons, trying to reach Wickram before the Aqua Guard did. He squeezed his way through the crowd of onlookers (they had come for the juggling but stayed for the carnage), saying, "Excuse me," and occasionally, "Raspberry soda" when someone gave his foam nose a startled look. Soon he was at the front, where the two battling boys, more dishevelled than bloodied, were being held apart.

It took two burly men to restrain the raging Wickram, but the orange-haired boy was being held just as effectively by a tough-looking woman who had a firm grip on his freckled ear.

"Ow! Ma, let go!" he squealed with embarrassment. "He started it! Stupid circus freak!"

Barnabas was alarmed by the tornado of fury in Wickram's eyes. He was also impressed by the boy's strength, which seemed almost enough to break him loose from the tight grip of the giants behind him. "You don't disrespect our circus, earthworm!" Wickram was screaming at the orange-haired kid in a voice hoarse with passion.

Barnabas looked around for Falstep, desperate for some help. They had to get Wickram away from his captors so they could all escape... and quickly! But the clown, whose intoxication seemed to vanish during his performance, was staggering unsteadily along the edge of the crowd with his tartan cap in his hand, smiling, bowing sloppily, and muttering, "A few farthings, if you can spare it. For the children..."

Barnabas ran his fingers through his hair in exasperation. He would have to get them out of there himself. He hurried over to Wickram. "Hey!" he yelled into the furious face. "Hey, Aqua Guard coming. Let's get out of here!"

Wickram, like a switch had been thrown in his brain, simply stopped being angry. His muscles relaxed, and he tumbled back against the chests of the man holding him. "Right, okay," he said. "Let's get moving. Hey, Sarbukkit," he told one of the men holding him. "You can let go, guy, I'm cool now. Seriously..." The men seemed reluctant to comply until Wickram said, "If I go all skull-cracked again, you can report me to my dad, okay?"

Whatever that meant, it seemed to do the trick. Within a few seconds, Wickram had grabbed Falstep by the arm and was leading the three of them away from the approaching Aqua guards. They ducked under a narrow stone arch into a tight laneway, and Wickram said, "'Step? Falstep?"

Falstep was counting the coins in his cap with intense concentration ("5, 15, 25, 27...") although he kept losing his place and starting again. ("*Dung!* 15, 25, 27..."). "We should do this more often..." he slurred.

Wickram took the cap and emptied the coins into his hand. He dropped half into the clown's jacket pocket and half into his own. Placing the cap back on Falstep's head, he crouched to look into the his eyes. "Right, we will, but now I need you to drive the mule cart. Can you do that?"

"Sure! Drive to the cool mart."

"The mule cart, right? Drive it to the Coppergate Crossroads, and we'll meet you there. Got it? If the Aqua asks you anything, say you didn't see the fight."

"And don't mention me at all," Barnabas added, dubious about the clown's ability to follow any instructions in his current state. But Falstep saluted them, turned 180 degrees on his heel and headed in the direction of the cart. Barnabas asked Wickram, "Is he in any condition to drive?"

"Don't worry," Wickram said. "Even if he passes out cold, the mules know their way home." He peeked out into the Commons for a second. "No one's watching. Okay, follow me." He squeezed past Barnabas and led them down the laneway at a brisk pace.

As they got farther from the Commons, the laneway widened into a meandering, pedestrian street, with three and four storey buildings rising on either side. The sunlight penetrated this concrete canyon randomly, lighting up one stretch and leaving the next in thick shadow. Most of the buildings were small apartment houses, and despite the obvious density of life here, there was a sense of happy chaos in the crowded neighbourhood. Tiny balconies hung off the upper stories, stuffed with planters full of spring flowers. Abstract murals in primary colours covered the facades. Hand-painted street signs told them that they were passing "Dorby's Abode," "Haven on Erd," or "The Cracked Bottom."

"This is the oldest neighbourhood in the Valley," Wickram said. "It's my favourite. Later on, they built everything on a boring grid."

In fact, the roads curved and twisted so much, that Barnabas had no idea which way they were heading. He could only stumble along after Wickram, trusting that the boy would bring them to safety. A wave of exhaustion passed through him; it wasn't even 11:30 in the morning, and already it had been an impossibly jam-packed and bewildering day. Barnabas was grateful when Wickram came to an abrupt halt in a small square.

A group of kids, maybe 8 or 9 years old, was playing some kind of kickball game that involved slapping buildings on each side of the square, like running bases while the ball was in play. But Wickram wasn't interested in the game. He had stopped in front of a little shrine in one corner of the square, built into the side of a building. Painted on the wall in bright colours was a rather homey double portrait of Father Glory and Mother Mercy. In this version, the woman's gently smiling face was turned directly out into the laneway at more-or-less eye height, while the man was painted in profile, looking up to the sky with grim intensity. And though the figures were painted, the crowns on their heads were metal pieces screwed into the wall, decorated with colourful glass jewels. A small, weathered table sat under the portraits. Fresh flowers were stacked up around its elaborately carved legs, and on the mosaic table top sat a metal box with a coin slot cut in the top.

Barnabas watched Wickram put a hand to his chest and lower his head. He mumbled a prayer, and Barnabas could make out the words "...blessing for our hard work, mercy for our unmet quotas..."

"I thought you didn't believe in this stuff," Barnabas said. "You were kind of making fun of the religion when you and Falstep were doing the play."

"Yeah, no, I'm not a believer. Most of us in the circus aren't. But it's kind of considered good form to do a little offering. My dad says it shows respect and makes people less suspicious of us."

Barnabas nodded although the answer raised even more questions that he would have to ask later.

"Anyway, I kind of like doing the offering. It's a cool ritual, and it's sort of nice to imagine there really is this lady looking down and helping you out when it all goes to dung. Ha! When you meet Graviddy, don't tell her I said that!"

"Who's Graviddy?"

"She's my girlfriend! Well, actually don't say that to her either. Anyway, she's utterly bitter-root about the Church of Glory. She made up all these dirty joke versions of the prayers. She once drew a moustache on the Mother!" Wickram sounded shocked, but their was a kind of awe in his voice, too. "Here, watch this."

From a little cloth bag hanging from his neck, he pulled out a coin which he dropped into the slot in the box. Barnabas heard the coin hit the others inside, and then he heard a little click and a whirring sound. Hissing steam begin to rise around the table, and after a few seconds, hidden lights behind the crowns on the heads of Father Glory and Mother Mercy lit up, making the jewels sparkle. Barnabas laughed in delight.

As if the act of staying still for two whole minutes was too much for him, Wickram jumped straight up into the air, and when he landed, he shouted, "Come on!" and began running. Barnabas groaned and ran after him through yet more narrow laneways. They had to stop as a packed trolley car crossed their path, but when it was past, Wickram hurried across the tracks, and a few meters beyond the tracks, he turned off the cobblestoned roadway and began climbing a steep, unpaved footpath. They soon came to the crest of the hill. A sturdy old bench with many names carved into its wooden slats was waiting for them under a dusty old maple tree.

"Have a seat, Barn. Enjoy the view."

Barnabas was just glad for the chance to rest. He pulled his backpack off and felt the cool breeze on his sweating back. Dropping onto the bench beside Wickram, he raised his head to check out the promised view: ahead of them was a large depression in the earth, shallow at the edges and quite deep in the centre, almost a kilometer wide and a little less than that the other way. The ground was muddy in some places, and pooled with brown water elsewhere, especially towards the centre of the depression. At the edge where the land was dry, scrubby bushes and clumps of grasses grew.

"Welcome," Wickram said with a sweeping flourish of one arm "to

Lake Lucid, the traveller's refuge, the sweetest of waters."

"This used to be a lake? When? Dinosaur times?"

Wickram's answer shocked him: "I can just about remember my folks taking me here to swim when I was little."

Barnabas looked around and saw that it was true. Along what were once the shores of the lake were docks, boathouses, and other buildings that now sat deserted. Two jetties thrust themselves uselessly out into the mud. Between them lay the broken bulk of a large boat. The remains of a colourful awning clung to skeletal piping above the deck. All of these signs of pleasures past were decaying, overrun with weeds, but Barnabas could see they weren't all *that* old. The day was nearing noon, and he squinted against the bright light. And squinting, he seemed to see the shimmering waters of the past — kids running on the beach, diving off the docks and raising white plumes of spray, families picnicking on the boat, enjoying the blessings of the summer after a long, hard winter.

From a large building off to the right, a low thumping began. The building sat on the edge of the former lake, and a dozen fat pipes extended out from it, like the limbs of an octopus. Some went into the lake bed, where they disappeared into the muddy ground. The rest of the pipes shot out from the opposite side of the building, running across the Valley floor in various directions.

Barnabas found the stark industrial wasteland profoundly ugly and disheartening — the kind of image he saw on the news from some place far away — an oil facility in the arctic or somewhere equally desolate. "Where did all the water go?"

Wickram flipped a thumb over his shoulder and Barnabas turned. He was looking back at the cliff, up at the City. "You drank it," Wickram said. "Cheers."

"Oh," Barnabas said, feeling like he should apologize. "But where does the City get its water now?"

"There's still groundwater under the lake, at least for a few more years. That's the water plant over there, sucking out what's left."

At that moment, though he didn't have the cell signal to actually talk to her, Barnabas clearly heard Deni Jiver's voice in his head: "This story is huge! You're a member of the Journalism Club, Barnabas. Get documentation." He reached into his bag and pulled out his phone. Thumbing open the camera app, he started taking pictures, the phone going, "click, click… click."

"Whoa!" Wickram called, sitting up. "You can't do that!"

"What?"

"Pictures! You're not allowed to take pictures. Not anywhere in the Valley."

Barnabas stared at him. "But … why not?"

"Ordinances! I think it's because of something Father Glory said. Wait, let me remember…" He closed his eyes and spoke inaudibly, his mouth working. "Right! 'The image is light, and the light is theft from the thing itself.' It's from P&P." Barnabas gave him a blank look. "You know," Wickram insisted. "The Book of Precepts and Perceptions."

Barnabas squinched up his eyes in confusion. "But what does it mean? How do you steal light?"

"It means that if you take a picture of, say, that tree, you diminish the tree. I mean, if you just take one, you would hardly notice. But say you take a hundred pictures and give one to everybody. Then they don't need to come see the real tree anymore. And they wouldn't even know or care if someone cut it down."

Barnabas thought about that for a minute. It sort of made sense, but then Deni was jumping up and down in his brain, screaming: *Conspiracy!*

"I see," Barnabas said. "But banning photography sounds to me like maybe there's a big cover-up going on. Like maybe they don't want evidence of the Valley getting out to the City."

This didn't seem to interest Wickram much. He yawned and said, "Whatever, you just can't take pictures." Suddenly, he shot to his feet. "But maybe take one of me, okay?" He looked around to see if anyone was watching and then threw his hat down on the bench. He pushed the hair back out of his eyes, put one foot up on the bench and crossed his arms over his chest, pulling back his lips and gritting his teeth in a sneer that seemed almost carnivorous.

Uncertainly, Barnabas snapped the picture. Wickram bent to check out the result. "Flamtasmic! Do you recognize it?"

"Uh, no…"

"I'm supposed to be Steve Raveeno! It's the cover of his 'Fast Chicken' album."

Barnabas had no idea what he was talking about, but Wickram seemed so excited that he put on a fake smile and said, "Oh yeah, that's right. Looks just like —"

"I know, utterly. Hey!" He pointed down the steep hill in front of them. "It's Falstep!" Barnabas looked down at the mostly-deserted road that ran along the edge of the dry lake, and there was the mule cart, making its slow progress. The little figure in the tartan cap seemed to be kind of slumped forward.

"Come on!" Wickram yelled, which might as well have been his motto, given the number of times he had already said it. Barnabas, whose own signature phrase could just as easily have been "What choice do I have?", grabbed his backpack and ran after Wickram, who was fearlessly navigating a path down the hill that was so narrow and treacherous, it would give a mountain goat pause. Barnabas somehow survived the descent, and a minute later, the cart clip-clopped around the corner. Falstep was fast asleep, chin on his chest, the reins slack in his hands.

"Told you," Wickram said. "The mules know the way. Good mules!" he enthused, patting their flanks as they passed. He jumped up onto the bench and reached a hand down to help Barnabas, who scrambled up awkwardly after him. They managed to get Falstep into the back of the cart, where he curled up and began snoring.

As the road left the lake shore and began to climb, Wickram reached into the back and grabbed his guitar. He started playing a lilting, haunting melody that conjured in Barnabas' head all the sadness he felt about the death of Lake Lucid. But then the tune shifted into a major key, and Barnabas noticed that they were heading up a hill on a series of switchbacks towards the plateau of meadow and forest he had seen from the top of the radio tower. The relief he felt at seeing something green and growing surprised him. He had never been anything but a City boy, but after the industrial wasteland he had just witnessed, he was profoundly grateful.

Wickram stopped playing and put his finger to his temple under his hairline. Withdrawing the finger, he contemplated the drop of blood on it.

"You okay?" Barnabas asked.

"Yeah, it's nothing. A good fight leaves you with some souvenirs, right?" He picked up his hat off the floor, banged it on the bench to get the dust off and plopped it on his head.

It was mid-day and the sun was strong; Barnabas envied him the hat. He told Wickram, "Personally, I try to avoid fights."

"What can I tell you? I don't let gricklickers put me down. That's what Falstep taught me."

"You're really good, you know. I mean, the guitar. It was… beautiful."

Wickram gave him a sceptical look. "You play an instrument?"

"Well, uh, no. Mom didn't want me to end up like… Um, my Dad's a musician. And my Stepdad used to teach about music at a college, so I know what's good when I hear it."

Wickram spat out onto the road and pulled his hat down until Barnabas could no longer see his eyes. "Whatever. It's not like it's good for anything. I mean, if I was up in the City in a real band, playing a Daniel Doob Deluxe Frogcaster, plugged into a Driven Scorpion tube amp, and it was in the Manhammer Dome in front of a huge crowd…" He trailed off, looking into the distance like he could see this dream concert happening.

As the they climbed the hill, the sides of the road grew increasingly lush with berry bushes and wildflowers. The buzzing of insects and the insistent chirruping of birds filled the air, finally drowning out the thump and grind of the water plant, which had followed them for half an hour. The road levelled out, and they entered a lane bordered by tall beach trees. Barnabas felt himself relax, maybe for the first time since he'd woken up on the floor of his room that morning.

A giant sign arched over the road, attached to the trees on either side. In the centre of the sign was an enormous eye. Radiating out from the eye's black iris were dozens of strips of copper, each ending in a star, like miniature comets. Some of these comets shot upwards from the eye to form a night sky, a firmament which surrounded the words: "Welcome to Pastoral Park. Home of Tragidenko's Circus of Humanity!!" And as joyous and wondrous as the starry eye and starry sky were, there was also sadness in the image, because from a corner of the eye, a single tear of blue glass hung suspended. It was like a warning: taking this road to the circus meant you might discover the key to untold wonders and happiness, or else you might drown in the sorrows of the world. Perhaps both in the same evening!

Barnabas got goose bumps. He felt an irrational joy run through him. "You know what, Wickram?" he said. "In my whole life, I've never been to the circus!"

Wickram replied coolly: "Really? I've never been anywhere else."

CHAPTER 10

The roadway continued to wind upwards under the canopy of trees until at last they turned a final corner and emerged into the sunshine. The sight that greeted them was — no other word for it — awesome. They were in a wide square, bordered by flower beds that were bursting with pansies and hyacinths. Behind the beds, forsythia and rhododendrons competed to catch the eye in ostentatious display. And scattered across the expanse of interlocking bricks were huge statues of clowns, acrobats and horses, carved in wood and vividly painted.

But the sight that quickened Barnabas' heart and made a smile spread across his face was the great circus tent. He had glimpsed it from the top of the radio tower, but that distant view hadn't prepared him for the majesty or the humour of it as it rose before him. The tent was easily five stories tall, and enticingly fat — like a cupcake on a plate, with its promise of sweet delight. The huge expanse of canvas was painted in swirling bands of red and gold and festooned with silver flags that blew in the breeze. Painted on the central panel was another great eye, like the one on the road sign, which lent the whimsical facade an edge of mystery and even menace. The main entrance to the tent lay at the end of a long walkway, lined with more beds of glorious flowers. Barnabas realized what the sight reminded him of: the picture of his mom and dad in front of the Taj Mahal on their honeymoon in India.

"That's amazing," he told Wickram.

The tall boy acted like he didn't care, but the grin he was trying to suppress betrayed his pride. "Yeah, it's not bad…" he managed.

The cart followed a road that circled around one side of the tent. A gate stood open, and as they passed through it, the peaceful scene changed in an instant. Three people in purple coveralls crossed their path, carrying enormous bundles of palm fronds and peacock feathers. A scrambled jangling of bells sounded to their right, and three bicycles flew by, ridden by three figures with their hair in enormous curlers.

"Something's up," Wickram said. "Everyone's in an utter stumblestorm…"

The cart was weaving between wooden buildings with signs like, "Canvas Workshop" and "Ropes and Rigging." Through the open doors, Barnabas could see a flurry of activity, voices calling out: "I need three number fours and a wrapped fall-net!" "I don't care if it's not finished — stow it in the travel trunk!"

As they passed a long building labelled "Wardrobe," two women ran out the front door and pursued the cart, spilling needles, measuring tapes, and spools of thread from their many-pocketed aprons. The younger one, with a tangle of bright-red hair and enormous black-rimmed glasses, was shouting, "There you are, Wickram! You stole my bolt!" She leaped aboard the cart with the agility of a goat and went straight for the pile of material in the back, stepping over Falstep as if his unconscious presence wasn't the least bit surprising.

"Hey, it's not my fault if you left it in the cart," Wickram retorted.

"I've been frantic! Glistich only just finished sewing the sequins, and I have seven jerseys to finish for tonight!" She bundled the material awkwardly into her arms, and only then did she notice Barnabas sitting in the front. "Who's this?"

Wickram shrugged. "Kid from Furrowing. Wants to perform Ikarian games."

The redhead gave Barnabas a doubtful look. "You're from Furrowing? What do you do there?" the woman asked. "Canary in the coal mine?"

Wickram interrupted her. "What's happening tonight? Everyone's running around like the tent's on fire."

The redhead replied, "Full dress rehearsal. The Maestro will explain. We have a meeting in 15 minutes in the Big Top. Hey, were you in another fight?"

"I slipped on a pile of stupid."

She shook her head in apparent disgust before turning to look behind them at the other woman, grey-haired and heavier, who was panting mightily as she trotted to keep up with the cart.

The redhead shouted at her, "Loosee, catch!" and heaved the heavy bolt of material over the back. "Don't drop it, honey! I don't have time to clean it," She turned back to Wickram and said, "Fifteen minutes. Make sure he gets there." She cocked a thumb at Falstep's snoring form before lifting a leg over the back gate of the cart and jumping.

Barnabas said, "Wow, people sure do jump in and out of moving carts a lot around here."

Wickram rounded another corner, and Barnabas smelled the distinct odour of manure and hay. They climbed a little hill toward a group of low stables. In several paddocks, horses and mules were exercising. Barnabas caught a brief, thrilling glimpse of a huge snow white horse just before it disappeared inside. Wickram brought the cart to a halt outside the building and began unhitching the mules.

"Hey, Barn," he called. "Go find Whistlewort. Tell him the cart's back. I've got to water and feed these guys."

He led the animals into the building as Barnabas climbed down, wondering where he should look. But just then, a man with a weather-worn face and an undisciplined crest of frizzy grey hair appeared from behind a big tower of hay. Bits of straw stuck out of his hair and from the weave of his woollen jersey as if he might be stuffed with it like a scarecrow.

"Are you Whistlewort?" Barnabas asked.

"Yer," the man grunted.

"Here's the cart. Wickram is feeding the mules."

Whistlewort didn't reply, just began checking the harness and the wheels. The tuft of hair on his head lifted and settled on each passing breeze. Eventually, he said, "Amazing. The fool boy didn't wreck anything this time." He looked into the back of the cart. "Tell him he forgot his clown." He then gave Barnabas the same close inspection he had offered the wheels. "And who are you?"

"Um, I'm from Frowning. I want to do, uh, Uncaring games." He stuck out a hand for the old man to shake.

Whistlewort ignored the proffered hand. "Ikarian games, you mean? Then it's funny you're wearing a clown nose, don't ya think?" Blushing,

Barnabas pulled off the sweaty red nose and pocketed it.

Muttering to himself in a tone that didn't sound too friendly, Whistlewort handed Barnabas Wickram's guitar, then asked, "And what am I supposed to do with those masks in the back?"

Barnabas said, "I don't know. They're not mine."

A burly man in a long, striped coat was running up to them. "They're mine! Oh, thank the Father; I thought they were lost!" He pulled the sun and moon mask on over his head, and its colours, Barnabas noted, matched his coat. In his full costume, the man no longer seemed human; it was as if some mythical creature had suddenly appeared in their midst. He grabbed the rest of the masks and ran off again without a word.

Wickram emerged from the stables, and Whistlewort barked at him, "You shouldn't let Falstep drink like that! What would your father say?"

"I don't know! I never listen to him!" Wickram undid the back gate of the cart and jumped in. He shook the clown on the shoulder. "'Step! Wake up!"

Barnabas heard the clown mutter, "Did I miss my cue?"

Wickram, with a surprising tenderness, helped Falstep climb down from the cart, saying in a soft voice, "Forget the meeting, you go back to the dorm and sleep now. I'll come and get you before dinner." He gave Falstep a little push, and he began to stagger off down the road. Wickram headed down another path, calling, "Come on, Barn." Barnabas grabbed his backpack and headed after him.

He turned and looked back at Whistlewort's diminishing figure. He wanted to say "thank you" or something, but the man was watching him with a dark scowl, shaking his head like the world had gone bad in his fridge.

They walked by a building whose windows all stood open. Inside, men and women were cutting wood, drilling, sanding, and nailing, and Barnabas stopped to watch. Someone in the shop shouted over the din, "Meeting time!" and they all put down their work and got ready to go. Barnabas saw that they were all using hand tools like the kind he had seen in the Crumhorn Museum. Something occurred to him. "Hey! There's no electricity here," he called to Wickram as he jogged to catch up.

"Nope. Pastoral Park: it's boring and dark," he rhymed. The carpenters left their shop and began walking behind them. From every direction, people were heading for the Big Top, which suddenly loomed overhead, eclipsing the sunny day.

"But why no electricity?" Barnabas asked. "The rest of the Valley has power."

"Purity of vision," Wickram said with evident sarcasm.

A girl emerged from an alley and began walking beside them. Though she was taller than him, Barnabas thought she was probably around his age. She was a strange character — both elegant and understated. Her pants and blouse were plain and black, but the dozen or so braids that emerged from her dark hair were each a different colour, all pinned together on top in a little rainbow peak. She wore no makeup, and her pale features kind of vanished in the general whiteness of her skin. Except her lips. Her lips were surprisingly full and pink.

"Who's this guy, Wickram?" she asked. Barnabas saw a large sketch-book under her arm, and, he noted, the bag she carried at her side was bursting with art supplies, including dozens of pencils in more colours than her hair.

Wickram answered, "Hey, Garlip. Yeah this is Barnabas. He's from Coursing. Brilliant on the mini-trampoline. Built his own rig when he was only seven."

"Really!" she said, looking Barnabas up and down a little sceptically. He felt himself blushing. "Can't wait to see your act, Barnabas. Or else you're just lying, Wickram." She waggled her fingers on the side of her head and ran ahead of them, up a small set of stairs that led into the Big Top.

"She called me a liar!" Wickram said, shaking his head in disbelief, and Barnabas would have said something, but Wickram suddenly threw a hand in the air and yelled, "Hey, Mom!"

The woman was sitting quietly on a low crate beside the wooden stairway where the girl had entered the tent. She jumped energetically to her feet and gave her son a wide smile. Barnabas didn't think she looked old enough to be the mother of a teenager. But when they got closer, he could see the shallow wrinkles in her brown face and the strands of grey in her long, straight black hair. She was noticeably shorter than the other members of the community, bringing to a total of three the number of non-giants Barnabas had seen so far in the Valley, himself included.

Her bright smile dropped as they got closer. "Look at you!" she said with a trace of an Indian accent as she reached up to touch Wickram's swollen lip. "I just send you to the station and you get into another fight? What am I to do with you, Pickle?"

"It wasn't a fight. It was nothing, Mom!" Wickram's voice was petulant, but he looked at the ground, embarrassed. She reached up to push back his hair and clucked her tongue at the cut on his temple.

"Right after the meeting, you come home so I can clean that!" She sighed, and her hand moved into his hair, caressing it tenderly for a moment before Wickram pulled back from her. Barnabas understood; no guy wanted his mom fawning over him in public. "And where is Falstep?" she asked. "Did he arrive safely on the train?"

"Yeah, sure. But when we got back, he didn't feel well. He went to lie down."

The look his mother gave him said that she knew exactly what was ailing the clown. "Honestly, I'd feel more secure if you were being watched over by a hungry bear than by that man!" She took a deep breath and seemed to shake off her anger. She turned to Barnabas and smiled warmly. "Introduce me to your friend, Pickle. Hello, I am Sanjani. You are the boy from Forming Guild who wants to learn trapeze? We did not expect you until next week."

"No, Mom, he's from the City! He has a RoamPhone Gen 1!"

Sanjani's mouth dropped open, and she put a hand to her chest as if she suddenly couldn't breathe.

"I'm Barnabas Bopwright," Barnabas said, trying not to be freaked out by her reaction. He held out his hand for her to shake. "Nice to meet you."

Instead of shaking it, she grabbed the hand protectively in both of hers. The smile returned to her face, but the smile was... complicated. Her warm coffee eyes were wet as she looked deep into his, and Barnabas wanted to pull away in embarrassment like Wickram had.

Perhaps sensing his discomfort, Sanjani dropped his hands. She looked around as if to see who might have overheard them. "Does anyone else know he's here, Pickle?" she asked Wickram in a quiet voice.

"Well, everyone's in the compound has been clocking him, but outside we kept him on the hush-hush. Put a clown nose on him so they'd figure he was from Pastoral Park."

She bit her lip. "We'll need a plan. And papers. Wickram, go inside. The meeting is beginning. It is most important." She reached into the cloth bag that hung from her shoulder and handed him a little paper package tied with string. "Here's your sandwich. You come right back to the house after the meeting, do you hear?" They watched Wickram disappear into the darkness at the top of the steps.

"Follow me, Barnabas," Sanjani said and began to walk away from the Big Top. "Where did Wickram find you? When did you come through the forest?"

He found the question strange, like she asking if he was an elf or something. "I didn't come through a forest. I came on the subway."

"You mean you got through the frontier without being caught? How is that possible?"

"It was sort of an accident. There's was this machine on the train, right? And I could hide behind it."

"I see. You were very, very lucky!" Her worry reignited the fear he had felt on the train. The word *Doomlock* began banging at his temples.

They were walking back the way he and Wickram had come, and soon the stables came back into view. Sanjani called out to Whistlewort, who was hammering a fence-post into the earth: "Whistlewort, my dear one, we need your help!" She steered them back up the path to the scowling man. He put down his mallet and crossed his arms over his chest. "This is Barnabas. He's from the City. Came through on the train!"

"Ikarian games, my ass," Whistlewort muttered. "On the train? That was damn foolish!"

"I didn't plan it. I was just —"

Sanjani put a reassuring hand on his shoulder. "No, no, dear, no one blames you," although Whistlewort looked like he did. She went on, "So, we'll need to take steps to keep him safe."

The man scratched his head. "Let me think," he muttered, sitting down on a stool which was really just a piece of log. Sanjani sat on another across from him, and Barnabas joined the circle, parking himself clumsily on a low tree stump.

Sanjani said, "First of all, he'll need identity papers."

"Well, I can whip those up fast enough. Good enough to fool any Aqua who don't look too close." He pulled his knife out of his pocket and began whittling the end of a stick. "But I'm thinkin' long-term. Been quite a while since we had to plead the case of a defector."

"I'm sure we can find him a place in the circus." She turned to Barnabas, her eyes moist again. "We'll be like a new family to you, dear boy, I promise." And then back to Whistlewort: "In a year or so, we'll take him before the Guild Council —"

"Who are not our friends these days, I will remind you."

Barnabas was following this conversation with growing agitation. "Excuse me," he said, but they didn't seem to hear him.

"Dimitri is trying to change that," Sanjani insisted.

"Dimitri, you'll forgive me, is a dog who keeps gettin' beat and goes on wagging his tail regardless."

"Excuse me!" Barnabas shouted, loud enough to get their attention. "Hi, sorry, I think there's a misunderstanding here… I don't want to stay in the Valley."

They both looked at him, confused.

After an uncomfortable silence, Whistlewort barked, "Then why the hell didja come here in the first place?"

"I told you! It was an accident!"

Sanjani leaned over him, looking concerned. "Really, dear? You don't want to stay? You didn't come here to… get away?"

He seemed to have hurt her feelings or… he didn't know what. "I'm sorry," he said. "It looks really interesting here, but I have to get back to my family. I have school and stuff."

She looked back at Whistlewort, who was whittling harder than ever, and said, "He's hoping to go home again. What can we do?"

Hoping? Barnabas thought, a little alarmed at the conditional nature of her statement.

Whistlewort checked the sharpness of the stick on one calloused fingertip. "Well, identity papers are the least of it. He'll need a whole backstory, an exit plan… And I never forged travel documents before! That's not gonna be easy."

"Thank you, my friend," Sanjani said, although Barnabas hadn't heard the old man promise anything. "Let us know what we have to do." She led Barnabas away.

Where the community had been buzzing with activity when he and Wickram arrived, now it was deadly quiet.

"Is everyone in the meeting?"

"Nearly everyone, yes. But Dimitri — Maestro Tragidenko, that is — told me everything this morning."

"What's happening? Is it something bad?"

"Oh, no. Perhaps pointless, as Whistlewort suggests, but an act of optimism, nonetheless."

The story clearly needed more explanation, but Sanjani didn't offer any. Since he had told her he wanted to go back to the City, she had grown quiet. Barnabas was sort of glad about that; he wasn't sure he had the head space for more stories, what with everything else he was trying desperately to absorb. More than once, as they wound through the empty streets, he was confronted with a view of the City up on the cliff. Each time he gave a little gasp of surprise. How long would it take, he wondered, until he accepted what he saw as his new reality.

They came upon a hill, dotted with small cottages. A steep, tree-lined road ran up the hill, and Barnabas followed Sanjani up it. Each vividly painted cottage they passed was unique in some way. Some were topped with little rooftop terraces, and some had postage stamp yards, planted with too many flowers. A life-sized topiary elephant stood in the middle of one yard. Another little house was covered in small metal plates that were attached to it like the scales on a fish. A gust of wind rose, and the house shimmered in the sunshine.

Sanjani waved at an old woman who sat in her front yard in front of an easel, painting. The woman waved back cheerily, but then she noticed Barnabas. She gave him a wary stare which he could still feel on the back of his neck after they passed.

He said, "That lady didn't seem too glad to see me."

Sanjani just nodded. "Day-Z remembers the early days of the circus when a lot of people didn't want us here and did what they could to disrupt the Maestro's dreams. She probably thinks you're a spy for the Guild Council."

"I'm not!"

"Oh, I know that, dear, but she spent time in Doomlock. After something like that, it's hard to trust again." Barnabas looked back one more time at the old lady and shuddered. Sanjani exclaimed, "And Look! Here we are, safe and sound back home."

They were standing at the end of the lane, just below the crest of the hill. In front of them stood a stout house, and small as it was, it was the only one on the street with a second storey. The building's yellow walls were so rounded, it looked like an enormous squash. The trim as well as the shutters around the windows were painted green. Spring flowers grew in window boxes below every window, and the stones leading through the tiny front garden were clean and shiny, like they had just been washed.

Sanjani opened the thick wooden door, and Barnabas followed her into the house, which was pleasantly cool and dim after their time in the strong sun. He closed the heavy door behind him. The house, despite being laid out on two floors, was no bigger than the apartment where he and his family lived. The main floor was one big room with the large table in the middle, bookshelves to one side, and a little kitchen area by the front window. Between the table and the kitchen was a pot-bellied wood stove with a shiny, metal smoke-stack that snaked up and out through a hole in the wall. The walls were rough plaster, painted light purple. There were few adornments, but principal among them was a large framed circus poster from some bygone century.

Barnabas was relieved to see that Sanjani had shaken off her dark mood like raindrops off an umbrella. She was humming to herself as she carried a metal watering can to the deep, ceramic sink and began filling it. She called over her shoulder: "Please, have a seat at the table, Barnabas. I will get you some lunch."

"Thank you," he said and sat down, pulling off his backpack and placing it on the floor beside him. Then he remembered. "Oh! I still have my lunch." He dug into the bag and pulled out the lunch container his step-dad had packed for him. He had an unsettling memory of the barbecued dinosaur from his dream, but when he opened the plastic box, he was greeted by the mundane reality of a hummus and pepper wrap. "I forgot this was still the same day. It seems like ages since I left for school."

"I imagine." She brought him a glass of fizzing, red liquid.

"Raspberry soda!" he said, recognizing the drink.

"That's right." She said, sitting opposite him. "It's a favourite at this time of year."

"You're from the City too, aren't you?" he asked.

Sanjani smiled. "How did you guess? Because I'm short like you?" she said playfully.

"We're not short!" he said. "They're all giants!" This made her laugh, and he felt a bit more relaxed. He asked, "Why is everyone in the Valley so tall, anyway?"

"I don't think anyone's exactly sure. The first recruits were chosen for their size and strength, but the next generation was born even taller, as was the one after that! Perhaps we eat better food. Perhaps it is the sense of purpose in our lives."

This answer confused him a bit, so he opted for an easier question: "How long have you lived here?"

"Oh, I was very young when I arrived. Not as young as you are, but barely grown up."

He chewed on his lunch contemplatively. "So, you meant to come to the Valley? I mean, it wasn't an accident, like me?"

"I meant to go somewhere other than where I was. I found myself in River's Edge Park one night and… Well, it's a long and strange story. Do you believe that sometimes a new life calls us, Barnabas? Perhaps the life we were supposed to be living?"

"I don't know. I think a lot of people just get stuck where they are. But then they just make the best of the life they have." He was thinking of his mom and of Björn.

"True, however some lives are better left behind and forgotten," she said. He wanted to ask what she meant, but it might have been part of that 'long and strange story' she was reluctant to tell. So he focused on eating his wrap, his cauliflower bits, his mini tiramisu.

The uncomfortable silence was broken when the front door flew open, and Wickram's presence filled the room like an airbag bursting open in a small car.

"Mom! Have you seen my math textbook? I've got school in half an hour." He hung his hat on a hook by the door and dropped his guitar in a canvas chair in the corner. "Hey, Barn!" he said, noticing his guest.

Sanjani said, "I put the book on your desk, Pickle. No, no, don't get it now. You come here and let me wash that cut." Wickram sighed elaborately and followed his mother over to the sink. His long legs could cover the length of the house in a few strides, and the whole room seemed even smaller now that he was in it. He winced a little as his mother dabbed at his temple with a wet cloth.

"How was the meeting?" she asked. "I hope everyone is enthusiastic about this opportunity."

"Of course they are. They would jump into Forming's smelters if their crazy old maestro told them to." Sanjani clucked her tongue at this as she applied ointment from a little glass jar to the cut.

Barnabas asked, "What was the meeting about?"

Wickram said, "We have to do a special performance tomorrow night for a group of delegates from the Clouding Guild." It was all Sanjani could do to hold him in place while she stuck a bandage on the cut. When she was finished, he strode over to join Barnabas at the table. "But Clouding hate us, so what's the point?"

Sanjani, wringing out the cloth, said, "The point is that the Circus has been in operation for 23 years, and we still aren't accepted by one of the major guilds. And that makes our position in the Valley too precarious."

Barnabas said, "I saw some of them on the subway. Falstep called them Clouders." He remembered their scary breathing masks and vicious dogs. "They really hated on him. What have they got against the Circus?"

Sanjani leaned against the sink and regarded him. "They are the most religious of the guilds. They live a very strict life and believe that our entertainment dishonours Father Glory and weakens the holy work of the Valley."

"What about Mother Mercy?" Barnabas asked. "Do they think it dishonours her, too?"

Wickram began thumbing through a magazine — a glossy movie preview, two or three years old. Without looking up he said, "Clouders don't like the Mother. She's all about forgiveness, and they're all about screaming at you for being a sinner."

Sanjani's tone was censorious: "And despite your views, Wickram, you will be a good host when they are here tomorrow night, and keep that famous tongue of yours in check. And now stop reading that silly magazine! You have a guest. Go show Barnabas your room. You have to change for school anyway. That shirt is grey with road dust."

"Oh sorry, Barn. Yeah, come on up!" He closed the magazine (smoothing his hands carefully over the cover as if it was a rare and precious book) and sprinted up the steep staircase at the side of the room.

By the time Barnabas got up the stairs, Wickram was already nowhere to be seen. Barnabas found himself in a narrow hall which ran between two small rooms. At the front of the house was a simple unadorned bedroom with several vases full of fresh flowers. It was obviously the parents' room. Wickram, meanwhile, was moving around noisily in the back bedroom. The door was closed most of the way, and Barnabas gave a short knock before he pushed it open.

If the rest of the house was simple and airy, Wickram's room was a veritable cave of clutter and culture. Every square inch of wall was covered in band posters and pages torn from magazines with stills from action movies as well as sexy pictures of their female stars. This amazing collage, Barnabas realized, was the only piece of the world beyond that he had seen so far in the Valley. Around the narrow, wooden bed were various musical instruments, including a button-accordion and several wooden recorders. In addition to the real instruments, Barnabas saw a collection of fake guitars and keyboards made of wood and cardboard — unplayable, but elaborately painted, right down to the manufacturers' logos. Wickram was shirtless, stuffing school books into a canvas bag.

Barnabas stood by the door with his hands shoved into his pockets. He always felt weird entering another kid's most personal space for the first time; he didn't dare touch anything or sit down.

"Nice instruments," he muttered, for something to say.

"Thanks. Do you like this one?" Wickram asked, picking up a fake electric guitar shaped like a lightning bolt. "I just finished it." He brought it up to his chest and raised the neck so it almost hit the ceiling. He began screaming the sound of a guitar solo, pretending to bend strings and play power chords. He was so serious and simultaneously over-the-top about the performance that Barnabas had to work hard not to laugh. He turned away and moved to the window so that Wickram wouldn't notice.

Straight across from him was the peak of the Big Top. No matter where you were in Pastoral Park, Barnabas was coming to realize, the huge tent grabbed your attention, a constant reminder of the community's work, a literal focus point.

Leaning out the window, he looked off to the left and was struck by a presence of equal power: the forest that lay behind the circus community and extended up to the great cliff. The season's new leaves were just opening on the closest trees, giving them a shimmery, blurred look. Beyond these was a thicker forest of tall evergreens, dark and dense, swaying together in the wind like the flanks of a huge, green dragon. As the wind blew through them, the dragon seemed to be breathing heavily in uneasy sleep.

Behind him, a wheezy melody started up, and he turned to watch Wickram playing the button accordion. The sound was like some old clown show, and it made Barnabas smile. But Wickram's face was serious, his eyes closed, lost in the music he was playing. He opened them and found Barnabas watching. He scowled and tossed the accordion down on his bed.

"Come on," he said, standing up. "You might as well go to school with me. You'll meet everyone." He pulled open a drawer in a tiny dresser and grabbed a t-shirt (a faded piece of merchandise from a long-ago Big Mouth Grouper tour). Pulling it on as he took off out of the room, he bounded noisily down the staircase.

CHAPTER 11

Sanjani snuck over to the kitchen window to watch they boys as they left the front garden and vanished down the road. She only dared do this for a moment; if Wickram caught her watching him with motherly concern, he would instantly whip himself into a fury and shout something like: "I'm not a helpless little puppy, Mom! I think I can manage to get to school without being carried off by an eagle!"

She lifted the full watering can out of the sink with two hands and carried it to the back door. Wickram was right, of course; she had bigger things to worry about than her 16-year-old son walking to school. There was the performance the following night, for one thing. What had Dimitri gotten them into? If it didn't go well, might their position in the Valley become even more uncertain?

And then there was the boy from the City. What a time for him to have shown up! He was like an unexploded grenade that had rolled into Pastoral Park. They would have to handle the situation very carefully. Then she thought of the poor boy himself, what he must be feeling — it was hard enough to find your place in the Valley even if you were *happy* to get away from the City.

Her back garden was a tiny patch, barely big enough for the few vegetables she planted. She began watering the tomatoes, the basil, and the parsley. The cucumbers she already regretted planting; there just wasn't enough room for the enormous leaves they would grow.

She had behaved poorly with Barnabas, rubbing her disappointment in his face. But she had been so delighted in those five minutes when she imagined that the boy was going to join them in Pastoral Park. As much as she was part of the community — and had been for 18 years — she was still the girl from the City, at least in the eyes of the oldest members of the circus. It would have been so nice to have someone around who might need her special sympathy, someone who was suddenly in need of a new mother in a way her own son no longer was.

If only Wickram wasn't so enamoured with that old reprobate clown! she thought. Falstep encouraged Wickram's wildness, the temper that got him in such trouble. She touched her own temple in the place where she had smoothed the bandage carefully over her son's cut, and tumbled down the cliff of memory...

She smoothed down the edges of the bandage on her forehead again and again as she stood silently in the hallway. It was like a little meditation, calming and centering as she looked for the courage to move. The little bag had been hastily packed, and with more sentiment than practicality, but she thought she had everything she needed. What did a person really need, after all? Acceptance, safety, love.

She backed slowly towards the door of the apartment, her eyes never leaving her parents' bedroom door. They were still asleep, though not for much longer. "To be in bed after the sun is up is to throw away the day's opportunity." That was one of the many maxims her father had shouted into her ears since she was young. He should have shouted them at her little sister too, but Kareena was somehow exempt, immune. Kareena, their baby, would stay in bed for hours without repercussion. Only Sanjani had to be perfect, but always failed to meet this lofty standard.

Then the heavy door was at her back. She felt behind her for the deadbolt, unlocked it with painful slowness. She willed its loud click to be just a little quieter today, but when it came, it sounded like a gunshot in the silence of the morning. She turned quickly, reaching for the doorknob, noticing the bruising on her wrist which had grown darker overnight. She pulled open the door, and then she and her bag were through and into the hall. The door closed too loudly behind her, but she was running now, running for the stairwell. It had to be the stairs, because waiting for the elevator (begging it to hurry, knowing the apartment door was about to fly open, that he would be upon her in his undershirt and uncombed hair, in his betrayed fury) was simply out of the question.

Only when she was on the subway, only when many stops stood between her and her father, only when she emerged into a neighbourhood where no one would think to look for her, did she breathe free. But what would she do now? She would walk the streets like a normal person. She was only 17, but already very grown up, she felt. She would walk the streets and look in the shop windows. She would read the paper in the library, maybe look in the classifieds for a job, or for an apartment. Her future belonged to her!

It was a beautiful late-September day, and the early morning chill was gone by 11am. She ate lunch in a café, feeling very grown-up. The total on the bill rather shocked her, considering how little money she had (taken from her mother's purse, the only thing that truly made her feel guilty). But today was a day to celebrate, so a little extravagance was called for.

Many hours later, with sore feet and growing hunger, she sat on a bench in River's Edge Park, watching the lazy, brown river pass by below her as the sun began to set. The day dimmed more quickly than she was ready for. Dusk flowed into the park like an inky presence, filling the space under the trees with the first pangs of doubt. The wind picked up, and soon she was cold. The only thing she had to eat was a plastic pack of soup crackers that she had slipped into her bag at the restaurant.

Now was the time to find a phone booth and call her friend, Dorothy. Dorothy was not exactly expecting her call, but Sanjani had hinted that someday she might need her help. But then a voice in her head said, "And what if Dorothy panics and tells? Or what if her mother doesn't believe your story and calls your parents just as you're settling in for the night in Dorothy's room?" She imagined herself in pyjamas, hair damp from the shower, helpless as the bedroom door opened to reveal her father, an invincible, implacable giant.

So she didn't phone. She stood, picked up her bag and walked. And soon she was crying.

The group of men was still far away. They were mere suggestions of danger, rough smudges that moved vaguely in her direction, whose shouts and intentions were still unclear. She walked away from them, trying to appear confident and certain of her path. But soon it was clear that they were following, and the only direction she could go was deeper into the groves of the park.

Before long, their shouts turned from teasing to threats, and they were running after her, incomprehensible silhouettes, monstrous and impervious to reason. She lost her way; their pounding footsteps seemed to come from all directions. Jumping over a short fence, she left the path to run through the underbrush. Branches cut her arms and her face, and more than once she tripped and landed painfully, bruising her knees, ripping her tights. But she stood again, running deeper into the woods.

It was terribly dark now. Surely too dark for the men to find her... yet she knew she wasn't safe. She found herself in a garden of giant boulders which stood together, cold and silent, like a herd of stone cattle. She made herself be still and listened with all her concentration for the sound of footsteps and snapping branches, but mostly she only heard her own breathing.

And then she did hear something, something like a voice which wasn't a voice, saying words which were almost just sounds, almost just the wind in the trees, or the falling of the leaves, or the distant rush and plash of the river. But she followed the voice, didn't she? And it led her on an unknown path through the garden of boulders. And there, in the darkness was a harder darkness, blacker than nothing. But from this nothing came a welcome exhalation of warm air... and the voice.

She was so cold, so afraid, wasn't she? There was nowhere on earth to go; she saw that now. She had made no plan other than escape, and now she knew that wasn't enough. This warm breath that rose from a nothing filled with whispers — maybe it was a path to oblivion, but it was a warm oblivion, and she would take it.

The darkness closed over her. The sounds of the world were swallowed, and her own breath, her heartbeat, and her footsteps grew louder. She knew she was no longer under the canopy of trees but in a cave, dank and close. Down into the earth the cave went, damp and descending. The path split sometimes, but whenever she had to make a choice, the voice seemed to call louder from one side and she followed it. Many hours must have passed by the time she entered a large chamber where the echoes of dripping water rung like glass. She was cold and hungry. Her feet ached, and her arm was numb from carrying her bag. Suddenly, she felt she was not alone. Not at all alone. Two by two, little points of red light appeared in the darkness. Eyes. Hundreds of pairs, staring and blinking. Were they friend or enemy?

She was afraid, of course, but she was also too tired to be afraid. And they had led her away from danger, hadn't they? So she asked, "What do you want with me?"

And then there was another light, a beacon that glowed far down another tunnel. A match? A candle? The glint in the eye of a dragon? But it was pure and white, and she turned from the staring, red eyes and followed it.

Time lost all meaning as she walked down and down, stumbling after the beacon despite her mortal fatigue. And then Sanjani was outside, back in the forest. But no, this wasn't the acre of trees in River's Edge Park; this was a real forest, tall and deep, and a stranger to the busy criss-crossings of human beings. The old lady was there. She led Sanjani to edge of the woods, and together they watched the sun rise over the Valley.

"Don't be afraid. You're home now," said the old woman, the light glinting off the blue jewel in her necklace which was an unblinking eye.

CHAPTER 12

Barnabas followed Wickram from the front door of his house, across the front garden, and out through the little gap in the knee-high, stone fence.

Here at the top of the street, they could see all the cottages. Wickram said, "Most of the people in the circus live in the dormitories, but some of the older denizens, the ones who were here at the beginning of the circus, live in these cottages. Personally, I hate it."

"Why? Isn't it better to have your own room? And some peace and quiet?"

"No way! All my friends live together. They have a blast, and I'm stuck here with my stupid parents and a bunch of old people who give me dirty looks every time I put a foot wrong or burp too loud. Hey, check this out!" He pointed up at a tall pole, intricately carved with colourful birds. On the top was a wooden box, and emerging from the box was a woven metal cable that travelled down to another bird-decorated pole on the other side of the road. From there, the cable connected to another pole and another, criss-crossing all the way down the street. Real birds sat on a couple of the poles, and more were perched on the cable itself.

"Wow, I didn't notice these on the way up. What are they?"

"They were built by this artist named Skeelix. She was kind of like an aunt to me. She died a few years ago, but we keep the system running."

"What do they do?"

"It's better just to show you." He pointed at a metal handle that was sticking out of the post. "Turn that," he said.

Barnabas took the wide handle in both hands and began to crank it counter-clockwise. After about 20 seconds, it got hard to turn.

He looked at Wickram, who said, "Yeah, that should do it. See the switch on the other side of the pole? Flip it to the left and get ready to be amazed."

Barnabas walked around the pole and reached out a cautious hand, pausing briefly at the last minute as if he might get an electric shock. But there was no electricity in Pastoral Park, so he flipped the switch. The handle began to turn clockwise, and a set of bells played a short a fanfare. Up above them, the doors on the front of the box creaked open, and a wooden bird, painted brightly in reds and yellows, flew out of the box, wooden wings flapping vigorously as it shot along the woven metal wire toward the next post.

"Come on!" shouted Wickram — his battle cry — and ran after the bird down the steeply sloping street.

And indeed, it was a beautiful thing: the mechanical bird zigzagging through the air, changing direction and ringing a bell each time it met a pole. And it was beautiful to run as fast as they could down the hill, testing the limits of stability, laughing and whooping, watching the actual birds take flight in alarm as their wooden cousin bore down on them. And for those giddy 30 seconds, all of Barnabas' worries were chased out of his life.

The bird beat them down the hill, of course, disappearing into the box atop the last pole, the doors slamming shut behind it. Down at the bottom of the cobbled street where it met the main road, the boys were bent over, hands on their thighs, laughing and panting.

Barnabas stood slowly and noticed that everyone who passed was looking at him, smiling, talking in low voices to each other and then staring some more. He reached into his pocket and pulled out the squashed clown nose.

"Should I ... ?" he asked Wickram.

"What? No, don't bother. If Whistlewort knows about you, then it didn't take more than an hour for everyone else to know."

"But won't I be in trouble if anyone finds out I'm here?"

"You're fine. At least here in Pastoral Park. We can keep a secret. Well, not from each other, but from the rest of the Valley. Let's go or we'll be late for school."

As they walked along the main road, more people waved to him or said, "Welcome!" One fit, middle-aged woman (one of the circus' veteran acrobats, Wickram told him after) stopped to ask him if he knew her uncle who lived up in the City. He just kind of gawped and shook his head, but she didn't seem to mind. It was like she was happy just to have met the mystery guest.

The boys didn't have to walk far before Wickram led them into a wide, concrete building full of large rehearsal rooms with high ceilings. In one, tumblers were flipping, vaulting, and forming human pyramids. In the next, a man and woman were balancing on each other's outstretched limbs, holding the poses in perfect stillness for many seconds while all their muscles strained with exertion.

Barnabas wanted to linger at each doorway to watch these incredible feats of strength and skill but Wickram was behind him, pushing him ahead, saying, "Don't rube out on me, Barn. You'll come to rehearsal this evening and see the whole thing."

They turned a corner and came to a room where chairs and desks had been set up to create a small classroom. Eleven kids turned their heads as the two of them entered. They ranged in age from around 10 to 18 (Barnabas was already learning to adjust his age estimates for the inhabitants' increased height). They all stared at him, and he saw a few heads come together to whisper.

At the front of the room, standing beside an old-fashioned blackboard, stood the teacher, a slender middle-aged black woman, whose tight grey curls were cut close to her head. She wore loose cotton pants and a short-sleeved tunic that showed off her powerful arms, with their clearly defined muscles.

She turned to glance at a big clock on the wall. "Well, Wickram, you're a little earlier than usual. Let's keep trying to improve on that, shall we?"

"Yes, Ma'am," Wickram said with a cocky smile and took hold of Barnabas' shoulder, steering him towards the back row where they took their seats.

The woman smiled at Barnabas. "And welcome to your friend. I'm Kalarax. I'm a tumbler in the circus, and I also teach the older children three days a week. I understand your name is Barbarous?" she asked.

"Uh, Barnabas. Nice to meet you." Word of his arrival was spreading fast, just like Wickram had predicted, though not necessarily accurately.

"Oh, forgive me. Make yourself at home. And I hope you can help enlighten us with some of your up-to-date City education."

He nodded, but thought that maybe she was being sarcastic. She picked up a piece of white chalk and turned to the blackboard. The other students all turned away from him except for one girl, possibly the oldest in the class. She had honey-blonde hair, short in the back, but with generous bangs that made a dramatic straight line above her large, green eyes. Those eyes were staring straight into his without apology or embarrassment, and Barnabas could only stare back.

Wickram suddenly elbowed him fairly hard in the side. "Here," he whispered, handing Barnabas a piece of paper and a pen. "You can use these." When Barnabas looked back up, the girl was turned away.

The first thing they studied was economics. It was a lesson in how much food, fuel and supplies the different guilds in the Valley required, and how those numbers were translated into manufacturing and agricultural planning. It was pretty interesting, and Barnabas learned that the Valley had approximately 8,000 residents. Most of these were members of the four guilds, but there was also a community of support workers plus, of course, Pastoral Park, home of Tragidenko's Circus of Humanity, the smallest segment of all, numbering 160 people.

From there, they moved on to poetry and then math. Barnabas found he knew some of what was being taught, but was totally unfamiliar with other parts. He dropped off to sleep for a few minutes in the middle of a lesson on groundwater and wells, but that was hardly surprising — he had barely slept the night before and spent the whole morning running on adrenaline. When he woke up, the teacher was gone, and one of the kids explained that they were supposed to be working on math problems until she got back. Of course, what really happened was they all got up and circled around Barnabas.

Wickram introduced the kids: "This is Soonie, Mooney, Beaney and Moe. Huro, Buro, Dromadop, Thumbutter, and..." his voice kind cracked for a second. "Uh, this is Graviddy." He was referring to the girl with the honey-coloured hair, whose amazing eyes were back on Barnabas. Graviddy, Barnabas remembered, the girl who was Wickram's girlfriend (a fact you were not supposed to mention), the one who had no patience for the church of Father Glory and Mother Mercy. She sat on the edge of a desk with remarkable poise. And you would think that remaining so erect would mean she was stiff and hard like a soldier. Instead there was a kind of buoyancy to her as if her spine were just naturally drawn skywards.

"Hi," she said. "Nice to see a new face. You going to be staying at the dorms?"

Wickram jumped in, speaking a bit too loudly and without looking at her. "No, he's staying at our house." For the first time since Barnabas had met him that morning, Wickram seemed awkward and uncomfortable. Graviddy wasn't looking at him either, but she didn't seem the least bit uncomfortable. Barnabas had witnessed this phenomenon before: a crushed-out boy and a girl who seemed to be utterly indifferent to the pain her existence caused him.

Another voice, in the corner behind him said, "What are you doing here, anyway?" He turned and saw the girl he had met earlier outside the Big Top, the one in black with the coloured braids. Her art supplies were spread across her desk, and she was just barely looking up from whatever she was sketching to ask the question.

Wickram said, "That's Garlip. Garlip, Barnabas."

Before Barnabas could answer her question, the littlest kid in the class, a boy of maybe 10 with his hair in a ponytail, said, "I heard you climbed on top of a train to get down to the Valley. I heard that you did it on a dare."

Barnabas' eyes went wide. "What? No! I didn't mean to come down here at all." He proceeded to tell the story, beginning where he fell asleep on the crowded train. This led to a side-lecture about just how crowded a subway could get in the morning, which in turn led to him providing half-remembered statistics on the population of the City, followed by a more accurate account of the number of subway stops, and finally, a short treatise on how supermarkets worked.

Kalarax returned, carrying a wooden box, and everybody more or less hurried back to their seats. "I see we got a lot of work done on the math problems. Fine, please do them as homework tonight. Who wants to play Snap Answers?"

They all seemed enthusiastic about this idea. They reconfigured their desks into a circle, and the box was passed around. Each student took three beanbags from the box, and Kalarax walked around, handing out question cards. The game began. Garlip was up first. She stood, looking at no one, her face a little grim, and began tossing one of her beanbags in the air, over and over. The boy sitting to her right turned over his first card and read the question out loud. It was a math problem which Garlip had to solve in her head. Kalarax started up a metronome, and after five seconds, one of the students threw a beanbag Garlip's way which she had to add to the one she was already juggling. Thirteen seconds later, she was juggling three beanbags and about to receive a fourth when she called out the answer. Kalarax confirmed it as the correct response and Garlip was able to drop the three bean bags, including her original one, into the discard box. The teacher made a note of her score on the blackboard, and the game proceeded.

Not everyone got math problems. Some question cards required the student to list a series of geographical places, or name the steps in a certain kind of mineral extraction. The scoring was complicated: correct questions gave you the most points, but the number of beanbags you simultaneously juggled also worked in your favour. However, the number of beanbags you still had at the end of the game would make you lose points.

The students were highly accomplished, not only with their answers, but with their juggling! Wickram, sitting on the edge of the teacher's desk, got an answer wrong with five in the air. Immediately, he had two more thrown at him, one by Graviddy, who seemed to lob it with more force than necessary. Still juggling, he stood up to give himself more room. And with seven in the air, tossing them just short of the high ceiling, he finally got the answer right.

Graviddy, for her part, said nothing at all, seemed not to be even thinking about the math problem she had to solve until she was juggling eight bags. She looked so poised and beautiful that Barnabas felt hypnotized. In a bored voice as if it had just occured to her that she should speak, Graviddy said, "x=9." She tossed the beanbags into the discard box without even waiting for the teacher's confirmation. Barnabas almost applauded.

When Kalarax declared the game over, the students all began tossing their remaining beanbags her way, and she juggled them effortlessly, three or four in the air at once, before letting them drop back into the box.

Graviddy won the game.

The teacher dismissed them when the big clock on the wall read 4:30. As they packed up their books, one of the kids climbed on a chair and wound the clock. They all walked out of the building together, in little knots of two and three, passing the rehearsal rooms, where the sweaty performers were still hard at work. Wickram ran ahead with two of the other teenage boys, and soon they were playing a very skilful game of hacky sack in a square across the road.

The kid with the ponytail, whose name was Beaney and who was the only one shorter than Barnabas, asked, "When are we supposed to do our homework? We're gonna be rehearsing all evening."

A girl whose name Barnabas had forgotten, answered, "It'll be a lot of stop and start tonight. Just bring your homework and do it during breaks."

Beaney said, "Yeah, but I'm stuck in the bottom of the clown car most of the time. I can't do anything unless all the other clowns move first!"

Something brushed against Barnabas' shoulder, and he turned to find Graviddy standing beside him. "Hi," he said with a smile, looking up at her. "You're a really good juggler."

"Oh, we all do that. You should see me do my silks act." Her big green eyes were shining on him like two spotlights. She was utterly unembarrassed by this intensity, and he was totally intimidated.

"Wow. Okay," he managed to say. "I guess I get to watch you perform tonight."

"No, Maestro Tragidenko wants me to rest. I hurt my shoulder last week and he needs me ready to perform for the Clouding representatives tomorrow night. I'm one of the stars of the show." She said this without apology, but it didn't sound like bragging. It was just a fact of life.

Now he was at a loss for words. He tried staring back at her with the same focus, but it felt too weird, and he looked away. "Oh, then I'll watch you tomorrow. I'll be here for a few days."

"I heard you were stuck in the Valley for at least six months," Graviddy said.

"No!" Barnabas almost shouted in alarm. "I-I'm leaving on Tuesday. I mean, I have to!"

"Okay; that's not what I heard. Anyway, you were pretty brave to come here like you did. I'm impressed."

He was going to start all over again saying that it was an accident, and that therefore he wasn't brave. But then he thought how cool it was that this beautiful girl who was a *star* was impressed by him, so he held his tongue. And she smiled at him — really the first smile he had seen from her — and it kind of lit up his insides like hot chocolate in winter. Without another word, she turned and walked away.

He looked around to see if Wickram was finished with his game, only to find the boy right beside him, staring at him with a suspicious look.

"Oh, hey!" Barnabas said with too much force and too much smile as if he had already done something wrong. "Are you, uh, going to show me more of the circus now?"

The suspicion cleared from Wickram's face as quickly as it had arrived. "We have 90 minutes until dinner. Let's go for a walk."

Little Beaney spun around and called, "Can I come, too?".

"No!" Wickram said with finality, and Beaney looked totally crestfallen until Wickram told him, "But you can come with us tomorrow, okay? You know where." This made the boy grin. "Come on, Barn," Wickram said and headed down the road. Barnabas gave the others a quick wave goodbye and followed.

They had only gone a short way when Wickram veered off onto a narrow path through a meadow that glowed in the late afternoon sun. A thin fog of bees buzzed around their ankles, darting among the buttercups and clover. The path led them through tall stands of berry bushes which soon swallowed the view of Pastoral Park and the Big Top.

"I guess you thought the class was pretty boring," Wickram said, twisting and raising his arms to avoid the scratchy canes of the bushes.

Barnabas wasn't tall enough to do this, and he was quickly covered in scratches. He said, "No, it was cool. That juggling game was totally —"

Wickram cut him off. "She's gorgeous, isn't she?"

"Graviddy, you mean?"

"And so smart and talented. Everyone's kind of in love with her."

There was a deceptive ease to his voice, and Barnabas felt like he was being tested. "She's a ... really good juggler," he said in a carefully neutral voice.

"She likes me, you know. She just doesn't show it."

Wickram pushed a cane out of his way and it snapped back on Barnabas, catching him in the wrist. He winced. "Yeah, I'm sure she does," he said encouragingly. "I could tell."

"But everyone loves her," Wickram said again. "Especially my dad."

Barnabas didn't know how to reply to this weird factoid. The sun suddenly vanished as they left the bushes behind and entered the woods — the same woods he had seen from the window of Wickram's bedroom. Light filtered through the sparse canopy of new leaves. He heard little rustlings and dartings in the undergrowth as they walked, two clumsy invaders in a world of small birds and mammals.

Wickram kept his voice low as if he didn't want to alarm the world of the woods more than they had to. "Mom says the whole of the Valley used to be like this — dense trees from the edge of the cliff, right up to the shores of Lake Lucid.

They came to the banks of a narrow, burbling river. A stone bridge crossed it and led on to a path that vanished into the woods beyond — the darker forest of thick evergreens. Barnabas was about to walk onto the bridge when Wickram grabbed his arm. "We don't go into the old woods," he said. "It's kind of out of bounds."

"Why?"

"Weird stuff happens there. They say there's a witch or something. That she killed lots of people before. Made them into jerky."

Barnabas started to laugh at this. It sounded like something you would tell kids to keep them from straying and getting lost. But then he stared into the shadows across the bridge and felt a troubling doubt. Maybe it was just because of Wickram's spooky story, but the old woods seemed to emanate an aura of ancient stillness and mystery. "You don't really believe that, do you?" he asked.

"I dunno if it's true or just road apples. Sometimes a bunch of us say we're going to spend the night in there. But we never get around to actually doing it."

Wickram moved off the path and sat on a rock that hung over the water. Barnabas joined him, asking, "But we're safe here on this side?"

"Oh yeah! No one's ever been killed on this side." He said this with great authority. So they lay there peacefully on their backs on tufts of thick, dry moss, and after a few minutes, Barnabas felt a sweet heaviness come over him. All the stresses of the day were put on hold. He was able to just relax and enjoy the peaceful plash of the water and the intermittent cries of jays and blackbirds.

Wickram asked, "You ever been in love?"

Barnabas thought about Deni. "No. Not really," he replied.

"It's kind of the worst thing in the world," Wickram said, pushing the hair out his eyes and fixing Barnabas with a weighty look. "But kinda perfect, too, you know?" He let the curtain of hair fall back into place.

Barnabas didn't know. Not exactly. Did Deni love Cal? He knew his mom loved Björn, but he was pretty sure she also still loved Harold "Brownbag"

Bopwright. And even though she cursed him anytime his name came up in conversation, her eyes still misted over when she looked through old pictures from her first marriage, back when they were all together. Did love ever make you really happy? He wished there was someone he could ask, because the answer seemed pretty important.

They dropped the topic and went on to talk about the other kids in the class, about what they did in the circus. Barnabas answered more questions about City life, about apps and togs and smart billboards. The afternoon was warm, and the sound of the stream lulling. Soon, Barnabas felt himself drifting off to sleep. He was just deciding to give in to this delicious impulse when Wickram suddenly sat up.

"Dungbutter!" he shouted. "I forgot I'm on serving duty at dinner!" He cocked his head up at the canopy of trees. "Where's the sun? Looks like it's already 5:30… Come on!"

The peaceful interlude was over, and Barnabas found himself running again after the tall boy.

CHAPTER 13

Barnabas chased after Wickram, back through the woods and the streets of Pastoral Park, to a large sky-blue building on a wide square. This was the community dining hall. Barnabas entered a minute after Wickram, and found his new friend already racing around, putting bowls of salt and jars of honey on the large wooden tables. Each table was surrounded by ten gleefully mismatched chairs as if the circus community had assembled the collection piece by piece from countless yard sales.

Wickram put Barnabas right to work, barely pausing to bark orders at him even as he ran back and forth, in and out of the kitchen. There were a few others on serving duty, all of whom were doing their work considerably more calmly than Wickram. They introduced themselves to Barnabas but did not give him any tasks; they seemed to accept that he worked exclusively for Wickram.

By the time the population of Pastoral Park began to flow into the dining hall, the space had been transformed from empty, echoing warehouse to an over-sized but nonetheless homey dining room. The smell of spices filled the air, and each table sat expectant with mismatched plates and cutlery, and small vases containing the last of the season's tulips, in all the colours of the rainbow.

Barnabas saw the older kids from class, including Graviddy, entering together and heading for a table in the corner. They were loud and exuberant, and he was looking forward to joining them. But before he could walk there, Wickram appeared at his side, put an arm around his shoulder, and steered him to another table where a group of adults was sitting. They greeted him eagerly, and Barnabas knew it would be rude to leave. He smiled through his frustration. He had a pretty good idea why Wickram was keeping him away from the kids' table: he was trying to stop him from talking to Graviddy. He wanted to find Wickram and say, "I'm not interested in your girlfriend." Except, she wasn't officially his girlfriend. And maybe he *should* be interested.

At the front of the room, someone got up to make community announcements, and finished by wishing everyone health and peace.

"Health and peace," they all replied in unison. The kitchen doors flew open and the evening's servers, including Wickram, appeared with trays of food, starting with radish-apple soup, and continuing on to grilled rabbit and mashed taro. It was all very fresh and good, cooked with bold, aromatic spices, and all washed down with the best apple cider Barnabas had ever had.

The men and women at his table turned out to be landscapers and groundskeepers, the ones responsible for the beautiful gardens in front of the Big Top. They asked him polite questions about his life in the City, though they already had their own ideas about the life of a typical City dweller.

"Living and working in those towers all day, they see so little sunshine that their doctors make them go lie on tanning beds every week just so their skin doesn't turn transparent and fall off," said one.

Another knew with certainty that, "Everyone has to compete for their jobs. They have special tournament facilities where you have to try and shoot your opponents with balls of paint. The winners get the good jobs. The losers are forced into work that is basically slave labour. But you have to take it or you'll starve."

Barnabas tried to explain that this wasn't exactly true, but they gave him a pitying look, like he was too brainwashed to understand. One woman did want him to tell her everything he knew about River's Edge Park. She had heard that it contained some of the most beautiful landscaping in the world, and it was her dream to visit it someday. Barnabas couldn't really name the plants or anything, but whatever he managed to remember about the park seemed to enthral her.

He had a question for them. "Is this show for Clouding Guild a big deal? Are you nervous?"

An older man named Sarjen made a puffing sound with his lips and said, "Nervous? Nah. It's a bit of pressure, trying to impress those humourless, rodrammed grobs, but if the Maestro wants to give it a try, we'll do our best."

Barnabas looked around the room. "Is Maestro Tragi-something here?" he asked.

A woman with fingernails which were cut short but painted bright yellow said, "Tragidenko. No, he's in the Big Top with the department heads. You'll see him during the rehearsal. Now, he's nervous!"

Sarjen, picking his teeth methodically said, "The worst part of the whole thing is we invited the Clouders to have dinner with us. We'll have to spend 10 minutes praying before we can eat a gromlicked thing!"

"And twenty minutes after dinner, too!" laughed the woman.

Someone tapped Barnabas on the shoulder, and he turned around to find two of the kids from that afternoon's class there: Buro and — he had to think for a minute... "Thumbutter!" he said out loud.

"Yeah, and I'm Buro. Come over to our table for dessert."

So he did, and either by accident or design, he ended up sitting next to Graviddy after all. He began having a much better time than he had with the adults... except for when Wickram brought out the tray of desserts and gave him an annoyed look. When Wickram was done serving, he returned, and everyone shifted around to make space for him. Not surprisingly, he put his chair between Barnabas and Graviddy.

Soon it was time to head over to the Big Top for the rehearsal. As they left the dining hall they found Falstep sitting on a bench outside, enjoying the dregs of the day's sunshine.

Wickram grinned and ran over to him. "Hey, you got your head on straight now?"

The clown appeared fully in command of his senses. He was wearing a wide-brimmed purple hat, and he pulled it down at a cockier angle and said, "Let's just say the world is showing me its smiling face now instead of its backside."

A group of men and women emerged from the dining hall and soon surrounded Falstep on his bench. Barnabas realized these must be the clowns. They weren't wearing any funny wigs or big shoes or anything, but just the way the way they banged into each other and reacted with exaggerated, outraged, wide-mouthed faces was hilarious.

"Hey, kid," Falstep said to Wickram. "Get me a plate of food, will ya? I gotta go rehearse my people."

Wickram rolled his eyes and headed back toward the dining hall, but he didn't really look unhappy. Barnabas watched the clowns head for the Big Top, wondering whether he should wait for Wickram to return. But then the kids came by and swept Barnabas into their midst, following the clowns toward the rehearsal.

Inside the huge tent, the group dispersed, heading for wherever they needed to be. Garlip lingered a minute. She pointed to their left. "Sit over there in front of the red pillar. That's the best seat in the house."

"Are you going to watch with me?"

"No, I'm apprenticing with set design. I think the paint crew probably needs some help." She looked him in the eye for a second, then blushed and looked away. "Enjoy the show," she said and strode quickly away, holding her art supply bag tightly to her chest. He pondered both her discomfort and her retreating posterior until she vanished behind a curtain.

And now Barnabas was alone to take in the marvel that was the Big Top of Tragidenko's circus. Rows of benches were wrapped in a large semi-circle around the circular stage — the "ring," he remembered it was called. Two main poles rose up from either side of the ring, shooting high into the air where they acted as the main support for the tent. Halfway up them were two platforms, like the crows nests on an old sailing ship, with trapezes and dozens of other ropes tied to them. Even higher, catwalks crisscrossed between the poles, just under the tent's roof. Gas lamps hung from the catwalks and from the polls themselves, flickering warmly, filling the tent with a bright but somehow gentle light.

Behind the ring rose a series of gigantic curtains separating the performance area from the backstage. Barnabas watched various curtains being raised and lowered, revealing and hiding yet more curtains of different colours and elaborately painted backdrops. There was a whooshing sound above him and he looked up to see two huge spotlights firing up, each with a bright flame and a big reflector. Their operators began shining the spot beams around the tent, and it looked very glamorous to Barnabas — like a movie premier.

Everywhere there was life. Stagehands were stringing ropes and testing them; painters were touching up pieces of set; performers were stretching their muscles, chalking their hands, beginning to climb up towers, and up ropes, and lengths of fabric which hung from the towers. Musicians tuned their instruments and practiced complex figures together over and over until the complex became second-nature. A makeshift makeup area sprang to life at the side of the ring, and a line of performers proceeded to transform their everyday faces into the beautiful, otherworldly faces of the stage.

Off to his left, a group of people burst into the tent, engrossed in some kind of debate, hands gesticulating, everyone talking at once. And though anyone in the group might be said to have a big personality, they were all bland as butter compared to the figure in the centre. He was the very definition of *larger than life*. His tall, wide body was all but engulfed in a long coat of coloured patches. A floppy hat of more patches sat precariously on the mountain-top of his long, tangled hair. The hair reached down to his shoulders to form a continuum with his beard, which was itself long enough that the end was tied with a ribbon. Together, mane and beard turned his head into a thundercloud of hair, jet black where it wasn't shot through with bolts of pure white. The eyes in the centre of this cloud were black pools, but they were as bright and electric as lightning.

"Show me!" he proclaimed in a low and resonant voice that seemed to emerge from somewhere deep inside him, or from deep in the centre of the Earth.

"Guess who," whispered Wickram, who had appeared at Barnabas' side, silent as a cat.

"The… The Maestro?" asked Barnabas. "Tragidenko?" Wickram raised his eyebrows in acknowledgement.

A woman with a shaved head who had entered with Maestro Tragidenko shouted for the ring to be cleared, and it happened almost immediately. She ran over to the curtain to left of the ring and pulled it open. Three men and two women in tight suits of orange and blue with silver helmets on their head entered on bicycles. The bicycles were beautiful creations in shiny green. They reminded Barnabas of grasshoppers. Three of the bikes were of ordinary dimensions, but two had their seats, handlebars, and pedals extended way up high off the ground. These bikes were more like mantises. The performers began circling the ring. Barnabas realized that the two riders on the oversized bikes were the twins, Huro and Buro. The others bore a resemblance to them, and Barnabas wondered if they were all from the same family — Huro and Buro's parents and maybe their big sister.

They circled for another few seconds before the shaved-headed woman — their coach? — clapped her hands. The riders on the three ordinary bikes rode into the centre of the ring, circling intricate patterns around each other. They changed positions with startling precision, jumping up to balance on one foot on their seats, then spinning around to sit on the handlebars. The bikes passed within a hairbreadth of each other each time they turned. And just when Barnabas felt like he couldn't even keep track of everything that was happening, Huro and Buro, on their giant mantis bikes, pedalled into the centre to join the dance.

The act had started in silence, but now the band was starting to play along, instruments joining in one by one as the players hurried to their places.

Five bikes at two levels were circling and spinning in the ring. The cyclists began trading places, making remarkable jumps from the high bikes to the low, from bikes going in one direction to those running the opposite way. The whole routine ended with what looked like an imminent, five-way crash but turned into a frozen tableau with each bike up on one wheel, supporting each other in what could only be a metaphor for teamwork and community.

Barnabas was surprised at the soaring emotions that arose in him — just two minutes of movement, just five people. Now the cyclists dismounted, and everyone in the whole tent grew silent. All eyes were on Tragidenko, who was running his fingers through his long beard and blinking rapidly.

"Yes!" he said with enthusiastic finality and strode off, disappearing behind the curtain. The helmeted performers and their shiny-domed coach breathed a collective sigh of relief and gave each other short, exuberant hugs. Buro noticed Barnabas and pointed him out to Huro. The twins grinned and waved before following the rest of their team backstage.

With this drama over, the hubbub in the tent grew again. Acrobats began practicing moves in the ring, and three carpenters climbed up into the audience to hammer a new guardrail in place.

Barnabas looked over and found Wickram rising from a crouch behind a bench as if he had been hiding. But from whom? From the Maestro? He asked, "What do you do anyway, Wickram? Are you in the band?"

"Nope, I'm a stage-hand," he said, sitting up. He pointed across the ring. "See that curtain? The red one, just to the left of the big black one in the middle? That's my curtain. I have to pull it aside for a bunch of entrances and exits and then make sure it gets back into position."

"That's it?"

Wickram frowned at him. "What? Don't you think stage-hands are important? How do you think all the curtains move, and the props and apparatuses get where they have to go? Magic?"

"No, that's not what I meant. It's just... you seem really creative, and I thought maybe you'd be doing music, or drawing sets or —"

"Well, I'm proud of my work! The stage-hands are like a family. We watch out for each other, and we do everything so perfect, no one even has to remember we exist."

Barnabas was trying to pull together an apology, some combination of words that wouldn't get him in more trouble when Maestro Tragidenko swept in through the centre-stage curtain and strode to the middle of the ring.

"Attention! Attention is desired and required!" he called. From behind every curtain, members of the troupe emerged. Up on every ladder and across every rigging strut in the vast space, work stopped again, and heads turned toward the ring. Five or six trap doors opened in the floor, and all the clowns, including Falstep, peeked their heads out. Wickram got up and went to stand with a group of men and women in loose, faded black clothing who must have been his stage crew "family."

"My darlings, my darlings," the Maestro said to the members of the circus company, wiping his sweating brow. "You have made many beautiful things full of love. I am humbled." His voice was exotically-accented, rising and falling in a full-bodied sing-song, and the company seemed to hang on every word, smiling with gratitude at his praise. "We don't yet precisely know what is this show we are making, yes? And some of the wonderful work will be tossed on the fire — with regret and humility — so that even greater creations will rise from the ashes.

"But tomorrow, despite all this yessing-and-noing, this guessing-not-knowing, we must put on a polished performance!" He rocked back and forth on his heels, turning slowly to look at everyone with his warm, piercing eyes. He threw a fat finger in the air. "So! Tonight, we are seeing where we are being." Tragidenko turned around and looked out at the audience, which comprised Barnabas, Sanjani (who was serenely knitting), some of the landscapers, and clutch of pre-school kids.

Tragidenko continued: "And you, our dear, dear rehearsal audience…" He looked at Barnabas. "Some new to us…" he stretched out his hands as if to hug them all. "You will help us to see, to understand, to truly know in our hearts how far we have travelled on this sea of confusion, and how close we are to the shores of TRUTH!"

Barnabas started to applaud, but no one else did. He shoved his hands under his arm pits and scrunched down in embarrassment.

"So! We will commence with the tightrope tango and run straight through, pausing only if mortal danger presents itself…" He laughed a low, phlegmy chortle. "Straight through to the end of Act I!" He clapped twice, and the company moved purposefully to their starting positions.

Wickram waved at Barnabas to come join him. Barnabas hurried down the aisle, climbed into the ring and went through the gap in the curtain that Wickram held open. He found himself in the backstage world of the circus. A huge place itself where dozens of performers and technicians had established themselves in their own little territories.

Wickram said, "I thought maybe you'd like to watch from backstage here tonight."

"Can I? That would be great."

"No problem. Tomorrow, you'll have to be in the audience, though."

Wickram started pulling off his clothes and changing into his own set of stage-hand blacks. And as Barnabas looked around, he saw a lot of people changing; a lot of really beautiful, toned bodies, all stripping and dressing with a performer's lack of shame. He wanted both to look and look away.

Now in his black clothing, Wickram tested his curtain, giving the rope a few short tugs when a pulley stuck. Another man in stage-hand black stepped up to Wickram and tapped him on the shoulder. Barnabas guessed he was the man in charge of the team, since he was the oldest and had the most tools at his waist.

"Okay, you're here," the man said. "That's a start."

Wickram looked uncharacteristically sheepish. "Yeah, Givney, of course I'm here."

"But are you awake? That's the question."

"Yeah, of course, I'm —"

"You only have four cues in this section, right? That's just four things in a row to get right. Now, I'm thinking that's more than you've managed in the last three weeks. But, I'm also thinking: 'Smart kid; knows better than to disappoint me again.' Am I right?"

Wickram straightened up tall and shouted, "Yessir!"

"Good, 'cause I'm watching."

Givney walked away, checking the placement of equipment, checking off items on a clipboard. Wickram was red with embarrassment and looking at the floor, so Barnabas figured he's leave him be for a minute. He wandered through the backstage, which was lit up with small, battered kerosene lamps. Performers were trying out little bits of choreography. Wardrobe people were crouched beside them, sewing on feathers and repairing seams on their jackets. Giant set pieces were being wheeled into place. Masks, hoops, juggling clubs, teeter-totters, and torches were laid out on tables, waiting for their moment in the spotlight.

Everywhere he looked, Barnabas could see intense focus. Sure, people were smiling and telling jokes (a man dressed head-to-toe in green feathers stood with a mandolin player from the band singing a dirty song), but each in their way was getting ready to be their best, for themselves and for each other.

Someone tapped him on the shoulder.

"Hey!" Wickram said. "Don't wander off, we're about to start. You gotta stay by me or you'll get in someone's way."

They returned to Wickram's curtain and found Givney standing there, arms crossed over his chest. He said, "You're already away from your station?"

"Sorry, sir!"

"Four cues, Wickram, just four cues."

Wickram gave Barnabas a stool to sit on and showed him where he could peek through the curtains and watch. A stage manager gave the five-minute call, and all the chatter backstage stopped. The atmosphere was electric, like the moments before a summer storm.

Soon, the Stage Manager called "places!" The house lights dimmed, and the show began.

And it was double magic for Barnabas: the spectacle on stage and the activity backstage. Out in the ring, sometimes only steps away from him, tumblers, jugglers, and clowns performed amazing acts of dexterity and hilarity. High in the air above him, trapeze artists and tightrope walkers defied gravity. They made his heart stop as they flew through the air, caught at the last instant by a pair of arms that had not been there a moment before. In the audience, front row centre, sat Maestro Tragidenko, whispering and gesticulating to a large woman with tiny hands who wrote down everything he said, her face as calm and still as the Maestro's was expressive.

Barnabas jumped back, startled, as Wickram opened his curtain and a half-dozen women on unicycles flew past him on their way offstage. A couple of them turned their heads to check out the short stranger in their midst.

Barnabas had a sudden memory of being backstage at the Malibar Theatre when he was a kid, watching his father performing with a band on the famous stage. He remembered the sense of belonging to the privileged few who were important enough to see the show from that special vantage. Had his mother been there beside him? He was very young then, so she must have been. But he only remembered watching his father, applauding loudly along with the enthusiastic audience after each of his solos.

And then Graviddy was onstage. Surprised, Barnabas whispered to Wickram, "I thought she was resting tonight." But she was not performing; just standing onstage in position, looking up at the lengths of white fabric — her "silks" — that hung from the rail above her. Without leaving the ground, she moved her arms and turned circles to remind herself of what she would be doing up in the air the next night, and giving the band and the lighting people a chance to practice their timing. She came offstage through Wickram's curtain (that was cue two of four, Barnabas noted) but acknowledged neither of them. Barnabas found he was a little hurt by this snub.

There was a flurry of movement. Lights flashed and flickered, sets pieces representing trees were rolled on, and a veritable army of nymphs and faeries rose from the trapdoors or lowered themselves from the rigging. And just as suddenly, Maestro Tragidenko was there in the backstage, and this time he was close enough that Barnabas could smell the mixed aroma of wood smoke, sweat, and flowers that emanated from his towering mass.

He put a huge hand on Wickram's shoulder and pulled him closer, gesticulating at the stage and whispering. "There! There! Imagine a solo guitar playing! Something sweetly flying in *arpeggios* of light and mystery. A sound which grows and ebbs, like waves. Perhaps a flute enters and sings a counter-melody, something like only you can compose for it, yes?"

Barnabas watched Wickram stiffen, his jaw grow tight. "I don't think so," he said in a low growl, continuing to watch the action onstage. "Will you go away? I'm working here." He pulled the cord to open his curtain, and an acrobat in a deer's head mask flipped his way past them and onto the stage.

As Wickram closed the curtain, Tragidenko leaned closer, putting his arm right around the boy's shoulders. "But, yes! Yes! You hear what the band plays now? They are good people, but their music, it is sentimental, not worthy of the spectacle. It needs subtlety, grace, and a core of iron. Do you not dream of making music like this? Music that can raise up the hearts of your circus family and the hearts of the audience? If I were like you, young and talented —"

Wickram shrugged off Tragidenko's arm violently, turned on him with eyes full of fury and said, none too quietly, "But you're *not* like me! You keep thinking you understand me, that you know what I want, but you don't listen! You don't care what *I* want out of *my* life! What *I* think!"

Barnabas jumped back, like the clock was running down on a time bomb, and detonation was imminent.

Tragidenko threw up his hands and looked for some kind of guidance from above — from God, or the people manning the spotlights, or whoever might listen. "He doesn't want this!" the man said, raising his voice. Everyone backstage turned and stared their way. Barnabas looked out on stage and saw that even the performers were giving little sideways looks. Someone in the band missed a beat. Tragidenko, his eyes like the craters of twin volcanoes brought his face close to Wickram's. "You want to be musician, to be *artist*. But when you get a chance to make music for something *majestic*, for something bigger than your own little *play-acting*, you are too singular, too important!"

"Something *majestic*!" Wickram imitated with derision. "Meaning something *you* want!"

From across the backstage, Givney shouted, "Wickram!"

But Wickram's engine was fully revved-up now, and nothing could slow him down. "Maybe I'll just walk out of here and go work in the foundries at Forming! Then who will you have to manipulate and pester?!"

Tragidenko laughed, a dark laugh that made the end of his beard swing like a pendulum. "Oh, excellent! A poignant image! You in the foundries! Will you bring your mother along to serve you cold drinks when the furnaces grow too hot?!"

"Wickram! Wake up!" called Givney, but it was too late. A group of nymphs was struggling to pull aside Wickram's curtain so they could get offstage. "Crump!" Givney yelled and ran over, pushing Wickram aside and pulling the curtain cord.

Barnabas watched Wickram freeze, staring in disbelief. Tragidenko, for his part, seemed to shrink into himself. His furious eyes grew soft and ashamed. Sheepishly, he murmured to Givney, "My fault. I interrupted the boy—"

Life flowed back into Wickram, who shouted, "No! It's my fault! I screwed up. I quit! You were right about me, Givney: I'm useless! I resign my position in the circus!" He turned and ran, disappearing into the darkness at the back of the tent.

The show had ground to a complete halt. Tragidenko grabbed his beard in both hands, pulling it hard and squeezing his eyes closed, his whole body shuddering. Everyone was silent, staring at the Maestro for ten seconds, until he opened his eyes, shook himself like a wet dog, and strode quickly through Wickram's curtain, which still stood open. He clapped his hands loudly and declaimed, "All right, all right, technical difficulty. Let us take that exit as read. Please set up for next scene: the clown wars!"

With Wickram gone, Barnabas felt like he had no right to be backstage. Furthermore, he was scared of getting in the way and causing more "technical difficulties." He crept off the way Wickram had gone, trying hard not to trip over anything in the dark. Deep in the shadows, at the edge of the tent, he saw a bluer darkness in the midst of the black. He felt a cool breeze and heard the sound of frogs chirping, and soon found a gap in the tent. He walked down a small staircase into a meadow behind the Big Top.

It was almost completely dark now, the sky black but for a band of dark blue to the west. Some stars shone in the sky, though the ambient glow of city light was just as bad down in the Valley as it was in the City. Looking up in the direction of the cliff, Barnabas could see the windowless backs of the Tower District's buildings silhouetted against the glow. Then he noticed a single row of lights high up on one of the towers as if there were windows facing the Valley after all—but just a few, and on just one tower. He almost lost his balance in a rut in the ground, and when he looked back up toward the tower, the row of lights had been extinguished.

Ahead of him, he could just make out Wickram's form, sitting on a rock with his back to the Big Top. Barnabas approached cautiously and said,

"You okay?" Wickram turned around, and Barnabas could see his wet eyes glinting in the moonlight.

"Yeah. No. I utterly flat-stomped it!" He shook his head, and Barnabas thought he might start crying for real. "Four flippin' cues! I couldn't even get four cues right."

"Well, Tragidenko distracted you!" Barnabas said, climbing up to sit on the rock beside him.

"That old goat! He rashes me like nettles! I can't think straight when he starts talking like that!"

"I just don't get how you can afford to talk to the head of the circus that way. What if he fires you? Throws you out?"

Wickram laughed, harsh and brittle. "I wish! Don't you get it? He won't throw me out." He took a deep, shuddery breath. "He's my father."

CHAPTER 14

There is a place at the edge of sleep where the waking world still seems like a dream. The light is filtered as through a gauzy curtain; the sound like a sweet song played on a flute in the next apartment. It's a place without danger, without responsibility where the future doesn't weigh on you, and regret doesn't poison your heart. Barnabas loved that place.

He still remembered times like that when he was with his parents — his mom and his real dad, not Björn — coming home from one of his dad's gigs. Little Barnabas would be curled into the corner in the back seat of their old car with his dad's saxophone case propped up across from him, an object of sacred mystery. He would drift in this land of semi-wakefulness, listening to his parents talk, listening to music on the radio, watching the street lights forming magic refractions through the smeary windows. It was like flying through outer space, and he remembered feeling truly free and safe.

It was like that now, waking up... wherever he was. There was birdsong and fresh morning air, the sounds of wooden wheels and animal hooves, the smell of fresh bread. Warm, red light smiled kindly behind his closed eyelids, and he felt like he was floating, free at last of every trouble and worry. Maybe he would just lie there forever. Then he heard a snickering sound, very close. He opened his eyes to find Wickram's grinning face close above his.

"Wakey-wakey, Barn." The boy was cheerful and his breath smelled of milk. The close-up face retreated quickly as Wickram stood to his full height, way up near the ceiling. "I guess you caught some good winks. When Mom came in and woke me up, you didn't move a muscle. We thought you were dead."

Barnabas' head felt heavy with confusion, and it took him a few seconds to realize where he was: on the floor of Wickram's rock-shrine bedroom, in Sanjani and Dimitri Tragidenko's house in Pastoral Park, across from the circus' Big Top, in the Valley, where everyone worked to maintain the City — his city — which teetered on the edge of the cliff above them. He sat up quickly, which made him feel woozy.

Wickram was combing his hair straight in a tiny mirror that hung from the wall, humming a song, and looking his usual cheerful self. Last night's miseries — the fight with father, quitting the circus — seemed to have melted away in the morning sun. "I've got to get to school," he said. "I already had breakfast and everything."

Sleep was still clinging to Barnabas, threatening to pull him under again. "Okay, give me a minute. I'll..." he yawned extravagantly.

"No don't worry. Mom says you're staying with her this morning." He grabbed his book bag and headed for the door. There he turned back and said, excitedly, "I'll be back at noon, and then I have an utter thrillkick surprise for you!"

Barnabas nodded, yawning again, and listened as Wickram barrelled down the stairs, yelled goodbye to Sanjani, and slammed the door of the little house. He got up and did his best to straighten up the bedroll Sanjani had made for him on the floor. Examining his rumpled self in the mirror, he sighed. He had slept in his clothes, and they were all wrinkly, but they were the only ones he had, so he couldn't do much about his appearance. He ran Wickram's comb through his hair and tried not to worry about how he looked.

The last half hour of the previous night were a little vague in his memory. Sanjani had found Barnabas and Wickram sitting out in the meadow on the rock, and Wickram had run away from her into the night. Barnabas had followed her home, stumbling like a zombie in his fatigue. He barely remembered her helping him settle in on the floor of Wickram's bedroom, and then... oblivion.

As he left the bedroom, he wondered why Sanjani wanted him to stay with her instead of following Wickram to school. Did Whistlewort already have whatever travel documents he needed? Falstep had said there was a train Tuesday, so he would have to stay in the Valley until then. Was Pastoral Park willing to take the chance of hiding him? At the top of the stairs, he was brought up short by a passionate voice from below.

"I expose all of us to terrible danger!" cried Maestro Tragidenko in his distinctive voice from somewhere at the back of the house. "These Clouding maniacs and their heartless dogma will convince the Guild to throw us out!"

The man appeared at the bottom of the stairs, Sanjani right behind him, helping him into the jacket of his grey pinstriped suit. Though the suit itself was conservative, he wore a purple shirt underneath it, and a shiny gold bow-tie around this neck. Barnabas backed up into the shadows, where he could watch unobserved.

As the Maestro buttoned the jacket, Sanjani reached up and stroked his beard. "You have to stop worrying, Dimitri! Clouding doesn't control the Guild. And most of the rest love the circus and appreciate all the joy you have brought to the Valley. Tonight, you will even show Clouding that we are a positive force." She pulled an apple slice from the pocket of her apron and brought it to his lips. With a mischievous smile, he snapped it up like a dog. Sanjani giggled, and a deep, glutinous laugh rumbled out of Tragidenko.

"You are right, my darling. Enough of my glooming!" he said, straightening his bow tie in a mirror by the door. "I must go meet Kelvin and discuss lighting cues." But before he reached the front door, he looked up and spotted Barnabas, crouching at the top of the stairs. "Oh, hello, hello, little guest!"

Barnabas, embarrassed to be caught eavesdropping got awkwardly to his feet. "Hi," he said and descended the staircase. The Maestro seemed to grow to the size of a mountain as Barnabas approached him. His hand was swiftly enfolded in the vastness of Tragidenko's and shaken vigorously.

"I hope our humble home was sufficient shelter from the storms of life," Tragidenko said in his startling, enthusiastic tone.

"It's great," Barnabas managed.

"Everyone is treating you well? Your needs and desires are adequately met?"

"Yes. I-I guess I just don't know what will happen with the documents that —"

Tragidenko moved the big hand to Barnabas' shoulder, giving it a warm, sweaty squeeze. "Not to worry! We don't let our friends down! You are our friend, no? You are my son's great friend, I can see that already! You will be a good influence on him?"

Barnabas had no idea how to answer this and just opted for the best smile he could muster. Tragidenko pulled an enormous gold pocket watch from his vest and checked the time. He spun on his heel, and headed for the door, grabbing a striped fedora from a hook on the wall. The large peacock feather sticking up from its band brushed the top of the door frame as he exited.

Barnabas felt kind of run over by the man's oversized personality, but he had more pressing concerns. "Uh, Sanjani? Is there, you know, a washroom?"

"The outhouse is in the back. Go through that door there. You can wash your hands here in the sink afterwards."

With that business taken care of, Barnabas followed Sanjani back into the streets of Pastoral Park. It was much more humid than it had been the day before. There was a thin haze in the sky, but strong sunshine was cutting through it, even at this early hour. Barnabas could tell it would be a hot day.

The streets were relatively deserted, and Barnabas asked, "Where is everyone?"

"At work. In rehearsal or the workshops. Or at school."

"Any word from Mr. Whistlewort about my travel documents?"

"Patience, Barnabas. It will all work out."

He wasn't so certain of this, but he moved on to another question. "I know it's not really my business," he began. "But, um, is everything okay with Wickram and his dad now? What happened after I went to sleep?"

Sanjani didn't seem to mind the question. In fact, she seemed more than pleased to vent some of her frustration. "They both needed to sulk. Wickram probably ran to the clowns' clubhouse to act like an idiot with Falstep. I'm sure Dimitri — Maestro Tragidenko — went back to the Big Top to pour over plan's for tonight's show, filling his head with details so he did not have to think about his son." She turned and smiled wearily at Barnabas. "And then they both snuck back into the house in the middle of the night, like they are so clever — like I do not hear them. I *always* hear them."

They arrived at the dining hall, where breakfast was buffet-style to accommodate many different working schedules. They took their food trays outside to a picnic bench in the grassy area in the centre of the square.

"I know you came from the City," Barnabas said to her as he shovelled mushroom omelette and fresh bread into his mouth. "But what about the Maestro?"

"Dimitri also came from the City, but quite a while before I did. Did Wickram tell you what I do here in the Valley?"

"No."

"I'm an historian and archivist. I get funding from the Guild Council to do my research and writing. So, let me offer you a little history lesson, since you're an honoured visitor to our community." He nodded, and she began. "Wickram explained to you how the Valley came to be the support system for the City?"

Barnabas thought about the little play that Wickram and Falstep had performed in the cart. "Father Glory. He did this big speech in the market, and the people followed him. And then he became a god."

He hoped his words weren't blasphemous or something, but Sanjani laughed brightly at this summary. "Roughly speaking, yes. However, before he 'became a god,' he was President of the Unified Guild Council. He held that position for almost 30 years until he died in his fifties of lung cancer. But you're right; by the time he died, he had long-since become Father Glory. A deified personage to many, though not to me or to most in the circus. The people who succeeded him followed his Book of Prayers and Precepts — the set of philosophies and rules he created — to the letter. But there was growing discontent in the Valley, and in an act of what could only be called radical desperation, the Council elected a man named Punjant as President. Punjant believed only radical changes could keep the people of the Valley loyal to the needs of the City.

"Unlike most of his predecessors, Punjant visited the City often. The Guild Presidents before him would just do their twice-yearly visits with the Mayor in his apartment in Delphic Tower, and then scuttle back down the hill. But Punjant loved to walk the streets of the City to see how the people lived, to see what motivated them and gave their lives meaning and contentment.

"One day, in a poor quarter of the City, he came upon a sandwich-board sign, sitting on the sidewalk in front of a nothing-special door in the side of an industrial building. Nothing special, except that the door had an image painted on it: an eye with a tear in the corner."

"Oh, like on the sign when you come up the road. And on the Big Top!" Barnabas exclaimed. "But what did it say on the sandwich board?"

"It said, 'Circus of Humanity! The Great Tradition Lives On! Shows at 12, 3, 7, and 9!' Punjant checked his watch. It was just coming on 3 o'clock. Curious, he went inside, paying the two dollar admission to an eager man at the door. He was led into a large, empty warehouse that smelled of old diesel oil. In the centre was a circus ring. Ropes and trapeze bars hung from the ceiling. Teeter-totters, balance beams, and trampolines were pushed against the back wall.

"Punjant and a few homeless people were the only audience. The whole set-up seemed to have 'failure' stamped upon it before the show had even begun. But then it did begin — and what a show!

"Punjant, growing up in the Valley, had never seen a circus, or really any organized performance like this. The most they had down here in his lifetime were song competitions, focussing on work songs, or songs about finding love and settling down to a life of duty in your guild. He delighted in the acrobatic skill of the tumblers, the daring of the trapeze and silks artists. And the clowns had him hysterical with laughter, brushing tears from his eyes! They were led by an amazing one-legged clown named Onestep Fruntovuvver — our own Falstep's father. Immediately, Punjant imagined bringing this laughter and all the wonder of the circus to the Valley.

"He made his way backstage after the performance, and there he met Dimitri, who was terribly young then. Dimitri had started the company with nothing but a desire to revive lost circus arts. He found a group of men and women who had been stars of the circus in their day but were now old and mostly destitute. He brought them together and made them teachers to a group of new, young pupils. My husband's gift was always to inspire.

"After two years of training and rehearsal, they had begun to perform, but they could not find an audience. They were terribly in debt and on the verge of giving up the day Punjant accidentally found them. In many ways, he was as much of a dreamer as Dimitri. He promised the circus a home in the Valley with all the funding they needed, and an audience hungry for their talents. It was a rash promise to make, considering he needed to convince the Guild Council, but he succeeded. There was no doubt in anyone's mind that the morale of the Valley needed improving, and in the end, representatives from three of the four guilds agreed to the plan."

"All except Clouding, right?" Barnabas asked.

"Exactly. The council members from Clouding said, 'We must find our inspiration in the Book of Precepts and Principles. The wisdom of Father Glory is all anyone needs in this life.' 'But Mother Mercy loves to laugh,' Punjant reminded them." Sanjani looked up over Barnabas' shoulder and said, "Isn't that right, dear?"

Barnabas turned and saw Garlip — with a big, steaming mug in her hand — just sitting down at a nearby table. She was wearing the same black pants, but today she was in a grey t-shirt, and her multi-coloured braids were hanging loose around her head like decorative streamers. Seeing her there in the morning sunshine made something kind of shift sideways in Barnabas' chest, like a little train derailing. It was not a feeling he had been expecting when he awoke that morning.

"That's right, Sanjani. 'The mother delights in delight,'" Garlip quoted in a rather stiff, declamatory voice. "'She knows the laughing heart is more open to grace.'"

Garlip and Barnabas stared at each other for a few too many seconds, until Barnabas spontaneously said, "Hi," and then "I like laughing, too." He cringed inwardly. His ability to talk like a normal person seemed to be a casualty of the train derailment.

Sanjani picked up their trays and said, "Garlip can tell you more about the ways of Glory and Mercy than I, Barnabas dear. Why don't you stay here with her. I have to get down to work."

Sanjani left, and he moved to join the girl, sitting on the opposite side of her table and in the opposite corner. Her mug was full of black coffee, and he watched while she sipped it noisily.

"How are you doing?" Barnabas asked.

"Fine." She sipped again, looking off into the distance.

He waited to see if she would say any more, and when she didn't, he asked, "Why aren't you in school?"

"I was working with the set crew until 3 am. Painting mostly. They said I could sleep in, take the morning off."

More silence while he thought of what else to say. The conversation was like running out of momentum halfway up a steep hill, over and over.

"Why did Sanjani say you knew more about, um, the religion stuff?"

This question seemed to engage her more. She put down her mug and turned to look at him. "Me and my parents were pretty devout before we joined the circus."

"Were you in Clouding Guild?"

Her eyes narrowed. "Ugh, no. They don't *own* the Great Plan, you know! We were in Forming. My parents designed factory systems there, but what they really wanted was to build apparatuses for the circus. It took years to get approval, but when I was 10, we moved to Pastoral Park."

"And then you stopped believing?"

"They did first. I mean, maybe they already didn't really believe back at Forming, but it wouldn't have been cool to say it there. Then we get here, and pretty soon we're not even praying before we eat. I was furious!" She slurped coffee as if for emphasis.

"Really? Why? Sorry, there was just never any religion in my family, so it's totally a foreign —"

"Why? I felt betrayed. I guess with all the changes — I had to leave all my friends and my school and the church and everything — I just wanted to feel that Mother Mercy was still watching out for me, that even though we weren't in a guild anymore, we were still building the Celestial City."

"The Celestial… you mean the City? My city?"

"No… Well, that's part of it, but… Come on, I'll show you."

She led him across the square to another building, and he wasn't surprised, given the delicious smells rising from inside, to be told it was the bake house. They walked around to the side of the building where a mural was painted across the stucco, brightly coloured and rendered in intense detail. They sat in silence on the grassy slope opposite the mural, taking in the elaborate artwork.

"This is the schematic of the great plan. At least my version of it. I painted it two — almost three years ago," she said with apparent nonchalance, but she was watching him for his reaction.

He didn't have to fake his enthusiasm. "You did that? It's amazing."

"It's okay. The perspective sucks and the anatomy's wonky. I didn't know *anything* about colour theory yet." She tilted her head as if trying for a more objective way of seeing it. "It has energy, I guess. Look. Down at the bottom is the Valley, right?" Barnabas recognized some of the geographic landmarks and some of the buildings, including the Commons and the hill with Pastoral Park on it.

"Yeah, I see," he said.

"Then there's the City on the cliff. The Temporal City, we call it. But above that, that's the real thing: the Celestial City."

The city on the cliff — Barnabas' home — occupied only a thin layer in the painting, a series of shiny towers, rendered without much detail or distinction. But then above that, perched on clouds exploding with so many sunbeams, it looked like bombs were going off in mid-air, was another city. This one was lovingly rendered in a wealth of decorative and fantastic detail — towers, bridges, parks, walkways suspended high above the earth. Everything glowed and sparkled. And in the sky to either side of the buildings were hazy portraits of Father Glory and Mother Mercy as if formed from clouds themselves. Father Glory's eyes were hidden behind his glasses, but Mother Mercy's were large and tender, and she looked out at the viewer with calm reassurance.

The image produced an odd sensation in Barnabas' heart: less a derailment than an opening. He felt the presence of something larger than himself, a kind of order, a kind of universal love that was incredibly comforting and attractive. "Amazing," he whispered. "But what is the Celestial City?"

"Father Glory told us that while we built the Temporal City in our daily work, what we were really doing was building the Celestial City, brick by brick. 'Our sweating backs and straining muscles are a testament to our devotion,' He said. And when we die, we get to live there, in the great metropolis of our creation. And as long as people in the Valley believe and strive, we in the afterlife will continue to see the urban improvements manifest around us, an eternal tribute from our children to us."

Barnabas' head reeled. "That's what everyone believes?"

Garlip didn't answer. She crossed her arms over her chest and said, "I painted and painted for weeks, praying all the time, barely eating. Everyone was worried about me, but my parents told them to just let me do it. And then when I was finished, I sat right here on this hill and cried."

"Because you were so proud?"

"Because I didn't believe anymore. Like the last drop of religion I had went up on that wall, and there was nothing left in my veins. And after that, the world was only what I could see. The Valley was the Valley and the City was the City."

Barnabas looked at the mural with fresh eyes. Now he saw not just the early experiments of a talented artist, but also a testament to loss. He looked back at Garlip, but this time found himself staring at her profile, and the full lips that gave her pale face so much distinction. He wondered what it would feel like to kiss those lips.

She caught him looking, her brows scrunching up. She stood and brushed the grass off her behind, and he tried not to get caught staring at that, too.

"I'll show you the sets and props workshop if you like," she said, her voice grown a little quiet.

They set off down the road, in silence for a while until Barnabas said, "You know Mother Mercy in your mural? She kind of reminds me of Graviddy."

This remark earned him a glare, but there was a blush under the glare.

"Yeah," she said. "Everyone has to have a crush on her at some point. It's kind of a law of the universe."

"Oh! I'm not! I mean, I don't have…"

But Garlip grinned wickedly at him. "No, of course not. Wickram would never allow it!" They both laughed at this, and it broke the tension. She arrived at the workshop and spent the rest of the morning there. As they left, they saw Wickram and Beaney coming down the road, on their way from school.

"Hey! Barn!" Wickram called, running to greet him. "You ready for your adventure? Hi, Garlip," he added parenthetically before ignoring her utterly. "We're just heading back to my house to pick up lunch; then we're on our way."

Beaney joined the group. "Barnabas, you're going to love it. It has all the best —"

Wickram put the kid in a headlock. "Shut it! I want it to be a surprise."

They had reached an intersection, and Garlip turned to walk down the other path. "You boys have fun," she called.

"Wait," said Barnabas. "You can come, if you want…"

"Thanks, I was just there."

"Yeah, Barn," Wickram said in exasperation. "She was just there. Get your engine out of neutral, come on!"

Wickram hurried them up the hill to his family's house. Beaney waited in the yard, but Barnabas followed Wickram inside where they found Sanjani at the big table, sorting through old photographs from Valley, presumably from the days before Father Glory had forbidden photography.

Wickram yelled down at her as he raced up the stairs, "Mom, we're in a rush. Did you make us all lunch?"

"Hello to you, too, Pickle," she called after him, moving photographs from one pile to another. "Did you have a nice time with Garlip, Barnabas?"

He felt himself blush, which coloured his little "Yeah" in a way he hadn't meant to.

"That's good." She got up and went to collect a picnic basket from the kitchen counter, which she handed to him. It was heavy with food and drink. She went to the kitchen window and called out, "Hello, Beaney dear. Would you like some raspberry soda?"

Wickram was already thundering down the stairs. He was now wearing a "Steve Raveeno — Acoustic Live" t-shirt.

"No time, Mom, I have a cart reserved. Let's go, let's go!" he shouted and headed for the door.

Sanjani called, "Hold it! You know that dinner is at 5:30 and the call is 7:00? It is a performance day, Wickram; you cannot be late."

"Circus hours have nothing to do with me anymore, Mom. I resigned last night!"

"Don't act so certain of everything, young man! And in any case, it's Beaney's call, too. Be back by 5:00."

She marched up to him, straightening the fall of his t-shirt. She pulled his little leather change pouch out of the top of his t-shirt and tucked several coins into it. "Buy your father something he will like," she said. "He is very nervous about tonight." Wickram rolled his eye and tucked the leather pouch back under his shirt. "Five o'clock," she repeated.

"Then stop holding us up, Mom!" He opened the door and marched out. Barnabas hurried to follow.

As the boys walked down the road, Sanjani called from the door, "In fact, I want you back at 4:30! You boys will be all dusty from the road, and you should shower before dinner!" Barnabas noted that her Indian accent was more pronounced when she was shouting.

"Goodbye, Madam General!" Wickram yelled back over his shoulder, and began whistling a marching tune.

CHAPTER 15

Before too long, the three boys were out on the dusty road. Barnabas wondered whether they were in the same cart as yesterday, and being pulled by the same mules. He felt like asking might be some kind of insult, like not recognizing someone's mother the second time you meet her. He and Wickram were up front and Beaney was in the back, though the kid was mostly standing up and hanging on Wickram's shoulders.

"Barnabas," Beaney said, "Did you like the circus last night? I'm one of the clowns!"

"I know," Barnabas replied. "And I liked it a lot."

Trucks frequently cozied up behind them and then passed terrifyingly close on the left. It was like the whole world was in a hurry except them. Today, instead of taking the road beside the dried-out Lake Lucid, they drove along a wider thoroughfare that was pointed more-or-less straight at the cliff and the City. Barnabas felt a pang; his home was so close, but completely inaccessible. He watched the cliff grow higher as they approached it, the towers looming more and more threateningly over them, eventually casting a massive shadow across their passage.

But the loom and gloom only seemed to be affecting him. Wickram was in a great mood, apparently not caring about last night's fight with his father, nor the schism between him and circus life. He seemed to be simply enjoying the day and devoting himself to the project of keeping Beaney laughing hysterically. He sang songs with dirty lyrics and did imitations of different circus personalities, including his father:

"You are all my children, *yes?* And I love you the way the dynamite is loving the detonator, *yes?* Like the top of my head is loving the little drop of bird shit that falls from the sky. The little shit made with love and com-*passion* by the smallest sparrow. We, my dear artistes, must be like that little shitting sparrow in everything we do here!"

The sweet morning air was filling incrementally with the smell of smoke and the sound of mighty machines. They turned a corner and were soon passing an enormous factory complex whose buildings stretched out on both sides of the road. Tall chimneys spewed dark smoke, and monstrous trucks passed through the gates, hauling huge stacks of grey metal girders on long trailers. Most of the people Barnabas saw on the factory grounds were wearing masks and goggles, and he could understand why: his own eyes stung, and his mouth tasted like metal and ash.

Beaney shouted over the din, "This is the Forming Works, where the Forming Guild works. Look how busy they are! There must be a new tower or bridge or something going up in the City."

A truck the size of an ocean liner pulled up behind them, and Wickram steered the cart onto the shoulder to let it pass. Barnabas was surprised to see the mules were unperturbed by the noise. He figured they were used to all the sounds of the Valley. As they drove away from the factory area, the foul air cleared.

They were moving parallel to the cliff now. Beside them was the safety fence that separated the rest of the Valley from the area known as the Tumbles. If it hadn't been clear enough before, Barnabas could now see that you would not want to be inside that particular perimeter. The rain of cliff rocks and dirt was constant as was the endless cascade of consumer goods from the City above: toaster ovens, canned produce, premium-sized bags of dog kibble... falling, crashing to the ground, raising plumes of dust, like a ballroom of dancing ghosts.

Barnabas craned his neck up to look at the line of towers. "Do you have your binoculars?" he asked, and Wickram pulled them out from under his seat. Focussing on Delphic Tower, Barnabas saw a single set of windows facing the Valley. They must have been the same windows from which the light had been shining the previous night. And thanks to Sanjani's story about how the Guild Council Presidents visited the Mayor of the City in Delphic Tower twice a year, he could guess who in the City had that one-of-a-kind view. It was Mayor Arthur Tuppletaub, and all the mayors before him. They lived up there and looked out those windows every day at the great secret they kept from the Citizens.

Wickram suddenly shouted, "Hey! Hey! Shift your eyeballs front-wise, Barn, my man — this is it!"

Barnabas lowered the binoculars and stared down the road. They were approaching a huge sign that straddled the road on wooden posts. The text was pieced together out of junk — chipped ceramic plates, bike wheels, broken appliance parts, long filaments of rusted wire. Barnabas read it as Wickram spoke the words out loud with almost religious fervour: "Presenting a Fabulous Feast of Fallen Finery! A Cavernous Cache of Cascaded Curiosities! Welcome to THE DROP SHOP!!"

Across the bottom of the sign was a large arrow, pointing to the right, in the direction of the cliff. Wickram turned the cart, and they followed the long driveway towards a large warehouse, built right up against the safety fence of the Tumbles. Like the text on the sign, the walls of the building were pieced together out of different materials, from metal to wood to plastic. Only the roof presented any kind of unity: a huge peaked sheet of galvanized steel. Despite the motley appearance of the windowless warehouse, it looked strong and a little imposing as if something dangerous and secret might be going on behind its walls.

"This is the place, Barn," Wickram said, his tone reverential. "The Drop Shop is everything you ever wanted, and more." His smile turned off long enough for him to say, "Well, you're from the City, so maybe it's not so skull-cracking for you but…" The smile turned back on, brighter than before. "It's my little oasis in this cultural desert."

Wickram pulled the cart to a halt to the right of the battered steel door. He jumped down and tied the reins to a fence. Beaney jumped down to join him, and he and Wickram ran up to the building. As he pulled the door open, Wickram turned back and called, "In any case, Barn, it's the only place in the Valley that's got chips and pop!" He and Beaney vanished inside.

Barnabas left the cart reluctantly. There was something about the place he didn't like, though he had no idea what that might be, nor any reason why. Maybe it was the loud churning of the gas-powered generator up against the wall of the building. It sounded to him like a dog growling a warning. He put a hand on the stiff mane of the closest mule and gave it a reassuring pat as though it was the beast and not him who felt uncomfortable.

The door opened again, and two women in red coveralls exited, carrying out a beat-up table saw which they brought over to a nearby parked truck. Barnabas had a weird impulse to run up and ask them for a lift back to Pastoral Park. He scolded himself for being ridiculous and instead followed his friends inside. The heavy door had swung itself shut on silent springs, and he had to use considerable strength to swing it open again.

Barnabas had been expecting the inside of the building to be as dark and forbidding as the outside, so he was more than a little surprised to be hit by a tsunami of light, colour, and sound. Music came from everywhere — multiple marching band recordings, clashing in a bright cacophony, an operatic tenor keening loudly above them. The crazy array of lighting included lamps and lanterns, neon signs with white tube teeth advertising a dentist's clinic, rotating disco spotlights in primary colours, and stark fluorescent fixtures like those in a hospital morgue.

But what was the Drop Shop? It was something between a dollar store, an antiques emporium, and a funhouse. There were appliances at one end, dismantled by their fall down the cliff, but rebuilt Frankenstein-style, and polished to a shine. Dozens of bicycles hung from chains on the ceiling, some of them with their pedals and wheels turning eerily on hidden motors. All kinds of art hung from the walls, from posters of pop stars to oil landscapes in gold frames.

Aisles of shelves were filled with merchandise: books on one shelf, tools on another, games, medical supplies, garden gnomes, and gaudy lamps. Off to his left, Beaney was standing on a step stool, rummaging through a box of action figures. Wickram was running up and down the aisles, pulling down various objects and shouting things like, "Oh my God! It lights up when you shake out the salt!" and "Look! A golf magazine with a 3D hologram cover!"

A voice as rich and over-sweet as toffee spoke right into Barnabas' ear: "What are you looking for, young man? *It falls from the skies, a brand new surprise!*" He turned in alarm to find himself facing a middle-aged woman in too much makeup and a mountainous hairdo that was so stiff and shiny, he wondered if it were made of plastic. The ample chest of her simple blue coveralls was festooned in glittering costume jewellery; butterflies, flowers, and fairies all tried hard to out-sparkle each other. No less shiny was her smile which, showing dozens of frighteningly white teeth, seemed to cut her face horizontally in two.

Barnabas returned his own weak smile and said, "Uh, no thanks. Don't need anything now."

"Everyone needs something, young man," she said in a voice as fake as her smile. "Wouldn't you look just fine in this!" She pulled a dusty bowler hat off a nearby table and plunked it on his head. *"It falls from the skies, a cunning disguise!"*

Annoyed, Barnabas removed the hat and tried to hand it back to her, but she had turned away. She raised her hands in the air and said, "The bounty of the City! Things fall over the edge every day, and my Georgie goes out to collect them! Risks his life in the Tumbles, he does, just to keep our little business going. *It falls from the skies, our wondrous supplies.*"

Barnabas looked around at the shelves of merchandise and the piles of boxes that stood by the wall, still unpacked. Everything had fallen over the cliff — each object, lost to someone from the City. Wasn't that stealing? He followed the sound of Wickram's voice, and found him in front of a shelf of old paperbacks, all of which must have slipped out of backpacks or back pockets, living a lonely life on the streets before finally falling over the edge.

"Check it out, Beaney," Wickram was saying as Barnabas approached. "It's another 'Billy Brazen, Boy Spy' book. My dad loves those."

Barnabas peered down at the old, yellowed book whose title was "Billy Brazen and the Submarine Pirates." On the crowded cover, the curly-blond hero was in scuba gear, treading water and facing off against a shark while a company of pirates, standing on the back of their black submarine, laughed at his plight.

Beaney, wearing a pair of 3D glasses that should never have left the movie theatre, said, "Get it for the Maestro. He's so stressy about tonight; it'll make him feel better."

"Well, Mom wants me to. I personally don't care."

Barnabas saw that this wasn't true; he was clearly delighted to find the book. A handwritten sticker on the battered cover read: "11 farthings AS IS."

"How much is a farthing?" Barnabas asked Wickram.

"It depends on the season. At this time of year, we sometimes go out and pick chantarelle mushrooms. A full basket can earn you around 50 farthings."

The shopkeeper was at his side again, grinning her awful grin and saying to Barnabas, "See? A treasure for everyone. There must be something here you desire…" She glanced down at the bowler hat, which he was still holding, and raised her eyebrows.

"Uh, thanks, no. I'm good," he muttered, thrusting the hat back towards her, but she walked away without taking it.

Just then, the whole building shook. All the illumination of all the overhead fixtures was dwarfed by a shaft of sunlight as a great door in the side of the warehouse slid open with a wrenching shriek of metal on metal. The man who dragged it open stood dramatically silhouetted. There was something heroic about him, standing in that big square of light, helmeted and proud. With a grunt, he pushed a huge flatbed trolley ahead of himself. It was covered with more junk, and both he and the cart were sending up great clouds of dust as he entered.

"It's my Georgie!" the shopkeeper shouted in delight. "Back again from the Front!"

Now that he was inside, he seemed less impressive than he had a minute before — a middle-aged man in soiled coveralls and thick black goggles, in need of a shave and sweating profusely under a badly scuffed football helmet. He huffed and puffed with the effort of sliding the giant door shut again. It slammed into place with a resounding bang.

"Thank the Lord you weren't killed, my love," the woman said to him, throwing her meaty arms around his chest. "It sounded like the whole world was coming down out there today! Oh, and I need you to fix the compressor on the fridge." To the boys, she said, "He's so clever with his tools!"

"Unhand me, woman," he said with brusque rebuke. "I can hardly breathe as it is!" He coughed, letting loose another cloud of dust, this time from his lungs. Straightening, the man cursed and tossed the helmet and goggles to the floor, wiping his eyes on his dirty sleeve. He raised his head and Barnabas jumped back, startled. It was the man he had seen at the train station and, later, outside the school — the man who had startled Mayor Tuppletaub and then climbed into his limousine.

"Glower," Barnabas gasped.

"Yeah, of course Glower," said Wickram with evident enthusiasm. "George Glower, the owner of the Drop Shop. Why? You've heard of him? Is he famous up in the City, too?"

Barnabas didn't answer. What was Glower doing here in the Valley?

Barnabas put on the old bowler hat and pulled it low as he skittered sideways behind Wickram. Not content with this as a hiding place, he dived into an aisle of farming equipment, and peered out at the dusty man through a scrim of chicken wire. There was only one person in the Valley that might recognize him as a resident of the City, and that was George Glower. Barnabas reached into his pocket for the crumpled red clown nose and slipped it on.

Her eyes shining, the shopkeeper approached the cart and immediately began sifting through the objects on his trolley. "A good haul, was it? Lots of precious… Oh, Georgie! A hair dryer! And a pair of roller skates! Oh, just one. Don't make no never mind. I'll sell it for top dollar, don't you worry."

"None of that garbage matters, Greta," Glower answered. "Look at this!" He lifted a long red box off the cart and blew the dust from its surface. It was something like a toolbox, but made of wood, smooth and richly finished with red lacquer. Glower opened it carefully to reveal two lines of little blue pyramids, and one orange cube. He removed one the pyramids and turned it slowly in his hand, examining it with intense concentration. The man's voice lowered to a husky growl, full of awe. "It's what I've been looking for. You see? It must be some sort of laser communication system. But if I can boost the signal, I can use it for remote triggering of the…" He stopped suddenly, noticing Wickram, who was waiting nearby like a good dog hoping for a treat.

"Uh, hi, Mr. Glower," Wickram said. "Did you find any more issues of 'Shredder'? The guitar magazine? You know I buy them the minute you get them in."

Glower looked suspicious. He quickly replaced the blue pyramid in the box and slammed the lid shut. "What? What do you want from me?" But then he seemed to collect himself. "Oh yes, you're Tragidenko's boy, right? No. No 'Shredders.' Only a case of old Amateur Sociologist magazines and some real estate fliers." He turned to the shopkeeper, and hissed, "Get them out of here, Greta! I have work to do."

"But Georgie, we're supposed to be open until seven today!"

"Get them out!"

Greta turned to Wickram, her look of annoyance visible for just a second before she turned her 50 megawatt smile back on. "Sorry, love, no 'Sledders' today! But look at that: Billy Brazen, is it? That's a *fine* book you've picked out. Oooh, the adventures you'll dream up after you read it!" She began shepherding Wickram towards the cash, pulling Beaney from a display of used postcards as she passed him. The boy clutched his action figure and staggered after her while she enthused, "And what a price I'm going to give you on that lovely doll, you precious little darling. You'll think I'd died and been reborn an angel." She pulled them towards the front counter, where an ornate, old-fashioned cash register of polished brass awaited.

Barnabas watched all this from his hiding place. Greta had lost track of him, he realized, although he knew he didn't have long until she figured out one of her customers was still on the loose. He watched as Glower again lifted the lid on the red box. The man was visibly excited, muttering something, and Barnabas strained to hear.

"I can do it, yes, I can! I could move the whole timetable up. Do it next week. Boom! And down the bastards all go…" his voice became inaudible as he moved towards a smooth black door at the back of the warehouse.

The door had no handle, but beside it was a digital number pad. Glower punched in a long code, and a light above the door turned from red to green. From somewhere behind the wall came a loud *clunk* and the whir of gears. The heavy door opened smoothly.

Leaning forward, Barnabas caught a glimpse of a very different room — uncluttered, orderly, with long, shiny work benches and bright lighting. He pulled back into his hiding place before he could be noticed. He walked down to the end of the aisle of farm equipment and headed back across an aisle of dress clothing and art supplies, laying the groundwork for a plausible story of getting lost in the vastness of the store.

Barnabas looked back up the central aisle and saw Wickram and Beaney up at the cash. As he hurried their way, he glanced at the battered trolley, sitting by the big loading bay door, loaded with its bounty from the Tumbles. A little glint of light amid the debris made him slow and then stop. It was nothing — just a tiny reflection, like you might get off a camera lens, but something about it seemed… familiar. He gasped and ran to the trolley. As he pulled the object loose, he dislodged a pile of decorative tin boxes which clattered loudly to the ground. But he didn't care; he was holding something he thought he'd lost forever: the *diaboriku!*

"What are you doing, boy?!" called Greta, running to him from the front of the store. "Those items haven't been catalogued! Come back tomorrow if you want to purchase —"

Barnabas held up the *diaboriku* indignantly. "But this is mine! I dropped it yesterday in the…" He was on the verge of telling the whole story to the woman, who now stood in front of him, furious, eyes burning like a dragon's. But he couldn't tell her! That would mean admitting he was from the City! He would get himself arrested as an illegal stowaway in the Valley or whatever. And he would get his hosts at Pastoral Park in deep, deep trouble.

Her eyes flashed with anger and her cheeks reddened. "It's not yours, you greedy little boy! That is legal property of the Drop Shop!" Like a snake striking at its prey, she shot out a hand to grab the device. But Barnabas was faster; he pulled his prized possession against his chest, just avoiding the red-lacquered nails.

"No!" Barnabas replied sharply. "It's mine!" He knew he sounded like a two year old, but he could neither explain nor accept defeat.

He saw Wickram and Beaney running his way. Wickram, his face a mask of embarrassment, yelled, "Barn, man, it's not cool. It fell into the Tumbles, so it belongs to Mr. Glower. You gotta let it go!"

Barnabas dodged around Greta and ran up to Wickram, whispering desperately, "It's from my brother. I lost it in the City yesterday! It rolled down the street, and then it must have rolled right over the edge of the cliff. I'm the only person in the City who has one; it has to be mine!"

Shooting nervous glances at Greta (who was standing behind them like a stick of dynamite waiting to blow), Wickram said, "Not according to the agreement, man. Guild Council granted Mr. Glower salvage rights to anything falling from the City."

"That's right, you miserable thief!" Greta hissed. "*It falls from the skies, I don't apologize!*" Barnabas ran behind Wickram and watched the last traces of the affable saleswoman vanish behind this great green creature of greed.

In a voice like gravel on glass, she said, "Those toffy bastards in the City think the universe owes them their easy lives. But they're careless little children!" She laughed harshly with evident hate. "They spend their dollars and buy more and more and more and more, until it slips from their pudgy little fingers even as they're coveting the next, the next, the next treasure. But too late! It's gone. It's *mine!* You want that shiny little toy, child? You can trade it for your farthings tomorrow!"

Barnabas bit his lip. His brain was swirling in a fog of anger and humiliation. It wasn't fair, he didn't deserve this attack! And there was no one on his side. Still, he couldn't bring himself to just hand over the *diaboriku*. Greta began moving forward, nails raised like 10 little swords. Wickram was still in front of him, but he was not a willing shield. Barnabas needed a plan, and fast. He looked around and saw the open door to Glower's back room. Shoving Wickram forward at Greta, he made a break for it.

There was no logic in the plan, and as he entered the back space, he had no idea what he would do next. He looked around. The room was like a combination of an appliance workshop and a scientist's lab. Machines big and small, from air conditioners to motor scooters, were in various states of repair. But there were also homemade devices, lengths of cable and switching, packed densely into old coffee pots, some with timers — digital and analog — strapped to them. Down at the end of the room was an even stranger object: a diorama of the City, built out of wood and modelling clay. Why would Glower make such a thing, if indeed he had made it?

There was a little gasp behind him, and Barnabas swung around to see a kid emerge from a room to the side of the workshop. It took him a second to recognize the slight form and gaunt face in this new context, but then he saw it was Galt-Stomper, whom he'd last seen (had it really only been the previous morning?) with Glower at Admiral Crumhorn Station.

"Don't I know you...?" the boy murmured. The situation was getting out of hand. Barnabas stood frozen, not knowing how to proceed.

The next voice was behind him, and when he heard it, Barnabas actually said, "Yipes!" like he was in a cartoon. He spun around and saw Glower rise from behind a broken dishwasher, holding a C-wrench.

"What are you doing in here?!" the man barked. "This part of the Drop Shop is not open to customers!"

Barnabas, still frozen, willed the angry man not to recognize him beneath the bowler hat, behind the clown's nose. A third voice caused Barnabas to again spin on his heel.

"He stole that whatchamahoozis right off your cart, Georgie!" shouted Greta in outrage. She was about to storm into the workshop, but then she balked at the threshold, pulling her foot back at the last minute. Barnabas had the distinct impression she was not allowed in the room.

A presence loomed up behind him, blocking the light of the overhead fluorescent. "Give. It. To. Me," said a deep and chilling voice. Barnabas turned — slowly this time — and found himself toe-to-toe with George Glower. Veins were standing out in the man's temple, and he was grinding his teeth audibly. The large hand he held out was vibrating with rage. Terrified, Barnabas dropped the *diaboriku* into the sweating palm and backed away.

"Are you finished disturbing me?" He was addressing them all but looking in particular at Greta as if everything were her fault.

Everyone nodded, and Wickram said, "Yessir," in a pinched voice. He came forward into the workshop with every kind of apology written all over his movements, and grabbed Barnabas by the upper arm, pulling him back towards the door.

Glower snarled, "If this thief is the kind of companion you bring to my store, perhaps you should be barred access."

Wickram's face paled. "N-no sir," he stuttered. "Won't happen again. I swear."

When they reached the door of the workshop, Greta's red-clawed hand fell on Wickram's shoulder, and she began to pull him across the store. Wickram's hand was still gripping Barnabas' bicep, and he was dragged after them. The three of them formed an odd parade, stumbling toward the exit, with Beaney running after them, bringing up the rear like an excited terrier.

Soon, the three boys stood outside, blinking in the sunshine.

Wickram turned a desperate, angry gaze on Barnabas and said, "Dung-buggies, Barn! You almost got me banned from the Drop Shop!"

"But my *diaboriku*..." he tried to explain as they walked toward the cart.

Suddenly, the door of the store flew open again, and Barnabas continued his life as a cartoon character, this time shouting "Woop!" Glower stepped outside, carrying a large sheet of stiff paper that flapped in the breeze. With quick, assured movements, he taped the sign to the door. He retreated inside without looking at them, slamming the heavy slab of metal after himself.

The sign, hand-lettered in bold, block print read: "The Drop Shop will be closed until further notice."

INTERLUDE: JUNE, 1911

"Mr. Mayor — Your Honour — I do not advise you to enter these streets on your own. It is a neighbourhood of ruffians and coarse-bred, desperate men. Allow me to summon a team of police officers to escort you to —"

Lawrence Glorvanious spun on his heels and snarled into his Deputy's face: "I am not a little girl, Stanton! I am not a fragile academic, unaccustomed to the grit of the streets. I will go alone, and that is the end of the discussion!"

The Mayor left the gawping civil servant standing at a noisy intersection, next to a man doing a brisk trade in flavoured ices on this sweltering day on the cusp of summer, and plunged into the clutter and dilapidation of the neighbourhood known as Scraptown. He was sweating in his black suit as he side-stepped piles of manure and other ordure, and trying to reconcile the map he was holding with the narrow, chaotic streets around him. If there was an antithesis to the Platonic order of the City to come, this was it.

His passage through the quarter did not go unnoticed. Suspicious eyes glared at him, and small knots of people halted their work to wonder at this wealthy man's incursion into their world. The Mayor tried to march with confidence as if he were certain of his way. Two street urchins, no more than nine years old, had begun to dog his heels, stretching out dirty palms in his direction. They followed him for many blocks before he finally shook his silver-tipped walking stick at them, and they scuttled away into the shadows.

How could it be that his son had lived here in this filth, with these uncultured paeans for four years? When Florian had accepted the job of creating the secret workforce that would maintain the City, the Mayor had imagined his son moving into an office at the Municipal Building, sending underlings into Scraptown to recruit and train. But Florian had insisted that he must move here himself, so that he might truly know these people, gain their loyalty. How could father say no to son under these circumstances? How could he trust him with adult responsibility and then treat him like a child?

Since Florian had accepted the job, The Mayor had rarely seen him, only read the monthly reports the boy sent to City Hall and approved the mysterious, expense sheets which contained line items such as, "Inspirationals." Last year, his son had even failed to return home for Christmas. Advisors had been telling the Mayor for years that he must take control of the situation. What if the boy was actually hiding out, unable to admit his failure? What if — they said it with practiced delicacy — he was not in complete possession of his sanity? But Lawrence Glorvanious had refused to doubt his son. The memory of those passionate eyes made him believe. At least they had done until recently.

When the fourth spring came round since that cold March meeting in his office, the Mayor decided it was time to see for himself. And "himself" was precisely what he meant. If his son had failed, he was not going to have a coterie of clucking underlings or a phalanx of coppers see his disgrace. No, he had to go alone.

He stepped into an alcove and pulled out the map again. He had passed a clear landmark a block earlier — a fountain, now dry and vandalized. His destination had to be nearby. Stepping from the shadows, he called out to a woman walking by with a basket of strawberries: "Good lady!" Startled, she almost dropped her basket.

"Yes, sir?"

"I am seeking a building called, I believe, the Comforting Arms." It was a peculiar name. Was it a hotel? Had Florian abandoned his duties to become an innkeeper?

"Oh, I see! You're nearly there, sir. Right around back of the dye works. Just that way."

He handed her a shiny nickel for her trouble and was startled when she handed back a paper cone of strawberries. He rounded the dark, stinking dye works, eating one of the bright berries that was threatening to spill out of the cone... and there it was.

It was a wonderful edifice of new brick and sturdy wood, only two stories high, but proud and commanding. The windows were stained glass and featured, to the Mayor's surprise, images of some of the great buildings he was planning to erect in the new City. There was the new City Hall, there the library, and there the waterworks, all rendered in clean line and bright colour. Above the majestic front doors was a bronze relief of a pair of outstretched hands, welcoming him to — the words gleamed in the mid-morning sun — The Comforting Arms.

Many people were climbing the steps of the building and entering through the broad double doors. Although their clothes were patched and faded, they were clean, and worn with pride. Everyone's hair was combed, and their hands and faces scrubbed. There were men and women and a few babes in arms. Shockingly, a Negro was among them, and a Chinaman. Carrying the cone of berries before him like a bouquet of flowers bought for an *amour*, he climbed the steps himself. It was only when he was walking among the arriving crowd that he noticed they were all unusually tall.

Inside, there was a small, neat foyer with twin staircases to the right and left. The growing crowd, however, was moving straight through another set of double doors into what was, apparently, the sanctuary of a church. On either side of the door, a greeter — one man and one woman — wished each new arrival "Glory be!" or "Raise your eyes to the City of God." One plucked the cone of berries from his hand and said, "Thank you for your offering. The Father will be most grateful."

Unnerved, the Mayor said nothing. He went inside, sat in a pew at the back of the sanctuary, and waited to see what would happen. And what happened when a little over half the seats were full, was that a pair of doors on the stage slid open, apparently unaided, with a little hiss and puff of steam. Out stepped his son.

Florian Glorvanious was not a boy anymore. Though only 22 now, he seemed to have gained a gravity that surprised and impressed his father. There was more meat on his bones; he wore a dignified brown suit with a green tie, and round, wire-rimmed glasses. A moustache was the final touch — adding years to his face. Florian walked to the lectern with confidence and looked around at the congregation, which had grown silent and expectant.

In a commanding voice Lawrence Glorvanious had never heard before, his son said, "The Lord loves his labourers. He loves the man and the woman whose hands are dirty with the honest work of digging in the earth to bring forth the raw materials that build the City."

"Glory to the Father," the congregation answered, and the sound of the deep, unified voices coming from these tall people made the Mayor catch his breath. He thought, *Why don't my speeches command this level of respect?*

"Soon, my brothers and sisters," Florian said, "We will travel to our Promised Land. And there we will bend our backs to the task of supporting the Earthly City. Remember, for every brick set in place on Earth, one will be laid with divine love in the Celestial City."

The men and women, white and dark, around the Mayor said, "We are the servants on Earth, the masters in Heaven."

When he looked back toward the stage, the Mayor saw his son had noticed him, taking him in with cool appraisal. In fact, there might have been the smallest turn of a smile visible beneath that moustache.

"Your Honour," Florian called, coming to greet his father after the service. He was making his way slowly through a throng of his followers who were pressed in around him as if to bask in his presence. They didn't seem to realize that their Mayor was also in their midst. When Florian finally got through the crowd (they towered above him like he was walking in a forest), father and son shook hands formally. The Mayor realized he was being treated not as the elder, but as an equal. Insulted, he was about to do something to remind his son who had the power here, but then he understood that he did not have it. He looked at the love and reverence in the congregation and understood that they would protect his son from any insult or injury.

Still holding his hand, Florian said, "Mr. Mayor, I am so pleased you have found your way to The Comforting Arms. All who love the Father and his workers are welcome here."

Mayor Glorvanious was flustered. "This is… quite an accomplishment, my son." He understood that Florian had done just what he had been tasked with: he had put together a loyal and strong workforce. What the Mayor hadn't envisioned was that their loyalty — or was it worship? — would be to his son.

"Thank you, sir. Our congregation has grown quickly. We already have our first babies born within the community — fine, strong children who will grow tall and full of faith. We await the day when we will travel in glory to the Promised Land." The religious language disturbed the Mayor. Still, if it worked to unite the people, it might be an excellent strategy. But was it strategy? He stared into his son's fiery eyes and saw only unblinking sincerity.

A beautiful young woman, with long chestnut hair and dark eyes, had moved into place beside Florian. When the young man realized she was there, the set of his shoulders relaxed, and his serious countenance softened.

"Mr. Mayor," he said, "I would like to introduce you to Julianna, my fiancée."

The girl held out a delicate hand which the Mayor shook automatically, even as his mouth dropped open. She was obviously of Scraptown, not an appropriate match at all for a Glorvanious! He needed to get Florian alone, to remind him who he was. Whatever nonsense he might be spewing to these people, it was vital he remembered what standards he must uphold. He had to remember the loyalty that was owed to his family!

But it was too late. Already his son was bidding him goodbye, making apologies, saying that his duties called him away. He promised to continue sending his reports, but warned that the church's expenses might be increasing significantly over the coming months. And then he and his fiancée were borne away by his followers. Before she vanished, Julianna gave the Mayor a little merciful smile as if she understood the Mayor's confusion.

Damn her! Lawrence Glorvanious thought as he was left alone in the sanctuary. *Who is she to understand me!?*

Part III:

A Night of Laughter, Tears, and Adventure

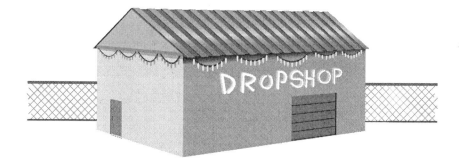

CHAPTER 16

Barnabas hated being angry. Being angry was just a bad idea. Sure, there were lots of things every day that he could be angry about. He could be mad at his father the way Thelonius was, never forgiving the man for divorcing his mom. He could be mad at his mother, who used to invent games and laugh all the time, but who now filled their lives with stress and tension, with schedules and deadlines. Then there was the way Principal Rolan-Gong had believed the Mayor without even asking Barnabas for his side of the story. There were just so many valid reasons to be furious.

But what good would it be to be angry about any of it? If he was angry all the time, like some kids, like Wickram maybe, who would want to even be around him? When Björn came home from the job he hated, did he want to see some pissed-off teenager? In the end, it really wasn't so hard to just be cheerful and polite. Being angry just made more problems.

So, he kept his cool, even on days like this when it was really, really... *really* hard. They were returning from the Drop Shop, and Barnabas had chosen to sit in the back of the cart this time, back turned to the boys up front. On the driver's bench, with Beaney at his side, Wickram babbled ceaselessly, and Barnabas wasn't sure how much more he could take.

"How could that be true?" Wickram asked in a mournful moan as they clip-clopped along a dusty, rutted dirt road. "Mr. Glower would never close the Drop Shop. For one thing, I would die!" They hit a pot-hole, and

Barnabas accidentally bit his lip as the cart jerked down and up. Wickram's voice switched abruptly from misery to enthusiasm: "Hey, Beaney, did you see that new game they had for sale in the sparkle corner? Like a mini-pinball but with spinning cats and, like, a fly swatter thing!"

Barnabas thought that the boy's brain was like one of Deni's old vinyl records; if you accidentally bumped up against the player, it would jump to some other random track.

As if to test this theory, they hit another pot-hole, and right on cue Wickram jumped tracks again, apparently deciding it was music time! He started to pound a beat on the bench between his legs and whistling enthusiastically. Barnabas cursed under his breath. They were taking a so-called "scenic route," but all Barnabas could see around them was dust and debris while they bounced uncomfortably along the rutted dirt road.

Wickram began singing in a high, strained voice, "'BEAUTY'S IN THE EYE! WHEN YOU BEHOLD HER!' Hey, Barn! Do you know that song? It's by Big Mouth Grouper. I love them. When's their new album coming out?"

Barnabas turned and shouted, "It's not! They broke up, okay? The lead singer is doing commercials for Moderated Assurance now!" Wickram and Beaney spun around in surprise. "It's just not fair," Barnabas screamed at them. "The *diaboriku* is mine! Yesterday I didn't even know this stupid Valley existed, and now there's some stupid rule that I can't even have what's mine. I mean, I *lost* it and then I *found* it again, but now I can't *have* it! It's BULLSHIT!" He punctuated the word by punching the side of the cart. Pain flared across his knuckles.

The two boys up front were amazed, slack-jawed, and Barnabas felt his face redden. There were tears in his eyes, and he gritted his teeth against them. This was why he hated losing his temper. As soon as he let his emotions go, they would slide out of control like rocks in an avalanche, picking up speed and power until he was buried under their weight.

He looked up at the City, wishing he was there, and that he could just forget about everything he had seen in the last 24 hours. And then maybe he could forget about the day before with the Mayor and Mr. Klevver. And while he was at it, could Thelonius please *not* have sent him the *diaboriku* in the first place? Cal Kabaway could make it work no problem, but he couldn't, and it just made him feel stupid, like he was a disappointment to his brother.

And then he thought, just let history re-spool all the way back to when it was him and his mom and dad, happy in their old kitchen, laughing while the smell of garlic and oil filled the air — before divorces, before new marriages, before corporate parents, before grade point averages and career pre-planning seminars.

Wickram and Beaney were still staring at him, not sure what to do or say, and Barnabas turned away in shame. Now he'd done it; he had destroyed the day for all of them with his selfish tantrum. They drove in silence, and Barnabas rubbed his sore knuckles and picked off the skin that had torn loose. Before long, the road evened out. It wound past little groves of ash trees and big colourful rocks that looked like a giant's child had abandoned them after play. Barnabas couldn't decide if the rock formations were natural or if some big machines had set them like that. There was something whimsical about the effect, something light and effortless and yet artistic in the way the huge, heavy objects were arranged.

Beaney tapped him on the shoulder. He was holding out one of Sanjani's sandwiches. "Thanks," Barnabas said.

Beaney smiled and said, "These rocks are called the Fumble-Bunnies. We used to play here a lot when I was little."

Barnabas' voice was a little rough with emotion. "I guess this is the scenic route, after all." He gave Beaney a crooked smile, and the boy sat down beside him.

The three ate their sandwiches in silence. Barnabas spotted a pair of deer in one of the little groves and pointed them out to Beaney.

His mouth half full of sandwich, Wickram suddenly said, "Really? Big Mouth Grouper broke up? That drags the mud *utter*. I wanted to see them perform at the Manhammer Audio Dome some day."

Barnabas found a bit of tissue in his pocket and blew his nose. He felt calmer now, purged. "Well, maybe they'll do a reunion tour in a few years," he said. He reached down and lifted the bowler hat up for them to see. "I think I accidentally stole this."

Beaney's eyes went wide, but Wickram just laughed. "Accidentally, you say."

"Seriously! I was still wearing it when that Greta woman kicked us out!"

Beaney climbed back up to the front bench and put a hand on Wickram's shoulder. "Can I hear the song again?" he asked.

Wickram threw back his head and shouted the lyrics to the heavens, pounding the bench with a heavy backbeat. One of the mules brayed.

***

The minute they got back to Pastoral Park, Beaney ran off to rehearse some special move he wasn't sure of for that night's performance. Wickram was in considerably less of a hurry.

"I'm free as a bird," he said as they left the stables. "I had to do something for every circus performance since I was six, but not tonight!" They were passing under a big birch tree, and Wickram jumped up to catch a bough, swinging himself up onto it.

Barnabas looked up at him. "But don't you feel, I don't know, sad or weird? Are you sure you can't ask Givney for your job back?"

"I don't care, got it?" He swung around the bough, hanging down from it by one leg and one arm. "Now I can do anything I want tonight!"

"Like what?" Barnabas asked, but Wickram was attempting a dismount that didn't work, and he ended up on his ass on the ground. Barnabas stuck out a hand to help him to his feet.

Even this ignominious fall didn't seem to upset Wickram. He laughed and said, "We better go if we want to shower before dinner." The bathhouse was solar-powered, Wickram explained as they walked, so late afternoon was actually the best time to get hot water.

When they left the bathhouse, damp and refreshed, the sky had grown overcast. They hiked up the hill to the family house. When they entered the cool, stone building, they found no one downstairs, and no one responded when Wickram called out. The dining table was covered in so much paper that the dark wooden surface wasn't even visible. One side of the table was all clippings, photographs, and official documents from Sanjani's archival work. The other was pages of lighting cues and performance notes scribbled in Maestro Tragidenko's busy, flowery handwriting. There were little cartoons all over the margins of his pages: clowns being fired from cannons, rabbits in military uniforms. In the middle of this nest of notes was a top hat covered in shiny purple velvet. It was circled by an orange hat band, and a large orange flower sat on the rim. Wickram seemed to be considering the hat carefully.

"Is it your dad's?" Barnabas asked.

"Yeah, he performs in that one." He reached into his pocket and pulled out the Billy Brazen book he had bought at the Drop Shop. He laid it carefully on the top hat, pausing for another moment to consider the arrangement. "Come on," he said. "I'll get you some clean clothes to wear."

They were just a few minutes late for the early, pre-show dinner hour. Wickram had supplied Barnabas with a promotional tie-dyed t-shirt from a guitar company that had more and brighter colours than anything Barnabas would have chosen for himself. He was also wearing borrowed socks and underwear, but he was obliged to stay in his dusty jeans as Wickram didn't have any pants small enough to fit him. For some reason he couldn't exactly enunciate, he had decided to wear the stolen bowler hat. Maybe he just wanted to dress up special for his first circus show.

Sanjani waved at them, and Barnabas waved back with a smile. Wickram barely acknowledged her. He brought Barnabas over to a table where Huro, Buro, Thumbutter, and Garlip were sitting. Barnabas was busy exchanging shy smiles with Garlip when he realized that Wickram had walked away from the table without a word.

"Hey, Wickram, where are you going?" shouted Garlip, but the boy didn't stop. "That was weird," she said to Barnabas.

Thumbutter, with a mouth full of stew said, "Now that he's quit, he thinks he's too good for us." She was a body builder, Barnabas had learned on the previous day's walk in the woods. She was training to anchor a balance team, and all that training meant she was always hungry. Barnabas was hungry too, and he was glad to see there was a plate of hot food waiting for him. Or maybe it was Wickram's he was eating; but no one stopped him, so he tucked into it with gusto.

Buro said, "I think Wick's depressed that we're all getting ready for a show and he's not."

His twin, Huro added, "He's going do a delve and wallow for a whole month, you'll see."

"He didn't act depressed today," Barnabas told them. "We were at the Drop Shop. He said he feels free."

"He was just fog-minding," Garlip told him, and when he looked at her blankly, she explained: "Thinking about anything other than his problems. But now that we're in pre-show, it's utter real." She shouted over her shoulder: "Graviddy! Go talk to your boyfriend, he's sliding drain-down."

"Leave her alone," Huro said. "She's getting in the zone."

"The Zone…" Garlip murmured and rolled her eyes. Barnabas turned around and saw Graviddy sitting by herself at another table. She was staring at the table, nodding slightly, as if hearing music in her head. She had a plate of food in front of her, but she was just picking at it with her fork. Her usual brazen confidence was nowhere to be seen.

"And she's not Wickram's girlfriend," Buro added quietly, seriously, and Barnabas wondered if he was a possible rival for her affections. He remembered Garlip's words: "Everyone has to have a crush on Graviddy at some point."

Beaney ran into the dining hall, holding a plush dolphin toy as long as his forearm. "Look!" he told all the kids at the table. "I got it! Utter bullseye!" He leaned way back until he was staring up at the ceiling and balanced the dolphin's plastic nose on his own nose. He began walking around with an exaggerated strut, arms outstretched, hands doing little razzmatazz waggles.

The table gave him enthusiastic applause, and Thumbutter patted the seat beside her. "Flamtasmic, kid. Now sit down and eat. We haven't got a lot of time." She pushed a plate of chilli, bread and broccoli in front of Beaney, and he dug in hungrily.

"Hey," Buro said. "They're here." The whole table, along with everyone at every other tables turned to watch the delegation from Clouding Guild enter the dining hall. The background hum of conversation died away and then rose again to a loud buzz like a hive of bees before a storm.

Barnabas had been expecting them to look like he'd seen them on the subway, in heavy suits with elaborate breathing apparatuses. Instead they were dressed simply in identical dark pants, plain leather shoes, and loose grey tops like mini ponchos. Both men and women had short cropped hair. They looked like muscular monks. Whistlewort and other older citizens of Pastoral Park were showing the group of around 15 Clouders to their tables. The hosts were full of smiles and broad gestures, but the guests in grey and black kept their faces stony.

The dining hall door opened again, and in walked Maestro Tragidenko with a woman, not very tall by Valley standards, but wide and strong. She looked like she had been carved from a single stump of 100 year-old oak that had fallen in the forest one day with a shattering, self-important boom. And while Tragidenko, in his wide-lapelled pin-stripe suit and gold bow-tie was the very picture of merriment, she was scowling. She surveyed the hall with grave mistrust like she was assessing the danger to her people and readying herself to order a sudden retreat.

"That's Carmmin," Huro told Barnabas. "She's the Speaker of Clouding Guild."

"There's no kids," Barnabas said. "I figured they'd bring their kids to see the circus."

Garlip shook her head. "No, of course not. They wouldn't expose them to our kind of blasphemy," she said bitterly.

"Gonna be a reaaalllllly fun show," Huro muttered.

Most of the Pastoral Park population started getting to their feet, grabbing their belongings and heading out. "Call is in ten minutes, kids," someone said to their table as they passed by. The teens rose to follow, but Garlip, Huro and Buro stayed in the exit door a minute, taking the measure of the evening's audience. They were seated around two tables with the elders from Pastoral Park scattered among them.

"First person who catches one of them smiling gets five farthings," said Buro.

"Utterly," said Huro. "But you'll see: Falstep will get a laugh out of them. He's the greatest clown in history."

Barnabas thought of the Clouders and their confrontation with Falstep on the subway. *The Father is sickened by your triviality,* they had told him. It didn't bode well.

The visitors from Clouding Guild had begun to pray in unison, their heads lowered. "O, Father Glory, who sets us to work for our bread. We praise You, Father, and thank You for the endurance of our limbs, for the steadfastness of our purpose, and we shall be ever-vigilant, ever true to Your holy principles. The Earth is bountiful for those with the strength to tap its riches." The hosts from Pastoral Park had their heads bowed too, but Barnabas didn't see their lips moving.

Looking at Garlip, he was surprised to see that she was reciting the prayer along with the Clouders. She caught him looking and stopped, crossing her eyes and sticking out her tongue at him. "Let's go entertain the servants of God," she said drily and led him from the dining hall.

CHAPTER 17

No one offered to bring him backstage, so Barnabas found a good seat in the audience and watched all the pre-show action. Despite having seen the circus from behind the curtain last night, he still found himself grinning with anticipation. He even felt a weird nervous excitement, like he himself was going to perform. After about 15 minutes of waiting, he couldn't sit still anymore. He carefully placed his bowler hat on his seat to reserve it (although the audience would probably number no more than 20), and ran up the aisle to exit the tent through the main gate.

The sun was still up, but the sky was full of dark mountain ranges of cumulus clouds, and he wondered if there would be a storm later that evening. Out in the parking lot were a small bus and a big truck that must have belonged to the Clouders. Circling around the Big Top, he came across a collection of little houses, no bigger than garden sheds. Some probably were for storage, but others were clearly inhabited, painted bright colours, light shining from their open windows. He wandered between them, listening for signs of life. From one came the voice of an opera singer doing warm-up exercises, her voice climbing higher and higher with each cycle: "Mi-ay-ee-ahhhhhh, oh-may-yoo!"

Then he passed another little house, and from within, he heard Falstep's voice: "I'm serious, stop drinking my hooch! Make yourself useful; hand me the brush and the black paint. No, the thin brush. If I painted on my eyebrows with that one, I'd look like the Grouch!"

"This one, right?" came the reply and Barnabas recognized Wickram's voice. This must have been Falstep's dressing room. He considered knocking on the door and joining them, but he wasn't sure that was the right thing to do before a show. He decided to go ninja and spy on them — just for a minute.

Falstep's window was above him, and Barnabas reached up to grab the window ledge. He climbed up, bracing his foot on a tiny outcropping of decorative moulding, and peered in. The clown was seated in front of a big mirror with bright kerosene lamps burning on either side. The desk in front of him was covered in makeup, brushes, sponges, tweezers, and other paraphernalia that he used to transform himself from an ordinary man into something almost but not quite human: a circus clown. Or was a clown the most *human* type of human of them all? Three or four brightly-coloured wigs sat on a table to his right. Behind him, a wardrobe overflowed with costumes. The room also had a bed, beside which lay a pile of well-thumbed books and several liquor bottles of different degrees of emptiness. Perhaps Falstep didn't just get dressed here, but actually lived in this little room.

Most of his face was already covered in pure white makeup. His lips were bright red. A painted-on tear, like the one in the circus' sign, hung down from one eye. Falstep took the proffered brush from Wickram (who had to crouch slightly under the low ceiling) and drew on a pair of raised eyebrows, that gave him a look of curious surprise.

Wickram sat on the unmade bed. He picked up a brown bottle from the floor — it might have been the one Falstep bought the day before at Maize's Tasties — and the contents sloshed around noisily. He lifted it to his lips, tilted his head back, and took a long swig. Lowering the bottle, he burped quietly.

"Hey!" Falstep said, eyeing him in the mirror. "What'd I say about leaving my hooch alone?"

Wickram shot him back a smile full of innocent mischief and put the bottle back on the floor. Maybe it hadn't been his first drink of the evening since his eyes already looked a little glassy. He asked, "Who's the Grouch?"

Somewhere behind Barnabas, the opera singer started up again: "Mi-ay-ee-ahhhhhh, oh-may-yoo!"

"Red wig," Falstep ordered, and Wickram got to his feet to retrieve it. "Wait! Make it the blue," Falstep said. "Yeah, blue tonight. This is going to be some *serious* clowning." Wickram handed him the wig, and he began to fit it in place, his eyes focussed intently on the image in the mirror.

"The Grouch," he said as he pressed the edges of the wig smoothly against his forehead and temples, "was one of three great clown brothers: the Grouch, the Harp and the Chick. They made movies, and people all over the world loved them. My Dad said he learned more from them than from any other clowns he ever saw or worked with. Nose!"

Wickram gingerly picked up the bulbous rubber appliance, which had been lying on a stained white towel. Falstep put it on with great precision and smoothed on more white makeup to cover the edges as he continued his lecture: "From the Grouch, my dad learned merciless wit, from the Chick, bottomless confidence. But it was the Harp, he told me, who was the purest clown that ever lived. An amoral animal spirit! Pure joy, pure anarchy."

"That last one sounds like you," Wickram said, sitting back down on the bed and surreptitiously picking up green, pyramid-shaped bottle and sneaking a sip. He winced as it went down his throat.

Falstep seemed to miss this stealthy manoeuvre. Rubbing blush on his cheeks, he said, "Anarchy? Nah, I'm just kind of crumpin' around out there, trying to be one-tenth the clown ol' Onestep was. And hey! If I come back to my dressing room tonight and there's nothing left for me to drink, there will be misery aplenty in Pastoral Park!"

This time, Wickram's expression was sour. "All right, fine, I don't want your lousy liquor anyway." He burped loudly.

Barnabas' fingers were aching from hanging onto the ledge, and his toe on the narrow moulding was starting to cramp. He jumped down to the ground in expert ninja silence. Wickram's face appeared above him in the window, and Barnabas pulled himself up tight against the little house so he wouldn't be seen. Wickram said, "I don't get why you went into your father's business anyway. It's like a slizzy prison sentence." He shouted into the evening air, his voice already slurry with drink: "I'm a free man, going my own way!"

Wickram pulled his head back in, and Barnabas figured this was a good time to move on. He continued his circumnavigation of the Big Top. Coming around the bend, he spotted Graviddy standing outside beside a little doorway — really just a flap of tent pulled back and tied off. She was wearing a tight costume — sparkling white with stripes of different purples. He suddenly lost the desire to be invisible. He wanted to talk to her; maybe about Wickram getting drunk. He wanted to know if his new friend did that a lot, and if they should be worried. Or maybe he just wanted to talk because he was kind of thrilled by her.

He was about to walk over and say "break a leg" (which is what you were supposed to tell performers, he remembered) when she suddenly lurched sideways and vomited into a clump of bushes. He quickly hid himself behind a tree, feeling embarrassed on her behalf. But was she sick? Did she need help? Apparently not, since she stood herself up matter-of-factly and wiped her mouth with a handkerchief before slipping back inside the tent. Barnabas wondered if she threw up before every show. Maybe that was part of "getting into the zone." If so, it was weirdly impressive.

He finished his circuit of the Big Top and went back in through one of the side entrances. The atmosphere had changed in his absence. The pre-show lights were on now, casting mysterious beams around the tent, golds struck through with little blasts of red and green. A palpable electricity hung in the air: the promise of magic. The ring was ready for the show, though quite a few performers were still out there, stretching, juggling, getting their minds and bodies ready for what was to come.

Barnabas took his seat again, moving the bowler hat to the chair beside him. Amid the bustle in the ring, he spotted Givney. He was busy teaching someone Wickram's curtain cues. Barnabas had still been kind of hoping that Wickram would un-quit at the last minute and be part of the night's performance, but now it seemed impossible.

He thought again about Wickram. He wondered if he should go back to Falstep's trailer, try and make him stop drinking, distract him or something. Would it be the right thing to find Sanjani and tell her? That idea felt like betrayal. Barnabas didn't have much experience with alcohol and drugs. He didn't go to a lot of parties, and the kids that used the illicit substances did so in closed bedrooms or in darkened backyards where he wasn't invited to go. He wasn't sure he wanted to be. Anyway, Falstep was with Wickram, he reminded himself, so maybe he should just leave it alone.

A man with grey hair and small round glasses walked into the ring carrying a clipboard and checking off items on a list. When he got to centre stage, he announced in a strong voice: "The call is 15 minutes. Fifteen minutes, everyone. And the house will be open in five minutes. Everybody please make your way backstage and keep your voices low. Thank you."

The performers cleared the ring, and a few minutes later, the band entered and took their places on a little stage to the right of the ring. They began to play a kind of comedy tango, the clarinet weaving a high, woozy obbligato over the sexy beat of the rhythm section. Barnabas was just getting into the song, tapping his feet to the rhythm when the group from Clouding was led into the Big Top. The Speaker, Carminn, entered first, again surveying the room as if some mysterious beast might be lurking in any corner. Most of the group looked just as stern, but Barnabas noticed that one guy of about 18, the youngest in the contingent by far, seemed to be mesmerized by the sights and sounds in the tent and was just barely holding back his smile.

Just after the Clouders took their seats, a long drumroll began, and the lights dimmed. The drumroll grew and climaxed in a cymbal crash as a curtain parted at the back of the ring. Illuminated by a bright spotlight, Maestro Dimitri Tragidenko swept onto the stage and marched to the centre of the ring. He was dressed in a long, shining great coat of purple satin. The purple and orange top hat, that Barnabas had seen back at the house, was perched on his head at a rakish angle. The Maestro's eyes sparkled with excitement, and his brilliant smile shone forth from the centre of his beard like the sun breaking through storm clouds.

"Ladies and Gentlemen," Tragidenko proclaimed. "Honoured guests! Welcome to a night of laughter, tears, and adventure. This is the show of shows! The elegance outpouring! The imagination made manifest! Welcome to Tragidenko's Circus of Humanity!!"

Barnabas clapped loudly, but the applause from the small Clouding contingent was so restrained, it seemed to suck the energy out of his enthusiastic contribution. He looked around, and the Big Top suddenly seemed really empty. Nonetheless, the first group of performers burst into the ring in a series of somersaults and leaps. Barnabas recognized the tumblers he had seen rehearsing in the school building. Soon they were climbing into their elaborate human pyramid. It had seemed incredible enough before when he had listened to them breathing hard and grunting with exertion, their bodies slapping against the mats. But now, in their costumes, under the lights, with the music twirling and soaring, it all seemed effortless and unearthly, like they could fly with no more thought than a flock of birds.

The tumblers were followed by the first of the trapeze acts, men and women spinning through the air, saved again and again from certain death by strong hands which appeared at the last minute to save them. Next came the clowns, emerging on a series of ridiculous, mismatched bicycles, crashing into each other, flying over handlebars into each other's arms. One of the bicycles flew apart in mid-jump, and the clown, still holding the handlebars, let his momentum carry him into the audience. He ended up standing above Barnabas on the arms of his seat, looking around in shock. He handed Barnabas his handlebars and ran back to the stage.

It was all as wonderful as Barnabas could have hoped, that is until Falstep ran up the steps to the Clouding group, trying to find a volunteer for the next part of his act. He met a wall of resistance so stony and cold that his perpetual motion was brought to a dead halt. Carminn had her arms crossed over her chest, and the others all followed suit. Barnabas noticed the young Clouder drop his gaze to the floor, like he was embarrassed. The group's refusal to be engaged was almost comical in itself, but really not. Under his manic smile, Barnabas could see — just for a second — a look of panic cross Falstep's face before he ran back down the aisle as if he were being chased by a swarm of bees.

Something was spoiled in that moment. The performers kept giving it their all, the band played its heart out, but that wall of crossed arms seemed to have cursed the atmosphere. Barnabas wanted to compensate for Clouders; he applauded until his hands hurt and even tried a few cheers, but these just felt embarrassing.

The only time the magic returned was when Graviddy appeared in the centre of the ring. She raised her arms to the heavens, and the heavens answered with long lengths of white silk that unrolled from overhead into her outstretched arms. She began to climb the silk, her limbs taut, her spine arched elegantly. And it all looked so easy, so perfect that Barnabas just gasped. And when she was high over the ring, wrapped now in her silks, she suddenly let go and spun downwards, catching herself just above the stage.

A male dancer twirled out from behind the curtain and caught her hand. Running and leaping with the grace and power of a gazelle, he circled the ring, pulling Graviddy along as she hung from the silk by one wrapped ankle. As the man ran faster and faster, the connection between them grew more strained, until suddenly they broke apart and Graviddy flew up into the air, still spinning, disappearing into the darkness at the top of the tent. The dancer stood alone in the ring, legs wide, back arched, panting heavily. His arm remained stretched heavenward as he looked up with longing. Barnabas was doing the same. Was Graviddy supposed to represent something here? Was she the ideal that human beings could and should aspire to, or was she something other — something more than human, a sublime creature he had dreamed into existence?

The spotlights went out, leaving little afterglows in Barnabas' eyes, and then the house lights came up. It was intermission. When he stopped applauding, and his soul returned to earth, he turned around and looked at the Clouding contingent. They all seemed to be leaning towards Carminn, their foreheads creased. Those closest to the Speaker were conferring with her, quietly but with emphatic hand gestures. She was nodding slowly and waving her hand at the ring, then up toward the darkness at the top of the tent.

The only one not in the conference was the young Clouder, who was walking down toward the ring, staring around at the lights and colours with a look of gratitude and wonder. Meanwhile, all around the tent, performers were peeking out through cracks in the curtains, or staring down from trapeze stations, watching the deliberations of the Clouders.

Carminn nodded solemnly and stood up. Immediately, the members of her group got to their feet as well. "Sensash!" she shouted at the young Clouder, who ran back up the aisle to her side as if she had cracked a whip. The Clouding contingent followed her out the exit. The curtain at the back of the ring shot aside, and Maestro Tragidenko hurried up the aisle and ran out after them out. The whole population of Pastoral Park seemed to explode from backstage or down from the heights, following their Maestro out into the parking lot, and Barnabas ran out with them.

The group from Clouding were climbing into their bus, all except Carminn, who was making her away over to the big truck. Barnabas watched Tragidenko hurrying after her, shouting, "Wait, please! The show — it is only half over!"

Carminn's truck looked like a cross between a pickup truck and a whale shark. The huge grill and massive fender were like a set of steel teeth, giving the vehicle a carnivorous look.

As she climbed up into the cab, Carminn answered, "Oh, yes, it's over for us."

Tragidenko was sweating heavily when he caught up to her. "But did you not see? Did you not understand that our performance... it was a celebration of human power, of the creative potential of a community? Working together just like we all do in the Valley. Like you do to honour Father Glory."

She looked down on him from the driver's seat. "You know what I saw? I saw vanity! I saw brazen acts of frivolous nonsense that insult the concept of decent, holy work!"

Barnabas, standing back at the entrance of the Big Top with the circus company, could feel their anger rising like humidity against his skin.

Tragidenko kept trying. "No, no, you are not understanding the metaphor. When the dancer reaches for the flying girl… He is all of us striving to be *more*. He wants to be more than a lost animal hiding in the earth. He wants to touch the infinite!"

Barnabas had to admire his perseverance, the way he kept his temper in the face of these insults. Tragidenko seemed to believe that if he only explained it right, he would change their minds. But it was obvious to everyone else that he was throwing himself against a brick wall, hoping against hope that a door might magically appear there. Carminn slammed her door and started the engine, which was shockingly loud in the quiet of the evening. Banks of headlights on the front of the truck blazed into life, bathing the circus troupe in a harsh, accusatory light.

She leaned out her open window. "If it were up to me," she said, "This place would be torn down, and we would teach you people how to get your hands proper dirty, be of some use to the Father."

She threw the vehicle into reverse and did a three-point turn, kicking up more dust than seemed necessary. The bus with the rest of the Clouders followed her down the road, black smoke and diesel fumes filling the air in its wake. Before the bus disappeared in the dust, Barnabas thought he caught a glimpse of the young Clouder, Sensash, staring out the grimy back window at them, looking forlorn.

"Wait!" Tragidenko yelled after them as the sound of their engines receded, and now he did sound angry. "We have prepared a reception after the show! With fermented elderberry wine!!" He spun on his heel and spat on the ground. "Bah!" he said, and dropped his scowling face to his chest. After a tense minute, he raised his head, looking more weary than angry. "Well, we tried." He gave them a little smile. "You, my beautiful children, were sublime. You respected your audience even when they did not respect you. I am so, so proud."

"Yeah, sure…" said a quiet voice behind Barnabas. He turned around and saw Falstep, sitting on the ground looking utterly dejected. No one else seemed to have heard him.

"What will we do now?" asked one of the trapeze artists.

The Maestro wiped his brow. "Now, we will sit together as friends, perhaps drink a little of the wine and remind ourselves that tomorrow the great curtain of life rises again. We will…" He paused and cocked his head. The sound of engines, which had faded to nothing, now seemed to be rising again. They all looked at each other, not knowing what to make of this. Why would the Clouders be returning?

But it wasn't that stony, unsmiling gang. Three large trucks pulled into the parking lot and came to a halt with a snort of air brakes. Dozens of people — hundreds! — began jumping from the backs of the packed trucks, and others climbed down from the roofs. And they looked excited, flashing delighted smiles, with baskets of snacks and bottles of drink under their arms. They headed for the entrance to the Big Top waving at the circus performers as they hurried in to take their seats. The performers, beaming, waved back and ran inside the tent themselves.

Barnabas, utterly perplexed, stood where he was, trying to understand what had happened. He saw Sanjani climbing out of the cab of one of the trucks, helped down by the driver. She walked over to her grinning husband and said to him, "Oh, Dimitri, I took one look at those sour apples at dinner and realized they'd be gone by intermission. So, I jumped on my bike and headed for the Forming compound. I knew they'd be delighted to get a sneak peek at the new show!"

He hugged her tightly and peppered her face with myriad kisses. But then he pulled away and tugged at his beard. "But do we just do the second act now or…"

She took his hand, "Start from the top, old man; these people came for a show!"

CHAPTER 18

As Barnabas made his way back inside through the chattering, enthusiastic crowd, he expected to find his choice seat taken. But there it was, empty, guarded by the loyal bowler hat that he was really starting to think of as a friend. He settled in as the audience began to clap rhythmically, demanding that the show begin.

Everything was different this time. Having an appreciative audience who laughed and gasped and applauded in all the right places made the performance come alive in a way he hadn't even known he was missing the first time around.

At intermission, he wandered among the people of Forming Guild and listened to them gushing about their favourite parts and performers. A lot of them mentioned Falstep, but even more enthused about Graviddy. They had noticed her in years past as a promising performer, but she had, apparently, surpassed their expectations. "I was utterly moth-lighted," one said.

At the climax of the second act, Graviddy burst into the ring, riding a magnificent white horse. Catching the ends of the silks that dropped down from above, she flew off the horse's back and into the air, twirling like a comet circles the sun. Barnabas couldn't resist sneaking out his phone and taking a movie of her. On the screen, she was a little incandescent streak of white, a heavenly body, made of light and star stuff, burning with the heat of a meteor.

The disastrous evening had turned around so spectacularly that the members of the circus troupe looked a little shell-shocked as they took their many bows. The people from Forming stayed after for the reception out in the garden, augmenting the food and drink with the snacks they had brought. Lanterns were hanging from trees, lighting the area softly. The accordion and violin players from the band were standing under a big oak tree, playing lively little tunes that sounded like tango and ragtime as people sat in chairs or on the grass, laughing and sharing stories.

Barnabas was hanging back shyly, content to watch everyone enjoying themselves, until Garlip and Thumbutter emerged from the Big Top and swept him into the crowd. "Let's wake up the night birds!" Thumbutter yelled, raising a fist in the air.

"You were great," Barnabas told her, remembering her part in a balancing act. Thumbutter started doing a little victory dance, and Garlip rolled her eyes. Barnabas wanted to compliment Garlip too, but he felt pretty lame when all he could come up with was, "Uh, the sets were really... pretty."

They reached the food table and started loading up their little plates with goodies. She told him: "Thanks. I worked on some of the costumes, too. My dream is to be the lead designer. One day, maybe."

"Barnabas!" yelled Beaney, running up to him. "Did you see me?" The white makeup on his face was imperfectly cleaned off and his hair was still standing up in spikes, the tips painted red.

"Sure, I saw everything. The clowns were great. And you didn't drop the dolphin; way to go!"

A strident, slurring voice behind them. "Yeah! *Way to go* as they say up in the *City*." Barnabas and the other kids turned around to see Wickram heading their way with a distinct stagger. "A triumphant performance, sure to go down in the anals of time!"

Garlip crossed her arms on her chest. "The word is 'annals.' Are you drunk, Wickram?" Barnabas saw that Wickram was holding Falstep's green, pyramid-shaped bottle.

Huro and Buro ran in behind him. Huro said, "Hey, Wick, don't run away from us. We're just trying to help."

Wickram spun around quickly, overshooting a bit and almost tumbling over. "Help? I don't need any help! I'm helping you wonderful circus people to *celebrate!* What a triumph. You sent the Clouding scruds scattering and skittering. HUZZAH!" He toasted the moment with a big drink from the green bottle.

Buro walked up to Garlip and Barnabas. "Help us get him home before his parents see, okay?"

Barnabas asked, "Does he get like this a lot?"

Garlip shook her head. "No. I mean, a little bit sometimes, but not like this."

They watched Wickram elbow his way to the food. People were staring at him. At that moment, Graviddy emerged from the Big Top. She took one look at Wickram and clucked her tongue, shaking her head in disgust.

"Hey!" Wickram yelled. "It's the great star, descended from the heavenlies to touch the groundy ground." He dropped to his knees in the grass and bowed until his chin was on the ground.

"That's really top grade, Wickram," she said. "Utterly mature."

Wickram jumped to his feet and staggered over to Barnabas, leaning down and resting too much weight on his shoulders. "Look at her, Barn! She's so beautiful. Even with hair tied up in an old lady bun. Even in that ratty old t-shirt. She's prettier than any girl in the whole circus!" Barnabas felt choked with embarrassment by this declaration as well as by Wickram's pungent, alcoholic breath.

And that was when Sanjani slid out of the darkness, her face shifting through a range of emotions. "Wickram, you need to come home with me right now. Right. Now."

"But it's a celebration, Mom! We're all just happy as hell. Right, everyone?"

Her shifting expression coalesced into anger. "I know why your friends are celebrating. Through their dedication and effort, they put on a great show tonight. You, on the other hand, have chosen to quit the circus. You don't deserve to be the centre of attention here, do you?"

Wickram's mouth dropped open. His eyes were huge and shiny, and he seemed to be having trouble focussing on his mother's face. He looked from side to side as if seeing his friends for the first time. Then he looked at Graviddy, but she turned her back. A gust of wind shook the trees, and the rustling leaves seemed to hiss at him.

Sanjani's face softened again. "Come home with me, Pickle. You will feel better in the morning." She held out her hand, but he backed away from it, tripping over a chair and landing on the grass. Huro and Buro hurried forward and helped him to his feet, their hands under his elbows. But when he was standing again, he yanked himself away and ran off in to the night. Barnabas noted, kind of impressed, that Wickram had never let the green bottle fall from his grasp or its contents spill.

"Wickram!" Sanjani called after him, but he was good and gone. She sighed and said to them all, "If you see him, children, please try and get him to come home. Or else find a safe place for him in the dorm. You were all wonderful tonight. Dimitri and I are very proud."

As she wandered off, Barnabas also drifted away. He was an outsider. He had no right to be discussing what had just happened with the group of kids, who had been friends for years, maybe since they were born. On top of that, he didn't want to hear them turning against Wickram, if that was what they were going to do. Despite the boy's craziness, Wickram had been kind to him and offered him friendship in this strange place. Barnabas hoped there would be some way he could repay the kindness.

Wandering around the darkness at edge of the garden, he came across Maestro Tragidenko and Falstep, sitting half-hidden on a stone bench in a little grove.

"No, no, my friend, my dear, dear companion, you were glorious tonight!" Tragidenko said in a warm, emotional voice, putting his big arm around the little man. Falstep, Barnabas saw, was crying.

He pulled himself back into the bushes where he could watch unobserved. Falstep's crying was as out-sized and theatrical as his clowning. He brayed like a donkey, blew his nose loudly on a huge polka-dot handkerchief and sobbed, "Why did I let them throw me off like that? I shoulda known what kind of audience they would be! I shoulda known, I shoulda tried harder. Then the Clouders would have stayed! It was my job to win them over and I *crumped* it! Utterly!"

"Balderdung and nonsense! There was nothing you could have done, my friend. I too dreamed that the impossible would happen tonight, but they were not here to be won over and wooed. They were hard as nails. They were the nails and the hammer both!"

Falstep dropped his face into his hands and wailed, his body shaking with his sobs. "They'll screw with us, Dimitri, you watch! Those Clouders won't rest until we're down in the Furrowing mines! My father, *he* coulda made them laugh. He coulda made them love us all."

"Never! Not even dear, dear Onestep would have been able —"

"Yes he would! I'll never be half the clown he was!"

But before Tragidenko could say another word, Sanjani rounded the corner and stood in front of them, hands on her hips. "You!" she cried, staring more nails and hammers at the clown. "You will stop giving my son liquor!"

Tragidenko's face twisted in alarm for a moment before he raised a hand in the air to calm his wife. "Please, darling, not tonight. We will discuss this in the morning when everyone is recovered again, yes?"

But she didn't want to be appeased. "He is a just a boy, Falstep! He looks up to you, heaven knows why."

His face blurred with tears, the clown shouted back at her: "I didn't give him the booze, okay? He took it! You want me to wrestle him to the ground? Tie him to a tree? He's not a baby, and I'm not his nanny!"

The wind was rising now, and she had to raise her voice above it. "You do not know the meaning of responsibility!"

"Sanjani, darling, please…"

Barnabas pushed himself deeper into the bushes and escaped from this scene too. All he wanted was to find some peace. Climbing through the little thicket and out the other side, he almost walked straight into Graviddy, who was all but invisible in the dark.

But she didn't seem surprised to see him. "So much drama tonight," she said in a level, somewhat amused voice. Barnabas wondered if she had been following him around.

He tried to sound as above it all as she was. "Yeah, you'd think they would be a in a good mood. I mean, except Wickram…"

But Graviddy didn't want to talk about Wickram, apparently. "You had your little drama today too, from what I hear." She started walking, sticking to the shadows as he had, like she too was an outsider.

He hurried after her, still confused by her words. "Wh-what? What drama?"

"I hear you lost something and found it for sale at the Drop Shop."

"Oh. Did Wickram tell you?"

"Beaney. Anyway, I agree with you." She turned and watched the cheerful people at the reception. The food and drink were all gone, and the group from Forming Guild were leaving, waving and calling out their good nights to the people of Pastoral Park.

Barnabas kept his voice low (though he wasn't exactly sure why): "You agree with me how?"

She began to walk again, her long elegant legs striding away. "That round thingy is yours. I don't care what treaty that old crocodile Glower has with the Guild Council. I say it's yours, and I think we should get it back."

Running to keep up, Barnabas asked, "Do you think he'll charge a lot for it? Besides, the Drop Shop is closed. Until further notice."

"Oh, I'm not suggesting we buy it back at some point in the uncharted future when Glower and that greasy Greta tell us we can. I think we need to get it tonight."

They rounded a little copse, and there in the darkness, glowing faintly in whatever scraps of moonlight the cloudy night offered, stood the white horse on which Graviddy had entered the ring. Barnabas remembered catching a glimpse of it at the stables when he'd first arrived at Pastoral Park. The horse's flowing mane and feathery tail were shifting in the rising wind. It looked utterly unearthly.

Her voice full of amusement, she said, "Want to go for a ride?"

CHAPTER 19

It wasn't his first time on a horse; Barnabas had spent some miserable hours at a summer camp circling a corral on a pony, clouded by flies and wishing he was in his bunk reading comic books. But this wasn't the same thing. No, not all. He was galloping along the road on a huge, white stallion, his arms wrapped tightly around the waist of a beautiful, exotic girl while the wind howled around them, making the sparse trees that lined the road dance and sway. The ground seemed a long way down, taunting him with threats of sudden calamity.

Barnabas peeked out from behind Graviddy's back and looked up at the City. It was a bright ball of light high up on the cliff, with the tower district in the foreground, cutting a dark silhouette. As he looked up, the rectangle of light that marked the Mayor's apartment snapped on, like the distant beam from a lighthouse, shining out over the rough seas.

Graviddy was leading them along the same route he had taken in the cart that morning with Wickram and Beaney, but what had seemed a long journey was now flying past in a blur. They rounded the corner and found themselves passing the Forming works. The road here was illuminated by powerful lights on high poles. A shift of workers was defying the night, and giant machines roared on, tirelessly. What would those workers think if they happened to look up and see the white horse fly by?

As they left the factory area and plunged back into the darkness, Barnabas pressed his cheek against Graviddy's back. He could feel the spine just beneath the t-shirt, her strength, her warmth against his cheek. The air on his arms, in contrast, felt cool and damp.

"I think it's going to rain," he called out. "Any minute!"

"Don't worry, we're almost there."

"Are you supposed to take the horse out at night like this?"

"Are you supposed to be in the Valley at all?" she snapped right back, and her sassy spirit made him smile.

A few short minutes later, they reached the turn-off to the Drop Shop. Graviddy brought the horse to a halt, and Barnabas could hear it breathing heavily in the stillness of the night. She jumped down from the saddle and helped him climb down, before pulling a flashlight from her pack and leading the horse down the embankment. The drooping branches of a willow tree hid the stallion from anyone passing on the road. Graviddy fed him an apple from her bag, talking to him in quiet, soothing tones, the way Wickram had talked to the mules.

In the distance was a low grumble of thunder like a great dragon rolling over in its sleep. The wind shook the willow tree, and Barnabas thought he felt a drop of rain. "I wish Wickram was here," he said.

Graviddy snorted. "Oh, like he'd be a lot of help in a secret operation tonight."

"I mean, I wish he was here and not drunk. The Drop Shop is kind of his place."

She was shining the flashlight into her bag, checking its contents. "Wickram has very strange loyalties. Falstep, Glower... When the one he should be listening to is his father."

"Oh?"

"I'm not saying, 'Follow the path through the woods your parents blazed before you.' That's from the Book of Prayers and Precepts; I don't care about the P&P. No, it's just Dimitri knows that Wickram is a flamtasmic composer, and he wants to give him the chance." She said this with great conviction, and Barnabas realized she didn't think Wickram was just a lovesick buffoon.

"You call Maestro Tragidenko 'Dimitri'?"

"He's like an uncle to me."

Barnabas saw a light on the road, piercing the unbroken darkness. "Look!" he said and she turned around. It was a truck, its engine noise growing steadily as it approached.

"Get down," Graviddy said, and they ducked behind a bush. Less than a minute later, the truck was close enough for Barnabas to recognize it by its banks of blazing lights, and by the massive grill, like a set of teeth clenched in anger.

"That's Carminn!" he whispered urgently, and Graviddy nodded, her eyes wide with surprise. The truck was right above them now. It turned sharply and headed down the driveway towards the Drop Shop, which stood dark but for a single bulb glowing above the door. The watched the truck pull up to the building, and Carminn climb down from the cab and vanish inside.

Graviddy stood up. "This is getting interesting. Come on!" They scrambled up the embankment and began jogging down the long driveway. Graviddy ran easily, head held high, but Barnabas was hunched over, like a spy, looking all around for eyes in the night. Somewhere in the Tumbles, there was a shattering crash like a sideboard full of grandma's best dishes had met its sad fate. Barnabas cringed.

They passed Carminn's parked truck and ducked around the corner of the building.

"We need to get up on the roof," Graviddy whispered.

Barnabas answered, "I saw a ladder on the wall this afternoon." He was sweating and panting from the run, and she wasn't, which was kind of embarrassing. "Down this way." He led them along the side of the building until they reached the base of the ladder, which was bolted to the wall.

Barnabas said, "Where's your flashlight? We need to see what's up there."

But before Graviddy even pulled it from her bag, a flash of lightning lit up the entire valley. The darkness returned immediately, but they had seen enough to get their bearings. She began to climb, and just as Barnabas put his foot on the first rung to follow, the thunder arrived. At the top of the ladder, he found Graviddy's hand waving in front of his face. He grabbed hold and let her help him up over the lip.

"Okay?" she whispered.

"Yeah, are we there?"

As if in answer to his question, another flash of lightning erased the night. In that brief moment of illumination, Barnabas saw a raised hatch up near the apex of the sloping roof.

"Almost," she said. The thunder arrived more quickly this time. Then out of nowhere, she told him, "I mean, he thinks that unless he's singing his songs in front of 10,000 rubes up in the City..."

"Wait. Who are we talking about?"

"Wickram! He thinks that unless he's up in your Manjammer Drone being a superstar, he's an utter failure. I just want to shake him sometimes!"

"Man*hammer* Dome," Barnabas said, and the lightning flashed again. In the brief moment of illumination, she looked pensive and vulnerable. "I thought you didn't like him. But you do, don't you?" Maybe she would have replied, but the thunder arrived, sooner and louder than ever. "We better hurry," he said. "Before we get fried by lightning."

The slope of the roof was gentle, but every step made the steel surface creak and pop obnoxiously, and they were obliged to creep forward slowly on hands and knees. When they arrived at the apex of the roof, Graviddy lit up the hatch with her flashlight, and Barnabas was relieved to see it wasn't locked. He slid the single bolt aside and lifted the hatch just as the rain began to fall. Graviddy went first, stepping onto a ladder that led downward. Barnabas followed, carefully lowering the hatch above him.

They were standing on a narrow walkway that ran under the peak of the roof, the entire length of the Drop Shop. All the lights were on inside the building as if in defiance of the oncoming storm. The rain began to fall in earnest, drumming loudly on the steel above them.

"Excellent!" Graviddy said. "They won't be able to hear us with all that racket."

Barnabas stood on tiptoe to peer over the wall of the walkway; Graviddy, a Valley giant, only had to lean out. They saw that they were above the main part of the shop. George Glower and Carminn were standing in one of the wide aisles, talking with grave enthusiasm. The drumming on the roof, Barnabas realized, was also preventing him from hearing what they were saying.

He could hear Greta, though; her voice, keen with aggravation, seemed more than capable of cutting through the sound of rain on the galvanized roof: "Oh, that's delightful. You two just catch up on school days or what-have-you while I do all the back-break!" She was packing up boxes with merchandise from the shelves, and dragging them over to the trolley that Glower used for his collecting runs. Strands of her heavily lacquered hair were standing up like charmed snakes, and sweat was pouring down her forehead, leaving long furrows in her thick makeup.

"It's madness, Georgie!" she screamed in Glower's direction, though he didn't appear to be listening. "You give me four days notice to pack up all our treasures! I'm going to have to abandon two-thirds of the total inventory. Thousands of farthings left behind for ruination and devastation — it's a disgrace!" Out of some obscure corner, Galt-Stomper ran through, carrying a little folding table. "You! Boy!" Greta shouted after him. "You stay and help me with the bundling and the twining!"

But Galt-Stomper, his face its usual mask of fear and determination, didn't even slow down. He ran right through into Glower's secret workshop, whose big mechanical door was standing open. Graviddy and Barnabas crept back along the walkway until they were over the workshop. Barnabas had more time to be impressed by the workshop than during his earlier visit, which had been brief and panicked. He saw precision measuring tools, metal lathes, welding equipment, and a dozen devices he could not name. On one big table, a set of plans lay open, its curling edges weighted down by whatever lay at hand: a set of callipers, a magnifying lenses, an elegant ceramic bowl half full of peanuts.

Down at one end of the room, Galt-Stomper was setting up two chairs and the folding table in front of the model of the City Barnabas had seen that afternoon. The boy climbed up on a step ladder to focus the small lights that were illuminating the diorama, then gave the whole set-up a last check, and ran back out of the room at full speed. The walkway shook as the workshop's hydraulic door slid shut with a decisive *clunk*.

Graviddy tapped Barnabas on the shoulder and pointed downwards. "Is that it?" she asked, voice raised above the maddening staccato of rain on steel. There, sitting casually on a table amid other random, forgotten objects, was the *diaboriku!*

"Oh my God!" he shouted, though his voice was drowned out by a thunder clap.

Grinning, Graviddy bent down and pulled a bunch of shiny white material from the bag at her feet. Barnabas recognized the silks from her performance. With great care, she tied the long, flat rope to the handrail of the walkway. She pulled out a container of powder and applied it liberally to her hands. "Rosin," she explained. "I'm all hot and sweaty, and don't want my grip to slip."

"You're going to climb down and get the *diaboriku*?"

"You bet. I'm going to do a full three-and-over fall to a leg swing. Then when I have it, I'll —"

"Why don't we just use that ladder at the end of the walkway?" he asked, pointing. Graviddy's eyes narrowed, and she swore some obscure Valley swear. But the point was rendered moot as the walkway shook with the opening of the workshop's security door. Peering over the edge, they watched Glower and Carminn enter.

The hammering of rain on the roof had grown lighter, and Barnabas could hear Glower calling, "Greta! We're starting!"

Greta appeared in the door, wiping her brow with a handkerchief. "As if I have time for your little pantomime! The shop is closing; I have to move everything! The particulars couldn't interest me less."

"You need to see this," he insisted, and she threw up her hands in exasperation. Glower yelled, "Galt-Stomper! Get in here!"

The boy arrived instantly, trying to negotiate a safe path around Greta, but she grabbed him by the shoulder — painfully, it appeared — and said, "Oh no, Georgie. If you want to waste my time in here, this little grub is going to move all those boxes to the loading dock." She turned Galt-Stomper around and sent him back to the shop with a kick in the pants. Licking both palms, she smoothed her lacquered hair back down and entered.

Glower began to show Carminn round the workshop, and Greta drifted along behind them, bored, her hips swinging to some melody in her head. Barnabas strained to hear the conversation, but only caught curious snatches:

"...she won't tell a soul..."

"...won't matter after Tuesday ... a whole new order..."

"...now is the time for resolve... ruthless and bloody ... the Father will forgive..."

Glower brought the two women over to look at the open plans on the work table and began gesturing excitedly with big sweeps of his hand.

"I don't like this," Barnabas whispered to Graviddy.

"I know. We'll never get your toy now," she replied.

"No, I mean ... What are they up to? Why is Carminn here, and why are they packing up the Drop Shop? I have a bad feeling." He looked down the walkway to the ladder. Did he dare?

"Where are you going?" Graviddy hissed urgently, running after him.

"I've got to hear what Glower's telling them!" The end of the walkway, beside the wall had a square hole in it through which the ladder extended. His stomach was tightening with fear, but Barnabas grabbed the top of the ladder and gave it a testing shake. It held solid and made almost no noise.

He put his feet on the rungs.

"What if they turn around and see you?" Graviddy hissed.

"They have their backs to me. They're busy with the plans or whatever. I can do this!" He wasn't sure where this confidence was coming from, considering he could practically see his pounding heart tenting the front of Wickram's tie-dyed t-shirt. But he couldn't shake the feeling that something big and bad was going on, and he had to find out what it was.

He moved as quickly as he could without making too much noise. Glancing over his shoulder, he saw the trio still bent over the big papers although Greta was tapping her foot impatiently. All he could do was pray they would give him another minute.

He was halfway down, and already he could hear their voices more clearly:

"I don't know how long I've had the notion. But there wasn't a day I didn't ... revenge for all the ... inflicted on me."

"I understand, Glower. The arrogance of ... just grows stronger every year. The Father weeps to hear the ... from their insolent mouths. He is begging us to ... in his honour."

"Will this take very long, Georgie?"

Infuriatingly, the ladder ended some two metres above the floor. He took a second to curse this bit of design madness, and then wondered how he could possibly jump the distance silently. The answer came a moment later: another bolt of lightning. He only had to wait a few seconds for the great *Ka-Boom!!* which shook the building, and in that moment, Barnabas jumped. He hit the ground and rolled, finding shelter behind one of the work benches. Peering between the legs of the bench, he saw that Greta had turned at the sound of the thunder. He had missed being caught by maybe a second.

From his vantage point, he also had a better view of the diorama. There was the cliff, and at the top of it, the buildings of the Tower District, each one crafted with care in wood, painted with no little attention to detail. The scale was impressive; the tallest of the buildings stood a good 40 centimetres. Beyond them, the rest of the City was just a suggestion of architecture, with a bunch of green modeling clay in the back, standing in for Riverside Park. The diorama's broad base was skirted by black fabric that hung to the floor like curtains over whatever table must be holding it up.

"But I don't understand," Carminn asked him in her guttural voice. "You told me we were still weeks away, and now you want to do it in such a hurry. Tuesday, for Glory's sale!"

"Because I found something out in the Tumbles! A find so fortuitous it almost makes me believe that your fictional Father Glory intervened."

Greta guffawed and slapped Glower on the shoulder. "Oh, you're a naughty boy, you are, Georgie!"

Carminn pounded on the table. "Do you want me to leave? You dare insult the Holy Father like that? Do you think you can do this without me?!"

Greta sneered and said, "Georgie doesn't need you at all, you frumpy old elephant."

"Enough, both of you!" Glower barked. "This is serious. Follow me."

To Barnabas' horror, they began walking his way. He scuttled like a crab under the workbench, dodging the legs of several stools. He reached the end and rolled out. The groups was now standing right above the spot where he had been hiding. Barnabas ran across the floor bent over and hid behind a tool cupboard. Peeking out, he saw Glower was holding the red box he had found in the Tumbles. He opened it and pulled out two or three of the little blue pyramids.

Greta leaned in for a better look. "Ooh, a lovely cerulean, that is."

Glower handed Carminn of one of the pyramids, and she turned it over in her rough, plump hand. "What is it?"

"I'm not completely sure what it was originally intended for," Glower replied. "My best guess is a wireless communication system that uses lasers as the signal medium. This is the control node." From the box, he removed an orange cube which he placed on the table.

Impatiently, Carminn dropped the pyramid onto the table. "We don't need to communicate with anyone! We need to tear them screaming from the sky."

"Oi! Easy on the merchandise, girlie!" Greta snarled.

Glower snatched up the little pyramid and put it back in the box. "No, you don't understand, which frankly doesn't surprise me, Madam Speaker." A dirty edge of glee had entered his voice. "I'm going to use them as remote triggers. Standing in the one place in the City where I have line of sight on every building in the Tower District, I will… Well, why don't you take your seats and I'll show you." Carminn glared at him. Their collaboration, Barnabas thought, was not an easy one for either of them.

But then Barnabas saw that his hiding place would be visible to them when they moved to the chairs in front of the diorama. He looked up towards the walkway and saw Graviddy shaking her head in disbelief or panic. Barnabas lowered his head and looked around for a solution; there was really only one option. He squatted low, ran, and dived head-first through the black skirt that hid the base of the diorama. He smoothed the curtains closed behind him and tried to pant as quietly as he could.

He turned to look upwards and saw a faint light entering his little dark cave. The diorama, he realized, wasn't on a table. The legs were attached to the model itself and he could see the whole of the underside. Getting up carefully on his knees he found himself looking out from behind the diorama's cliff face, which seemed to be a painted mesh. From the outside, it looked solid, but from Barnabas' vantage, it was a window. In front of him, barely two metres away, Carminn and Greta were lowering themselves into the two chairs, Carminn's wide form all but eclipsing the dainty wrought-iron seat. Glower picked up the remote control from the folding table and stood behind them. All three were staring at Barnabas, but they could not see him.

"Is all this arts and crafts really necessary?" Carminn asked. "Seems like a crumping waste of time."

Greta gave the diorama an approving nod. "I think it's lovely, Georgie. We should put it up right by the cash as an *objet d'art!*"

Glower seemed to be only half-listening, his eyes wide, licking his lips like a dog anticipating the bone he will get after the meal. Voice rising with excitement, he told them: "It's important to visualize a project as clearly as possible before you begin. When those great City fathers were planning their metropolis, they too commissioned intricate, cunning models. In fact, I know just where they're stored now!" He laughed abruptly, and thunder returned the sentiment. Barnabas felt goose bumps rising on his arms.

Glower pushed a button on the remote, and the lights in the rest of the workshop dimmed, leaving only the spotlights that shone down on the diorama. They all stared at it — and unknowingly at Barnabas — with growing anticipation.

The owner of the Drop Shop, his eyes glowing with mania, said, "Those architects of the past planned the construction of the City so carefully; can we do any less for its destruction?" Raising the remote control, Glower pushed another button and right above Barnabas' head, there was a sharp *bang!* that scared him so bad he came close to screaming. A piece of the diorama disconnected itself and he saw, through the face of the cliff, one of the tower models falling into the Valley.

He dropped to the floor, covering his ears with both hands as the next explosion came, and the next and the next. And one by one, the towers of the City diorama fell into the Valley: the Jezebel! The Neverlander! Greatest Hiltz! Delphic Tower! His nostrils burned with powder smoke, and his ears rang painfully. Lying on the floor, knees curled up to his chest, Barnabas looked up at the holes above him where the towers had stood. Through the ringing in his ears, he heard Glower laughing like a child, up past his bedtime, demented by a sugar buzz of anarchy. And then Carminn, too, was laughing as the lightning flashed, and thunder shook the Drop Shop.

Under the diorama, unseen in the heart of the action, Barnabas was in a bad way. His heart pounded, and he felt like he was going to throw up. The immensity of the horror was too much to be contained by his body or comprehended by his mind. The maniac Glower! He was actually plotting to knock over the tower district, crash it into the Tumbles, along with all the people who lived and worked in those buildings. Barnabas wanted to scream; he wanted to thrash his limbs on the ground, but he had to hold it in, hold it in and not get caught. People willing to do something so terrible wouldn't hesitate to kill a witness, especially a nothing kid like him, a fugitive in the Valley, who had stuck his nose in where it didn't belong. But there was more than his personal safety to think about: he was the only one who knew, the only one who could tell the world and *stop Glower! Stop Carminn!*

He gritted his teeth and concentrated, trying to take in every word they were saying.

"Georgie," Greta cried. "Are you mad?! We have a good business here! Why would you do such a lunatic thing?"

Carminn and Glower took no notice of her. Carminn said, "But even with these new triggers, isn't Tuesday too soon to be ready?"

Glower laughed again, "That's the beauty of it! With the laser trigger, it's so simple. I'll need to work fast, but don't forget: I've been preparing for months. I have complete access to the towers. All of them!"

Afraid of missing anything, Barnabas got slowly back up on his knees and looked through the mesh — although the fallen towers now blocked most of his view.

Carminn was on her feet, pacing, counting off something on her fingers. "And you have enough explosive? I could allocate some more if you —"

Glower rubbed his sweating head absently with one broad palm. He was staring at the broken diorama with wide, gleaming eyes, giving Carminn his back. "Don't question my calculations!" he said. "I told you what I needed, you provided it. It's all in place."

Greta's face suddenly filled Barnabas' view as she examined the broken diorama with fascination and wonder. Barnabas dropped back down to the floor.

Carminn was sounding more agitated now. "But maybe *I* need more time! I'm only working with a handful of people inside Clouding, and this will be a major operation! After the fall, we'll have only a short window to assert control of the guilds and —"

Again Glower interrupted her: "What you do after the day of reckoning is entirely your affair. As long as I'm exempt from prosecution, I am content to let you rule over your little kingdom."

Barnabas saw Greta's shadow pull away from the diorama. "Not so fast! Georgie and I have the rights to everything that falls into the Tumbles. *Everything!*" she shrieked. "When those towers come down, it will be the greatest windfall of our lives, and *he* may not care what happens afterwards, but I do! *We have a contract!*"

Carminn's tone was contemptuous. "A contract with the Guild Council! After Tuesday, the Guild Council will cease to exist. Clouding Guild will be in charge!"

"Oh no, no, no, no, no! You and your people honour our contract or Georgie isn't making his little fireworks for you."

"Greta, please…"

"Shut up, George. This time you listen to me. I want your word — your blood and guts oath on this, you sanctimonious cow!"

"You ridiculous market-stall harpy," Carminn spat. "We are trying to establish a Holy Order for the majesty of Father Glory, and you just want to keep on selling your blasphemies and pornographies. Fine! Go ahead, you have my oath! Now, Glower, you're leaving for the City tomorrow?"

Their voices were growing quieter. Barnabas got back on his knees and peered out. The trio was heading for the door of the workshop.

Glower said, "Yes, at 1130 hours. Make arrangements." He pushed the button and the hydraulic door slid open. They exited into the shop.

Barnabas didn't hesitate. He dropped on his ass and pushed himself out from under the diorama, feet first. He ran across the room and jumped onto the ladder, climbing quickly. He didn't give a thought to the noise he might be making; he needed to get out of this place. He needed to tell people — Sanjani, Tragidenko, Whistlewort — what he knew! And they would need to tell the Guild Council, or whoever, because there wasn't much time! It was already the early hours of Saturday, and in just three days… Boom!

At the top of the ladder, Graviddy was reaching out her hand, pulling him up onto the catwalk with her surprising strength.

"What was that all about?!" she demanded. "I couldn't hear a crumping thing!"

"But you saw?"

"Of course I saw! Major pyrotechnics!"

Barnabas went up on tiptoe. He had yet to see the destruction from outside his hiding place. And there it was: the towers toppled into the Valley, the cliff edge where they had stood scorched black. It was only a cheap model, but now that he understood what it meant, it looked sickeningly real.

He told her, "They're going to do it! Glower is! Blow up the towers! Crash them into the Valley!"

Graviddy started to say something, but it only came out as a groan. Her mouth hung open.

"We have to go," Barnabas said, feeling truly terrified for the first time in their night of adventure. He began walking shakily towards the hatch in the roof

"Wait," Graviddy called after him. "Go look down into the shop."

"We have to leave!"

"Do it! Where are they?"

"Th-they're all down by the front door. Carminn is leaving. Wait! Glower is heading back towards the workshop!"

"How long until he gets there?"

"What are you going to —"

"How many seconds?!"

"I don't know! Ten!" He turned to her and saw that she had wrapped her silks around herself, like she was a caterpillar halfway through spinning a cocoon.

She nodded, and a look of calm focus fell over her features. She put her hands on the railing of the walkway, took a breath and pulled herself up and over the side. Barnabas stretched up to watch, horrified as she spun down into the workshop, the silk unravelling layer by layer. And at the bottom of her fall, she swung upside-down in a graceful arc, ankles wrapped in the silks, arm stretching down to scoop the *diaboriku* off the table.

The hydraulic door began again to slide open. Nimble as a monkey, Graviddy climbed her silks, collecting the excess as she went. And as suddenly as she had leaped, she was back on the walkway, her face gleaming with sweat. With a satisfied smile, she handed Barnabas the precious sphere.

"Okay," she said, "Now we can leave."

INTERLUDE: MAY, 1914

nlike the last time when he had insisted on going alone, Mayor Lawrence Glorvanious entered Scraptown accompanied by his Deputy and an entourage of five policemen. Angry glances greeted them from darkened doorways, and the Mayor stood tall, knowing that to show fear would invite violence. Half of Scraptown had recently been annexed for the creation of a prestigious neighbourhood in the new City, and while most of the inhabitants had left voluntarily, some had to be rousted, a few arrested as an example. It was unfortunate, but change — even positive change — came at a price.

The Comfort Arms had continued to grow in the three years since his last visit. There were two new annexes, and some of his son's tall workers — white, negro, and oriental working side by side — were labouring enthusiastically, constructing a substantial outbuilding. The Deputy tried several doors in the main building, but only one opened. The Mayor followed him into a large, bright room where a dozen clerks were working. The men and women looked up at the entrance of this official brigade, but none rose to greet them.

"The Mayor is here to see Florian Glorvanious," the Deputy announced, and the clerks looked at each other in confusion before one finally rose and went out through a door at the back. The mayor massaged a knot of tension in his shoulder. After five minutes that felt like a lifetime, someone finally came to greet them, but it was not the Mayor's son; it was the chestnut-haired woman, Julianna.

"Your Honour," she said. "We bid you welcome. The Father is engaged with very important matters and has asked me to come and welcome you." She had grown in confidence and beauty, the Mayor saw. But the nerve! She had made this announcement — this insult! — without apology as if Lawrence Glorvanious were some travelling brush salesman.

"The Father?" he said, his consternation growing. "I am looking for my *son!*"

"I'm sorry," she replied. "My husband — your son, Florian — is often called 'Father Glory' out of respect."

Again, the Mayor found himself repeating her word back to her as if he had woken that morning a parrot: *"Respect?!"*

He was about to launch into a diatribe about a boy who did not know enough of respect not to rise above his station when Julianna's manner changed. Understanding and sympathy suffused her face. Her whole body seemed to soften as if to share his hurt. The words of anger caught in his throat, and twisted themselves into a torrent of warring emotions: pride that his son had become a leader, jealousy of the same, an ache of longing for the days when Florian was a boy — so bright and gentle and serious, calling in that piping alto: "Let it go! Let it go!" Then the father had released the kite, letting it soar into the heavens as the son ran with it, laughing with uncomplicated joy.

Julianna's voice caressed him: "It must be hard to have been so far from Florian these past years. But if you could see all he has done, the loyalty he commands, you would know you made the right decision in giving him this role." The Mayor looked down and saw her small, gentle hand holding his. His own hand, rough and wrinkled, looked clumsy and coarse in hers. He almost pulled away in a show of outrage, but that warm, smooth hand soothed his anger.

"Mr. Mayor," came a voice behind him — a man's voice, deeper even than he remembered. But what had he expected? The little boy's piping alto?

Mayor Glorvanious turned to his son. Florian was even more a man than three years earlier. He was broader, more solid. The moustache on his face was so full, it seemed to be a separate creature that inhabited his lip in a kind of symbiotic relationship. The Mayor saw no choice but to treat his son as an equal. They were in the domain Florian had built, with his Florian's followers all around them.

When they had departed to a private room, the Mayor told his son, "My advisors believe War in Europe is inevitable, imminent. Of course, as leader of this City, I will do everything I can to support the war effort." His voice grew quieter but more vehement. "But I will *not* lose what has been built here! This workforce you have prepared, my son, is everything. When conscription comes, I will not see them lost to the battlefields."

Whatever Florian thought of these words — they would be considered by many unpatriotic, to say the least — his face revealed nothing. After a silence, he said "What do you propose, sir?"

"The plan has always been for your people, the unseen engine of the new City, to *vanish*. Let it be now. It is time to lead them to the Valley, Florian, and to close the gate behind them."

Florian Glorvanious looked out the window, into a sky filled with billowing clouds, and whispered, "Into the Promised Land ..."

The Mayor seized on this. "Yes! It is time Father Glory led his people into the Promised Land, where they will fulfill their destiny!" His plan had turned out better than even he had ever imagined. With the religious fervour Florian had instilled in the workers, they would be eternally loyal. The Mayor was delighted with himself.

The sun suddenly broke from behind the high clouds and filled the room with light. The Mayor drew back, his chair squeaking on the hardwood, and squinted as the light haloed his son's head. For a moment, Lawrence Glorvanious wondered if this serious man before him, this icon of devotion, could really once have been that boy who had run with abandon, laughing as the kite flew higher and higher.

Part IV:

Hunting in the Dark for a Glimmer of Hope

CHAPTER 20

George Glower heard Carminn's truck roar off into the night, and he cursed her quietly but with great vigour. *She's just a means to an end, George,* he reminded himself. The Speaker of Clouding, with her privileged dreams of righteous power was like so many others he had met in his eventful life. They thought they were fulfilling their own destinies when, wittingly or un-, they were born to further his.

Glower realized that Greta was speaking, had been speaking since the moment Carminn had closed the Drop Shop's door behind her. But George had long ago learned how to block out inconsequential noise. He turned and looked at the woman like she was a biological specimen, an odd creature discovered on the underside of a leaf. He squinted and tried to hear her, but his mental filters, that allowed him to omit the pointless from his consciousness, were just too good.

"I have to prepare," he said, evidently cutting her off mid-sentence (how could it be otherwise, since she never stopped talking?) Her look of hurt as he turned away was just another curiosity — a feature of the leaf creature that some naturalist would write up in some obscure journal.

Soon he was alone in the quiet of his workshop, the only sound the patter of rain on the roof. He wondered idly where the boy was. Gone back to whatever hole he hides in, George supposed. He didn't know what would happen to Galt-Stomper after Tuesday, and he felt … not so much worried as curious. The boy was, for all his nervous ineptitudes, a good and useful helper. Still, George could not be expected to take care of everyone. After all, who had ever taken care of him?

The smell of the fireworks he had used in his demonstration still hung acridly in the air. He thought again of the moment the beautiful little hand-crafted towers had fallen, how his heart had quickened with excitement. But even though the demonstration had gone flawlessly, he felt weirdly empty. For a moment he was gripped by the terrible fear that he would feel just as empty when the real thing was done. But no! That was impossible. It would be an apotheosis, an unparalleled victory! Tuesday — just three days away — would finally bring the night of celebration that had been denied him nine years ago. A feeling of vivid, electric excitement passed through him — perhaps too much excitement, for he suddenly felt faint. He slumped forward, arms rigid, supporting himself with his palms flat on the workbench.

He felt faint. The world seemed to rush away, and he had to support himself, slumping forward to place his hands on the folding table. But he wouldn't sit, he was determined to stay on his feet.

"George, are you all right?" the woman asked him, concerned. She spoke with familiarity, like she really knew him, but he wasn't entirely sure which one she was. The name-tag on her smart, mauve jacket read "Nina," Some campaign functionary, higher or lower in a hierarchy that he had never bothered to comprehend. Under his hands on the table, his own face looked up at him, repeated a thousand times on a thousand flyers — flyers that had suddenly been rendered obsolete. Above the repeating faces, the same heraldic device: "A Tradition that Built the Past, A Vision to Build the Future!" and his name over and over, in confident block letters. This kaleidoscoping name seemed to mock him now, like the tedious voices of all those reporters calling to him at once, like so many seagulls on a peer: "George! George! George! Over here, George!"

"The results show your opponent surging in early returns."

"Are you going to concede the election?"

"Where do you feel your campaign fell apart?"

"Would you comment on allegations of campaign finance irregularities?"

He had brushed past the reporters into the campaign headquarters, imagining them bursting into flames in his wake. Would he comment? Lower himself to their level? Never!

Still feeling faint, he forced himself to stand, but immediately a fog obscured his vision and he felt himself blacking out. He gave a terrible moan, and another functionary, this one in no-nonsense navy blue, ran forward to slide an arm under his. He thought he recognized her as somebody significant. Her name-tag also read "Nina."

"George, please, there's still one thing to do and then you can go home. We'll have the text of your concession speech ready in five minutes. Please... just hold it together until then."

Hold it together? But that was the problem exactly! It had all fallen apart, fragmented into a million loose bits as if one minute he had been driving his car on the highway — a superb car, of excellent workmanship and distinguished lineage — when it had suddenly disassembled into an endless inventory of screws, flanges, belts, microchips, LEDs, carbon-steel lattices, precision performance parts, and redundant safety measures, all stretched across a kilometre of blacktop while he flew unprotected through the air, tumbling end over end into oblivion.

He felt that he was going to be sick. He lurched across the room and bent low over a garbage bin, vomiting prodigiously, his whole body involving itself in the act of purging. And it seemed that the remains of a thousand miserable campaign lunches, pancake breakfasts, booster backyard burger barbecues all exploded from him and rained down onto yet more campaign literature: "Vision! Focus! Giving YOU a voice at City Hall".

He was drenched in sweat and groaning, hugging the rim of the bin, and people were running to him with water and paper towels, trying to talk sense to him — as if he was vomiting out of perverse disloyalty to the team.

The retching finally stopped and he felt... better. Empty and clear-headed. He stood up and wiped his mouth with his sleeve. The faces staring at him all belonged to inconsequential strangers. His victory had been certain, the election his for the taking. And these slack-jawed fools, wallowing in their incompetence like a dog rolls in filth, had stolen it from him.

He was through with them.

George could dimly hear their shouted pleas as he left the building through a back door and headed out into a dark alleyway. He ran then, ran past the stinking dumpsters behind the restaurants, and rats scuttled out of his path. He came to the main street, full of action and light on this sweltering summer night. And he hated all these fools with their loud voices and their pointless revels. The City that had once been so glorious was sinking into a cesspool, and they didn't care. They didn't care that he alone could have rescued them.

"Let me be your saviour!" he had begged them. But no! They wanted his opponent, that fool... what was his name? Why bother trying to remember. It was over.

He ran across the street heedlessly, a delivery truck nearly ending his story. Maybe that would have been better... No! He was not the one who should be destroyed, all the others were. He imagined the City emptied of these fools. Without them, it would still gleam bright with promise, it would still burble with steam-driven genius. And he would walk the streets as Master, without all the idiot naysayers and vote-stealers, and then *he would finally get some real work done!*

Revolted by the howling crowds, he turned off the main street again and vanished behind, into the warren of laneways that good citizens know instinctively to avoid. But he had no fear. He was a survivor, a scuttling rat. He saw almost no one in his travels through the back passages of the City, and still fewer as the night wore on.

He was hungry. No, that wasn't it. He was tired. No, not exactly. He had to... get there. Where? To the end — the x-marked finish of this maze. What was it called? Oh yes: "The end of the line." Also: "Rock bottom."

He became aware that he was shouting. "I'm sorry! It wasn't my fault! Don't... Don't punish..." He slapped his hands across his treacherous mouth, but the sound of his voice seemed to echo on. He realized he was under a bridge, a mighty arc of steel struts that spanned one of the dirty trickles that fed the great river. Garbage choked the stream and garbage lined the concrete slope of the embankment. He dropped his hands from his mouth, but immediately screamed again, the sound exploding from him as the vomit had. And when the echoes finally died away, he thought he heard something. A murmur? The hissing passage of a small greasy animal? Or was it laughter?

"I'M NOT AFRAID OF YOU!" he shouted into the night, and he was proud of the hauteur of this pronouncement. He felt his sense of control returning. The night was hot and unbearably humid. Sweat soaked his shirt. (What had happened to his tie and jacket? He had been wearing those when he left his campaign headquarters.) And the voice returned, speaking all but inaudibly in a chittering whisper that, for all its obscurity, sounded perfectly reasonable. And with the voice came a breeze, deliciously cool. The whispering voice, the cooling breeze called him into the shadows under the bridge, and he accepted the invitation.

He disappeared into the darkness and followed the voices down into the underworld. And it was all right, wasn't it? There was nothing for him above.

And as the narrow tunnel steepened and a true chill entered his bones, he wondered if he was actually dying, walking willingly from this life into oblivion. But that was all right, wasn't it? What was the point of life if that which was owed him was denied.

The voices sniggered as if they found this idea amusing. Could they hear his thoughts? Anything was possible. The darkness was absolute, but he could feel that he had left the close confines of the tunnel and entered a great cavern. Little points of red began to appear in the darkness, little lights in pairs — red eyes, hundreds of them, watching him, waiting. It was one more event before one more crowd.

"Do you want to hear my acceptance speech?" he asked the assembly, and it seemed to him they did. "Citizens!" he proclaimed. "Tonight you have granted me a great honour, to take on the work I was born and raised to do, to carry on my family's tradition of service and leadership. Tonight when you tuck your children into their beds and lay your own heads on your pillows, I want you to dream. Dream of growth, dream of a future for your city that surpasses the glory of its past. And I will hear your dreams, and they will become my dreams. Or perhaps it is my dreams you are dreaming now! Perhaps I am already in your homes. That noise you hear in the night that awakens you, gasping, out of sleep — maybe it's me! Haha, a-hahaha! But do not worry. I am your friend, I am your father. I will lead you into the light!"

And even as George said the word, a light appeared to his left. It was just a faint glimmer, but he felt his heart gladden. He said nothing, but his lips formed words of gratitude. He walked to the light and found himself in another tunnel, descending at a gentle grade, and the light grew brighter and bigger, beckoning him with a promise of salvation. But I don't want salvation, he told the light. I want revenge! Still, there was no sense in turning back now, so he stumbled forward and emerged into a forest, deep and green and fresh of scent.

The old woman was seated on a rock, skinning a rabbit with a long, sharp knife. "Don't worry, George," she told him, wiping the gory blade on the hem of her dress. "You can have your revenge. You can have whatever you want. All it will cost you is your humanity — but that's no great sacrifice, is it?"

CHAPTER 21

The rain beat down on them relentlessly as they rode the white horse through the night. There were no gusts of wind, no rising crescendos of thunder; just a steady downpour that had soaked them to the skin so far back down the road, Barnabas could only suppose it was now soaking them to the soul. He and Graviddy didn't even attempt to shout to each other over the noise of the rain as they raced back to Pastoral Park. He didn't know what she was feeling as he held on to her tightly, but deep in his own belly, something awful was growing — a great, green worm, born of shock and despair, eating away at his sanity.

How was it possible, all he had learned in the last hour? The City compromised, the towers toppled! In his mind, he could see the great towers aflame, tumbling in slow motion down the cliff into the Valley. All the people in those glorious buildings would be killed, and everyone else in the City would be heartsick and fearful. He imagined his mother in that terrible tomorrow, afraid to leave the apartment like she had been in the months after his dad moved out.

And what of the Valley itself, gripped by the cold, iron fist of Carminn, its new dictator? Surely that was what Graviddy was thinking about as she urged the horse on through the darkness, because Carminn hated the circus with a vehemence that astonished Barnabas. When it came time to deal with the people of Pastoral Park, cruelty would inspire her creativity. Perhaps she'd send all the acrobats and clowns down into the mines.

Tragidenko and Falstep would end up chained together, breaking rocks in a quarry. He imagined Wickram red-faced in front of a smelting furnace, his guitar tossed into the heart of the inferno for fuel.

Feeling the rain abruptly lighten, Barnabas lifted his face from Graviddy's back and was surprised to find the dark shapes of trees rising around him. The leafy canopy on the road to Pastoral Park was sheltering them, welcoming them. The horse must have been tired from the long run, but it seemed glad to be home and picked up its pace, galloping through the parking lot, around the Big Top, and into the wide square in front of the dining hall. And as it came to a halt, sending gravel flying, many figures ran out from the building to intercept them. Barnabas recognized Sanjani, Whistlewort, and Kalarax among the faces as he and Graviddy were all but pulled from their mount. Barnabas stepped back into the darkness, out of the spotlight of their distress which, for now, was aimed entirely on her.

"Where have you been?!"

"We were flattened with worry for you!"

"This horse is not your personal pet, youngster!"

"Was this the tourist's idea?" *The tourist.* That meant him, Barnabas realized. This question, unsurprisingly, came from Whistlewort.

Graviddy stood her ground, hands across her chest, shouting down all comers: "This is a lot of teeth-cracking for nothing! I can take care of myself!"

And as Barnabas waited, cold and damp, the green worm of despair in his belly seemed to swell, to climb up his throat until he had to open his mouth and scream: "He's setting explosives in the City! He's going to blow up the towers and crash them down into the Valley!"

The whole group turned to him. There was no sound but the dull and constant rain which ran down his face and off his chin; only Barnabas knew that his tears were flowing with them. A gentle hand touched his arm; Garlip was standing beside him.

"Who's going to blow up the towers? What are you talking about?" she asked him gently.

And since it was she who asked, it was to her he spoke. "Glower! And he's doing it with Carminn." Saying it out loud should have been a relief, but right away he could hear how absurd it sounded, too huge and terrible to be possible.

The adults, who by now should have moved the party inside, stood looking at each other as the rain fell on their heads. Finally, Sanjani said to Graviddy, "Is this… true? Were you there, too, Graviddy?"

She gave Barnabas a desperate look before answering. "I was there. I saw… Well, they had this model of the City and… and they blew it up. But I didn't exactly hear what they…" The adults were again looking one to the other. "He's telling the truth!" she shouted. "I saw how they were talking!"

Whistlewort stepped forward and grabbed Barnabas by the arm. "You, Bulbous, come with us. We need to hear the whole story. Graviddy, take that horse back to the stable, dry him well and make sure he has food and water, then off to bed with you! No, Garlip, you too! Back to the dorms. This isn't your concern. And hold your gossiping tongues until we know something that doesn't sound like a tall tale." He turned to Sanjani. "Where's Dimitri? Still haunting the Big Top?"

"Probably. I'll get him."

Whistlewort was now pulling Barnabas into the dining hall like he was one of the stubborn mules from the stables; the other adults followed. They must have spent the last hours waiting there for him and Graviddy because several lanterns stood lit on one table, along with mugs of cooling coffee and an unfinished card game. Whistlewort deposited Barnabas at one end of the table, muttering, "Don't move." Kalarax emerged from the kitchen with a large towel which she draped over his shoulders, and one of the groundskeepers brought him a steaming mug of tea.

Sanjani and Tragidenko entered the dining hall, looking grim, and soon he had seven pairs of adult eyes staring at him as he shivered and sipped his tea.

"Start from the beginning," Tragidenko said in a deep, tired voice.

It took Barnabas a few seconds to decide just how far back the "beginning" was. He started by explaining about the *diaboriku*, how it had been lost in the City, and then found at the Drop Shop. Then he told them about Graviddy's offer to help him retrieve it. From there, Barnabas tried to remember every detail of their midnight trip to the Drop Shop although he was having trouble putting together the exact sequence of events. It was as if the whole narrative had become scrambled in his head when the deafening explosions went off around him. He felt like an idiot. He felt like a liar.

Tragidenko, seated directly opposite him, combed his beard with his fingers throughout the recitation. When there was nothing left to say, the

Maestro just shook his head. "But that is madness! What would be the point of such a … such a conflagration?"

Barnabas' voice shook as he answered, "Glower said it was revenge! Against… against the fools and the ones who didn't… I'm not sure."

Sanjani came to sit beside him. She put a hand on his hand. "And you say you met Glower in the City? The day before you came here?"

"Yes. I saw him once at Admiral Crumhorn Station, and then he was outside my school. I talked to him then." He was aware of flies buzzing at the windows, searching for a way out.

Sanjani gave him a sad look like she pitied him. "But Barnabas, dear, that's not possible. George Glower — anyone who moves here from the City, me included — we can't get travel passes. We can never go back."

Whistlewort said, "I'm not even sure we can get *you* back up there. Not legally anyway."

Barnabas felt his throat close around a lump — the anxiety worm returning. "But Glower was there! I saw him!"

Kalarax said in a reasonable voice, "Was he on the train with you?"

"N-no."

She continued: "He could never get past the Aqua Guard at the Frontier, Barnabas. Coming or going."

"Then he came some other way!"

"There is no other way."

Barnabas looked at Sanjani. "Through the forest… You asked if I came through the forest."

Sanjani shook her head forcefully. "It's not a highway! You can't just come and go. You have to be… guided." She seemed embarrassed, like it was hard for her to say these words in front of the others. And, in fact, they were all looking away, or down at the table, and Barnabas had a strong sense he better just shut up.

Tragidenko shook his long grey curls. "No! We cannot go to the Guild Council with this. Where is the proof? He is just a stranger — a boy we don't know! A boy who shouldn't even be here. And Carminn! Can you imagine this? After the Clouders and that… that terrible visit? No, we would be setting ourselves up for derisions and disasters." The man put his hands on the table and heaved himself to his feet, causing all the lanterns and mugs to dance and sway. "Everybody go to sleep now. This is nonsense. I am sorry, young man, but… No, not possible."

He turned and swept out of the room. Sanjani patted Barnabas' arm. "Perhaps you should go sleep somewhere else tonight," she said. "It's just, with all this, and Wickram not... himself..." Barnabas felt like he had been slapped, thrown out of his shelter into the rain and wind. Sanjani wouldn't even look him in the eye as she said, "Kalarax will help you find a place at the dorms." And with that she stood and hurried after her husband.

There was nothing more to be said. The mugs were cleared away, and they all filed out into the night. The rain was now just a drizzle, but the air was bleak and cold. It was the middle of the night, and Barnabas was exhausted, defeated and alone. As he followed Kalarax across the square, he became aware that people were walking beside him: Garlip and then Graviddy.

Quietly, as if the night couldn't stand any more agitation, Garlip said, "Here, you left these in the Big Top." She handed him his cell phone and his bowler hat. He smiled his gratitude, but mostly he felt guilty for almost losing them, like he had lost the *diaboriku*. As he placed the phone in his pocket and the hat on his head, he wondered if he should ever be trusted with anything important again.

Then Graviddy grabbed his arm, and stopped him in his tracks. "I'm sorry," she said. She looked down into his eyes, and all her usual tough confidence was missing. "Please don't think I don't believe you. I-I didn't know what to say when they asked me. And they were all so looming and fire-eyed, you know? I was weak."

Looking into those beautiful eyes, Barnabas felt his misery lift off him. He said, "No, you were fine. You were great!"

"No, *you* were. You were incredibly brave back at the Drop Shop. I was really impressed." She leaned down to plant a soft kiss right on his startled lips. Before his mind could settle again in his skull, she had pulled away.

And it was all just about as perfect as anything Barnabas could imagine, until he heard Garlip say, "Uh, guys?" Looking up, he saw Wickram, smudgy with rain and blurry with drink, staggering towards him, fists raised.

"You little weasel! You rat!" Wickram screamed, simultaneously grabbing Barnabas by the shirt like he was going to kill him, and leaning on him for support. The two of them staggered backwards a few steps, a pair of clumsy dancers, as Wickram shouted into his ear: "Riding off with her! Kissing her! All this time... thought you were my friend! You-you came down to the Valley to steal my girlfriend, you traitor!"

Wickram tried to stand up and punch him, but it was a wild jab that just half-caught Barnabas on the side of the neck, and sent Wickram spinning sideways. At that moment, Huro and Buro appeared from somewhere, catching the boy before he could fall over into a puddle.

"Whoa! Easy, Wick!," Huro said in a soothing sing-song. "You don't want to go hitting Barnabas. He's your buddy." The twins looked like two cowboys trying to capture a bronco.

Buro said, "Just a little misunderstanding, right Graviddy?"

Graviddy was furious, all her previous tenderness gone. "Great grick-licking pugglenuts, Wickram! Is this pathetic performance still going on? Or is this the second show?!"

Huro was still using his calming voice (though it was starting to sound desperate): "No, everything's fine, Graviddy! We were just heading off to bed, weren't we, Wick?" while Wickram tried to break free and get back to pummelling Barnabas.

Barnabas shouted, "Wickram, honest, I would never try and take your girl —"

Graviddy cut him off. "Shut up, Barnabas. And you, Wickram..." She marched right up to him and shoved a finger into his chest. "I will ride with who I like, I will kiss who I like. Is that clear?" Wickram stopped fighting. He slumped back against Buro, looking pathetic, his long hair hanging limply around his face like seaweed.

"Children!" Kalarax called out, and they all stopped where they were. "It's almost two in the morning. I think it's time we were all in bed." It wasn't expressed as an order, but they understood that it was. They got in line behind their teacher like a ragged parade of wounded veterans. Huro and Buro supported Wickram, who now seemed all but asleep on his feet. Garlip walked wearily beside Barnabas, no longer looking at him. Graviddy walked alone. No one spoke. Soon they were at the dorms, a series of two-story buildings of concrete, wood and glass. They were just passing through a playground that stood beside one of the entrances when a strong, bony hand grabbed Barnabas by the arm. Exhausted, his nerves frayed, he cried out and spun around, finding himself staring up into Whistlewort's weather-beaten face.

"You'll need proof," the old man said in a low, harsh voice, his eyes bright in the dark night.

"Wh-what?"

"Your story is crazy as a fever dream, but you got no reason to make it up. Who knows what madness goes on Glower's head. Look at him! Wandering around in the Tumbles all day, just daring Father Glory to squash him like horse fly! But Carminn? She's something altogether different. I know exactly what's cooking in that pot: lust for power, hot and spicy as a rabbit ragout."

Barnabas' heart was pounding. "But no one's going to help! Tragidenko said —"

"No, he's right — Pastoral Park can't be advocating for you; we can't afford to expose our belly like that. No, you need the Guild Council to take action on its own. But no one's gonna believe as much as a goat raisin that comes out o' your mouth unless you get some more proof. And if you expect the Council to go up against Carminn and the Clouders — well, you better have something crackin' good to show."

"How do I...?"

"Tomorrow. We'll do something about it in the morning. Now, you go sleep. Yer gonna need a lot of strength if you want to save your City."

The old man seemed to melt back into the night. When Barnabas turned around, the kids and Kalarax were all clustered by the entrance of the dorm, watching him in silence. It was time to go to sleep and as Whistlewort said, to gather strength for the fight ahead.

* * *

He was in a rowboat on a river. It was the rowboat from his uncle and aunt's cottage, chipped red paint across an aluminum landscape of dings and gouges. The oars squeaked in the locks as he pulled them smoothly through the crystalline water. The landscape, sumptuous with flowers and large lazy butterflies, sped by surprisingly quickly.

"You've gotten so strong," his mother said, and he smiled proudly. For once she was the passenger and he the driver. Of course, he couldn't see where he was going; this was something that had never made sense to him about rowboats: the way they plunged boldly into the future, while the driver could only see the past. But he felt happy, and his mother, under a straw sunhat, her eyes closed and her lips curled into a gentle smile, was happy too.

The current was swift now, and a roar was growing behind him. His mother opened her eyes and said over the rising din, "Whatever happens,

Barnabas, I love you." Alarmed, he tried to turn and see what was coming, but he found he could not move his head. He could only stare into his mother's face, calm and serious as she repeated: "Barnabas, Barnabas," more like chanting a mantra than calling his name. He tried to steer the boat to the riverbank, but he wasn't strong enough to fight the current. "Barnabasbarnabas…"And then they were tumbling over the falls, falling into the abyss…

"Barnabas…" Garlip said, shaking him, and he jerked awake, his heart pounding. The girl was sitting on the edge of his bed, Huro and Buro standing behind her. "You having a bad dream?"

"Not sure…" he managed. He remembered something about falling, but the dream had already faded to a fog of feeling, devoid of incident.

"'Cause you were barking and snarling in your sleep," she said with grin. "Paws running, the whole thing."

Huro put a hand on each of her arms and tugged her up to standing. "Okay, Garlip, no girls allowed here! Meet us in the playground in five."

Buro shut the door firmly behind them and re-joined his brother, staring down at Barnabas with something that almost looked like concern. "You okay?" he asked. "Ready to face the day?"

Their attention embarrassed him. "Yeah," he said, his voice hoarse. He cleared his throat. He was in the lower berth of a set of bunk beds, looking up at the springs of the upper berth.

"Whistlewort told us you might be in shock from, uh, everything last night," said Huro. "He said we shouldn't hurry you too much. But, anyway, if you could hurry *just a bit…*"

Barnabas sat up and put his feet down on the scuffed hardwood floor. He was embarrassed to find himself in just his underwear; he could hardly remember getting into bed. "What time is it?" he asked.

"8:30," answered Buro. "We let you sleep as long as we could."

Barnabas nodded, noting a soreness in his neck where Wickram had punched him. He felt a sudden heaviness at the thought that his new friend now apparently hated him. This moment of melancholy was like a rock thrown into a pool of sorrow, and out from it, ripples of misery spread, from miniscule to mammoth. First, there was the way the adults had acted, treating him like a liar and an outsider that they couldn't trust. Then there was the possibility that he would be stuck in the Valley for maybe months until they figured out a way to get him home. Only then could he think of the worst thing of all: the plan to knock down the towers. He had allowed himself not to think of this right away, like his brain had to warm up before it could cope with that level of epic hopelessness. He felt the weight of impossible responsibility pushing down on his shoulders. It was up to him to find proof of Glower's plan and convince the Guild Council to stop him. The task seemed impossible.

Huro and Buro, meanwhile, were moving swiftly around the small room which, Barnabas realized, must be their dorm. Everything was neat and tidy, the books on the shelf, the papers on the desk. A chin-up bar was screwed into the wall, and on another was a watercolour of two little boys, maybe 8 years old, standing on the handlebars of two bicycles, ridden by a man and woman, going round the ring of the Big Top.

Barnabas asked, "Is this your room? Is that your family in the picture?"

The twins were filling up their backpacks with all kinds of things — rope, water bottles, a telescope. "Yup," said Huro.

"And yup," said Buro as he pulled Barnabas' clothes, neatly folded, out of a dresser drawer and handed them to him. The twins were wearing denim shorts and bright, short-sleeved tunics as well as flat-soled shoes, kneepads and goggles that gave them a sort of insectoid look.

Catching something of their energy, Barnabas stood up and dressed quickly. He turned around to make his bed and found himself face to face with Wickram, who was lying on the top bunk. Startled, Barnabas called out, "Woop!" and put his hands in front of his face as if to ward off a blow. Except that Wickram was fast asleep, a trail of drool running from his mouth to pool on the mattress. As Barnabas stared, the sleeper's eyes slowly opened. The two boys stared at each other, and then Wickram's mouth moved. He was saying something, but it wasn't really audible. Barnabas thought it might have been "sorry," but it just as easily could have been "porridge." Wickram's eyes closed again.

On one of the desks, he spotted his few possessions: there was his bowler hat, and beside it his phone and the *diaboriku*. He put the phone in his pocket, but there was no reason to bring the toy and risk losing it again. Furthermore, he decided to leave the hat behind, too. This morning, he didn't feel like he had the right to wear such a fine thing, to be the guy who could be *that* guy. Maybe once he had convinced the Guild Council to save the City, he would again feel special enough to wear it.

He went down the hall to the washroom where he peed and washed his face. There was no towel around, so he dried himself on his t-shirt, only it wasn't his t-shirt, he reminded himself; it was Wickram's. He exited just as Huro and Buro were marching down the hall past him, now wearing what seemed to be leather aviator helmets. The twins swept him up in their wake, and propelled him out into the morning. They found Garlip in the rather rundown playground outside. She was leaning against a balance beam and drawing with a pencil in a black-bound sketchbook. The sky was still dotted with clouds, and the breeze was a bit stiff, but the sun was strong and promised a good day. Barnabas asked, "Are we going to the dining hall for breakfast?"

Garlip snapped her sketchbook closed and answered, "We already ate. Here." She pulled a fresh cinnamon bun out of a paper bag and handed it to him. Until the warm, buttery smell entered his nostrils and made his stomach growl, he hadn't realized just how hungry he was. He began taking big bites out of the pastry.

"Then where *are* we going?" he asked stickily.

"On an expedition," Huro said. "To get proof of Glower and Carminn's plan." He jumped up and grabbed the bar of the jungle gym and began doing pull ups.

Barnabas felt a weight lift off his chest. "You mean... you believe me?"

"Whistlewort does," said Buro as he jumped up and joined his brother. "So it must be true. He told us all about it this morning." The boys were surprisingly strong despite their slim frames, and clearly trying to outdo each other.

Garlip gave Buro a sharp look. "Who cares about the old mulemonger? We believed you from the start!"

The boys jumped down and led the group around the end of the dorm building where a large field of grass almost glowed with green vitality. And there, leaning against the wall were four bicycles.

Buro said, "Whistlewort offered us a mule cart, but we figured we'd make better time if we borrowed these from my family." He and Huro immediately started doing routine checks on the vehicles, feeling tire pressure with their fingers, spinning the wheels and squinting to gauge their trueness. Thoughtfully, the twins had provided Barnabas with the smallest of the bikes, though he was starting to get sick of being reminded how short he was compared to everyone else in the Valley.

The four of them mounted their vehicles and took some experimental circuits across the grass, ending up as if by mutual agreement facing each other in a conspiratorial circle in the centre of the field. Garlip said, "Okay, City boy. Where to?"

Barnabas was startled. "Huh? I don't know! I hardly know the Valley at all yet."

"Back to the Drop Shop?" Huro suggested.

Barnabas thought about this. "No, there's no way to sneak up on the place. Especially by day. Besides, they're packing everything up. Won't be any evidence left."

"Well, what else did Carminn and Glower say?" asked Buro. "Anything useful?"

Barnabas thought about it. "Glower said something about leaving at 11:30 today. Carminn, um, she said she would make the arrangements. What do you think that means? Is there a train going to the City this morning?"

"Nope, not on Saturday," Buro said, and Huro added, "Besides, Glower can't get a travel permit. So there's no way he could make it through the frontier."

Garlip bit off a corner of fingernail, spat it out and said, "If Carminn offered to make these mysterious *arrangements*, then it must be something over at Clouding Town. That's where we should start."

Having encountered Clouders a few times already, Barnabas wasn't thrilled with the idea, even though it made sense.

"A plan is born," said Huro.

"Sure, just Pastoral Park returning the visit," said Buro.

"Let's ride!" they shouted in unison, and Huro added: "But fast and quiet. We're kind of not supposed to be leaving Pastoral Park."

"Or taking the bikes," Buro added.

CHAPTER 22

Flying down the long, winding hill from Pastoral Park on a ridiculously effortless bicycle with the wind in his ears was, for Barnabas, somewhere between terrific fun and fundamental terror. Huro and Buro were whooping like howler monkeys (which was worrying, since they had just insisted the four of them make a quiet getaway), weaving in and around each other while Barnabas was basically hanging on for dear life. He could easily imagine one moment of inattention landing him in a pothole that would send him flying over his handlebars to a messy death. But, at the same time, he didn't want to pump his brakes the whole way down like a loser and end up at the bottom 10 minutes after the others.

Then Huro was at his side, saying, "Un-clench, man. It's more dangerous to ride all tense like that. Drop your shoulders, open your chest, and look up! That's it; feel the road through your wheels. Breathe. Good." And then Huro pumped his legs like a charging rabbit and pulled ahead, swinging his feet up onto his handlebars in an insane show of nonchalance as he swerved in front of his brother.

With this bit of professional advice under his belt, Barnabas actually enjoyed the final leg of the descent. He wasn't even the last to the bottom; Garlip, he saw, was still far behind him, and he stopped to wait for her. She rolled up a minute later, looking less than thrilled.

"Well, that was … exciting," Barnabas said.

She rolled her eyes and tightened the elastic that held her ponytail.

"Sometimes the performers forget that not everyone is a suicidal daredevil exhibitionist. Some of us just wield a mean pencil."

Barnabas laughed. "Hey, don't be modest. I saw you in class the other day; you juggle just like they do."

"Oh, we all have to learn basic circus skills, but some of us get laughed at more than others."

The twins were waiting for them down the road, so they started riding again, but now both of them were smiling. And who wouldn't be happy to be riding the road through the fresh morning air while the sun played tag with the clouds? For the first time in days, Barnabas felt like his life wasn't totally out of control. Heck, he had a *gang*! And they were all heading off to get the proof he needed to save the City.

He followed his new friends down a road he hadn't travelled before, southwest on an oblique trajectory toward the cliff. Huge, grey pipelines criss-crossed the landscape, carrying the groundwater from under Lake Lucid to a cluster of factory buildings on their left.

Garlip said, "That's Coursing Guild's main filtration and pumping plants. Some of the buildings go back 80 years or more. I love all the decorative stonework. If you look way up on those towers, you can even see statues of water nymphs and sea monsters."

She was right — architecturally, the buildings were beautiful; their honey-coloured stone and their sculptures reminded him of Admiral Crumhorn Station, and maybe the buildings were from the same period. But all the same, with dozens of pipes going in and out, the Coursing Works reminded him more of his biology class. They had spent most of the winter with diagrams of human anatomy, labeling all the ducts, tubules, alimentaries, and arteries that kept the body going. The whole Valley, he realized, existed to keep the City running in much the same way. And like the unseen organs just beneath the skin, the Valley was right there but hidden. Maybe it wasn't so surprising that generations of City leaders could keep it a secret from the public. Who wants to think about the guts when they could be concentrating on the pretty surface?

Once they rode past the Coursing Works, some of the pipes gathered together into one huge one that ran along the road beside them. Barnabas had lost sight of Huro and Buro, but then Garlip pointed upwards, and he saw the twins were riding on top of the giant water pipe, which hummed and hammered rhythmically under their wheels.

From the driver's window of a passing truck, a man yelled up to them, "Hey, get off of there! That's not safe!" The huge dog beside him in the cab barked its agreement. Huro and Buro saluted in unison and turned their wheels sharply so the bikes flew through the air. They bounced down onto a lower pipe, and then down into a ditch beside the road where they disappeared for a moment before springing back into view like wheeled panthers. Barnabas hooted in appreciation and pumped his fist in the air. The truck drove on, the driver shaking his head.

Further down the road, with the cliff looming overhead, they came to a small town. It consisted of short, unadorned housing blocks and communal buildings, all built from the same rust-coloured brick. Dominating the town as the Big Top dominated Pastoral Park, stood an imposing, red-brick church with two tall spires. Behind the church, right up against the cliff face, was a huge industrial building that spewed smoke and steam into the sky. This town, of course, was the home of Clouding Guild, who produced the steam that provided the City with power and heat. Myriad steam pipes emerged from the top of the plant and snaked their way up the cliff to the City.

The little bicycle gang was anything but inconspicuous as they rode through the streets of Clouding Town. The denizens that passed them were either dressed in simple grey, like the contingent that had visited the circus, or else in work clothes, from simple coveralls to variations on the masked monsters Barnabas had seen on the subway. More than once, massive dogs, wearing tool-encrusted harnesses barked at them savagely. Even so, none of the Clouders gave them more than a curious glance. Huro and Buro led them down an alleyway where they parked the bikes.

The twins pushed their goggles up on their foreheads and Huro said, "Where do we start?"

Garlip wiped the sweat off her forehead with her sleeve. "Everything at Clouding starts with a prayer, so I guess we better go offer our respects."

They were soon standing in the courtyard in front of the great church, looking up the wide steps that led to the massive front doors. Shiny steel panels on the doors were embossed with an image of Father Glory. The deity's hands were raised in fists, holding bunches of lightning bolts the way a child clutches wildflowers. He didn't look happy with the work of his earthly followers.

"Not the friendliest place I've ever seen," muttered Buro, sounding a little less sure of the mission.

Barnabas felt the cold, hard eyes of Father Glory boring into him as if the old god was wondering what treachery he was up to. Barnabas had to remind himself that this fierce steel personage was merely a long-dead Guild Council President, not some avenging deity.

"Are we even allowed to be here?" he asked. "It's obvious we're not from Clouding."

"Doesn't matter," said Garlip, cutting through their little worried clump and marching confidently up to the doors. "Any believers are welcome here. My family used to come on all the important festivals."

"Lucky you," said Huro, flexing and releasing his fists nervously.

Garlip smiled. "Check this out." She pulled down a lever beside the doors and, with a great hiss and a cloud of steam, they parted majestically. The group walked inside through the dissipating cloud. They found themselves in a large foyer at the back of the sanctuary.

Garlip explained what they were looking at: "The entrance to the Clouding Works is behind the church. You're supposed to offer prayer every day before beginning your shift. See? You leave your gear and your dogs in that holding area, and then proceed into the sanctuary proper."

Barnabas had to lean close to hear her. The huge hall with its high-vaulted ceiling ate up her voice and returned only garbled echoes. Suddenly the air was shaken by great bursts of organ. There was no melody, just some kind of random pattern of notes that didn't belong to any normal scale and failed to line up into a regular 1-2-3-4. It was powerful but not beautiful. Clouds of steam shot into the air from the organ's pipes which were everywhere in the hall, in little clusters of two and three, or in massive banks. They looked a lot like the steam pipes rising up the cliff outside.

"Come on, the service is starting," Garlip shouted over the organ's cacophony. "Just follow me in and do what I do." They walked like a line of baby ducks behind her, down the central aisle between the rows of pews. On the walls were more renditions of Father Glory, overseeing different accomplishments of the guilds. In these paintings, he appeared to be a normal human, wearing a black suit and tie and something on his head which could have been a hardhat or a halo, depending on how you looked at it.

But the truly impressive part of the sanctuary was up at the front. The whole area around the pulpit was in slow, steam-powered, clockwork motion. The sections of the stage were circling slowly, and the nave rose and fell as if floating on an ocean. Above it all stood a huge and much more stylized incarnation of Father Glory, supporting the whole world in his raised hands. This clockwork globe teemed with figures of working men and women who travelled in and out of little doors as they dug in the earth, stoked the furnaces, hauled the ore, or built houses. Steam escaped from vents throughout the diorama, including from Glory's nose and ears, leaving the air in the sanctuary distinctly humid.

Halfway to the front, Garlip stopped and lowered her head. She brought her closed right fist to her chest and then up to her forehead, saluting the churning spectacle at the front. The twins and Barnabas did the same in clumsy unison, and then followed Garlip into one of the rows of pews.

The organ's almost random spattering of dark notes gathered together into a single held chord, and then with another loud exhalation of steam, the rotating floor of the stage brought a priestly figure forward to his place at the pulpit. All movement and music stopped, and he began the service.

Barnabas checked the time on his phone: 10:47. He whispered to Garlip, "How long will the service take? If this is where Glower is going, he's probably already here."

"Just 20 minutes. There's a service every half hour. They're crazy fanatics, but they don't let it slow down their production schedule. Too bad we're not at one of the really busy services between 6 and 7 in the morning. We wouldn't stand out so much."

Barnabas had only been to houses of worship a few times in his life, always for some celebratory event — wedding, christening, bar mitzvah. As usual, he found it hard to focus on the words of the priest. He caught something about, "He loves the sweat of your brow and eases the ache in your back," but then he gave up and started looking around instead, peering through the lingering wisps of sacramental steam into the dim corridors that flanked the sanctuary.

"There!" he whispered, a bit too loud, pointing, drawing annoyed glances from the worshippers sitting nearby. He lowered his voice. "That's Carminn, isn't it? Just walking past those pillars there."

Huro squinted. "Not sure… Yes! That's her."

Buro nodded. "Looks like she's in a hurry."

"Let's go!" Barnabas hissed, rising to his feet.

Garlip looked alarmed. "No, we can't leave in the middle of the service. Everyone will notice!"

But Barnabas was already making his way back to the centre aisle. "We can't afford to lose her," he said over his shoulder. He started hurrying back up the aisle, hearing the others clattering loudly out of the pews and following him. At the back of the sanctuary, he turned and headed down the corridor where he had seen the lumbering figure. He wasn't exactly running, but he was being reckless; he knew should slow down and not draw so much attention to himself. But he couldn't afford to lose her! Time was running out!

"Well, Father bless me, if it isn't Tragidenko's Big Top!"

Barnabas stopped. He and the rest of his gang turned to face the young man who had spoken. It took Barnabas a few seconds to place the face. He had been part of the Clouding contingent that had come to watch the circus — the only one who had appeared to enjoy the show.

Simultaneously, Huro said, "No, that's not us," and Buro said, "So what? We're allowed to be here."

The young man put a finger to his lips and said, "You better follow me."

Garlip put her arms across her chest. "What? You're arresting us? You haven't got the authority to charge anyone from another —"

The young man raised his hands in supplication. "Be Calm! I'm not your problem. But there are others here who would be less than pleased by your visit."

As they followed the young Clouder, Barnabas turned back one more time, seeing Carminn disappearing around a corner. She was carrying something, about the size of a cigarette case, that swung in her hand on the end of a long chain. It was all he could do to stop himself running after her.

The young man led them through a small, anonymous door into a narrow, dimly lit hallway which was short enough that everyone except Barnabas had to stoop as they walked. But even with sufficient headroom, Barnabas didn't like being in the dark, cramped corridor. It seemed to be pressing in on him on all sides and making him feel queasy. They travelled down the long corridor for a minute or more before the young man opened another door that led into a small room. Mercifully, it had a higher ceiling. They all sat down at a large, round table, watching each other warily. Everything was furred in dust including a pencil that might well have been lying on the table untouched for years.

Like the other members of Clouding Guild that Barnabas had seen, the young man's body under his loose grey clothes was broad and solid. The wrists sticking out the sleeves of his tunic were as thick as fire logs and his fingers, interlaced on the table in front of him, looked like they could tear the tops off cans of beans without an opener. But his face was surprisingly delicate: pale, freckled skin under copper-red hair, with a thin nose and gentle blue eyes that looked at each of them in turn, curious but not suspicious.

"No one uses this room anymore; we can talk safely here," said the young man. "I'm Sensash. I'm a student, but I'm also a member of Clouding's Convention of Elders — the newest member, in fact. Inherited the post from my father when he died in January."

"I'm sorry," said Garlip.

Sensash bowed his head for a moment and said, "Thank you. Now, you're obviously not here to pray. Any fool can see that, and you're lucky that the only fool who did is me. So what *do* you want in Clouding Town?"

The twins and Garlip all looked at Barnabas. He hated being singled out, but it was for his sake that they were here, so he gathered up his courage and spoke. He introduced himself and explained George Glower's plot to fell the City's towers. This made Sensash's copper eyebrows rise, but it was when Barnabas told him about Carminn's involvement that he was truly startled.

He said, "What? Why would she do such a thing?" More than startled, he seemed angry, his hands uncoupling and forming two fists on the dusty table.

Barnabas, afraid he had said too much and ruined the whole thing, began to stammer: "Something about… like… She wants to take over… Council…"

It was Garlip who stepped in to save him from complete incoherence. "Come on, Sensash, isn't it obvious? You saw her at Pastoral Park last night. You know her better than we do! She wants an excuse to take over the Valley, make everyone utter bitterroot devotees, chop Mother Mercy out of the sacred family and, you know, end *laughter* forever!"

Sensash pushed his chair away from the table and sprang to his feet. He began pacing the room, sending up clouds of dust in his wake. They all watched, and Barnabas wondered if they should maybe just run away now before he called the Aqua Guard — or Carminn — and had them arrested. But then Sensash, staring into the corner of the room, said, "It's... terrible." Silence for a long held breath. "But possible." He turned to look at Barnabas. "You're not from the Valley, are you?"

Nervously. "No. How can you tell?"

"You don't fit in. Your size obviously, but the way you talk, the way you move." He shook his head, clearly trying to decide their fate. "What do you want here at Clouding?"

Stronger now. "To find proof for the Guild Council, so they can stop Glower and Carminn."

"And what can I do to help?"

Barnabas sighed with relief. "I don't know exactly. Glower said he's going to the City this morning. At 11:30. Carminn said she would, uh, make the arrangements."

Sensash pulled a watch on a chain from his tool belt and consulted it. "But there is no way up to the City from the Clouding Works," he said.

Huro leaned forward, "Yeah, but Carminn's here. And she looked kinda... purposeful."

"She was carrying a switching key," Sensash murmured. He raised his hands. "Come, quickly. It's already 11:15 and I think she's heading for the Routing Depot."

They returned to the tight corridor and Barnabas had to set his teeth against his discomfort. *What's wrong with me?* he wondered. But they were on the move now! Something was happening! At the end of the corridor was a door. Sensash pulled a key from his tunic and turned it in a large keyhole. Steam released from two vents above the door, and it slid smoothly open. He motioned for them to wait while he peeked around the corner and then waved them through the door.

"This passage is rarely used these days, but keep close to the wall and run back to the door if I signal you." They moved along quickly but silently until Sensash whispered, "Wait here," and disappeared around the corner. He reappeared after a minute, carrying a bundle of grey cloth. "I have an idea how to get Barnabas into the Routing Depot," he said. "But we'll have to wait a few minutes." He sat on the floor and indicated for them to do the same.

Barnabas whispered, "What's a Routing Depot, anyway?"

"It's where all the steam pipes converge before they head up to the City. It's where the individual line pressures are controlled. I think Carminn is going there."

Sitting cross-legged beside Sensash, Garlip whispered, "You said you're a student. What are you studying?"

"Oh, you know," he answered. "Steam and Spirit." They all looked at him blankly. "I guess you don't know. It's a combined course in Theology and Mechanical Engineering. It's pretty much the most common course at Clouding Academy." He peeked around the corner and motioned them to their feet. He shook out the grey bundle, which turned out to be some kind of long robe. "Put this on," he told Barnabas. It was like a monk's habit and Barnabas felt all kinds of dumb in it.

Sensash considered him. "Pull the hood up, and keep your head lowered. Let the hem drag; it will cover those shoes of yours. Those are utter wrong."

He took Barnabas by the shoulders and steered him to the end of the corridor. Together they looked around the corner. Barnabas saw a line of grey monks approaching, heads lowered. They looked just the same as he did, and they were all around his height. They all carried little twigs, holding them up in their right hands. At the head of the procession was an adult Clouding woman, dressed the same, but with her head uncovered and a menacing wooden rod in her hand.

Sensash, standing behind him, whispered in his ear. "When they pass, quickly join the line."

"Who are they?"

"Acolytes of the Vapour — it's a ceremony all the eleven-year-olds do." (*I'm the size of an eleven year old Clouder,* Barnabas thought, chagrined) "They're on their way to feed the holy fires. They have to walk through the Routing Depot to get to the Hall of Conflagration. You'll ditch the group there, find someplace to hide, and watch for Carminn and Glower."

The line was passing now, and he and Sensash flattened themselves against the wall. "Go!" he hissed.

Barnabas was about to say, *But I don't have a twig,* when Sensash pushed him forward. He almost tripped on the long hem of the robe, and he had to lift it to scramble into position. He got into the rhythm of the line and then let the robe fall to cover his sneakers.

The acolyte in front of him, the same height as Barnabas but still with the treble voice of a boy whispered, "Don't fool around, Marnn! You'll get us in trouble."

Barnabas wasn't Marnn, but he made a kind of high-ish grunt that he hoped would pass for an imitation. He tugged the hood down farther and stared at his feet as they walked. The line snaked around two more corners, before entering some new area where the tap tap of their shoes on the concrete floor produced a noticeable echo. Barnabas peeked up and saw that they were in a vast space with a high ceiling, many stories over their heads. Here, all the steam ducts came together and rose in parallel up the walls, like the pipes of a huge organ, before disappearing through the roof. Through the large, dirty windows above them, Barnabas could see the pipes strapped to the cliff face, climbing towards the City.

The woman leading the group was standing off to the side of the line, and Barnabas dropped his head again as he passed her. "Keep up!" she barked. "How can you be in step with the Mighty Father's plans if you aren't even in step with your classmates?" She gave him a sharp whack on the shoulder with her stick, and he yelped. It took all his self-control not to turn and tell her where to stick the stick. But his bigger problem was how to escape the group while under such careful scrutiny. The line turned the corner, leaving the woman behind. He knew he had only moments until she re-joined them. Immediately to their left was a workstation, covered in pressure gauges and levers, and he jumped behind it. Crouching there as the line moved on without him, he watched the woman pass and follow after her acolytes.

Barnabas held his breath and waited for the sound of their footsteps to vanish before he pulled off the scratchy grey habit. He rubbed his itchy back against a corner of the workstation, as he pulled his phone from his pocket. *11:25.* He ran back around the corner to the Routing Depot, where he thumbed on the camera and took a picture of the deserted room. A flash illuminated the space and the camera said, "Click!" Barnabas hastily turned off both flash and audio. Here in the cavernous hall, dozens of workstations controlled the passage of steam. The place looked like a control room at NASA, and the complete absence of people seemed eerie and wrong.

Barnabas heard voices. Ducking behind a workstation, he saw Carminn enter; beside her was George Glower. Instead of his usual coveralls, he wore a grey suit, a powder blue shirt and a pale yellow tie. His shoes needed a shine, but they were pretty decent dress shoes. On his back, clashing with his professional attire, was an enormous khaki backpack, complete with a sleeping bag rolled up at the top as if he was going camping. Barnabas snapped three, four, five pictures of them. Without a flash, the pictures would all turn out a little dark and blurry, but he hoped that viewed together, they would clearly show the identities of the pair.

"Where is everyone?" Glower asked, sounding tense.

Carminn looked over her shoulder as if making sure there were no witnesses. "I cancelled the shift. No one will be here for an hour." She walked Glower around the corner, into the other wing of the L-shaped room. Barnabas sprinted quietly across the floor and found a vantage point behind a locker, amazingly close to them. Carminn was mounting the steps up to where one of the biggest steam pipes began its climb up the wall. She pulled a key from her tunic and opened a nearly invisible door in the side of the pipe.

Glower climbed the stairs and stepped right through the door, flicking on a light inside. Barnabas could see that it was a tiny room with a single small bench — like a space capsule within the pipe. He zoomed his camera in on the door and began snapping pictures. Glower leaned out of the capsule to talk to Carminn, and Barnabas snapped even more.

"Everything's on schedule," Glower said. "You need to be ready on Tuesday. Everything will happen at 1430 hours."

He slammed the door, and Carminn hurried down the steps to take her position behind the closest workstation. She was holding the little box on the long chain that Sensash called the "switching key." It was covered in bumps and rods, and she fitted it into a corresponding depression in the panel. After she performed a complex sequence of button-pushing and dial-turning, Barnabas heard rumblings beneath his feet. The big pipe began to vibrate. Carminn stared at a gauge on the panel, watching the needle rise closer and closer to the red. When it reached some optimal point, she threw over the large lever in front of her. Hissing steam vented from two small nozzles, and the big pipe shook and rumbled as if it was going to explode. Barnabas could hear a terrible clattering sound inside which quickly diminished. Carminn's eyes ascended the pipe, looking through the rooftop window and up the cliff. Barnabas suddenly understood: the capsule containing George Glower had just shot up, like a cannonball in a steam-powered cannon, through the pipe and up to the City. That was Glower's secret route: a private steam-powered express elevator.

Barnabas raised the phone and took picture after picture , though there was nothing new to capture. He hoped he had enough evidence — *oh, please, let it be enough!* — to convince the Guild Council of his story. Then his responsibility would be over, and it would be up to them to save the City.

CHAPTER 23

Events were transpiring quickly. It had only been last night when Barnabas had uncovered the horrible plot on the City. By noon, he and his friends had already gathered the evidence they needed to back up his words. It had been enough proof to convince Maestro Tragidenko to contact the Guild Council and get an emergency session called for that evening. Soon, the appropriate authorities would know about Glower and Carminn's plans and they would take decisive action.

The last of the day was vanishing behind the trees as Barnabas, alongside Whistlewort, Sanjani and Tragidenko, crossed the dry lake bed of Lake Lucid in Pastoral Park's most luxurious mule cart, complete with padded benches and polished kerosene lanterns. Because of the gravity of the occasion, they were all dressed up in a manner the circus folk called "formal." To Barnabas' eye, it seemed more "carnival." Tragidenko, in a hunter green suit and orange cravat still looked like he was about stand up in the ring and announce the arrival of the clowns. Whistlewort was in a long yellow coat and pointy leather boots that made Barnabas think of a jazz musician from the '40s, while Sanjani's dress was printed with enormous, blood-red poppy flowers from whose capacious mouths, bright yellow bees peeped out. For Barnabas, the star witness, they had raided the circus wardrobe for a suit of mauve velvet and a thickly ruffled shirt that made him feel more like he was playing some young lord in a costume drama than testifying before the Unified Guild Council.

The Council building overlooked the former Lake Lucid, and it must have been a terrific location with a marvellous view back in the days when there was actual water in the lake. In fact, the building looked like a grand, historic mansion, and when Barnabas said as much, Sanjani told him, "Yes, it used to be the residence of Florian and Julianna Glorvanious."

"Glorvanious? Like Mayor Lawrence Glorvanious?"

"His son," the archivist told him. "But he's better remembered now as Father Glory, and his wife as Mother Mercy."

Barnabas, turning this new revelation over in his head, just stared at the mansion. The true story of the City was growing more detailed in his head every day. He had a clear image in his head of telling it all to Deni.

As they walked up the stairs to the entrance, Barnabas looked back and saw trucks converging on the Council building from both shores of the lake — the councillors on their way to this emergency meeting. A clerk met them at the door and seated them on a wooden bench, just outside the great oak doors of the Hall of Deliberations. The doors were flanked by stiff, unsmiling members of the Aqua Guard, who were holding what must have been ceremonial spears. Or did they really use those on offenders? Barnabas didn't want to find out.

The Council members were entering the building now, giving the four-some from Pastoral Park curious glances as they headed into the Hall. Sanjani explained to Barnabas, "The Unified Guild Council is made up of 14 representatives: three from each of the four guilds, plus two representing the Valley's support services."

"And none from Pastoral Park," Whistlewort said bitterly, getting to his feet and starting to pace. "Whenever we need something, we have to stand before them, hat in hand, like some poor relations. Twists my belly, let me tell you!"

The outside door opened again, and Carminn marched in, followed by two more Clouders. Her heavy footsteps echoed through the foyer. She spotted two other councillors, talking confidentially in a corner, and called out to them in a booming voice, "By the Father's Great Name, what is so important that I have to drive all the way here on a Saturday night? Is this one of Borborik's invented crises? The outhouses at the train depot need urgent painting or some such rabbit-scat?"

The two councillors appeared to be as in the dark as she was, and they all went inside together. Carminn turned and gave Tragidenko a dirty little look before she disappeared.

"Whatever happens," the Maestro muttered, "this will not be ending well." Barnabas felt the urge to apologize for all the trouble he was causing, but he just looked down at his feet and said nothing. This wasn't about him, he knew. For five minutes, the only sounds were muffled voices from behind the oak doors and the ceaseless tap-tapping of Whistlewort's hard-soled boots on the foyer's parquet floor as he paced up and down.

Then came the sound of shouting and commotion inside the Hall. The two Aqua guards in the foyer turned and dropped into a defensive posture, gripping their spears as if they might be serious about using them. The double doors flew open, and out burst Carminn, seething with rage, three more Aquas following her. Her hands flew up around her head like the guards were flies she was shooing away.

"What is this idiocy?!!" she shouted. "I have been a member of this council for 15 years!"

An older man, immaculately dressed, ran out after her. His long, fine grey hair fell over the shoulders of his elegant black coat, and his open hands were raised as if he could smooth out her anger from a distance. "Carminn, please, there have been allegations made. I'm sure... they *can't* be true... it will all be fine. Just —"

She was marching swiftly toward the exit. "I don't care what nonsense you get up to, Borborik. You're wasting my time and I'm leaving!"

Two of the Aqua Guard circled around to stand between her and the exit. "Madam Councillor," one said in a clear, cold voice. "I'm afraid we're under orders to hold you until Council finishes its deliberations."

"Hold me?!" she growled in disbelief, coming to a halt. The other three guards were around her now although no one was brandishing ornamental spears. Instead, they carried truncheons and devices that looked to Barnabas like maybe they were for shocking people.

The grey-haired man walked up to this little huddle, busily wringing his hands. "No, no, not *hold*... Just, we need you to *stay* —"

"I'm not a dog!"

"Stay here for... a little while."

Carminn didn't look scared; she looked dangerous. She turned to stare again at the four visitors from Pastoral Park in their bright clothing. "What are they doing here? What lies are they spreading about me?"

And then: "Who is that *boy*?! I don't know that boy!" Goosebumps rose on Barnabas' skin.

One of the Aquas stepped closer. "Madam Councillor. If you will please follow me to one of the side offices. I'm sure you'll be comfortable there."

She made them all wait, tense and unmoving, for 10 more seconds before she said, "Fine," a single syllable that seemed to convey a monumental forbearance and more than its share of threat.

They escorted Carminn through a small door. Borborik, the elegant, grey-haired man, wiped his brow, looking worn out by the encounter. He nodded to Tragidenko and then as he re-entered the Hall of Deliberations, said to one of the Aqua, "Bring them in in two minutes."

Barnabas and his circus cohort were soon escorted through the double doors and told to sit on another long bench at the back of the hall. The Hall of Deliberations — spacious and richly appointed with marble lintels and crown mouldings that glittered with gold leaf — might once have been the ballroom of the mansion. The Council members sat in a semi-circle behind small, old-fashioned desks of dark wood. Borborik sat in the centre, his more substantial desk on a raised platform. Above this platform was a vividly-coloured fresco featuring Father Glory and Mother Mercy watching a geyser of water shooting skywards from an industrial pipe. There was an empty desk on the left side of the semi-circle which must have been Carminn's. The two Clouding councillors she had arrived with sat to either side of this emptiness.

"I am Borborik, President of the Unified Guild Council, the body which has been appointed to rule over the Valley. You may address me as 'Your Eminence.'" His voice, though authoritative, had a gentleness to it, and Barnabas let himself hope that his case would be heard with open ears. "Young man, please step forward and stand at the Testimonial." He indicated a little platform with a lectern.

Barnabas turned to Sanjani, who put a hand on his shoulder and whispered, "Just speak the truth. Those who speak the truth are always heard." He nodded and, gathering his resolve, walked forward and up onto the Testimonial. The lectern was built for people of Valley stature, and it came up nearly to his chin.

Borborik pulled out a sheet of paper from his desk and cleared his throat. "I will read you details of the statement of Maestro Tragidenko of Pastoral Park, which I took down telephonically this afternoon." He cleared his throat. "Young Barnabas Bopwright, who stands before you, infiltrated George Glower's emporium, The Drop Shop, just before midnight last night in the company of a young performer from Tragidenko's so-called Circus of Humanity. Their goal was to retrieve some object which Young Bopwright believes is his property. While at the establishment, the young man claims to have witnessed a demonstration and overheard a plan to explode charges in the City's Tower District —"

Every member of Council reacted to this, crying out in disbelief or repeating the shocking words to each other for confirmation. Amid the hubbub, Barnabas heard one councillor say, "...never trusted Glower. He's from the City, after all."

Borborik raised his hands in the air. "Please, if I may continue... To explode charges in the City's Tower District this coming Tuesday, and cause some or all of the skyscrapers to topple down the great cliff and into the Tumbles.

"Putting aside for the moment the issues of trespassing and illegal entry, young Bopwright's story, while incredible, does require us to investigate further, especially as his account has been brought to us by Maestro Tragidenko, who is a friend of this council."

One of the Clouding councillors spoke up, a man with a sharply pointed auburn goatee. "Before we go any further, I need to know why the Clouding Speaker was removed from these proceedings. Why can't Carminn be here?"

Borborik dropped his head and shuffled the papers on his desk as if the answer might be hiding among them. Without meeting the man's gaze, he answered, "Councillor Fayrbrin, the reason for her removal will become clear when we hear from our witness." He looked across at Barnabas, standing at the Testimonial, and seemed startled for a moment at how he was barely visible above the lectern. Borborik cleared his throat and said, "Young Bopwright, we would like to ask you some questions."

"Um sure, Your Eminence," Barnabas replied and was taken aback at how the echo of his voice returned to him, sounding higher and more childish to his ears than it had felt leaving his throat.

Borborik asked, "Was Glower alone at the Drop Shop when you saw his demonstration?"

"Well, no, the other person who works there, Greta, she was around. And this kid, Galt-Stomper — he was in and out of the room..." Barnabas felt more than a little reluctant to go on because he knew his next words would not go down so well. "And, yeah, so was Carminn."

Councillor Fayrbrin burst out, "Carminn? Speaker Carminn of Clouding Guild?"

Barnabas turned to look at the man, whose goatee was pointed directly at his heart like a weapon. "Um, yes, sir. She was there. And she knew all about the plan."

"Councillor," said Borborik. "I will address the witness. If you have any questions, you may ask them through me."

Fayrbrin squinted his eyes at the Guild President. "Yes, Your Eminence. I am, actually, *curious* as to the origin of the witness's strange name. Is Pastoral Park now reverting to the City custom of given and family names?"

Barnabas, too nervous and impatient to wait for Borborik to ask the question, spoke up: "I'm from the City!"

Again, the room descended into noisy chaos. Fayrbrin leaped to his feet. "Eminence, Speaker Carminn was right; we are wasting our Saturday night here. Some interloper boy has flouted our laws, has infiltrated the Valley surreptitiously and with malicious intent. Once here, he has committed acts of trespassing and theft, and now he brings outrageous accusations against one of our most esteemed denizens, one whose holy life is unassailable. It is this Bopwright who needs to be on trial, not my Guild. Not our Speaker."

Another councillor called out, "How did he cross the Frontier?"

"What is Pastoral Park's role in hiding this fugitive?" shouted another.

This time, President Borborik actually picked up a gavel and banged his desk to quiet the room. "Councillors, I must be allowed to run these proceedings! There are indeed many irregularities here, and they will be addressed, I assure you. But first, Young Bopwright, tell me: do you have any proof to back up your assertions?"

"Well, yeah!" Barnabas dug into his pants pocket and pulled out his phone, excited to finally present his evidence. "I'm just glad I still had charge, 'cause it's getting low, but... here!" He turned the phone out towards the councillors with one of his pictures on it.

Everyone in the room leaned forward. One of the councillors put on a pair of wire-rimmed glasses and said, "What is it?"

"Oh, this is my phone." He turned it back around and swiped back to the first image. "I took some pictures at the Clouding steam plant.

Glower and Carminn. And they were —"

A silence washed across him, so coldly palpable that he looked up, finding the whole of the Unified Guild Council staring at him in horror, and then in growing anger.

Fayrbrin was on his feet again. "Your Eminence, this is a disgrace! The scripture forbids photographic images. Not only is this boy slandering one of our finest denizens, he has desecrated our Holy Steam Works with his device!"

The councillor with the glasses said, "I want to see these pictures!" She conferred with the others sitting around her and then added, "Forming Guild is in favour of this evidence being admitted."

The other Clouding delegate pounded on the table and stood up. "Mr. President, I move that these disgraceful pictures be destroyed immediately, and the witness be arrested and remanded into custody in Doomlock! And send Tragidenko there, too! He has been aiding and abetting this inveterate invader to evade the law."

From the back of the room, Whistlewort shouted, "You idiots! At least look at what the boy risked his tail to bring you!"

This led to a brief shouting match between different factions. Barnabas, clutching the phone against his breast, sensed that a lot of old resentments were being aired. It was like the kind of fights his mom and dad had on the rare occasions they met up now; supposedly about something small like what time to pick Barnabas up, but really about all the years of hurt.

The President again banged his gavel. "My dear councillors. Might it not be possible to separate the illegality of the picture-taking from the potential good the pictures could do in helping us determine what might or might not be transpiring? Let us put it to a vote."

The result of the vote was terrifyingly close — seven to six in favour of seeing the pictures. It suddenly occurred to Barnabas that not only was the fate of the City in the Council's hand, *so was his fate!* Doomlock! The deepest station on the secret subway line, a place whose very name evoked misery without end.

Barnabas asked, "Do you want me to pass the phone around or…?"

"No," answered the President. "Despite how it may seem, we do use photographic imagery in the Valley, but only for reference purposes, such as the surveying of building sites." He turned to the clerk, who was standing behind his left shoulder. "Bring the projection apparatus."

A few minutes later, Barnabas' pictures were being projected onto a large screen on one of the side walls. "Uh, I know it's hard to see, but this is the Routing Depot at Clouding. Uh, and that's Carminn there, with Glower."

"Could be anyone," Fayrbrin muttered.

"No, you can see — wait — in this next picture. That's them."

The room was silent again. The President exchanged glances with several councillors before turning to Barnabas and asking, "Is that all you have?"

"No! This part is important." He skipped through several pictures, trying to find the ones he needed. In the middle of the phone, ominous words in bold red letters appeared: 'Low Battery!' Barnabas looked up at the projection screen and, of course, saw the words there too. But he tapped the warning and it went away. "Here, look. It's a kind of, um, elevator. The steam sends it up to the City. See? That's Glower sitting inside."

A councillor who had not spoken before turned to the two representatives from Clouding and asked, "Is this true? Is there such means of transport?"

Fayrbrin was startled, all his former bluster gone. His eyes darted back and forth between the screen and his Clouding colleague. "We know nothing of such a… means."

The colleague stammered, "We will of course look for this… anomaly. Tonight!"

The President wiped his brow with a handkerchief. He was making copious notes on his pad of paper and muttering to himself. He half looked up and said in a tone far less decisive than before, "The witness will kindly step down."

A surge of desperation ran through Barnabas' chest. "Wait! What are you going to do about this? You can see I'm telling the truth!"

The President picked up his gavel and banged it three times, the sound echoing like a gunshot off the walls. "The witness will sit down! Now!"

Sanjani came forward and led Barnabas back to the bench. "Don't worry, dear," she whispered. Whistlewort patted his back; Tragidenko followed this with a squeeze on his shoulder.

The President turned to the Clerk. "Bring in the next witness." Barnabas had no idea who this might be until he heard a familiar strident voice out in the foyer: "Take your interfering fingers off my body, you brute! I can move on my own. You'll catch more flies with honey, remember that!"

Greta entered, looking a little worse for wear. The buttons of her pink knit sweater were misaligned, and she wore a kerchief over her dishevelled hair, strands of which stuck out from under the fabric like cold, hard spaghetti.

She took her place at the Testimonial, her chin raised defiantly, but her eyes darting nervously from face to face.

Borborik said, "You were apprehended driving away from the Drop Shop with a fully-laden truck of your merchandise. Why has the Drop Shop closed down?"

"We're doing inventory, isn't it? And giving the floors a good wash down. You wouldn't believe the filth people track across my floors. I say to Mr. Glower, I do, 'George! People are animals, and he always tells me —'"

"Where is George Glower?" Borborik interrupted. "There are allegations that he has illegally left the Valley, perhaps not for the first time."

"My George? Illegal? The idea! The service that man does for the Valley is incalculable! Just *try* and calculate it! You can't count that high!"

"Then where is he?"

"I'm sure I couldn't say. On a spiritual retreat, *mayhap*?" She examined the purple polish on her long nails.

"That boy there..." the President pointed at Barnabas with his gavel, "claims that this coming Tuesday, George Glower will play his part in a scheme to commit extreme and mortal sabotage. He says you know about this plan."

Greta twisted around and glared at Barnabas. "That boy!" she thundered, "is a liar and a sneaky little sneak thief! Got no respect for the ways of our Valley, he has!"

"And so, you stand with George Glower?"

"I do!"

"Even if on Tuesday the towers crash into the Tumbles? If such a disaster occurs, we will come and take you from your cell in Doomlock and charge you as a co-conspirator. Do you still have nothing to tell us?"

Greta's supply of quick replies seemed to suddenly run out. She stood blinking for a minute, then slowly looked around again at the Councillors. Turning back to Borborik, patting down the kerchief on her head, she said, "Well... I might have heard one or two... suspicious things over the last week. Nothing, you understand, definitive..."

"And did these suspicions extend to Speaker Carminn of Clouding Guild?"

"Ooh, she's a baddun, and have no doubt! A snake what's tempted my poor Georgie away from his honest, *lucrative* path into some foul abyss!" She suddenly howled like a cat whose tail got stepped on. "Ohhhhh, your Eminent Worshipful Honour! Have pity on a miserable lady what's got nothing but —"

"Silence," Borborik called, his manner changing abruptly. "The witness will be remanded into custody in Doomlock, pending the outcome of this investigation."

Greta's whining turned to a cry of fury: "You can't do that! I have a truck full of valuables parked outside, where any nefarious crook can pilfer all my hard-earned —"

But the Aqua Guard was already leading her out the door, and as it closed, Barnabas could hear her calling, "Wait until my George hears of this! You lot will be barred from the Drop Shop for *life*, you will!!" Barnabas felt a cold satisfaction at her arrest. The Council understood who the real villains were. Now they would help.

President Borborik lowered his head, supporting it with both hands as he pored over his notes. When he finally looked around at the members of the Unified Guild Council, neither he nor any of them seemed very sure what to do.

"Councillors?" he said. "We have some difficult decisions to make. The Clouding contingent will look into the matter of the illegal elevator?"

Fayrbrin half stood. "Immediately, Your Eminence."

A councillor from Forming said, "Yes, breaches of the Frontier are most serious. They undermine our whole way of life."

Another councillor stood and said, "Eminence, we must calculate where the towers might fall and form an evacuation plan."

"Yes," said another, "Not only for Valley denizens but with an eye to salvaging as much valuable equipment as possible."

Borborik added, "If, that is, there is any truth to the boy's accusations."

"Yes, *if*..." the councillor agreed, nodding vigorously.

"What?" Barnabas heard himself say. He sat up, looking around the room in disbelief. Could he be hearing what he thought he was hearing?

"And it begins," muttered Whistlewort, his voice just shy of a growl.

An older, rotund man in a striped poncho stood with some difficulty. He cleared his throat and declaimed in a voice like an old Shakespearean actor, "My esteemed colleagues, while this potential pending tragedy is...

would be very unfortunate, I hope it is not too early to consider the opportunities such events will… *might* afford the Valley: years of rebuilding, renegotiation of the terms of our contracts with the City, the emergency powers this Council might take on —"

Borborik sat up straight, putting out a hand in the man's direction. "Yes, Swarnish, I think such discussion — while valuable — might best be left to a time… to such a time… after… *in case of*…*if* it turns out there's any truth to the allegations…" he cleared his throat and the whole Council looked embarrassed.

At which point Barnabas leaped to his feet. "What are you talking about?!" The whole room turned his way. "You know this is true; this is *happening!* How can you sit there and… and just *sit* there?! You have to warn the City immediately. Call Mayor Tuppletaub! I know he knows all about the Valley; his apartment looks right down on it." He had moved to the centre of the room, turning and turning to take in the embarrassed, impassive faces that surrounded him, looking for some spark of compassion, or even simple acknowledgement.

A woman with short-black hair and a lot of black eye makeup said, "Young man, we meet with the City only twice a year. Our relationship follows traditions that date back for the better part of a century."

Barnabas ran his fingers through his hair. "But this is life and death!"

Fayrbrin answered coldly, "When the City needs our help, they ask for it. We don't tell them how to handle their affairs."

The two Aqua guards in the Hall had moved to stand just a few metres from Barnabas, one on either side. But he wasn't intimidated; he was too desperate for that. "Then if you won't do something, I will! I-I'll warn the Mayor myself. Put me back on the train and I'll do it! I don't have any *traditions* or whatever!"

"No, no, not possible," said Borborik. "At this point, the existence of this conspiracy is mere conjecture. As has been pointed out, Young Bopwright, you are an infiltrator in the Valley. Your motives are uncertain. Then there is the issue of your illegal photographs. A most serious matter."

"Most serious," others echoed. Barnabas turned to look back at the adults from Pastoral Park, who were sitting impotently at the back of the Hall. *Help me,* his eyes begged them.

Borborik stood, shaking his head so that his long, grey hair swept back over the shoulders of his coat. "It is the will of this Council that you be remanded to custody in Doomlock, where you will be held until the matters of your illegal entry and illegal photography can be settled with representatives of the City, at our next semi-annual meeting in two months time."

Tragidenko stood and called out: "Mr. President, I am asking you for some excellent reconsideration! Many lives, many dreams may be at the stake. This boy, he meant no harm. His actions were accidental or committed for the goodness!"

"Maestro," the President said, his voice growing cold. "The role of Pastoral Park in hiding this fugitive, in allowing him free access to crucial guild infrastructure is something this Council will also have to investigate. You have already stuck your neck out a good deal farther than you should have."

Tragidenko sat, shaking his head. Barnabas looked at the guards, who were standing tense and close. He looked back at the door and wondered, *If I just took off and ran, could I get out before they grabbed me?*

Just then, there was a huge crash outside. Shouting, running feet. The members of Council all rose in alarm. The doors flew open, and an Aqua guard, bleeding from his forehead called out, "Mr. President, Speaker Carminn has escaped. We were unable to apprehend her before she vanished into the trees."

One of the guards flanking Barnabas ran out into the hall to help. Barnabas took this as a sign. He, too would escape! As if sensing his plan, the remaining guard grabbed him firmly by the arm.

President Borborik lowered himself into his chair, and everyone else followed suit. "Well then," he said. "I want her captured by morning. See to it. And Maestro Tragidenko, this new disaster just confirms my resolve — young Bopwright must be kept in Doomlock, not only for his transgressions, but to keep him safe from Speaker Carminn's wrath." Barnabas looked desperately back at his companions. *How could this have all gone so terribly wrong?* he wondered. Sanjani started crying.

"Take him away," Borborik said.

CHAPTER 24

When Barnabas was 12, there had been a kid in his class named Henry, who, it was said, would eventually wind up in jail. Henry stole from kids, he stole from the office. He actually smoked! At 12! The shocking idea that jail awaited him, that jail was the inevitable endpoint of his miscreant path did not originate with the kids. It was overheard from their parents, who gossiped openly, assuming their children didn't listen to *that* kind of conversation. But the children did listen, and soon Henry was shunned by his peers. There followed further acts of vandalism and some mysterious crime so terrible his schoolmates were never told the details. And then Henry was gone — expelled or withdrawn or, perhaps, already incarcerated.

Now, as Barnabas considered the case of that poor, bedraggled boy who always seemed to have boogers in his nose, he wondered what had become of him. Maybe, in a new environment, Henry had changed. Maybe whatever was going on in his life that made him so unhappy got better. But maybe once the rumours started, they stuck with you and doomed you. Doomlock.

Could Henry's crimes have been worse than George Glower's, than Carminn's? Yet they weren't behind bars. Nope, Glower was about to make his dreams of revenge come true; Carminn was about to rise to a seat of great power. No, those people didn't wind up in jail. Henry did. Barnabas did.

There was a window high up on the wall of his cell, and standing on the cot on tip-toes, Barnabas could just peer out. There was no glass in the steel frame, just four solid, vertical bars. But he was ignoring the bars, looking between them at the moon as it shimmered above the dry mud that had once been Lake Lucid. The mist over the lakebed was growing thicker, and Barnabas could almost convince himself that it was water, that the lake was still there, fresh and inviting. It was late, maybe close to midnight. They had taken his phone away, so he couldn't be sure.

Sleep tugged at him, but he didn't want to sleep. The Aqua Guards were coming at dawn to take him from the little locked room here in the Guild Council mansion and escort him to the train station, where he would ride the subway down into the dark, to a cell without a window, two metres by two metres by two metres, in the hopeless place called Doomlock. Better to look now at the mist and the moon than to sleep. Better to feel the cold, fresh air wash across his face, and to keep himself awake to hear the robins when they started to sing.

Maybe something was wrong with him. He should be more scared. He should be crying, banging on the door, begging someone to save him. But right now he just felt cold and empty. Sitting down on the bed, Barnabas pulled the scratchy blanket over his shoulders and buttoned his ruffled shirt up to the neck. How had he failed to make them understand? Why did the Unified Guild Council not care about saving the City? Over and over, he replayed the events of the trial in his head, but he couldn't see anything he might have done differently.

Through the walls came a miserable wail, as it had come every hour since he had been locked up: "Aaaaaaaoowwwwwwwwwwwoooooooooooooo!" followed by "Georgie, my Georgie, why have you left me here? Don't you love me, my big pigeon? Fly down and save me! Save me from Doooom-lock! AAAAOOOWWWWooooooooooo!"

Barnabas covered his ears. He wanted to yell at Greta to shut up. Why didn't the guards tell her to shut up? But soon she again fell silent, and he just felt bad for her. Worse, her cries had cracked the wall around his heart that was keeping him from feeling the pain and fear himself. Now it was growing in him, the hopelessness of his plight, the dread of the darkness to come. Would he ever see his family and friends again? Who would even know he was locked away in the ground, under a Valley no one knew existed? He shivered miserably and tears fill his eyes.

He was moments from wailing into the night like Greta when he heard something. Whispers. The sound of a twig cracking. He stood up in the centre of the cell with the blanket still around his shoulders and looked up at the high window.

Quietly, but forcefully, a voice said, "Annnnnnd — HUP!" Shuffling, grunting. A face filled the window. Even in the darkness, Barnabas recognized Thumbutter.

"Hi, Barnabas," she said, and her mischievous smile shone in the moonlight. "We thought maybe you wanted to get out of there."

"Yes, please!" he whispered, grinning, wiping the tears from his eyes with a corner of the blanket. His heart filled with hope so quickly, he thought it might tear at the seams.

Someone from below handed Thumbutter a socket wrench, and she began to undo the bolts that held the barred window-frame in place. It took almost ten minutes, and Barnabas could hear strained curses from below. When she had the heavy frame loose, someone hissed, "For Glory's sake, don't drop it, girl!" Barnabas watched hands from below take the frame and lower it out of sight. Thumbutter pulled herself half into the window and reached out her strong arms.

"Come on, Barnabas," she said. "There's not much time!"

He, dropped the blanket, put on the velvet jacket, and hopped up on the cot. She pulled him through the narrow window, and only then did he see what was happening — Thumbutter was the top of a pyramid men and women, all sweating with the exertion of the long pose. He was passed down the face of the pyramid with disconcerting ease as if they had been practising this act — The Amazing Pyramid Jail-Break! — for months. As soon as he hit the ground, the pyramid disassembled around him in a series of leaps, thumps, and grunts.

Whistlewort was there, back in his usual dusty work clothes. "Okay, keep it quiet. Now, get yourselves back to Pastoral Park, but don't all travel together; it'll draw too much attention." He walked among the acrobats, patting them on the back, and when he reached Barnabas, he put his strong, bony hand on the boy's shoulder and looked him in the eye with surprising warmth. "Sorry you had to go through that," he said. He reached into his pocket and handed a surprised Barnabas his cell phone.

"They let you have it?" the boy asked. The acrobats were vanishing into the night around them. Thumbutter gave him a wink as she passed.

Whistlewort answered, "Well, yeah, If you call me lifting it from the Clerk's pocket 'letting me have it.'"

"Hey!" came a loud whisper from above, so loud that its designation as a whisper was in question. It was Greta, her face peering through the bars of the neighbouring room. Her kerchief was gone and her hair was wild as a Gorgon's. "You get me out of here or I'm going to scream blue murder, draw the guard right quick!"

Whistlewort laughed up at her. "Sorry, honey, they were so worked up about searching for Carminn, they only left one guard on duty here. And now he's tied up in the basement."

She let loose her miserable wail again and screamed into the night, "And what am I supposed to do?!"

"Rot in Doomlock, I guess," the old man replied breezily and turned away. "Come on, Barnabas, we only have a few hours until they realize you're gone. Lots to do." He began to walk away.

"Wait, boy!" cried Greta, and Barnabas turned back. "Please, you're going to the City, aintcha? Gonna see my Georgie...?"

He didn't know what to say. The woman may not have been as evil as Glower, but she had done everything she could in the Council meeting to get him worse trouble. But now she looked so miserable, all he could say was, "Yes, I think so."

"Just... Just let him know his darlin' Greta is deep in the deep, in deep, deep trouble, and she's counting on him. I was always there for him, you know. His help-meet. He won't let me moulder away. Never!"

"I... I'll tell him," Barnabas promised.

"Forget about her," said Whistlewort. "We gotta move!"

A fine chestnut horse was waiting around the side of the mansion. Whistlewort helped Barnabas up onto its back and then told him to wait a minute. The old man vanished into the night. Hearing a noise off to his right, Barnabas turned and stared into the stand of trees that flanked the mansion. He thought maybe he saw something, a movement, a big shape. And it was watching him. But then Whistlewort appeared, climbed up into the saddle, and they were off.

The ride was a weird echo of his previous night's journey with Graviddy, and now as then, people were waiting for him when the horse pulled into the main square of Pastoral Park. Huro and Buro, Garlip and Graviddy were there first, gathering around him, helping him down from the horse.

But unlike the night before, the adults were pressing close around him, patting his back, handing him homemade snacks and a bottle of raspberry soda. Everyone was pressing him for details of the trial, but Sanjani slid through the crowd and put her arm over his shoulder, leading him away.

"You will have to talk to him later," she said. "Time is short and we have much to do. Come, Barnabas." Lighting their way with a kerosene lantern, she led him out of the square. When they reached the main path, they found Maestro Tragidenko waiting for them, a huge hairy silhouette in a great coat. He enveloped Barnabas in a hug that could have encompassed a mountain.

"I'm heartbreakingly sorry, my boy. Last night, I was an unforgivable coward. But today, you are reminding me what it is to be brave."

Barnabas was startled. He looked at Tragidenko and Sanjani and blurted out, "I've put you in danger. Pastoral Park is going to be in trouble because of me."

The Maestro shook his head. "No, Barnabas, this is not because of you, or for your sake. You and we, all of us are together in this; we do what we can to save the City, yes? And again, I am sorrowful how much burden falls on you."

Sanjani said, "But we will do what we can to help. Let's hurry."

As they walked quickly through the night, Barnabas became aware of something behind them. He thought of the dark shape in the trees outside the Guild mansion. But when he looked nervously over his shoulder, he saw that it was Falstep following them, keeping a distance, but keeping pace. When they reached the little house at the top of the lane, Sanjani finally acknowledged the clown's presence.

"If you wouldn't mind waiting outside," she told Falstep a bit icily. "We have some things to discuss with Barnabas first."

Falstep raised his hands defensively. "Hey, I ain't here to cause more problems. I don't even have to be here if you don't want."

Tragidenko shook his head. "Sanjani, my dove, I think it is important that dear Falstep has a chance to —"

"That's fine!" she answered sharply. "I never said he couldn't. Barnabas, please come in."

Inside, they lit more lanterns. Barnabas saw his backpack was sitting on the table, along with the jeans and t-shirt he had arrived in, laundered and neatly folded. On top of them was his bowler hat, and he was glad to see it. Despite everything else he had to worry about, a sudden panic ran through him. He hurried over to his bag and went through the compartments. There in a side pocket, much to his relief, was the *diaboriku.*

He joined Sanjani at the table while Tragidenko lowered himself into the couch against the wall and watched them. Sanjani's voice was heavy with the seriousness of the situation, but Barnabas found comfort in her warm hands as she laid them on his.

"At dawn," she said, "the Aqua Guard will return to the Guild House and find you gone. They will assume, correctly, that Pastoral Park freed you and they will make their way here. That means we had better be on the move within three hours."

"Where are we going?" Barnabas asked.

"As you know, it is not easy to get across the Frontier. Obviously you can't take the train, and Glower and Carminn's secret steam elevator will be locked down tight by now. The only way, as you suggested last night, is through the woods."

The way she said it sent a chill through him. "Is… is that how you came to the Valley? Is it dangerous?"

"Yes, I found my way to the Valley by accident and yet not by accident. There were people — I suppose they were people — who helped me in my passage through the earth. And in the woods there was the old woman."

"The witch over the bridge…" Barnabas breathed. When he and Wickram had been in the woods by daylight, Wickram's story of the carnivorous old woman had sounded silly. But now Barnabas wasn't so sanguine about it.

"She is not a witch. Or perhaps that is as good a word as any, I don't know. She was kind to me; that's all I can say. Tonight, we will go through woods, and I will appeal to her to let us return to the City. Please try not to worry."

"You're going to come with me?" He felt a wave of relief wash through him.

"I never thought I would return there; I never wanted to. But we have no choice, do we? Glower must be stopped." Before Barnabas could ask her anything more, she stood up and walked to the base of the stairs. "Wickram?" she called. "Will you come down and join us?" There was no answer. She hesitated a moment and then climbed the stairs. Barnabas was half-expecting to hear an argument spring up from the bedroom, but all seemed quiet. He remembered that Tragidenko was still sitting there in the shadows. Barnabas turned to speak to him, but the man was asleep on the couch, snoring gently.

After a minute, Sanjani came down the stairs followed by Wickram. They sat, Sanjani beside Barnabas, Wickram on the other side of the table, not looking up at either of them.

"Hi," Barnabas said in an exploratory way. "You heard about everything? Glower? Carminn? The towers?"

"Yeah," Wickram replied, running one of his long guitar-picking fingernails down a groove in the table top. "I can't believe Glower would do that. Totally guts me."

"Yeah. Well, I'm going to the City to stop him. Me and Sanjani."

Wickram half raised his head and pushed aside his fringe of hair. Barnabas saw no anger in his eyes. Wickram asked, "Guild Council really won't do anything about it?"

"Nope. They just want to throw me in Doomlock."

"Slizzpots."

"Wickram," said his mother. "I have something to ask of you. I want you to accompany us to the City."

Wickram snapped to attention, sitting up straight, a head higher than everyone else at the table. "What are you talking about? I can't do that!"

Barnabas, just as surprised, almost blurted out, *He doesn't even like me,* but instead said, "Isn't it dangerous?"

Sanjani's fingers were steepled, pressed together hard. "Wickram... Pickle... Your friend needs your help to stop Glower and save the City." Wickram shot Barnabas a look, and panicking, Barnabas looked away from him, back to Sanjani. She said, "But there's something else. For a long time, I have been thinking it might be good if you got away from here... for a while."

Wickram's eyes narrowed in suspicion. "Oh, I see. You're sick of me, right? Sick of me fighting with *him.*" He stabbed a finger in his father's direction, and the Maestro as if in answer, let out a loud snore. "You just want a bit of peace and quiet for once."

Tears glistened in Sanjani eyes, but her expression also grew harder. "Whatever you think, Wickram, you don't know everything. Now, sit still and listen. It was me who sent Falstep to the City last week. I needed him to visit a school. A school for the performing arts that I hoped was still there. I wanted him to find a way to get you an audition."

Barnabas looked back at Wickram, expecting him to be excited. But Wickram just seemed shaken. "What are you talking about?" he said. "I can't just... I'm not from the City. Why would they...?" He began to tap his foot like a jack rabbit, and the table trembled in sympathy.

Sanjani continued calmly. "I had hoped that all this could happen later in the summer, that we would have time to arrange your passage legally. But now the future of Pastoral Park is in doubt. There will be no favours for Dimitri Tragidenko's son. I want you out of here with me and Barnabas tonight."

"Is that what you think of me? That when things get bad I'm just going to run away? No! If Pastoral Park is in trouble, I'm not going anywhere, I'm standing with my friends!"

"Wickram, we don't know what will happen with the Guild Council. But the door on this opportunity might suddenly close! Please, I have dreamed this for you a long time."

"Funny how you forgot to discuss it with me!"

Abruptly, Sanjani stood up and walked towards the front door. Barnabas wanted to shout, *Wait! Forget about him; we need to focus on ME!* But she wasn't running away; she opened the door and spoke quietly. "Please, come in. He needs to hear it from you." Falstep appeared in the door, and Sanjani stood aside to let him in. "Wickram, Barnabas, I will take a little walk and return later." She stepped out into the night, closing the door behind her.

Wickram was angry now; the air seemed to thrum with resentment. Falstep sat down across from him where Sanjani had been, and Wickram asked, "So what's this? You're on their side now? Going to lecture me on what to do with my life?"

The clown stood again. Planting his palms, he heaved himself up and somersaulted across the table, landing with a flourish beside Wickram. "Tada! Now I'm on your side! Just shut it and listen to me." Falstep pulled himself up to sit on the table, his eyes level with Wickram's, and said, "Take a look at your life. You're messing everything up, and everyone is worried about you — that is when they don't want to kill you."

"So, why am I getting banished from the Valley? Listen, I know what they want you to say: I should behave myself, remember who my dad is and do everything I'm told! Fine, I promise. That make you happy, O King of the Hypocrites?"

Falstep snorted in amusement, but he didn't sound so amused. "Okay, wise-bone, let's say you woke up tomorrow, and *poof*, none of us was here anymore — not me, not Dimitri, not your mom. No one to push you around or give a road apple what happens to you. What would you do with your life?"

Wickram put his chin on the table and draped his long arms across his head as if he were expecting it to start raining stones. "Nothing! Everything! I'd go and help out in the kitchen, or maybe join a road crew. Make myself useful!"

"And what about your music?" the clown asked.

Wickram's head snapped upwards again. "What about it?" He gave an angry nod in Tragidenko's direction. "I don't owe him my music. It's the best part of me, and he can't just take it… just take it away and make it his!"

"And so you'll go on strike — refuse to make any music at all. And then maybe get yourself good and drunk when that hurts too much."

Wickram rose to his feet and screamed down at the clown. "Getting drunk is good enough for you, you wine-soaked tree stump!"

Falstep jumped to his feet on top of the table, regaining the height advantage. "And who in the name of the Fathermothering dung pile told you to act like *me?!!*"

Wickram looked confused. "Because… because I wish I *was* more like you! You don't give a crap what any of them think! You make your own rules and-and if anybody doesn't like it, you tell them to go lick mule stones!"

"I am so sick of how much you think you know and how little you really do," Falstep growled at him. "Who are you to talk about me, and why I do what I do? Half the time I tell myself that if I only keep working day and night, *maybe* I'll be any good as a clown! The rest of the time I drink, so I don't have to listen to the voice in my head that says, 'You're old! You're slow! *You're just not krumpin' good enough!!'*"

Like a bomb had gone off between them, they both fell back down on their asses, Falstep on the table top, Wickram into his chair, which groaned tragically, like it too was about to collapse. They were both breathing hard, and Barnabas found himself doing the same.

Falstep climbed off the table and sat again in Sanjani's chair. After a minute he said, "You want to make yourself useful? Contribute something? Contribute your music. Audition for this school, see what they can teach you. There ain't nothing wrong with building roads, but when you can do something like you do on that guitar…."

Wickram took a deep breath. "But… where would I live?" he asked, sounding like a lost little kid.

"You have an aunt up there. Your mom's sister. She said you could —"

"Wait! No way! After what Mom's family did to her? There's no way I'm going anywhere near those slizpots!"

Falstep pulled half a cigar and a match from his breast pocket and lit up. "Nah," he said, puffing on his smoke, a look of contentment suffusing his features. "Your aunt's terrific. Flirted a lot with me, so you know she's got taste. She was never the problem, Wick; it was always the old man. And he… Well, let's just say he's not a problem anymore."

Wickram looked drained, just staring into space. "I don't know what to say."

Falstep shrugged. "Go, audition. If you think they're a bunch of wet-rumped rubes, you don't have to go. But didn't you always want to live up there? In all that blind chaos?"

"I don't know. That was a dream; this is utter real." Wickram turned to Barnabas. "Mom said I could help you save the City. But, Barn, what could I do that would be any use?"

Barnabas said, "I have no idea what I can do either. But it's got to be better with your help than without."

"Do you even want me? I was kind of a goat-stone to you."

"Yes, I want you to come. For one thing, you never seem scared of anything. Me? I'm scared shitless all the time!" Blushing a bit, he added, "Wick, you're my friend, okay?"

Wickram gave him a lopsided smile, but then he looked off into the corner, and his smile died. "You're not asleep are you? You been listening the whole time."

Tragidenko's phlegmy voice emerged from the shadows like thick, brown ink. "Not the whole time, but I heard enough."

Falstep stood and spoke a little sheepishly. "Dimitri, you know I never wanted to come between you and the kid. I wouldn't do that to you."

"Hey!" Wickram snapped. "Don't talk about me like I'm not here."

Tragidenko heaved himself off the couch with a cascade of groans and came to sit at the end of the table. "My friend, I think no such thing. On the contrary, I thank you for taking care of my son when I could not. Now, if you would please leave us, I will see you in the morning."

Wickram looked a bit panicked. "Hey, no, you don't have to leave!" But Falstep stood and went out the front door. Barnabas wondered if he should follow, but the Maestro hadn't asked him to, and so he just made himself very still and listened.

Tragidenko, usually so extravagant, so full of motion became very still. His hands were clasped in front of him on the table, and his shoulders were hunched forward. "Wickram, you said I wanted to take your music from you, make it mine. Firstly, I am wanting to say, this is not true, has never been true." He paused, cleared his throat and continued. "I want, more than anything, for you to exult in the glory of your own creations as I have in mine."

"Oh, road apples," Wickram answered. "Admit it, what you want is me to take over your circus — give up my life, so I can keep living yours when you're done. Well, it's not happening!"

Barnabas saw anger wrinkle the Maestro's brow. "Of course I want you to take over the circus! Why wouldn't I?!" He ran his fingers through his thick hair and growled in frustration. "Listen, listen… When you were born, I was so happy. Your mother was happy. We were making a place for ourselves in the Valley… and then you were there, this beautiful dumpling with this smile like the sunrise. I told myself I didn't care what you did with your life as long as you thrived, wrapped up in the glow of our love. But then… but then… I saw so early what a creative soul you had. I saw that everything around you was alive in your senses, and I thought, 'Oh, yes, this one… he is like me!' I was proud when I heard your beautiful little voice singing out louder than the other children, so tuneful, so sure. And as you grew, I pulled you close to my side, told you my dreaming's for each part of every show. 'The Maestro's little assistant,' they called you."

Barnabas gave Wickram a furtive look, but the boy was again hiding behind his hair, looking away into the dark beyond the lantern's glow.

"Then we found you the guitar, yes? At the Drop Shop, in the first days after Glower — my God, that *mad man* — opened his store. And your teacher, the coal miner from Furrowing, that poor man climbed out of the black pit in the ground and then climbed the hill to Pastoral Park just to teach you for an hour every week. I admit, I was jealous. Never had you given me such attention as you did that miner, hanging on his every word while he was here, making him show you every technique he knew, and then when had gone, spending the rest of the week upstairs with your guitar."

Wickram's voice shook a bit when he spoke. "So, why couldn't you take a hint? I knew what I wanted!"

"Do you think I was not happy for you? I was! And I wanted us to share this happiness, bring it into our circus!"

"Your circus."

The Maestro banged a big hand down on the table. "No! Not mine. Never *mine*! It is the lifeblood of all our community. We are a family and we all serve the Big Top!"

A tear was moving down Wickram's cheek, but his voice was defiant. "Well, I don't! I'm going to the City and maybe I won't come back!"

"Then go! Be happy!" said Tragidenko, but it didn't sound like a blessing. Wickram stood abruptly, and his chair tumbled to the ground. He ran out the front door.

Barnabas looked helplessly at Tragidenko and all he could think to say was another "I'm sorry," before he ran after Wickram. His friend was outside in the little front garden, sitting on a bench that had been built for someone smaller, maybe for him when he *was* smaller. He was crying, his shoulders heaving. Barnabas was debating whether to say something or just let him be when someone else called out from the darkness.

"Are you okay?" It was Graviddy. She came forward and stood at the garden gate.

Wickram looked up defiantly, gritting his teeth, wiping away his tears. "I'm golden! I'm cinnamon toast. So, what's up? You here to yell at me, too? Official Pastoral Park punching bag, that's me."

"No, I just wanted to say —"

"Right, that I don't own you and you can kiss anyone you like, got it!" He got to his feet and moved over to Barnabas, shooting an arm around his shoulders. "Well, so can I!" He bent down and planted a sloppy kiss on Barnabas' startled mouth. Wickram pulled away and stormed back to his bench, leaving Barnabas wiping his mouth in confusion. "See?" Wickram said. "You and me are just two free birds, flying free in freeville!"

Graviddy rolled her eyes and came through the gate, sitting beside Wickram on the bench. "You really are an idiot, you know that?" She put a finger on his lips. "Now shut up and let me tell you something: I heard you're going to save the City with Barnabas and Sanjani, and I'm really proud of you. Impressed even."

Her proximity was making Wickram nervous. He shifted around, try-ing to strike casual poses without much success. "Oh yeah?" he said. "Who told you that? Falstep? Maybe I didn't say yes."

"I have no doubt for one second that you're going. Because maybe you don't know it, but I know how brave and strong you can be. And I'll tell you what, I'm not kissing anyone else until you get back. Deal?"

"What if… what if I'm gone for a long time?"

She gave him a quizzical look. "How long?"

"I don't know. What if it's months? Or a whole year?"

Graviddy made a show of considering this. "I think I can hold out."

Wickram pushed the hair back on his head, suddenly the coolest guy in the world. "Oh yeah? And what happens when I get back?"

She jumped to her feet and vaulted elegantly over the garden fence. "I kiss you, the returning hero. I kiss you hard." And she ran off down the road, her footsteps light as a deer.

Barnabas came over and sat beside him. "Please don't kiss me again, okay?"

"Just making a point."

"I know. Still…"

"I'm an excellent kisser; don't complain."

Maybe they had been waiting to give Graviddy her moment alone with Wickram, but as soon as she left, Garlip, Huro, Buro, Thumbutter, and little Beany came up the road, into view. Soon, they were all sitting in the garden, talking with enthusiasm. Barnabas was glad for the com-pany — especially Garlip's — because he was beginning to worry more and more about what would happen in the next few hours.

Sanjani, returning from her walk, asked Wickram and Barnabas, "Don't you want to get a little sleep before dawn?"

Barnabas shook his head. "If it's okay, I just want to hang out with my friends. I don't think I could sleep anyway."

"Me neither, Mom."

So she went inside, and the kids talked about the night's adventures, the circus, what the future held for all of them. Wickram told them about the music school, and Graviddy tried to hide her sadness. Barnabas realized how grateful he was to have these new friends, and thought that maybe he deserved them. Later, he found himself alone in a corner of the garden with Garlip, who showed him her sketchbook by lantern light.

There was a beautiful drawing of Mother Mercy embracing the world like it was her baby. Garlip stared at that one for a long, silent minute. "I miss believing," she said.

"So maybe you shouldn't have stopped," Barnabas replied.

"No, it's like missing the way you used to have naps in kindergarten — some things are just sweet memories and have nothing to do with your life anymore."

Then they kissed for long time, and Barnabas began to think that, despite all the fear and uncertainty ahead, this was one of the best nights of his life.

The birds were singing loudly, and the eastern sky was edging from purple to orange when a woman ran up the road, calling "Maestro! Sanjani!" Tragidenko and Sanjani must have been awake, too, because they were out in the yard in a moment.

"Lights on the road, Maestro, heading this way," the messenger said.

"Barnabas, Wickram," Sanjani said. "It's time."

CHAPTER 25

"**B**oys, get changed! Wickram, it will be cold underground, so wear your blue sweater. And could you bring your old sweater down — the orange one with the embroidered mushrooms — for Barnabas?"

Sanjani had been packing and preparing food for almost two hours. She still didn't feel ready, but there was no more time. She loaded the food and drink containers into her backpack, and when that was full, topped-up Barnabas' bag, which was already heavy with his school books. Her mind was racing, wondering what else she and Wickram might need for however long they had to stay in the City. She again questioned the wisdom of this trip. Was it worth the risks — both the risks of the journey and the possibility they would not be able to return to the Valley? She caught sight of Barnabas pulling on his t-shirt over his small, slender frame. Such a delicate child should not have to face so much danger and responsibility alone; he had already braved so much. She watched him put on the absurd bowler hat with great dignity, and the poignancy of the gesture touched her. No, it was right to go — for *all* the reasons they were going.

Sanjani slid a flashlight into a side-pouch of Barnabas backpack. She told him, "Graviddy lent it to us. She says the batteries are quite fresh." Running to the foot of the stairs, she yelled up, "Hurry, Wickram! If we get caught by the Aqua Guard, all is lost!"

Wickram ran down the stairs a moment later carrying his guitar. The pack on his back was practically bursting at the seams.

Sanjani shook her head. "No, put that guitar away! How will you carry it through the tunnels?"

"I need it for my audition!"

"They will have guitars at the school. Go!" Wickram ran back upstairs and she knelt, removing impractical items he had added to his overstuffed backpack. This was no time for sentiment. As soon as Wickram returned, she hustled the boys out the door.

Dimitri was there in the front yard, rising up on his toes to peer down the road nervously. "All ready, boys?" he asked. They didn't answer, and Sanjani thought they looked a little shell-shocked.

She came and stood before her husband. They were both pulling hard on the reins of emotions that threatened to break free; they knew they needed to be strong now.

She said, "All right, Dimitri, we're going. Don't let Whistlewort start a fight with the Aqua. Just explain to them —"

"Yes, my darling, don't worry, we'll be fine. Just come back soon."

"I will," she promised, though she knew she might not be able to keep it. To walk away from her mate, not knowing if she would be able to return — how could the world ask such sacrifices?

Dimitri was trying to catch his son's gaze, and Sanjani watched Wickram stubbornly refusing to give it. "Good luck to you all, and god speed," the Maestro said. "Wickram, take care... of yourself and of Barnabas. And... remember that I am with you. Always."

Sanjani held her breath, wondering what hurtful comment their son might make in return, but he just shifted from side to side and said, "Don't worry about me. You just take care of everyone in Pastoral Park. Don't let anyone hurt the circus." He gave his father a small, shy look before turning away again.

Then they just stood there. They had to leave, but no one seemed willing to make the first move. "Wait a minute," she shouted, and ran back into the house. She returned a minute later, holding Wickram's guitar. "Take this," she told her son.

"I thought you said it doesn't make sense to drag —"

"No, I know! Just... take it. Think of it as a talisman. A good luck charm."

"Kind of a clunky good-luck charm," he muttered, though she could tell he was relieved. He pulled the strap over his shoulders, shrugging and twisting to find a place for it alongside his backpack.

Feeling the heat of tears rising behind her eyes again, Sanjani grabbed one boy in each hand and hurried out through the gate without a backward glance. She led them across the road where they slipped between the bushes onto a small path that led down the back of the hill, away from any approach the Guard might make. They hurried along in the dark without a lantern and without a word, stopping to check before they passed into any clearing or across any road. The gloaming was upon them, and Sanjani had a brief glimpse of the pre-dawn sky, splendidly pregnant with the day, before they entered the dimness of the woods.

They could not help but crack twigs beneath their feet or startle the small creatures of the undergrowth, but hopefully they were far enough away that no one could hear them. The path was familiar to Sanjani, one she had often walked alone when she needed to be away for a few hours. It was through these woods she had entered her new life, whose peace and joy she was daily grateful for. But she never forgot that she was an outsider, too. These sanctuary woods still connected her to the life she used to have. Now, she was leading her only child through them to his new life. Was she offering him a blessing or a curse? Or was tradition always both?

She soon heard the burbling of the river, and then, coming around a dense stand of young trees, she saw the stone bridge. The sun had risen, and little glints of illumination were starting to penetrate the gloom of the woods. One such glint caught the white hair of the old woman, standing in the centre of the bridge in her long brown dress, leaning on her sturdy cane of gnarled oak. It was like she had been waiting for them.

Holding the cane in both hands, the old woman raised it over her head and stood up straight as if to show them that she had no need of its support. "Stop!" she said, her voice like a strong west wind. "Speak your business."

The boys, who had been dawdling behind, caught up and stood beside Sanjani in a tight knot.

"I'm not afraid of ghosts," Wickram muttered nervously under his breath.

Sanjani called out to the old woman, "Hello! It has been many years since I've seen you. You are looking very well. I've come here with —"

"Silence!" the old woman shouted, and Sanjani caught her breath. Would she not even be allowed to plead their case?

The old woman pointed it at Barnabas. "You, boy! You are not from here."

Barnabas' voice was a hoarse squeak. "N-no." But then he cleared his throat and took a few steps forward. "I'm from the City. And I have to return there on very urgent business."

The old woman laughed. She flashed a rueful smile at Sanjani, who saw that one of her eyes had been replaced by a shiny, black stone. *Was it always like that?* Sanjani wondered, confused. She found it hard to keep her focus on the real eye.

The old woman said, "Everything is always so *urgent* for the young, isn't it?" She laughed again — a crackling sound, like grit thrown against glass.

But apparently, Barnabas was not going to be intimidated by her. He called back, "This *is* urgent! George Glower has returned to the City, and he's going to blow up all the Towers! Send them crashing into the Valley!"

The old woman gave him a rueful, haughty smile, and now it seemed like the black stone was the true eye in the pair. "*Glower*, as you call him, is just another blunt tool of destiny. How many years do you think those towers can go on, teetering on the edge like that? One hundred? Two? He's just hurrying along the demise of your noisy, boastful world. Why should I care?"

But Barnabas was not backing down, and Sanjani's respect for him grew. "Well, I care!" he said, then softened his tone. "Please, ma'am, you have to let me and Sanjani through. And Wickram, too..." he indicated his friend, standing behind him in stunned silence. Barnabas implored, "I have to at least try and save the City. Please let us pass."

"Wickram is my son," Sanjani said with proud smile as she stepped forward to stand at Barnabas' side. "Remember? You helped me when I came to the Valley. I was barely a child myself, and now I am a grown woman and a mother."

The old woman looked at her but said nothing. She moved her head in what might have been a nod of recognition. Maybe they were persuading her after all.

She beckoned Wickram with a crooked finger. He inched ahead, guitar hugged to his chest like a shield, until he was standing with the others. The old woman said, "So, you would bring your music to that place of corruption?"

"Yeah," Wickram answered hoarsely.

"Be careful, they will accost you in an alley and steal your precious tunes away. They will give them to a banshee with a million mouths who will wail them into a million ears. But neither the banshee nor the ears will understand what those songs cost you to create."

Wickram shot his mother a panicked look, and she smiled weakly, willing him to stay calm. The light was growing stronger around them, and Sanjani peeked back over her shoulder. How much time did they have? Were the Aqua on their way yet?

A tense silence dragged on and on before the old woman said, "Fine, I will let you take the path, though I don't promise you will survive it. Come across the bridge!" The boys went first. Sanjani turned around one last time, to look for the Aqua Guard, or maybe to say goodbye. Then, just as she was about to put her foot on the bridge, the old woman barred her way with the cane.

"No!" she said, coldly. "Not you. This is not your journey to make."

Sanjani caught her breath. Wickram and Barnabas, now behind the old woman on the bridge, looked at her for guidance. She said, "But... They are still children; they need my help!"

"Go away! Go back to your home; you have no place here." The old woman scowled and turned her back on Sanjani, her dress swirling around her ankles. Sanjani felt her heart break like she was losing a second mother. *I didn't do anything wrong,* she wanted to shout. *Don't punish me!* But this was not about her, she reminded herself. She reached out a hand to the boys. She saw it was shaking.

"Wickram!" she said, trying to keep her voice light. "Give me your backpack." He handed it past the old woman, who was standing rigid as stone. Sanjani crouched on the ground and transferred some more of the food and water to her son's pack. Then she held up a small, worn book with a soiled blue cover. "Do you see this?"

"Yeah. Mom, listen..."

"No, you listen to me. In this book, I have written the name and phone number of the music school as well your Aunt Kareena's number and address." She put the book in the front pocket of Wickram's backpack and closed the strap securely over it. When she handed it back to him, their fingers brushed for just a second. The tears could not then be prevented.

Sanjani watched the boys cross the bridge, the old woman following behind them. "Mom!" Wickram called one more time from the other side of the river.

Forcing a smile through her tears, she called back, "Go! You'll be all right, Pickle. I trust the old woman with my life."

Barnabas waved and said, "Thank you, Sanjani, for everything! I won't let you down."

Sanjani waved back, and kept waving as they headed down the path. Suddenly remembering something, she jumped up and shouted so that the boys turned back around: "Barnabas! Don't tell them about the Valley! Please, for all our sakes!"

He looked a little startled by this dictum, but nodded his agreement. Then they were gone, disappearing down the path into the dark pine forest across the river that the light of the new day had yet to penetrate. Sanjani wiped her tears away with her sleeve. Feeling tired and empty, she sat herself on a wide flat stone, wondering if she had made a terrible mistake bringing her son and Barnabas here, to walk this uncertain path through the earth. She hadn't even told them about the voices underground, the whispers of those unnamed creatures in whose hands the fates of travellers lay.

She wasn't sure how long she sat there, maybe half an hour or more. She knew she had to return to whatever disaster was manifesting itself at the circus, and she got wearily to her feet, finding her back stiff and her knees sore. She was startled by the sound of heavy footsteps and the shaking of the bushes back along the path to Pastoral Park. Her stomach clenched in fear and she prepared for the appearance of the Aqua Guard. But that wasn't who came around the corner. No, it was a woman in grey, large and formidable, and in a fury. It was Carmin.

***

She was the Speaker of Clouding Guild. This fact meant a great deal to Carmin, yet it was also so inadequate. True, she was proud to be the one who steered the most powerful and the most devout of the guilds. She had a platform from which to speak great truths, and people were obliged to listen. And yet, the limitations of her position were a constant source of frustration. The members of the other guilds, and worse, the denizens outside the guilds — those damned circus people, especially — could not seem to comprehend the simplest of truths: Father Glory was all-powerful and his precepts, though sometimes hard to abide by, were laid out with perfect clarity. You just had to do what you were told. How difficult was that?! No matter how prideful it sounded, it was nonetheless true that if Clouding Guild (and thus she) was in charge instead of the Guild Council, with its endless appeasements and compromises, the Valley would be purer, more tranquil, and mightier.

But in just a few hours, everything had fallen apart — and right before the days of her greatest triumph! She was a fugitive, stripped of her office, hunted like an animal. It was galling. She had no doubt that the situation could be rectified. All that had to happen was for Glower to complete his part of the plan. Then in the chaos that ensued, only she and her inner circle would be ready and able to take control and restore order. Her destiny as Prophet of the Rebuilding would be a certainty.

But for that to happen, she had to stop the boy.

Was she making too much of this one small unbeliever? He was just a weak City rat. But Carminn was too honest to fool herself. She was a sharp judge of character, and she saw in this Barnabas creature the tenacious grain of grit that could grind her great plan to an ignominious halt.

Following her escape from custody, she had waited for hours in the trees outside the Guild Hall instead of running somewhere safer. The Aqua Guard had left the building to pursue her, and she knew how easy it would be to get inside and take down whatever few guardsmen remained. Then she could snap the boy's neck and be gone in a trice. But the damned circus freaks had the same idea and beat her to it! She almost ambushed him again when the old man left him alone on the horse, but there hadn't been enough time. So she had followed them to Pastoral Park, and then into the woods. And now she was almost upon her quarry. Only the impious City-born wife of the abominable Tragidenko stood in her way.

"You're too late, Carminn" the small woman shouted at her defiantly, standing at the foot of the bridge. "Barnabas and my son have crossed the river. The old woman of the woods will guide them on their journey, and there's nothing you can do to stop them."

For all the woman's bravado, Carminn could sense her fear. *What is her name?* she thought. *Ah, yes...* She called out, "Sanjani, let me pass, and you will not be hurt." She moved slowly and resolutely down the path toward the bridge. Panic flickered in Sanjani's eyes and she reached down to pick up a fallen branch, a weighty cudgel that could inflict some real damage. Carminn smiled; she actually admired her spirit. Motherhood had given her enemy courage beyond her stature. Carminn understood this; she had three children of her own , though she hadn't had the time to raise them. But she knew that all she was trying to do for Clouding, for the Valley, was also for their sake. They might resent her for her absence, but they would someday appreciate what she had sacrificed for them. They would see that this, too was a mother's love.

Carminn didn't slow her advance. Sanjani backed up onto the bridge, swinging the heavy branch in front of her. "Get back!" she called. "You're a criminal! A murderer!" Carminn kept her breath steady. She watched the rhythm of Sanjani's swings. Then, in one swift move, just as the stick changed direction at the end of a swing, Carminn leaped forward and caught it in one big hand. Sanjani cried out as the branch was wrenched from her hand, and Carminn brought it down across her thighs, knocking her to the ground.

But this little mother was not done; with no weapon but savage anger, Sanjani tore at Carminn with her bare hands, trying to stop her crossing the bridge at all costs. Carminn lifted the frail City creature off the ground like a bundle of kindling and tossed her against the stones the bridge. Her head connected with an awful crack. Blood gathered around Sanjani's head as Carminn looked down at the fallen body. She sent up a short prayer to the Father that the little mother was not dead. Such bravery didn't deserve death. Then Carminn turned her back on her adversary and crossed to the far side of the river.

The woods were darker here. Overhead, pinpoints of brilliant, morning light broke through the dense canopy of pine needles — little dazzles that made the contrasting darkness below seem all the more threatening. The path was narrower here. It meandered dizzily, on and on, seemingly without destination. But at last, Carminn turned a corner and found herself in a clearing before a great rock wall. In the wall was a cave mouth, so black, it looked like an absence cut in the fabric of the world. Sitting on a log, blocking the cave mouth, was an old woman, rough and sharp as the pine trees around her. She was bending narrow branches into intricate shapes and tying them with sturdy twine.

The old woman spoke to her without looking up. "Another one? Are you trying to get to the City, too?" She snorted derisively. "Everyone demanding the river run backwards for their pleasure."

Carminn considered just pushing past her and into the cave, but she had a feeling that this was not wise. Unlike Tragidenko's wife, there was something in this old woman's bearing that implied true power.

"That looks like a trap for small animals," Carminn said, trying to sound friendly and unhurried.

"A woman has to find her dinner, doesn't she?"

"True enough. Actually, I don't need to reach the City. I just want to stop two boys. Did you see them? They are on a fool's errand, and I don't want them to get hurt. If I go into the cave, will I find them?"

"There's no telling what you'll find in there! Your destiny, I suppose, one way or another." The old woman looked up from her work, fixing Carminn with a double stare of flesh and stone. "Oh, yes, your destiny."

Carminn didn't like her life being explained to her by some heretical fortune teller. A little too harshly, she said, "My only destiny is the one written for me by Father Glory."

"Never heard of him." The old woman tied a length of twine around two branches and then bit the dangling end off with surprisingly sharp teeth.

Cautiously, Carminn moved closer, squatting in front of her. "The revelations of the Holy Father have not reached you? Don't worry; in the glorious days to come, His name will travel farther than ever before. I pray that all the heathens in the City will come to know it. I could come here and teach you, if you like! It would be an honour to bring the gift of peace to your soul."

"Ha! I have all the peace I need here in the woods — that is until you fools show up and disturb me." She put the trap down on the ground and began digging in the pockets of her dress. "I will let you enter the cave. But I had better give you something." She pulled out a single wooden match and handed it to Carminn. The old woman said, "When the darkest hour comes, light this match and you will see just what that destiny of yours looks like."

Carminn let a little laugh escape her. "Well, thank you, lady. But I brought my own lights!" She lifted her tunic to show several compact battery-powered lanterns, strapped to her work belt. "I do, however, appreciate your kindness." She put the match away in a compartment in the belt. "How much of a head-start do the boys have?"

"That depends how fast they're going." The old woman picked up her trap and her spool of twine and walked away from Carminn, saying, "Don't worry. I'm sure your Father Glory — is that his name? — has the situation well in hand." And with that, she disappeared into the woods.

Carminn frowned. Was she being laughed at? Fool of an old woman! She got to her feet and walked to the cave entrance, unnerved by the fetid smell and the chill, damp air that escaped from its dark mouth. For a moment, she thought she heard a whispering voice inside, and a seedling of fear unfurled in her heart. But when she listened closer, there was nothing.

"Bah!" she spat on the earth. "The Holy Father is architect and site manager. His blueprints guide my life!" She crossed her fists on her chest and, switching on one of her lanterns, marched into the darkness.

***

Forty minutes earlier, Barnabas and Wickram had followed the old woman away from the bridge and into the eerie darkness of the pine forest. Barnabas saw that Wickram was good and spooked. His head snapped right and left and then back to the old woman as if he was expecting doom to descend in one form or another at any minute. Barnabas felt pretty nervous himself although he wasn't really worried that the witch was going to eat them.

She was moving with surprising speed for someone so ancient. Barnabas trotted to catch up with her and asked, "Did you meet George Glower when he first came to the Valley? You obviously knew who I meant when I told you about his plan. What was he like then?" He was looking at her face, and stumbled on a tree root, falling out of step with her.

"I don't know anything about him," she answered, without slowing or looking back.

"Well, did he come to the Valley through these woods?"

"You expect me to remember all these details! Boy, I have lived a long life and have more important concerns than the comings and goings of restless wanderers." She added, "And watch your step. There's no doctor here to set your broken bones." He would have thanked her for her concern, but she didn't really sound all that concerned.

They came to a clearing. On the other side of it was a wall of rock with a dark cave mouth cut into it. The cave was not much taller than Wickram, and narrower than it was tall. It looked anything but inviting.

The old woman waved her stick at it and said, "There, that is the beginning of the path that might lead you home."

"What do you mean, 'might?'" Barnabas asked.

Wickram, who had fallen behind, emerged into the clearing and came to stand beside him.

The old woman sat down on a log in front of the cave, and Barnabas repeated, "What do you mean —"

"There are many paths within. Uncountable. One wrong turning and you would be lost forever."

Nervous as he was, Wickram snapped at her: "Then how in the krumping pit fire are we supposed to —?"

Barnabas gave him a whack on the arm and spoke with more diplomacy. "Is there some kind of sign, like trail blazes or something, that we have to follow?"

She shook her head. From a pocket of her dress, she pulled a spool of twine and a knife. As she spoke, she began cutting lengths of twine and laying them carefully on the ground in front of her. "No; no sign-posts reading: 'This way to the City, idiots!'"

"Then how —?"

"The Lurkers will either help you or they won't." She looked up at Wickram and laughed. "Your mother must be desperate to send you off this way."

Before Wickram could say anything intemperate, Barnabas replied, "We *are* desperate. And there is no other way."

The old woman nodded. "Well, let's hope your conviction makes an impression on the Lurkers." She reached into another pocket and pulled out a small, square object that bounced a tiny beam of sunshine into Barnabas' eye. "Here, this should help."

It was a little mirror in a simple wooden frame. The glass was dark and pitted in a few places and the wood worn, but it was still a mirror and it still did its job.

Wickram rolled his eyes. "She's messing with us. What's this for, lady? Maybe these Lurkers only help you if your hair is neatly combed?"

But it was to Barnabas the old woman responded. "If you have any hope of making your dreams come true, boy, you have to know who you are."

Barnabas looked into the mirror, wondering indeed, *who am I?* What he saw reflected back was a small, scared kid. He wondered how he could possibly be equal to the tasks that lay before him. And not only that — for the first time he noticed just how much his ears stuck out! Maybe that was why Deni liked Cal better than him. But Garlip thought he was okay... He shook himself loose from this train of thought and put the mirror into the front pocket of his bag.

"Thank you," he told the old woman, who shrugged and got to her feet.

Barnabas and Wickram watched her walk across the clearing to a tree. She began to cut off small branches with her knife, assessing each one carefully. After a minute of this, she turned and snapped, "Well? Aren't you going? I thought you were in a hurry!"

Barnabas almost said 'thank you' again, but she was clearly done with them. He nodded at Wickram, and the two of them approached the cave mouth. Barnabas paused before they entered, shivering at the cold that emerged from its black depths. He pulled out the flashlight from his backpack and shone the beam into the interior, illuminating damp rock and nothing else. He gave Wickram an uncertain look, and Wickram nodded back. Together, they entered the cave.

CHAPTER 26

The climb was steep, and the air damp and cold. All the surfaces were slick, and both of them fell a few times before they got the hang of walking on the smooth rock. Wickram, who had to protect his guitar, took the most painful falls. And that wasn't their only problem. At first, the walls had been farther apart, and the ceiling a little higher, but quickly all the dimensions had shrunk, and Wickram had to hunch over as he walked. He complained a bit about this, but it was Barnabas who was in worse shape.

He wasn't sure what was happening, but as the walls pressed closer, and the darkness became absolute save for the flashlight's narrow beam. Barnabas felt a terrible sense of dread suffuse his whole being. He finally stopped dead and stood there in the tunnel, listening to his loud breathing and feeling the pounding of his heart.

"What's wrong?" Wickram asked. "It's too soon for a break."

"I dunno. I-I feel really crappy. It's like... like the walls are going to squash us." He looked back the way they had come, but the cave's entrance was too far behind them to be seen. He felt like he was encased in rock. Buried alive. In fact, *he was!*

Wickram gave him a little push. "Come on, we have a long way to go."

Barnabas nodded. He pulled his bowler hat more snuggly onto his head and his hands back into the sleeves of his borrowed sweater. *I'll just have to tough it out*, he told himself. *The City is depending on us.* He began to climb the steep path again, trying to put the terrible feeling of unease out of his mind, but it wasn't going away. He remembered experiencing something similar in the narrow, unused corridor in Clouding Guild. Now, it was much worse. Maybe that was because here underground it was impossible to keep track of time, and the tunnel was so monotonously, horrifyingly the same that his panicked mind began to fear if it would never end. He tried to distract himself, concentrating on his footsteps, counting them in batches of 100. Every now and then Wickram's guitar would tap against the wall, and the close echo of the strings would make Barnabas lose count.

It seemed like forever before something finally changed: they came to an intersection, the path dividing into two, each choice basically identical to the other.

"Which way do we go?" Wickram asked as Barnabas shone the light first up one, then the other.

"The one on the right is a bit steeper," Barnabas said. "Let's go that way." *And we'll be up and out of this hell faster!* he thought.

So they took that path, and it was hard going. But Barnabas' panic was now driving him forward with determination. Then they came to another intersection. Shining the light down each of the two paths, he was overcome with doubt, like a layer of frosting on the cake of his panic.

"What should we do?" he asked, and he could hear the fear in his own voice.

"I dunno," Wickram answered. "Hold your flashlight down the left tunnel again. Look, isn't that another split up ahead?"

Barnabas squinted down the tunnel. "I think you're right." The meaning of this hit both of them at once. The old woman had said there was only one right path. Therefore each choice they made was a potential disaster. "So, we made one choice and we have a 50% chance of being wrong. After the next choice, we're 75% likely to be wrong and after that —"

Wickram interrupted, "And if we're wrong, we're lost underground."

"Forever."

"Nah, we would die in just a couple of days after our water runs out."

The longer they stood there, the more the panic was consuming Barnabas, so he turned around and started hurrying back the way they had come, falling on his ass as he shimmied down the steep, slippery slope, but jumping to his feet each time and continuing.

Wickram, following behind him more cautiously was shouting, "Hold it, don't go all spinning dog on me!"

But Barnabas wasn't slowing down and when he got back to the first intersection, it was all he could do to stop himself from running the rest of the way back down the tunnel and out into the forest. Wasn't there some other way they could get to the City? There had to be! He jumped when Wickram laid a hand on his shoulder.

"Hey, hey, Barn! Guy! Easy man. Sit down, take deep breaths."

Barnabas found himself complying, putting his head down to his knees to hide from the unending darkness. Wickram was rubbing his back and it was all he could do to stop himself from screaming. But after a minute, the sharpness of the panic receded.

"Better?" asked Wickram. "You're claustrophobic, Barn. I heard about it from some people in Furrowing Guild. They figure out they can't work underground. Some of them have to join other guilds. Just your luck, huh? You didn't know?"

"I was never underground like this before. Not in any caves or anything."

"Okay, well, it's good we stopped. We gotta figure out how to navigate down here. I don't see any signs or markings or anything."

Barnabas had taken off his backpack and was doing an inventory of its contents, just to distract himself from his misery. He picked up the mirror the old woman had given him. He held it in front of himself and shone the light up on his face. He looked terrible. He got to his feet and joined Wickram in searching for some clue. As he turned around, he suddenly caught sight of something in the mirror up the corridor to the left.

"What?!" he shrieked, which caused Wickram to shout in return.

"Glory! What is it?!"

"I–I saw something up that way." They shone the light up the corridor, trying to see as far as they could.

Wickram shook his head. "No, there's nothing. You're just jumpy. Maybe the old witch said something that we missed... like if we take the first letter of all her sentences, it will spell the answer!"

Barnabas ignored this. He picked up the mirror again, using it to look over his shoulder as he turned slowly around. And there! Up the left-hand corridor — two glowing, red lights. The way they moved together made them look (*oh god*) like a pair of eyes! He spun around and peered up the corridor, but he saw nothing. He shone the flashlight again, and again nothing. Turning off the beam completely, he put his back to the corridor and tried the mirror again. The red eyes had returned.

"Th-there's something there," Barnabas said, his voice quavering. "A pair of eyes." Wickram spun around and looked up the corridor, and when he did, the eyes in the mirror vanished. "No!" Barnabas told him. "Look in the mirror."

Wickram squeezed down beside him. "Holy Mother Mercy..." he breathed.

Barnabas turned on the flashlight between them and they looked at each other. Barnabas said, "The old woman mentioned... Lurkers."

"Whatever," Wickram said, his voice tight and high. "We obviously don't go up the path with the red-eyed monster, right?"

Barnabas really wanted to agree with this logic, but he couldn't. "No, she said the Lurkers had to help us or we would be lost. We..." he swallowed audibly. "We have to go toward... whatever that is."

Wickram opened his mouth as if to object but then closed it and nodded. "Just shine the light again. Make sure it's not hanging off the ceiling or anything." But there was nothing, and so Barnabas led them up the slope. It was a shallower incline than the way they had originally gone, which was a relief. After about five minutes they reached another intersection.

"Now what?" Wickram asked. Barnabas turned off the flashlight and turned his back. He used the mirror to look up each of the two new tunnels. Up the path to the right, he saw not one, but two sets of eyes. He turned on the flashlight and led Wickram that way. After a few more such choices, Barnabas was feeling confident about their system. On the other hand, the number of Lurkers ahead of them was growing with each turning. He had to wonder if they weren't just wilfully following some carnivorous predator straight into its nest.

"How's the claustrophobia going?" Wickram asked him as they marched along briskly, trying to fight their nerves with sheer momentum.

"Thanks for reminding me. I kind of want to throw up, but I'm trying not to think about it." Barnabas noticed they were speaking in whispers.

Wickram had more questions: "Why do we only see the Lurkers in the mirror?"

"Maybe they close their eyes if we look right at them. They're shy."

"Then why don't we see them with the flashlight?"

"I don't know," Barnabas snapped, annoyed that Wickram expected him to be the expert. And then as if they had jinxed the device by talking about it, the flashlight's beam began to flicker. Barnabas gave it whack with the palm of his hand and it stayed on for a few more seconds before failing completely.

"Shit!"

"What do we do *now*?!" Wickram whined in his ear.

"Just… keep going." They stumbled forward in the dark, and Wickram kept stepping on his heels. "Watch where you're going!"

"In case you didn't notice, it's pitch black in here!"

"Ow!" Barnabas said as he collided with a wall. He rubbed his forehead. At least he hadn't broken the mirror, which he was still holding. He calmed his mind as much as he could and tried to get oriented. Behind him was the corridor they had walked up, in front of him was a wall. Barnabas reached to the left and felt another wall. To the right, there was nothing. "Put your hand on my shoulder," he told Wickram and they began to move along more slowly in that direction.

After a few minutes, he could hear their footsteps start to echo. The air seemed to be moving on his face. Were they in an open space? He reached in front and to the sides, but he could feel no walls. He made himself perfectly still and opened his senses wide. Small shufflings, a little snort, and a smell: dank, rank and alive. In front of him, not more than two meters away, a pair of red eyes opened. And then another to his left, and then more and more until there were tens, hundreds.

In the diffuse pink light of all those eyes, Barnabas could almost see. There seemed to be large forms everywhere, but he couldn't make them out. He slowly brought his backpack around in front of him and pulled his phone out. He turned it on and raised it slowly, using it to light his surroundings. He gasped and Wickram gave a short, sharp "Krump!"

They were indeed in a large cave, and the Lurkers were all around them, squatting on the ground and on rocky outcroppings. They weren't *not* human, but with their red eyes and long white hair that hung straight down over their shoulders and backs, they were certainly strange. They squatted like monkeys, and Barnabas wasn't sure if their bodies were covered with pale fur or some kind of rough garment. His phone's screen went red again with the low battery warning, and reluctantly he shut the device off. He needed to save the last of the power for when he got them back up to the City. If he got them back.

With the phone off, the red eyes were again the only illumination in the cave. The Lurkers seemed to be waiting.

"Say something," Wickram hissed at him, but Barnabas didn't know how to talk to these creatures. He felt like he didn't even have a voice.

A hand dropped down to clasp his shoulder; he could feel its sharp claws piercing his borrowed sweater and threatening to poke through his t-shirt too. He only had time to say, "Wait!" before he and Wickram were hustled forward, out of the big cave and back into one of the claustrophobic corridors. He heard Wickram's guitar bang briefly on the wall. After a few minutes of this forced march, they found themselves tossed together.

"Where are we?!" Wickram called in the darkness. Barnabas slowly circled around until he had determined that they were in a closed cell, smooth stone all around them as well as above their heads and below their feet. He couldn't even find whatever door they had been pushed through. They were buried deep underground, and even if he could find his voice again, there was no one to hear his scream.

***

Carminn climbed through the tunnels resolutely, lighting her way with one of the electric lanterns. At intersections, she made notations on the rock wall with a piece of chalk. She had doubled-back several times, trying to figure out if there was any underlying order to the design of these tunnels. They were clearly not natural, so someone must have had some plan in mind for their layout. But what if it was all haphazard? One tunnel following another over time, built willy-nilly without forethought? She couldn't expect some subterranean animals to think with the same logic as a child of Father Glory. She stood at an intersection, scratching her head when she suddenly heard a whisper.

"Who's there?" she called, repressing the nervous shiver in her breast with an iron will.

There was no answer, but she decided to walk in the direction the whisper had come from. Her lantern started to blink on and off and abruptly died. Cursing quietly, she clipped the dead lantern back on her tool belt and took out another. At the next intersection, she stopped and listened, and sure enough more whispers emerged from one of the two tunnels. Her second lantern died a short while later, and this time, with only one working lantern left, she knelt in the tunnel and took the two dead ones apart. The battery contacts were wet, almost sticky, with condensation. After she had wiped them with the hem of her tunic, the lanterns flickered to life again. The whispers grew louder and more insistent as she re-clipped the lanterns to her belt and got back on her feet.

"Yes, yes, I'm coming. If you had any decency, you would show yourselves!"

But no sooner had she said that when the tunnel opened up into a wide cave. Shining her light all around, she saw a vast space with ledges and walkways of stone at different levels. The high ceiling was a gallery of dripping stalactites. Tunnel mouths opened everywhere, suggesting that the whole underground world was complex as an anthill. And everywhere, there were creatures — identical as far as she could tell — squatting on every surface, occasionally moving around to huddle close to each other. Though their shape was human, they were clearly animals. They were grooming each other, scratching themselves shamelessly! And all were staring at her with their beady red eyes. She saw little that she would call intelligence there, and the fact that they had not shaped their world with more ingenuity proved it.

But she could not afford to speak to them as animals; they outnumbered her and, more importantly, she needed their help. Slowly, so as not to cause alarm, she stepped up onto a wide flat rock in the centre of the cave. Keeping her eyes on the assembled throng, she crouched slowly and removed the two lanterns from her belt. She unfolded the little feet on the backs of the lanterns, and stood them on the rock beside her. She switched them on and rose again in their bright beams, lifting her arms wide.

"The blessings of Father Glory upon you, great congregation!" she called. "I am Carminn, Speaker of…" she stopped. She was about to say 'Speaker of Clouding Guild,' but she saw no reason not to embody her new role here and now. "I am Carminn, Prophet of the Rebuilding! It is the will of the Great Father that I should meet you today, at the dawn of the new age, for it is abundantly clear that you are to play a role in this momentous transition."

Carminn looked around at the blinking red eyes. Did they even comprehend? The animals had stopped grooming each other; perhaps that was a good sign.

"I presume you know of the City that rises over your heads, of the millions of lost souls who walk its streets. In two days, the great towers of that city are destined to fall — fall as the giants of old fell. The earth will shake with their collapse, and the air will be filled with the cries of anguish at the death of old dreams. This tragedy is the will of Father Glory and must not be prevented. But in the wake of this tragedy, new dreams will be born: a world of purity and pious humility where we will all build together in the name of the Great Architect. Raise your hands in the air and feel his strength flow into you!"

Carminn raised her arms over her head, and all around the cave, the creatures did the same although they seemed to be not so much reaching for heaven as surrendering to a gunman. Nonetheless, they understood her! She lowered her arms and continued:

"Hail, Father Glory! But I am sad to inform you that there are those who would derail the Holy Engine before it can enter the Station of Grace. Here, in your mighty halls..." she looked around for effect, trying not to betray her disgust with how these monsters actually lived, "...there are two young heretics who, in their arrogance, seek to save the towers and to let the City... Uh, you may lower your arms now... Thank you. Heretics who would let the City carry on in its degenerate path!"

The beasts were completely still now, watching her with fascination, or so it seemed to her. She had them! Her voice grew more intimate. "And now, I ask you, in the name of the Holy Future, to bring those deluded young men to me. I will lead them back to the Valley, where we will kneel together and pray for strength in the coming time of tribulations." It was better, she knew, to tell this tale than speak the truth. The boys had to die, but it would be hard to explain the rightness of that path to these coarse and credulous creatures.

Carminn gasped when a heavy, hairy arm descended on her shoulder. She turned and stared into its red eyes. The creature's smell filled her nostrils, but she managed a smile. He... it... led her down from her stage, and she decided she would follow the creature. She believed in her Glory-granted powers of oratory. She would trust the Holy Father.

***

Barnabas woke confused from a troubled sleep, raising himself up stiffly on his forearms. At first, he thought he couldn't open his eyes, but then he realized that they were open; there was simply no light to see by. Understanding that he was still in the stone cell, he moaned and lowered himself back to the hard floor.

"Wickram?" he said, huskily. He cleared his throat and repeated louder,

"Wickram?!" hearing an edge of panic in his voice.

"Wha…?" The other boy snorted. There was a pause. "Oh."

Adrenaline spiked through Barnabas' body, bringing him to full, jittering wakefulness. His mind was turning quickly, offering a complete and vivid recap of the whole nightmarish situation: trapped underground by creatures who didn't talk, in a stone cell with no door, under kilotonnes of rock. Almost immediately, he felt the fear and nausea of the claustrophobia descending again. He groaned miserably.

Out of the thick, inky darkness, Wickram asked, "How long have we been asleep?"

"I have no clue. What the hell are we gonna do?" He whimpered, and there was no way to prevent the tears that started rolling freely down his cheeks. They would die here underground. The towers would fall, people would die, and Barnabas was powerless to prevent it. A stupid, embarrassing sob escaped, and he hit the ground with his fist in aggravation.

Wickram said, "Hey, hey, Barn, don't worry! Let's just… I dunno… take stock."

Barnabas heard him moving around. He heard the guitar bump against something, the strings ringing, and then Wickram was right beside him, with a big comforting hand on his shoulder.

"Where's your backpack?" Wickram asked, his voice remarkably gentle. "Oh, I got it. Let's drink… eat some fruit, okay? Would you like that?

Wickram put an apple in his hand, and he sat up and took a bite. They ate their little pitch-black picnic in silence, and Barnabas was grateful for something to do, and grateful that he wasn't alone. He sniffed back his snot and wiped his nose.

"You know," he told Wickram, "You're the most confusing guy in the world."

Wickram laughed. "Flamtasmic! Do I get a plaque?"

"No seriously, in the last two days, you've been this enthusiastic tour guide, then you were a jealous, drunken creep who punched me and knocked me to the ground, and now you're being all… well, really nice."

"So you're saying I should choose just one personality and run with it?"

"This one's okay," he said with an unseen smile.

"Hey, I got your little ball toy here, the one you got back from Glower. What does it do, anyway?"

"It makes monsters."

"Oh yeah? Maybe we could use some of those. They could fight off the Lurker dudes, and we could get out of here." Barnabas could hear him pushing the buttons on the *diaboriku*. "How does it work, anyway?"

"I don't know. I can't figure it out," he answered distractedly. The panicky tightness of the room was starting to overwhelm him again. He put his head against the cool stone wall and groaned.

"You okay there, Barn? Just lie down and relax." Barnabas did as he was told, stretching out on the floor while Wickram shuffled around again. Then he was tuning his guitar, and then he was playing. It wasn't a tune — not at first — but an undulating river of arpeggiated chords that was somehow soothing. As the music flowed around him, Barnabas felt like he was floating free of his body. And as a melody began to take shape among the chords, Barnabas' fear and nausea receded, at least enough that he felt human again.

"I wish my brother Thelonius was here. We need someone brave like him."

Still playing, Wickram said, "What makes him so brave?"

"Well, for one thing, he's part of this group called the Innervaders. They go into all these places you're not supposed to, places with "No Entry" signs. They just want to find out what goes on there and see stuff that's kept hidden from the public."

"Hunh," Wickram said.

"What?"

"Well, that sounds like you. You snuck into the Drop Shop, into the Clouding Works…"

"No! That's not the same! The Drop Shop was Graviddy's idea. And I had no choice about Clouding. I had to do that if I wanted to get proof for the Council."

Switching to loud, Flamenco-ish chords, Wickram said, "If you say so." But then suddenly he stopped playing. Barnabas opened his eyes and saw a faint pink light in the cell, just enough that he could make out Wickram, sitting with the guitar in his lap, staring in shock. Barnabas turned to his right. Where he could swear there had been a solid wall before, there sat a dense crowd of Lurkers, their red eyes glowing — dozens of them, stretching back down the corridor. The creatures began whispering to each other in little sibilant crackles. Soon the "discussion" was over, and the Lurkers began to retreat, backing away down the tunnel. Barnabas sat up urgently, afraid the cell would close around them again.

"Wait!" he cried, but that was exactly what they were doing; they had paused a few metres away. "Wickram, they want us to follow them."

"Do you think we should?"

"Yes! Come on!" He placed his hat back on his head and repacked his bag. He couldn't make the mirror fit inside, so he carried it. "And keep playing guitar!" he told Wickram. "That's why they're letting us go, I think!"

Like some crazy parade, the boys followed the Lurkers through the dark tunnel, Wickram bringing up the rear, playing a dissonant marching song. They soon arrived in the big cave which seemed to be their central meeting place. Barnabas was surprised to find a wide, flat rock in the centre of the space, lit up by two small electric lanterns.

"Wickram," he whispered. "Get up on that rock and play for them."

Wickram shook his head vehemently. "Not unless you get up with me!" he hissed back.

"But it's you they want to hear!"

"Yeah, but it's you who better talk us out of here. Otherwise maybe they'll just keep us as entertainment, bring us out once a day to perform. And, by the way, if that's what happens, you better learn to do magic tricks or tap dance or something."

"Okay, okay, come on."

Together they got up on the rock. The lanterns flickered on and off from time to time, and Barnabas was afraid they were going to go dead like his flashlight had. Wickram continued to play quietly, and Barnabas tried to gather his thoughts. Thankfully, his claustrophobia wasn't as bad under this high ceiling.

He could see the creatures closest to them, and beyond that, he could see hundreds of pairs of eyes. *Well,* he thought, *I have their attention!* "Hello, uh, Lurkers," he said. "My name is Barnabas Bopwright, and this is Wickram. We're sorry to, you know, invade your home like this. We would never have, but it's the only way we can get back to the City. You see, there's a big, big problem. Someone wants to do something, um, bad up there. And a lot of people will be hurt, and die even. I know the two of us don't look all that strong or anything, but we're the only ones who can stop Glower... Oh, he's the one that's going to do it — destroy the towers."

He realized that they probably had no idea what the towers were or what a "Glower" was. He was making a mess of it! He looked down and noticed he was still holding the mirror. He looked again at himself in its dark depths. His face still looked like a kid's, all soft and smooth, hardly a hint of a moustache yet. What was it the old woman had said? *If you want your dreams to come true, you have to know who you are.* But who was he? Not a hero! But then he thought about what Wickram had said about him being an Innervader like Thelonius. And thinking about it, he had to admit it was sort of true. It didn't matter that he had reasons why he did what he did. The fact was, he had done it! He looked again at his image, and he could kind of see something in his eyes. They didn't look the eyes of a scared kid, after all. They looked steady and clear. They looked brave.

He raised his head. "Listen, I don't know what you know about the City or the Valley. I don't know if you believe in anything, like God or Father Glory or... or working hard or making money or whatever. Heck, I don't know what I believe, except that everywhere I go, I see people who are just trying to live. And they all have problems and they're all worried about stuff. The kids are worried about what the world will be like when they grow up, and the adults are worried what will happen to their kids. There are bullies everywhere but also good people. And-and some people who are trying to be good sometimes mess it up."

Wickram muttered, "Hey, don't bring me into it."

The lanterns both flickered ominously, and Barnabas felt that his thoughts, too, were faltering. But then he knew where he was going: "I just believe — I *really* believe — that even if you want the world to be one way or another, you have to think about everyone — all the different kinds of people... and try not to hurt any of them with your plans. I think that if the world is going to get better, it won't be by knocking down the towers and rebuilding on top of the rubble and the dead bodies!"

Wickram stopped playing and said, "Barn, enough with the sermons. Just tell them what you want."

"What I...? Oh, right. Uh, so please — *please* — let us out of here. Help us get back to the City, okay?"

One of the lanterns chose that moment to flicker out. The Lurkers, who had all been staring at the improvised stage, turned to each other and began speaking in that strange chattering whisper. The sound soon filled the hall, like a swarm of locusts was passing overhead. Then, just as quickly, it died down.

"Barn, look!" Wickram was pointing way up the cavern wall off to the left. There, in one of the many cave doors, leading to one of the innumerable corridors of stone, a light was flashing on and off.

"That's it!" Barnabas breathed. "They're letting us go. That's the way!" He turned to the great crowd of Lurkers and said, "Thank you! Thanks!" but the creatures were dispersing, moving off into the interstices of their world to do whatever business filled their lives. One Lurker, however, came forward and stood before them. He held out one of his large, clawed hands, palm up. Barnabas couldn't bring himself to actually take the hand, but he motioned to Wickram. The two of them came down off the rock to stand beside the creature, who turned and led them up and up, towards the light.

***

Carminn was sitting on a rock in the small alcove where they had brought her, presumably while they discussed what to do for her. Her lantern, flickering intermittently, lit up walls stained in rainbow hues by dripping mineral water. A little spring of cold, clear water burbled up out of the ground, and she made a cup of her hands to drink. It was necessary to wash down the food the creatures had brought her. The stew of grubs and pale roots wasn't exactly appetizing, but she understood it was an offering, and so she felt obliged to accept it. These simple creatures clearly wanted to be led on the path to Father Glory, and she was prepared to take on that responsibility along with all her others.

One of the creatures entered the alcove and beckoned to her, lowering his head so he did not look her in the eye. "Don't be afraid, child," she said as she got to her feet. "My Lord accepts all who are prepared to dedicate the strength of their limbs to His glorious works."

She followed the creature back to the main cave. The congregation was much smaller than it had been, and she presumed these were the leaders, whatever that meant in this kind of primitive society. She took her place on the stone stage. One of the lanterns had gone out and the other was flickering. She would have to clear the moisture off the contacts again when she had a moment.

Two of the creatures came forward, one carrying what appeared to be a mat of woven mosses that he place reverently on her shoulders like a cloak. The other held a twisted ring of roots, and with this he crowned her.

Despite the primitive simplicity of the creatures, she felt touched and honoured. The two backed away from her, their eyes averted, and she couldn't help but smile, a rush of motherly affection filling her breast.

"Thank you, my children," Carminn said. "I thank you for this honour, and I accept the responsibility of being your prophet, of being chosen to open your eyes to the brilliant light of the Holy Truth. When the towers have fallen and the great work of rebuilding commences, I will send missionaries here to teach you. You will have the honour to serve the great mission, and the riches of your underground world will at last find purpose."

Sensing it was time to show them her natural authority, Carminn let the smile drop from her face and took on a stern demeanour. "Now, you must help me; there is no more time to lose. Bring me to the boys so I may stop their wrongheaded interference. Help me to reach out to them, and I will always be merciful to your people in the new age to come."

The creatures turned to each other and chattered in their staccato tones. The creature closest to her, the one who had crowned her, raised its hand. Down at the bottom of the cave wall, over to her right, a light began blinking in one of the many corridor entrances.

"That is my path?" she asked, and the creature gestured towards it. She considered stopping to retrieve the two lanterns at her feet, but now that the creatures were helping her, she wasn't so worried. She turned on her remaining lantern and headed across the great cavern toward the blinking light.

The light vanished as she stepped through the entrance. She began making her way down the long corridor of sleek rock, her lantern like the last star in a dying universe. She stopped when she reached an intersection, but then, down one of the two paths, she saw a distant light wink on and off. She took that route and soon came to another intersection where the same happened. She plunged on into the underworld.

She was almost running now, suddenly nervous about how far ahead the boys might be; she had waited a long time for the damned animals to finish their deliberations. The taste of their disgusting repast fouled her mouth. She was suddenly aware of the musty smell of the moss cloak around her shoulders, and the scratch of the crown on her head. She threw them off as she hurried along, following one beacon after another, not daring to wonder why she was descending instead of climbing…

Her lantern went out after the seventh or eighth intersection. A voice inside her said, *This is the path to doom, sister; go back.* But there was no way, she realized, that she would be able to retrace her steps. She cursed herself for not marking the turnings as she had when she first entered the cave from the woods. Fear began to take hold of her, but then she remembered the teachings in the Book of Precepts and Perceptions: *"Do not doubt the Father's path. Trust in his blueprint for the world and you will never be lost."*

Yes, she had to have faith. She had won the creatures over to the great truth. Proof of this came at each intersection where they provided direction. She started walking on in the darkness, hands stretched out in front of her. The ceiling was growing lower, grazing the top of her head, and she was forced to walk crouched over. Then her outstretched hands hit a wall. She felt her way to the left, but there she found another wall. The same to her right. She concluded she must have gone the wrong way at the last turning. Time would be lost in backtracking, but what choice did she have?

She turned around and started forward, but somehow there was a sheer wall of rock ahead of her, too. "I've lost my bearings in the dark," she said out loud, trying to quell her growing unease. She circled slowly with hands outstretched, kicking something that clattered like a pile of sticks. It was impossible, but there was rock all around her. And above her. Her back was aching from walking crouched over and she sat down on the ground. "Father, take away my fear..." she muttered. She attempted to get her lantern working again, but no amount of wiping or adjusting would bring back its light.

She was breathing quickly now, her panic rising. The damp chill of the small space was climbing into her bones. Then she remembered the wooden match the old witch had given her! With a shaking hand, she dug the match out of the little pocket on her belt. She almost dropped it as she tried again and again to light it against the metal heel of her boot, but then it struck, filling her nose with sulphur. She turned her head so her sneeze wouldn't extinguish the small flame.

Through watering eyes, she looked around the cell. There were no doors, just smooth walls, the ceiling so low, she wondered how she had even half stood before. She turned slowly and behind her saw the clattering sticks she had kicked. But they weren't sticks; they were a pair skeletons — human apparently — who had died here in this cell, perhaps many years before. She moaned in terror. The match had used itself up and it burned her fingers so that she had to drop it abruptly. It hit the damp stone and sputtered out.

Carminn sat in absolute blackness, buried in her own sarcophagus, and the old witch's words rang in her ears: "When the darkest hour comes, light this match and you will see just what that destiny of yours looks like."

* * *

"I can't take this anymore," Barnabas said shakily. They had been climbing in the darkness for what seemed hours, and the terrible feeling of the walls closing in on him had never left.

Wickram's encouraging voice rang with a cheer that had, over time, grown a bit ragged. "Sure you can, Barn! We're almost there!"

"That's what you said an hour ago!" But he kept going. The only way out of his claustrophobic misery was to get out of these tunnels. And the Lurkers were helping them! At every intersection, lights had flashed ahead to guide them up the right path. But Barnabas felt himself running out of the mental and physical resources to keep going. He stared down at the ground he couldn't see, imagining his feet as they took one step and the next, and the next…

"Hey," Wickram called. "Look at that."

Barnabas didn't look up. "Another light? Must be the next intersection."

"No, but it's different. It's red. It's square!"

Barnabas stopped and then he did look up, tilting his hat back on his head. Squinting into the distance, he saw that the distant red light *was* square. Rectangular, actually. And it had a word on it. Despite his exhaustion, he began to run, his cramped legs stumbling a bit, and soon he was close enough to see it clearly. It was a blissfully familiar sign; it said, "EXIT."

It was an ordinary, everyday exit sign above an ordinary steel door that was painted a dull industrial beige, and the door would have looked utterly normal if it hadn't been fitted into a wall of rough-hewn stone at the end of a long tunnel of stone. The sight was so incongruous that Barnabas laughed. He put his hand on the shiny doorknob and turned it. The door swung inwards, and holding it open, Barnabas looked back at Wickram in utter bewilderment. Wickram just shrugged and walked through. Barnabas followed and found himself in a nondescript hallway of some utterly ordinary office building. The other doors in the hallway had room number signs that read "B-25" and "B-27." They were in the basement of a building. A City building.

Barnabas let go of the door, and it swung closed, locking itself with a click. He turned back to read what sign might be on this amazing, ordinary door that led down to the secret Valley of hidden wonders. The sign read, "No Entry."

"Come on," he told Wickram. "We're here."

Part V:

Walking the Tightrope
without a Net

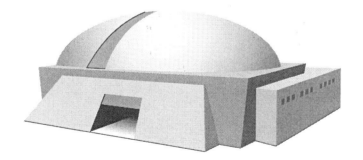

CHAPTER 27

"**G**round floor," said the mellifluous automated voice. "Going up."
The doors slid open, and bright light from the lobby poured into the elevator along with the roar of the morning crowd.

"Let's go," Barnabas said.

But Wickram hesitated. "Wait! Is that the whole trip?"

"Yeah, we went from the basement to the lobby."

Wickram began fingering the elevator buttons and seemed startled as they lit up under his fingers. "Does this mean there are 26 stories in the building? Can't we take a ride?" He pushed more buttons, smiling at the light show.

People were filing into the elevator and giving the boys exasperated looks for their poor elevator etiquette. Barnabas grabbed Wickram's arm and pulled him out into the lobby. "Come on, we're in a hurry," he said, but now he was smiling too. The sight of people in business attire, carrying briefcases and KonaBoom Coffee cups, of couriers pushing through the revolving doors, checking addresses on their phones filled Barnabas with sweet relief. He was home.

He turned and saw Wickram stumbling behind him, pirouetting to avoid collisions in the onrushing crowd, chirping, "Oops," and "Sorry!" every few steps. He reached Barnabas' side and fell into step, a little too close. The guy at the security desk was watching them suspiciously, and Barnabas steered them through the revolving doors and out onto the sidewalk. He caught sight of their reflections in the shiny, steel siding around the building's entrance: dirty, dishevelled, and slightly wild-eyed from their 24 hours underground. They were anything but inconspicuous.

He looked up at Wickram, about to explain what they would do next, and caught the boy's stunned expression. Wickram's eyes were darting wildly from billboard to car to pedestrian to pedestrian to pedestrian — hair, shoes, phones, dogs on jewel-studded leashes, people handing out flyers for fur sales. His mouth was working as if he was about make some comment , though he managed to say nothing.

Barnabas thought of how bewildered he had been in his first hour in the Valley. So, despite his feeling that they had to hurry, he spoke gently: "Come on, Wickram, I think I know where we are. This must be Greyshiver Street. That means Gumber Square is one block west, and we can pick up a Blue Line train on the far side of the square. He began to step into the crowd, but Wickram wasn't with him. He was frozen in place beside the doors of the building, hugging his guitar to his chest.

"How do you ... how do you get in?" Wickram mumbled in confusion. He meant into the crowd. Like, how do you take the first step? Barnabas had never thought to ask himself this question; it was just something he had always known.

"Uh, well you look for a space I guess and then you just ... Never mind. Just put a hand on my shoulder and move when I do." They set off but it was like pulling a wagon that didn't always turn the way you thought it would. He wished he had enough money for them to just jump into a cab, but he didn't. They crossed at the lights, and as they reached the far sidewalk (thankfully less crowded), he heard Wickram gasp.

Barnabas turned to see what was upsetting him now, and there they were: the great skyscrapers of the Tower District, sticking into the air like the splayed fingers of some mighty earth-god. The boys stared in silence. The sense of majesty and permanence that these great buildings had always conveyed had been replaced in Barnabas' mind by an all-too-clear vision of them bursting into flames, teetering and tumbling backwards into the abyss. If the idea had shocked him when he'd seen Glower's model, now the sheer scale of the horror finally sank in.

"Krump..." Wickram choked out.

Barnabas noticed a new wave of pedestrians about to descend on them, and he pushed Wickram off the sidewalk and into the relative peace of Gumber Square. They found a scruffy parkette with a semi-circle of benches, and Wickram slumped onto the first one, panting like he'd run a marathon. A siren, a jackhammer, the gut-thumping bass line seeping from a passing car — Barnabas watched each city sound register as a twitch on Wickram's face.

"Easy, man!" Barnabas said. "It's just … normal. It's just the City; there's nothing wrong."

"Yeah, yeah," Wickram said, managing a weak smile. "It's great! Great. I just didn't realize it would be so, you know, busy!"

"Yeah," replied Barnabas doubtfully. "Enjoy." He pulled off his backpack and reached inside for his phone. He turned it on and waited through a nerve-shredding minute for it to power up. When it did, the battery warning came up right away, and Barnabas dismissed it angrily, thinking *I know the charge is low! Don't waste power telling me!* Then he saw that he had 23 text messages and 14 voicemails. Twenty-one of the texts were from his mom, and he figured the voicemails must be too. He bit his lip guiltily and then forced himself not to think about it. He checked the time: 8:10. Good, he wasn't too late. He dialled Deni and chewed on his lip some more through three rings, four, five …

"Barnabas!!" she screamed, answering the phone.

"Yeah, I'm —"

"Oh my God, your mother keeps phoning here, and I had to program both my moms' phones to forward calls from her to my phone. And now I'll have to keep the phone in my lap all day in class in case she texts, and I'm not even supposed to have my phone on during —"

"Deni, listen!" Barnabas shouted. "This is an emergency, and I'm about to run out of charge. We're on our way to your place." He did a quick calculation in his head. "We'll be there at 8:45. You'll have to be late for school, sorry."

"But wait… What do you mean 'we?' What kind of emergen…" and the phone died.

Barnabas whistled out a sigh of relief. He kissed the phone and dropped it back into his bag. He assessed Wickram carefully. "Hey, you feeling better? Ready for a new adventure? We're going on the subway."

Wickram did indeed appear calmer. He was staring at City people go by in their fancy suits and haircuts like he was birder on his first trip to the Amazon. "Yeah, just needed to get my bearings. Now I'm greased and humming. Lead on!"

Luckily, Barnabas had just enough change to buy Wickram a one-way subway ticket. As he slid his own transit pass into the turnstile and navigated them to the right platform, he was unusually conscious of all these routine actions. His well-rehearsed City smarts, that he never had to think about from day to day, seemed oddly miraculous to him after his five days in the strangeness of the Valley. In contrast, Wickram was an awkward ostrich; he had to swipe his pass three times before the reader registered it. He kept stepping left into people's paths when Barnabas would have known to step right, totally mistimed his entrance into the crowded subway car, and then didn't know how to negotiate a hand hold on a pole before the train lurched into motion.

But Barnabas herded him like a dim sheep through the change onto the Red Line and then, five stops later at Gimlit Station, back up to the street. The security man at Deni's building almost didn't recognize him, and Barnabas remembered that he and Wickram looked like two street kids who lived behind a dumpster. But then the man said, "Oh, Barnabas, I'll ring up to Ms. Jiver and tell her you're here."

As they rode the elevator, Barnabas said to Wickram (who was watching the floor number display and silently mouthing the numbers): "Remember what your mom told us before we left."

"It was probably something about clean underwear, right?"

"No, she said don't tell anyone about the Valley. Just... just say that you met me when you came to see my dad play a show."

"But what do I tell her if she asks where I —"

At that second, the elevator door opened, and standing right there in the hallway was Deni. She screamed when she saw them, and Barnabas thought her reaction seemed a little staged — like she had been rehearsing this dramatic moment.

"What have you been *doing*?!" she shouted, and then, "Who in the world is this?!" when Wickram stepped out into the hall.

"This is Wickram. Wickram, Deni. Can you let us in before anyone else sees us?"

She nodded. "Yeah, you look like pickpockets out of Oliver Twist." She led them quickly down the hall to the open apartment door and the boys tumbled inside. Barnabas shrugged off his backpack and collapsed into a low, canvas chair in the front hall. Deni's apartment had always been a second home to him, and finally getting here after days in the new and uncertain was a bigger relief than he had expected.

Wickram, in contrast, handed Barnabas his guitar and moved right into living room, looking around, exclaiming, "Wow," and "Quality!" He leafed through thick, glossy magazines on the coffee table — esoteric journals of political thought and interior design — and then found a dimmer panel on the wall and began to play with the lights. Deni stared at him in the shifting patterns of bright and shadow as if some exotic monkey had wandered in.

"I really like your dorm!" Wickram enthused, turning all the lights up to full brightness.

Deni blinked in response and said to Barnabas, "Explain…that."

Barnabas' brow furrowed as he tried to figure out how and what to tell her; the task seemed overwhelming. Suddenly the hours of climbing through the domain of the Lurkers caught up with him. Through a huge yawn, he said, "It's… complicated."

Wickram came and sat on the floor beside Barnabas. There was a cardboard box to his right, and he reached in to pull out a small prehistoric fertility figurine, rendered in bright red plastic.

"What's this?!" he asked, turning it slowly in his hands, examining its wide hips and huge breasts, a little slack-jawed. The box was full of the figurines in many primary colours.

"They were give-aways at a women's health fundraiser," Deni explained, a little flustered. "Look, my moms will both be gone all day, so you can hang out here. But I have go to school now, at least for the morning. What do you need?"

"Food," said Wickram, raising his head.

"Sleep," added Barnabas. "And can we shower, Deni?"

"Yes!" Wickram shouted in agreement. "And do you have any clean clothes?"

"Oh, and a charger!" Barnabas added, holding up his dead phone.

"Right," Deni answered matter-of-factly, taking the phone from his hand and the figurine from Wickram's. "Follow." Passing the kitchen, she pointed and said, "Anything you want from the fridge, *except* the stuff in the Sigram's Deli bags — that's for a candidate's fundraiser here tonight." From the linen closet, she pulled out two big, fluffy towels and handed them to the boys. They followed her into her bedroom, where she dug through the lower drawer of her desk and brought out a charger cable.

She plugged in the phone. "There. And you can sleep on my bed." She wrinkled her nose at them. "I'll change the sheets later. Boys' clothes, I'm afraid, are at a premium in our household. I'll see what I can dig up at school. Anything else?"

"No. You're a life saver, Deni," Barnabas said.

"I'll be back at 1:00, and then I need to know everything. Everything!"

As soon as she was gone, they ate ravenously and took turns showering. After 10 minutes, Barnabas forced himself to step away from the luxurious hot water that seemed to soothe his every ache, mental and physical. Making his way back to Deni's bedroom, he had only to look at the inviting fluffiness of her bed for sleep to drag at him like a merciless riptide. A minute later, he was already half lost to the world when Wickram crashed down on the mattress beside him.

The last thing he heard before he fell utterly unconscious was the tall boy muttering, "Do you think Steve Raveeno is playing anywhere tonight?"

***

Three hours later, Barnabas snapped back to consciousness shouting the word, "Glower!" Or maybe shouting the name in his sleep had awakened him, heart pounding, confused. From somewhere nearby, he heard jazz music and the sound of laughter. The laughing voice was familiar, but he couldn't place it. The adrenaline rush began to fade, and the heavy hand of sleep threatened to pull him back under. He forced himself to sit up.

His head felt like it was stuffed full of puffed rice, and he had to follow a strange path of associations back to reality: Joan Miró print on the wall... like something Deni would have... wait, she *does* have that print... oh this is her room... this is her bed... did I have sex with Deni and I can't remember it...? no I was sleeping with Wickram... I was *what...*? no not like that... Lurkers... Valley... blow up the towers... "GLOWER!" he shouted again, and this time he woke up all the way.

The laughter in the next room stopped, and a series of faces appeared in the door of the bedroom — first Deni's, then Wickram's (what the hell was he wearing?), and then, surprisingly, Cal Kabaway's.

"What did you just say?" Deni asked, entering the bedroom and sitting down in her desk chair.

"Uh," Barnabas began, then checked to see what he was wearing. Last time this had happened, in the Pastoral Park dorms, he had been dressed only in underwear. But no, this time, he was still wearing jeans, although his torso was naked and he felt shy enough to pull the sheet up around his shoulders. The jazz record was still playing in the next room — some woman singing in a smoky, bluesy moan, and a tenor saxophone answering her. He assumed it was a recording of his dad.

Wickram came and sat on the end of the bed. For his part, he was dressed in a brand new set of brown and blue sweats, the zippered top bearing the old logo of the Junior Juggernauts School from before the re-branding.

The tall boy explained to Deni and Cal: "Barnabas is shouting about George Glower. He runs the Drop Shop. It's a really great store full of flamtasmic haul, except that he turns out to be skull-cracked and lethal."

Cal, still at the door, began to laugh, and Barnabas realized that was who he heard before. Cal said, "Barnabas, your friend here is really entertaining. I have no idea what anything he says means, but I think he's been telling us that he grew up in a circus and something about a steam-powered cathedral." Cal was leaning nonchalantly against the door frame like he owned the place, like he was an old family friend. Barnabas, who had been coming here since he was a little kid, found this confusing and irritating.

Wickram laughed too, like the joke wasn't at his expense. Deni leaned toward Barnabas enthusiastically. "We've been trying to get some deets on your week with your dad," she said, "But Wickram is a little hard to follow. Where exactly did you go?"

Barnabas surprised himself with how confidently he spun his tale: "Well, Dad played three different cities. We saw the sights, caught up with each other." All through his adventure in the Valley, he had imagined telling Deni everything. Sometimes he was practically dictating notes to her in his head. And once he learned about the plot to destroy the towers, he had longed to be able to compare notes with her, get her advice on how they would stop Glower. And instead, here he was, lying to his best friend. If he could tell her the real story, he knew how happy she would be. At age 15, she would be a junior journalist with the scoop of the century!

But Sanjani had told him not to tell anyone about the Valley! Why? Well, for one thing, the story was obviously so monumentally huge and such an insane reversal of everything they had grown up learning that maybe no one would believe him. That would only make his mission more difficult. But there was more: the Valley was a unique, living culture. It may have started as just a grandiose plan set in motion by Lawrence Glorvanious himself, but it had become something real, something special. There was a religion which at first he might have dismissed, the way Graviddy did. But it was special and kind of beautiful when you heard people like Garlip and Sensash talk about it. And then there was the Big Top; an amazing, creative community that maybe could only exist in that special place. What would happen to all of this if he let Deni reveal it? It might all melt away like a snowflake in the glare of the sun.

So he manufactured a look of gratitude and sincerity and told Deni: "I was shy around him at first, but it was a really special time. Dad-son time. I mean, you would have got more out of the music than me, but —"

"Oh, the music was brilliant!" Wickram enthused, getting into the spirit. "I didn't know the trumpet could make sounds like that."

"Saxophone," Barnabas said quickly.

Wickram nodded manically. "Right, what I meant."

Barnabas knew he sounded convincing because Deni got a dewy look on her face and said, "You are just so lucky! But I don't understand what your big emergency is. What's up with this Glower guy? And what does it have to do with Wickram's circus? And a witch in the woods?"

"Ignore him," Barnabas said, giving the tall boy a sharp look. "He just has an amazing imagination. He's here in the City to audition for a music school. On my dad's recommendation!" Wickram walked out of the room, and a minute later they heard him tuning his guitar.

Deni's expression had changed from dreamy to curious. "So the emergency…" she prompted.

"Right. We met George Glower on tour. He's kind of friends with the Mayor and he wants us to bring him a message. He said it's really important. Something about the election." This was Barnabas' current and only plan: get to Mayor Tuppletaub and tell him Glower's terrible plan. There was some truth in the tale he was telling Deni: Glower did know the Mayor; he had gone off in the Mayor's limo after the talk at the school. A sudden horrible thought crossed Barnabas' mind: *What if the Mayor is in on the plot?!*

"A message from Glower. Okay. And this message is…?" Deni asked with a suspicious edge to her voice. Wickram walked back in, absently playing a jaunty little march on his guitar, like the theme song of a bunch of wooden toys who have come to life in the old carpenter's magic workshop.

"It's private," Barnabas said with high seriousness. "Very, very private message."

Deni screwed up her lips. "Are you sure this Glower isn't just another figment of guitar boy's imagination?"

Barnabas scrambled out of bed and retrieved his phone, already thumbing through the menus as he brought it over to Deni. "Here! Glower is real! I have pictures of him! This is him in the steam works at Clouding... um, it's sort of a branch of the municipal steam works. Never mind. What's important is —"

"That's not George Glower," she interrupted.

Barnabas froze in confusion. "What? Yes it is. I was there. I took the picture!" Wickram stopped playing.

Deni snatched the phone from his hand and flipped from picture to picture, peering closely at the screen. "No, I know him. I mean, it's been years, but he was here in this apartment a few times when I was just a kid. This was even before he ran for Mayor. He was just this random engineer back then. Mom-Amy was setting up some foundation or something, and she thought he would be useful for fundraising. You know, given his name."

"His name... is George Glower," Barnabas insisted.

"No, it's George Glorvanious," she replied.

Barnabas felt his brain do a back-flip. "Glorvanious?! As in Lawrence Glorvanious, the great Mayor?"

"Lawrence's great-grandson, yeah."

"Wait. So... Florian's grandson?"

"Look at you! When did you learn so much City history? No, his grandmother was Florian's sister, Dolores. She kept the family name when she married. Hold on." Deni pulled her laptop from her school bag and opened it on her desk, typing quickly. "Here. In the City Courier, seven... no eight years ago. 'Glorvanious Campaign Collapses after Last Minute Surge by Rival, Dudley.' If I remember correctly, George was the favourite to be our next Mayor, but there was some scandal in the last week of the campaign — illegal donations or something — and he tanked on election day. I was eight. That was when I got interested in municipal politics."

Barnabas looked over her shoulder at the screen. Beneath the headline was a picture of the man himself, younger, leaner, dressed in a suit and tie, but clearly the same person he knew as Glower. The weirdest thing was the smile plastered across his face. It was hard to imagine George Glower of the Drop Shop ever smiling. Although now that Barnabas looked more closely, the smile was more like some uncanny special effect — mirthless and cold, manufactured for the media.

"Oh my God," Barnabas said, peering over at Wickram, who had his elbow on his guitar and his chin in his hand, listening intently. "It's him."

"That's not all," Deni continued. "The night of the election he disappeared! His campaign staff said he was acting weird; he was sick or something. Then he was just gone. Poof! And no one has seen him since."

Wickram said, "That works, Barn. The Drop Shop opened back when I was nine. Hey, Barn, can I use your phone and call that music school about the audition?"

"Not now, Wickram."

The sound of gunfire and screaming monsters erupted from the living room. Wickram started in fear, and Deni said, "It's just Cal. We have a new ImmersionStation 4D and Cal's on it all the time, gunning down the undead."

Wickram's eyes widened further. "The 4D? With Shatterclash Integrated Sound Intrusion?!"

"Uh, I think so," she answered uncertainly. Wickram threw his guitar onto the bed and ran for the living room.

Barnabas was replaying the words "Cal's on it all the time" in his head. He'd only been in the Valley four days! How could Cal already be a fixture in Deni's house?

"Hey, you're covered in goose bumps," Deni said. "Hold on." She slipped from the room, returning a few seconds later with an identical set of sweats to Wickram's. She turned her back as he changed.

He asked, "What are these anyway?"

"Track team from back in the Pleistocene era — like 18 years ago when the school first opened."

"Our school had a track team? I can't believe it."

"No, they just ordered the uniforms; the team never happened. They've been sitting in boxes down in the store-room all these years, waiting to be plundered." She turned back around and looked him over. "Score! I got your sizes right." Barnabas sat on her bed and she joined him. "I can't believe Glorvanious is back and that you ran into him," she said. "Small world."

"It's starting to feel like it."

"Isn't it illegal to vanish like that? Maybe you should go to the police."

"No, I have to talk to the Mayor. He'll know what to do with this... secret message."

She scowled. "Is this something to do with those secret subways you were babbling to Tuppletaub about?"

The embarrassing memory made him squirm. "I'm sorry about wrecking your interview. But we were right — Tuppletaub knows about... everything!"

She grabbed him by the shoulders and shook him. "You and your vague vagueness are driving me crazy! Okay, give me five minutes. I have to send Calvin back to school." She quickly left the room, calling Cal's name.

Alone for the moment, Barnabas looked at himself in the full-length mirror on her closet door. In the team track suit, he looked like some lanky athlete instead of his usual style which was basically awkward nerd. If he squinted his eyes at the image, he could almost believe he was someone strong, competent, and popular. Maybe he was up to the task of stopping Glower. Maybe he *could* save the City!

Buoyed by this bit of rented confidence, he strode into the living room, just in time to see a sight of shocking horror: Deni and Cal were kissing with unabashed passion. The blues singer on the record was crooning, *"Black velvet nights, black coffee, and my lonely life... "* while Brownbag Bopwright answered her with a broken-hearted sax lick. The vinyl melancholia was punctuated by bloodcurdling screams and rocket fire from the game Wickram was playing on the living room couch.

Barnabas felt a hot, sick surge of embarrassment, and his new-found confidence blew away like a fart in a tornado. He dragged his eyes away from the apparently endless kiss and slunk toward the foyer to pick up his backpack. He wanted to be quiet and cool but instead managed to upend the bag. Of course, the top was unzipped. Books and juice bottles hit the ground, and the *diaboriku* bounced out and rolled into the living room where Calvin interrupted the epic kiss to put a foot on it.

"Hey," he said, bending to pick up the device. "You found your monster machine! Did you ever figure out how to work it?" He walked to the foyer and handed it to Barnabas, who snatched it back.

"Sure! Of course," Barnabas snapped, the lie burning his throat. "By the way," he declared. "I also kissed someone this weekend!" He immediately felt like an idiot for saying this.

It didn't help when Wickram shouted over his game, "In fact, you kissed two people!" The heat rose in Barnabas' face.

"That's awesome," said Cal, and Barnabas couldn't tell he if he was making fun or really congratulating him. "Well, good luck with your top-secret emergency, man. Bye, baby!" he called to Deni and slammed the door on his way out (which Barnabas never would have). He looked up at his oldest friend, who was busy putting the jazz record away. She began straightening her clothes and hair, deliberately not catching his eye.

"Baby?" Barnabas asked in an icy voice. He started re-packing his bag with quick, angry movements. "Seriously, Deni, I've been gone four days! When did all... all this happen?"

She looked at him, blushing. "Well, if you really want to know, it was your fault! Or, I mean, I have you to thank for helping me find *true love!*" She turned and headed for the kitchen, and he followed. Pouring them glasses of orange juice, she said, "The day you left, Barnabas, I was such a mess! And Calvin took me to the coffee shop and got me a Kona float with organic vanilla bean ice cream. He just really *listened*, you know? He has a sensitive soul. That's because he's known a lot of pain in his life."

"You'll forgive me if I don't start a charity for him. I'm preoccupied with getting an important message to Mayor Tuppletaub."

She instantly forgot all the Cal drama. "You know more than you're saying," she accused. "Barnabas, you need to tell me everything about everything right now," she said, her voice rising in excitement.

"No, I really don't." He snapped at her and she gasped. They drank their orange juice, glaring at each other in silence until Barnabas said, "I just want to know how I can find Tuppletaub and talk to him."

"Hmm, too bad you're being so difficult. Because I know exactly where he's going to be this afternoon."

"You do not! You're making that up."

"The Executive Committee of City Council is meeting at 3:00 today — a special closed session to push a bunch of motions through before the election."

"How do you know that?"

"Mom-Amy is working for the Utilities Chief on his re-election campaign. Look at that printout on the wall behind you; that's his schedule for the whole week."

Barnabas got up and examined the busy grid. The Executive Committee meeting was listed for that afternoon, just as she said. The Utilities Chief, he noted, was also fully booked on Wednesday, and Barnabas could only think how all those meetings would be abruptly cancelled if Glower — no, Glorvanious — succeeded in his Tuesday plans.

"So," Deni said. "You need to get into that meeting. To bring him a message of crucial importance for the election." She slurped her juice audibly, not taking her eyes from him. "From his unlikely friend, George Glorvanious, who vanished mysteriously but reappeared at one of your dad's gigs... Have I got that right?" She waited for him to say something, but he didn't. "Maybe a message about secret subways?"

"Deni, I really don't know anything..."

"TELL ME!"

He made a loud, ugly grunt of exasperation. "There's nothing to tell! I was away with my dad, I met Glower, I have to talk to the Mayor. Now, will you help me or not?"

He wasn't used to confronting Deni like this and frankly it scared him. She was fixing him with that look of hers that made everyone — her parents, her teachers, now probably Cal — give her whatever she wanted. But if in a mere four days she had found love, it seemed that he too had found something: an inner determination that could not be shaken. Fate had handed him a job, and he knew that nothing was going to stop him from doing it. Not the Aqua Guard, not the Lurkers, not Mayor Tuppletaub, and not Deni Jiver.

And she must have seen this determination because shockingly she said. "Fine. I'll try to get you in." She flipped a thumb in the direction of the living room where the war against the zombies continued. "Is he really good on that guitar?"

"Really, really good."

"Sometimes the Exec Committee starts their meeting with some local entertainment. It's some new initiative to make it look like they care about the arts. I think Mom-Amy could convince them that a little concert by one of the City's young prodigies would get them in the mood to wrangle with development deals and gridlock strategies."

"Oh my God, you're a genius!" He wanted to run up and hug her, but the sudden memory of the epic kiss made him stay in his seat.

"But after you meet him, Mr. Bopwright," she said, actually wagging a finger, "You tell me everything you learned."

She poured another glass of juice and brought it to Wickram, who took it, murmuring "Thanks," but not taking his eyes from the screen.

Barnabas wandered past them to the window and looked out at the view — hundreds of streets, thousands of buildings, millions of people. "He's out there somewhere," he said quietly and a shiver went through him. "Where the hell are you, George Glorvanious?"

CHAPTER 28

Rush hour was just beginning as Barnabas and Wickram rode the northbound Green Line train in their matching track uniforms. Wickram, Barnabas noted, was not as freaked out by the crowds this time. In fact, the tall boy kept engaging strangers in conversation.

"Do you ever eat at Drumburger?" he asked one surprised woman. "I read on the back of Movie Monthly that the swizzle steak sandwich is a tasty treat you'll want to repeat."

As the train rattled through the tunnels, Wickram examined a handful of change. "My first earnings in the City!" he told Barnabas with a grin. He had started playing his guitar on the platform while they were waiting for the Green Line train and, much to his surprise, several strangers had tossed coins into his cap, which he had carelessly dropped at his feet. "Maybe I'll be playing the Manhammer Audio Dome sooner than I think!"

They exited the subway at Glorvanious Place, taking the staircase that lead up to the Civic Plaza, right at the feet of a huge statue.

"Whoa, who's that?" Wickram asked.

"Lawrence Glorvanious, the mayor who turned this place from a mill town to a great city."

It was an impressive bronze statue, the figure of the great Mayor four times live-sized. He was wearing a stylish suit, but on his head was a kind of miner's helmet with a big headlight, and he was leaning on a shovel, looking off seriously into a prosperous future. At his feet was a miniature of the city streets and its new buildings as they would soon be built. The Mayor was a colossus — creator and Godzilla at the same time. A plaque on the base read, "We are ever grateful."

"Glorvanious…," Wickram said. "That's a name I'm hearing a lot today. He looks like Father Glory."

"He's Father Glory's father."

"No kidding? I wonder who was taller."

At the far end of the Civic Plaza's expanse of black paving stones stood the main municipal buildings, a cluster of colourful, geometric shapes. First, on the right, was the red cube of the Principal Court, to the far left, the blue sphere of the Administrative Complex. In the middle was City Hall itself, the tallest and most beautiful of the buildings — a 22-story pyramid of dark green glass whose top five floors, right up to the pointed peak, were encased in pink marble.

They entered the massive lobby — the base of the pyramid, and thus the widest floor in the building — and Barnabas walked up to the large, raised reception desk with Wickram in tow. He was about to say "hi" to the man behind the desk, but the man was staring into space, his brow furrowed. Barnabas wasn't sure whether to speak or not, but then the man shouted into his headset, "The loading bay doors are only 3 metres high. You gonna have to come in through the basement!" He jabbed at his touchscreen and muttered "Idiot…" before turning to look down at the boys, a smile appearing on his face. "Can I help you?"

Barnabas cleared his throat. "Uh, yes. Yessir. We're, um, performing today for the Executive Council meeting. We were supposed to —"

"Names?" the man snapped, turning his attention to his screen, typing quickly on his keyboard. The smile was already gone, like holding it for longer than three seconds was too much to ask of someone with such a busy schedule.

"I'm Barnabas Bopwright. And this is Wickram."

"Wickram what?" the man asked, typing aggressively, like he'd already had enough of their antics.

Wickram came forward and leaned against the desk. "What do you mean 'Wickram what?'"

The man answered like Wickram was an imbecile. "You got to give me *both* your names. That's how it works after kindergarten."

"I don't have —"

"Tragidenko!" Barnabas said quickly. "Wickram Tragidenko!"

"That…" Wickram said in an offended tone, "…is not my name."

The man began to type again, and Barnabas gently but firmly pushed his friend aside. "Don't mind him, sir. It's kind of a nasty divorce, you know?"

Barnabas turned around and hissed, "Will you please be cool?! I'm already freaking out."

"Not my name!"

"That's how it is in the City. You'll need to have a last name for the music school, too."

The printer on the reception desk began to whine, and the man pulled two squares of paper from it and handed them to the boys. He said, "Peel off the backing and wear these the whole time you're in the building." Without pausing, he jabbed at his touchscreen and said into the headset, "Ms. Doublegrey, your performers are here."

A minute later, Barnabas saw a woman across the lobby heading their way, her heels clicking on the marble floor like a bomb that was getting set to blow. She was like something out of a TV show — the glamorous detective, here to solve the mystery that no one else could. Her luxuriant curly brown hair was tied behind her and falling over the back of her grey suit jacket. Under it was a satiny, pearl-grey blouse and a simple string of pearls. Her glasses were large and black-framed and gave her the appearance of never missing a trick. She exuded so much professional aplomb that Barnabas immediately began to lose the stubborn certainty that had been propelling him into this mad adventure. *What will I say to the Mayor?* he suddenly wondered. *What if I fail?*

Ms. Doublegrey didn't waste a movement. Her eyes locked onto his as she arrived in front of the reception desk and only wavered for the quarter second it took to check his name tag. "Barnabas Bopwright, welcome to City Hall. And Wickram Tragidenko! Your guitar has so much character! Is it very old?"

"Just Wickram," he said tersely.

"Well then, you can call me Joyce. I love your school tracksuits. Very retro." She checked her watch. "Okay, we better hurry; follow me!"

She used a key card to call an elevator (not one of the ordinary public elevators!) and punched the button for the seventeenth floor, the highest one on the panel. As soon as the doors closed, her phone said "ding." She pulled it from her jacket pocket and said, "Yes, Miss Coomlaudy? The briefing documents are waiting in your desk. Yes, I included the budget. No, the unredacted budget. Very good." She hung up just as the elevator doors opened on seventeen.

They followed her down the hall and through double doors with a gold embossed sign that read, "Executive Council." Inside was basically a boardroom, the decor modern but warm — metal beams painted cool grey, red-hued wood, and wall-to-wall carpet that muffled the sound. Large east-facing windows bathed the room in daylight. There was an alcove off the main room; frosted glass covered most of the opening, leaving a narrow doorway to one side. Behind the glass, Barnabas saw three seated figures, heads bent in discussion. He could just catch the murmur of their conversation.

Ms. Doublegrey said to the boys, "The meeting starts in 25 minutes. Now, if you wouldn't mind, I need you to give me a little preview of your show. The last performer turned out to be… well, embarrassing." Barnabas gave Wickram a nervous look, but his friend just nodded with no sign of concern. Ms. Doublegrey sat down in one of the Councillor's chairs and sat down, crossing her legs. "So, Wickram plays guitar. What is you do, Barnabas?"

Before he could answer, "Nothing!" Wickram said, "He sings." Barnabas felt like his stomach had just gone back down in the elevator without him.

Ms. Doublegrey smile encouragingly at him. "Great! I can't wait to hear you talented boys." Her phone said "ding," and she frowned down at it and then shot a nervous glance toward the alcove. "Yes, Miss Coomlaudy?" she said into the phone. Her brow furrowed and she told the boys, "Back in a second." She crossed to the alcove and became another silhouette behind the frosted glass.

"Barn, look!" Wickram exclaimed. He was over at the big windows. Barnabas, trying to get his brains to work despite his panic, joined him. "There!" Wickram pointed, "The Manhammer Audio Dome!" The sunlight was reflecting off the closed dome, which meant there was no afternoon game being played; on such a fine day in May, the roof would have been open if there was a game.

Wickram was pressed right up against the window as if getting those few centimeters closer made a difference. "Do you think we can go there later? I want to see it so bad."

"Maybe… Wick, listen. I'm just here at City Hall to meet the Mayor… I'm not a performer."

"Just sing anything, I'll follow along."

A man and a woman, dressed in black and wearing white aprons, entered the room, pushing in trolleys of food and drink for the meeting. They began setting up a buffet table in one corner.

Barnabas lowered his voice. "You don't understand, Wickram. I don't *know* anything!"

Wickram laughed like Barnabas was making a joke. "Don't worry," he said. "I'll make it work."

Before Barnabas could respond, Ms. Doublegrey returned, her crisp, professional smile back in place. "All right," she said. "Let's hear what you've got!"

Leaving Barnabas by the window, Wickram moved to the middle of the room. As he tuned his guitar, he pretended he was addressing an audience: "Thanks, ladies and jelly-men. This is a piece I composed last year." He started to play the same beautiful melody that Barnabas had heard on his first day in the Valley.

Ms. Doublegrey was bouncing her foot rhythmically, enjoying the song. She applauded, though the song wasn't over. "Very good! Lovely. Now, Barnabas, you're going to sing something with him?"

Barnabas moved to stand beside Wickram. "Uh…" he said, which was about all the patter he could manage. His mouth was dry as the Sahara. He asked, "Will the Mayor be here soon?"

"Oh, Mayor Tuppletaub sent his regrets. He had some important business to attend to." Barnabas' heart sank. Why was he even here, then? And if he couldn't ask the Mayor for help, how else could Glower be stopped? And why was Ms. Doublegrey staring at him like that? *Oh yeah.* He was so preoccupied, he had forgotten all about singing.

Wickram jumped in to save him: "Hey, lilies and geraniums, this is an old folk song from the place I grew up. It's call and response, so you all sing along with Barnabas." In a scratchy, bluesy voice, he belted out, "Sing yeah, yeah," and Barnabas found himself mechanically replying, "Sing yeah, yeah!"

Wickram continued, "For a Valley girl," and Barnabas echoed him. The routine was so straightforward that Barnabas had no trouble acting like it was all planned. He even managed a feeble smile. The song continued:

I said to my mama (*I said to my mama*)
I'm ready for life (*I'm ready for life*)
What guild should I go to (*what guild should I go to*)
To find me a wife? (*to find me a wife?*)

Ms. Doublegrey began clapping along, joining with Barnabas in the echoes, while Wickram dug in harder on the slap and ching of his guitar.

A girl from Clouding (*a girl from Clouding*)
Will do you proud (*will do you proud*)
Sing yeah, yeah (*sing yeah, yeah*)
For a Valley girl (*for a Valley girl*)

Despite himself, Barnabas was getting into performing. He looked around the room, first to his left at the food servers (one of whom gave him a thumbs up), and then in front of him, at Ms. Doublegrey and the imaginary members of the Executive Council. He pictured them in their seats all clapping and singing. Turning all the way to the right, he was brought up short by a figure standing in the entrance to the alcove. It was an old woman, small and wrinkled, but dressed immaculately. The scowling face beneath her snow white coiffure, with its sharp nose and piercing eyes, reminded him of a hawk. Wickram, oblivious to this hostile new audience, continued:

A girl from Forming (*a girl from Forming*)
Will keep you warm (*will keep you warm*)
Sing yeah, yeah (*sing yeah, yeah*)
For a Valley girl (*for a Valley girl*)

The hawk-faced woman was joined by two equally-wizened old men, one with white hair, one with a shaved head. All three were frowning their disapproval. Maybe they just didn't like the performance? But then the old woman turned and started whispering sibilantly into ears of her companions and gesturing at him and Wickram. What did they want? Why did they look so concerned? It was only then that Barnabas really heard the song they were singing. With a sinking heart, he understood what the censorious looks meant meant: the three old people knew about the Valley and weren't happy to hear these two strangers singing about it openly. The elderly trio retreated to the alcove, and Barnabas forced himself to look back at Ms. Doublegrey; keeping the smile on his face now actually hurt.

Barnabas wished Ms. Doublegrey would cut them off as they made their way through the verses about girls from Furrowing and Coursing. Finally, with a couple of more "yeah-yeahs" and a big guitar flourish, they were done.

"Very good!" enthused Ms. Doublegrey. "You boys have a seat and…" Her phone went "ding." She and Barnabas both looked toward the alcove. "Excuse me for just a minute," she said tightly, rising to her feet. "Why don't you boys get yourselves something from the buffet?" She disappeared again behind the glass.

Wickram was over at the food in a flash, but Barnabas edged his way toward the alcove. The whispering behind it was fierce now, and at one point it rose into a clearly audible, "Immediately!" Barnabas, drenched in sweat, moved over to Wickram, who was holding up a croissant, examining it curiously.

Wickram took a bite, made an appreciative noise and said, "See, Barn? Told you it would be fine."

"Wick…" Barnabas began, but then Ms. Doublegrey was back beside them. Her smile looked as fake and painful as the one Barnabas had worn.

"That was wonderful, boys," she said, "but I need you to follow me. There are some people who wish to speak to you. Barnabas, take your backpack, and Wickram, don't forget your guitar." They followed her out of the room and down the hall. Barnabas looked back and saw that a couple of security guards had fallen into step behind them. With Doublegrey in front and security behind, there was no way to escape. Wickram was bouncing along happily beside him, looking at the pictures of long-gone City Councillors on the wall.

They reached a large steel door. Ms. Doublegrey opened it with her keycard and ushered the boys through. Inside was a stairwell, with staircases going up and down, and in between them a caged-off elevator shaft like the ones Barnabas had seen in old movies.

Ms. Doublegrey pushed the call button, and when the elevator arrived, descending noisily and majestically from above, she pulled open the metal gate and motioned them inside. "You'll go up to the top floor and wait," she announced. She was all business now, and her smile had vanished as if surgically removed. Wickram had to stoop a little under the low ceiling as they walked into the small elevator. The rest of the negligible space inside was abruptly filled with the bulky presence of the two guards who entered and turned their backs on the boys, pinning them against the back wall.

With a jerk, the elevator began to rise, grinding slowly along its tracks. Through the bars of the elevator and the cage walls of the elevator shaft, Barnabas could see Ms. Doublegrey vanishing beneath them, a dark look of betrayal on her pretty face.

Barnabas peered up at Wickram, and his tall friend's calm smile made him fume with anger. "Why did you choose that song?!" he snapped. "It's all about the Valley!"

"What? She loved it, Barn."

He spoke slowly as if explaining to a child: "You told them we knew about the Valley and now they're bringing us in for questioning. We're in trouble!"

Wickram frowned. He shook his head and muttered, "There's no pleasing critics." Barnabas would have thrown up his hands in exasperation if there had been room to do so.

The elevator was moving upwards through the top floors of the pyramid. The scene around them could not have been more different from the rest of the airy, modern building. In the rooms beyond the elevator, there were no windows, no lights at all but the reading lamps on dozens of old-fashioned, wooden desks. The desks were piled high with stacks of papers. Manning them was a small army of sallow, harried clerks, filing, stamping, stapling pages as if the digital age had never arrived. And naturally as the elevator ascended towards the tip of the pyramid, each floor was smaller than the one before, adding to the sense of airless density. Barnabas felt his claustrophobia returning.

The elevator rose through one final floor (where the desks were pressed right up against the elevator shaft, and the clerks in their dismal habitat peered in at them like raccoons) and then finally came to a clanging halt one floor above. The guards pulled open the gate, and the boys stepped out into a large room without desks, without clerks. The space, lit from windows high above, was a square, five meters on a side, and the sloping walls rose to meet each other in a point, some seven meters overhead. They were at the very top of the pyramid.

One of the guards stepped back into the elevator, and the machine disappeared again through the floor, its noisy rattle diminishing as it descended. The other guard stood to the side of the elevator shaft, silent as stone and unknowable behind his mirrored sunglasses. Barnabas decided not to be intimidated by him. He stepped forward to examine the beautifully appointed room that seemed to be frozen in some distant past — perhaps the 1920s with its art deco futurism. There was a chair in each corner of the room and four more at the corners of the elevator shaft, a matching set, all elegantly curved and upholstered. The walls were lined with bookshelves, filled with well-thumbed, leather-bound books. Barnabas carefully took down a few titles, checking the dates. He found nothing more recent than 1929. On a second shelf were a series of enormous bound volumes. He laid one down on the carpet and opened it up, finding architectural blueprints and city plans inside.

Wickram tapped him on the shoulder. "Hey, Barn, can I borrow your phone for a minute?" Lost in the wonder of the book, Barnabas handed it to him absently, and Wickram asked. "And how do I work it?"

Sighing, Barnabas took back the phone. "Who are you calling?"

"The music school." He pulled out the worn blue notebook Sanjani had handed him at the bridge and showed Barnabas one of the pages. "Here's the number."

Barnabas dialled and handed the device back to Wickram, dropping his head again into the book of plans. They weren't reproductions, he realized. The paper was creased and stained with use, and small, faded pencil notations were visible in the margins. These were the actual plans used to build the City. They might well have been touched by Lawrence Glorvanious himself! On the page he had open, he found Gumber Square, and from there began tracing his finger down streets he knew. He was only dimly aware of Wickram talking in the background.

"Yeah, I'm supposed to have an audition. No, I don't have an application reference code. I didn't apply in line. Online, whatever."

Barnabas found another volume with the words "River's Edge Park" on the spine in gold. Here were the original designs for the great park, and it was basically the same as the park he knew today.

"Yes, Falstep came to the school… You told him I could call anytime… That's right! The little clown! Uh-huh, yes he sure is. Utter suave. Ha! He said that to you? Well, then you must be really beautiful. He's a flirt, but he never lies. No, I don't have a phone number for him."

Barnabas reverently touched the spines of the other volumes, overwhelmed by his proximity to these pieces of history. He barely registered the return of the clanking elevator until the gate was pulled open with a bang. He turned and saw the three old people making their way out of the elevator slowly; the old man with the shaved head was using a walker and wheezing loudly. The old woman's hawk eyes were still staring at Barnabas like he was a mouse she wanted to snatch up for dinner but this time, her thin lips with their bright red line of lipstick were twisted in a wry smile.

"I see the artefacts in this room interest you. That's a point in your favour. Do you know what this collection is, young man?"

Barnabas replaced the book he had been reading and stood up to face her. "No, ma'am."

"It's the personal library of Lawrence Glorvanious. We must never let go of the past, for it will never let go of us. As you saw coming up here in the elevator, we are still processing its bottomless legacy of paperwork."

The old man with the white hair said to him, "Your name is Bopwright. Are you, by any chance, related to Brownbag Bopwright?"

"He's my dad."

The man nodded, his heavy eyelids rising a millimeter, a fraction of a smile making the subtlest of changes in the ancient, wrinkled face. "He is the true heir of Sonny Stinson. Please tell him that."

The old woman waved this triviality away with a gesture of her bony hand. "We have things to discuss," she said, and she and her colleagues moved to sit in three of the padded chairs in three of the corners.

Barnabas, in turn, sat in the chair opposite her, at one corner of the elevator shaft. Wickram sat cross-legged on the floor beside him, quietly handing him back the cell phone.

"I am Summer Coomlaudy," said the old woman, looking like a queen on her elegant little throne. "But in this place, you may address me as Prime Prelate. I have held this position for more than 50 years, and I am only the third to have done so since the days of Mayor Glorvanious. My colleagues and I serve Council in several functions, but perhaps most importantly, it is we who meet with representatives of the Valley's Guild Council on a twice-yearly basis and make sure they understand the needs of the City they serve." Her eyes widened and she leaned forward intently. "It is clear from your faces that you know exactly what I'm talking about — that you are disturbingly familiar with the Valley. Have you been there?"

The boys looked at each other. "Yes, ma'am," Barnabas answered. "We just got back to the City this morning. Well, I got back; this is Wickram's first time here. He was born in the Valley."

The three elders looked back and forth at each other as if trying to decide what to do next. The bald man said, "How were you able to cross the frontier? It is designed to be impregnable."

This was a trickier question, and Barnabas decided not to mention the return trip through the land of the Lurkers. "There was a big machine on the Yellow Line train. I squeezed in behind it on the way to school and fell asleep. Next thing I knew, I was down in the Valley!"

The Prime Prelate turned to the bald old man and said curtly, "Memo to the Transit Authority." The man nodded, whipping out a pad of paper and a gold-plated fountain pen. She looked the boys over with her fierce gaze. "There are many other questions that need answering, but the one that might get us most quickly to the heart of the matter is this: why did you arrange to come before the Executive Committee on the very day of your return from zones unknown and forbidden?"

With excited conviction, Wickram spoke up: "Glower!"

"Glower? What is that?" said the white-haired man.

Barnabas answered, "He means Glorvanious, Ma'am, Sirs. George Glorvanious left the Valley two days ago. He's planning to —"

"I'm sorry," the Prime Prelate interrupted, and Barnabas realized what a strong voice she had for someone so old and frail. "Did you say George Glorvanious? Are you suggesting that he has been in the Valley since his disappearance?"

"Yes, Ma'am. We came here today to talk to the Mayor. Mayor Tuppletaub knows Glorvanious and I figure maybe he can stop him in time!"

The bald man said in a high, breathy voice, "Stop him from what?"

So Barnabas told them. He told them about what he'd seen at the Drop Shop, about Carminn and Glorvanious at the Clouding Works, and about the Guild Council, who refused to do anything to help. Throughout his story, the three old people were silent and still, barely even blinking. Barnabas was expecting, as he told them about the Council's inaction, that they would break their silence, pound their frail fists in disbelief and instantly call upon a phalanx of police and soldiers to descend on the Towers and defuse the explosives, to take to the streets with a team of dogs and roust Glorvanious from whatever spider hole he had crawled into.

Instead, they laughed.

Summer Coomlaudy, a cruel light shining in her eyes said, "While I am surprised that the less-than-illustrious great-grandson of our formidable founder found his way to the Valley, I'm not surprised to hear that his hateful little heart has come up with such a grand and futile scheme."

Confused, Barnabas asked, "Futile? It looked pretty real to me. And it's happening tomorrow! He said so!"

The white-haired man, still chuckling said, "Mr. Glorvanious has been away too long. He has no knowledge of the GateKeeper system that protects our glorious Tower District. Without access codes to the tower buildings — a different code for each, with three levels of encrypted redundancy — there is no way he has been able to infiltrate, much less sabotage anything."

The bald man wheezed, "GateKeeper is without equal and without flaw. The protocols are considered foolproof 97 times out of 98 with only a 1% hypothetical failure rate. Little George's attempt at terror will be no more effective than his mayoral campaign. I expect him to vanish again in humiliation."

The Prime Prelate was getting to her feet, a process which made her wince a little. "Still," she said, "It would be wise to round him up before he can cause any unrest." She began to walk towards a small, round window like a ship's porthole between two bookshelves.

Barnabas hurried up to her. "You mean, you're not going to do anything? What if he's found a way to get around (what did you call it?) GateKeeper?!"

Without turning, she waved him away. "You need to trust your elders, young man. It's our job to protect to the City, and we're better qualified than you are."

Barnabas wanted to scream with frustration. *They aren't going to do anything either!*

She brought her face close to the window and said, "So, that troublesome fool is back, is he?" She made a tongue-click of annoyance as she looked out on the City. "Where are you, George Glorvanious, you naughty man?"

CHAPTER 29

George Glorvanious was, in fact, buying groceries. George had found a beaten-up old shopping bag hanging on the back of Stefan's front door, and now he was filling it with discounted vegetables at a nearby Chinese green grocer. His friend — it was a strange word to use, George knew, but it was the closest descriptor he could find — was asleep again, and if there was to be any dinner that night, George would have to be the one to prepare it.

Stefan was not well and slept most of the time now. He had never been particularly strong; even in the days when they worked together as young engineers, he had been laid out for months at a time by various illnesses. These protracted absences had lost him more than one job, and though George had helped him find others, the trajectory of his career had been downward from the start. *Some people just weren't cut out for success,* George thought. Seven more years of living in isolation below the poverty line, of never having a doctor examine him for his persistent cough and weight-loss had taken their toll. Now he was clinging to the cold, damp edges of life like so much lichen on a rock.

Still when Stefan had opened the door of his tiny, dirty apartment three months earlier and found himself looking into the long-absent face of George Glorvanious, he had let him in without hesitation or demand for an explanation. He didn't ask why George had vanished seven years earlier, or why he had returned now. George showed his gratitude by fixing the plumbing (the bathtub faucet had been providing no hot water, apparently for months) and by helping with the cooking.

"It's only for a few days, Stefan," he had promised, but Stefan didn't seem to care. Nor had he been surprised when George returned two weeks later, and then repeatedly over the period when he was setting his grand plan in motion. Perhaps Stefan was glad for the company or perhaps, like George, he was indifferent to human companionship. Still, George had felt a strange sense of satisfaction as they sat together in the living room each evening, sharing the silence. Stefan read his tattered paperback editions of Russian classics while George sat at the dining room table, writing notes, or as he had done last night, making careful adjustments to his triggering system. The little blue pyramids and the orange cube that sent them their commands were a little temperamental, but George soon had them working reliably. Then George had helped Stefan to bed before settling himself down on the lumpy couch with its acrid smells of spilled food.

As usual, Stefan didn't ask him what he was up to when he was out all day Sunday and most of the day Monday. George thought, *A wife would never be so respectful of my privacy.* He could almost imagine settling in here for good in this sanctuary from the cruel and self-satisfied world outside. But tomorrow was Tuesday, the irrevocable day of justice. He didn't even know if he'd be alive 24 hours later, so there was little point in planning for the future. He had one wish only, and he hoped it would come true: to be walking up the centre of Grand Avenue after the towers were toppled, savouring the terror and misery around him. He wanted to see the faces of the people as their foolhardy sense of security was pricked like a soap bubble.

George returned to the apartment with the groceries and walked up the three flights through the garbage-strewn stairwell. The lock on the apartment was broken and the door was just slightly ajar; all the lights were on inside. Alarmed, he put down the groceries and pulled out a gun from his jacket pocket. Dropping into a defensive posture, he slowly pushed the door open and moved cautiously into the apartment. He passed the kitchen on his left, but there was no intruder there. *Who had broken in?* he wondered, his brain racing through scenarios. Did the Aqua Guard follow him? Did Tuppletaub betray him? Impossible… the Mayor would be implicating himself! He burst into the living room, weapon at the ready, and there he learned the truth. The leavings of the Emergency Medical Team were scattered across the stained carpet: torn packets from IV leads, caps from hypodermic needles.

The front door creaked and George, hiding his gun, turned to see Stefan's neighbour standing in the doorway. She carried in his groceries from the hall, putting them on the kitchen counter. "The ambulance took him to Crestwell Presbyterian," she said. "He didn't look good."

It was just after 6pm when he arrived at the hospital, and he cursed the fact that he had to spend this last evening before the big day here when he should be alone, quietly focussing his mind. He asked for Stefan's location and lied that he was family. In fact, Stefan had no family other than his brother, a lawyer on the west coast, who had never cared what happened to him. An orderly led George back through the Emergency Department past any number of casual disasters, past families flattened with boredom or shining with gratitude. They finally arrived at a sad cubicle in a distant corner. A nurse emerged from behind the curtains and offered her condolences. She seemed sincere, but George was not the best judge of these sorts of things.

They wanted him to sign forms — for the coroner, for the insurance company — but he told them that in his haste, he had forgotten his wallet and all his ID at home. He promised to come back the next morning and take care of the paperwork. When he returned to the apartment building, the neighbour was waiting for him. "He's fine," George assured her. "They'll keep him in the hospital for a day or two, just to be sure." She crossed herself before closing her door and fastening its many locks.

Back in the apartment, George fried up the eggplant and tofu and put up a pot of brown rice to cook. He wished he had bought white rice instead; the brown was taking forever and he was terribly, terribly hungry. Usually he could control his appetites better than this, but tonight his hunger knew no bounds. It made him want to scream. His mind, usually so disciplined, danced with a lifetime's memory of food: salty potato chips and crisp apples, those fried bananas they used to sell at the Harvest Fair. The summer night he had tasted candy floss and lip gloss on Ellen Varney's mouth and desired nothing more in life than to stuff himself with spicy fries and kiss her until the sun rose.

But, no, life demanded more of him. The name Glorvanious demanded more; that's what they all told him. So he learned to control his appetites, to be patient, hard-working, and abstemious. "The reward will come," they had promised. "The day of triumph!"

The rice was ready at last, and he almost wept with relief. He ate quickly, without grace, gobbling the food down with animal grunts, but he didn't enjoy it. He would have derived some satisfaction from seeing Stefan eating it. But simple enjoyment for its own sake was beyond him; he had long ago lost his taste for taste. No appetite mattered, no friendship mattered. There was only the striving, the day of honeyed triumph that would justify every sacrifice... even if there was nothing beyond that finish line but featureless oblivion.

With the dishes washed and stacked, he read through his notes again. He opened the wooden box and checked the contents. The orange cube was there, but only one of the blue pyramids remained — the rest were in place, ready to do their job. He turned out the lamps and sat on the couch with the box on his knees. The lights of the living city moved across the walls, and the muted reverberations of its raucous exclamations echoed in his ears. He thought about nothing and about no one. He waited for morning.

CHAPTER 30

Summer Coomlaudy, the Prime Prelate, turned from the porthole window and smiled at Barnabas, eyes twinkling. "You boys must be hungry!" she said with surprising grandmotherly zeal. "Why don't you wait here and I'll have Ms. Doublegrey bring you sandwiches. Does that sound good?"

"Utterly! Thanks," said Wickram.

But Barnabas said, "What about Glorvanious? I mean, no offense, but what if he does have a way of getting through PeaceKeeper?"

"GateKeeper..." the bald man corrected wearily.

The old woman patted Barnabas on the shoulder as she headed for the elevator and he repressed the urge to flinch away. "As I said, we will go find George and make sure he's not planning any other nonsense. Now, it's been very nice meeting you, but we're busy people, and we have to get back to work." She gestured to the guard, who opened the elevator's metal gate.

Barnabas wanted to say that the meeting had been her idea and that he and Wickram had been given no choice in the matter. But he just kept his mouth shut as the three old people entered the elevator.

"Roast beef or peanut butter?" the Prime Prelate asked before the doors closed.

He was going to press her again on the urgency of the situation, but a sudden suspicion overtook him. From some deep hollow inside him, Barnabas found a bright, guileless smile to put on his face and said, "The roast beef sounds great! Wick?"

Wickram nodded enthusiastically, "Yeah, sure, either. Or both!"

"Wonderful," answered Ms. Coomlaudy, and turning to the security guard, she said sharply, "Come with us." The guard squeezed himself into the elevator.

"Regards to your father," called the white-haired man from behind the obfuscating mass of the guard. The doors closed, and the elevator descended noisily.

Barnabas took a deep breath and let it out slowly. "Let's get out here," he said. "Fast."

"But... Ms. Doublegrey is bringing sandwiches! That makes this a paying gig, Barn!"

"Wickram! They're not going to bring us sandwiches! They're going to arrest us, or... or hold us without trial or something!"

"You're skull-cracked, Barn. They were so nice."

"Think about it! It's their job to keep the Valley a secret! And they didn't even take what I said about Glower seriously! They're not going to do anything to stop him. As far as they're concerned, we're the big threat here — you and me! Because we know about the Valley!" The cool blue fear that had been rising him changed to blood-red anger. "Dammit! This is how I almost ended up in Doomlock. What is wrong with everyone?! First, the Guild Council just covered their asses. Now these idiots don't even believe Glower's smart enough to get past their GateKeeper thing! What do they think he's been doing in the City for months?!"

Wickram picked up Barnabas' discarded fear. Looking around nervously as if an army of guards was about to jump out from behind the bookshelves and grab them, he asked, "What do we do now?"

"We get out of here. We try to find a way to see the Mayor. We're in luck; they think we're just stupid kids, waiting here for our sandwiches. They should have left that guard. Come on, we're going down the stairs."

"We'll be seen."

"We'll be fast."

Barnabas pulled on his backpack, and Wickram shouldered his guitar. They began running down the staircase that circled round the elevator shaft. A few of the pale clerks looked up momentarily from their work as the boys ran past, but they didn't seem too interested. But then the clanking elevator began making its way back up, sliding right past them as they flew down the stairs. In it was Ms. Doublegrey and a security guard. She looked shocked to see them, but she reacted quickly. Before the elevator disappeared from sight, she already had her phone to her ear.

"Hurry!" Barnabas yelled.

"You were utter right!" Wickram yelled back. "She did NOT have any sandwiches with her!"

They reached the bottom of the staircase. Barnabas was scared they would need a key card to get out of the stairwell, but from inside, it was a crash door, and the boys burst through it. They ran past the Executive Committee meeting room (where the committee members were now crowded around the buffet) and headed for the main elevators. A few people were already waiting, and the boys stopped beside them, trying to not look conspicuous, despite the fact they were dripping sweat and panting like overheated dogs. Barnabas spotted a guard in dark glasses talking on a headset, but he couldn't tell if the guard was looking at them or not. The elevator mercifully arrived, and the boys pushed in ahead of the other people, prompting someone to snap, "Mind your manners!"

Back in the lobby, Barnabas sensed a new tension in the air. Maybe it was his imagination, but there were more guards than before, and they seemed to be moving around with greater purpose. He grabbed Wickram by the arm and pulled him behind a large potted tree. "Look," Barnabas said, peering out between the frilly leaves. "That's a tour group. We're going to join them. Take off your guitar and keep it low, out of sight."

Hidden in the middle of the group of tourists, like two sardines in the centre of a vast school, they moved around the lobby, listening to the history of the City all over again: Lawrence Glorvanious, the subway, the Tower District. Barnabas wondered if maybe the long-dead Mayor was sending them a message: *save my City!*

The school of tourists swung as close to an exit as they were likely to get, and Barnabas grabbed Wickram again, pulling him loose and running through the revolving doors into the sunlight. They dashed across the Civic Plaza, and Wickram waved up at Father Glory's father as they ran past. They kept running until they were two blocks away, in a little scrap of park with nothing but benches and a drinking fountain, where they were separated from the sidewalk by a line of waist-high bushes.

Panting, holding his side, Wickram gasped, "I-I can't believe we got out of there!"

Barnabas allowed himself to enjoy the brief moment of triumph. "The only sport I ever played was softball when I was 11. I wasn't much of a batter, but I knew how to hustle. I could get to first base on even the crappiest hit."

Wickram lay down on the grass. "I have no idea what that means. But thanks." He moaned. "I still wish we could have waited for the sandwich."

Barnabas pulled out his phone and dialled Deni. "Hey, can we come back to your place now? We're hungry."

Deni screamed into the phone, "ohmygod, Barnabas! Your mom!"

He sat up, alarmed. "What about her?"

"She's on her way over here! She said that it's high time you came home, and that if something is wrong — she thinks this is about you and Mayor last week— then you should discuss it with her and your step-dad."

"Crap! What are me and Wickram supposed to do now?"

"Forget about you! What am I going to say to her when she gets here?!"

Barnabas rubbed his forehead. He felt terrible about lying to his mom and worrying her like this. But there just wasn't time! He could either go home and make her feel better or else stop Glower from blowing up the whole Tower District! He told Deni, "You'll just have to figure something out. The Mayor wasn't even at the Council meeting."

"Did you tell anyone about Glorvanious?"

"Yeah, and they didn't believe he was a problem."

"Is he?!" She sounded excited.

"Never mind. I've got to go to the Mayor's apartment at Delphic Tower. I've got to sneak in somehow." He thought about the GateKeeper system and his heart sank. Glorvanious might be smart enough to defeat the high-tech security, but how could he possibly do it?

Barnabas could hear a clicking over the phone and knew Deni was tapping her teeth with her pencil, which was one of the things she did when she was thinking. "Where are you? Exactly?" she asked.

"Corner of Quarter-round and Chuck. In the parkette."

"Okay, don't move. He'll be there in 15 minutes."

"Wait… Who will?" but she had already hung up. Immediately, his phone rang; "mom," read the display. He shut off his phone. He got to his feet and started to pace nervously. All his problems seemed to be tangled together into one invincible knot. He spotted two policemen coming along the sidewalk and ducked back down behind the line of bushes.

"We shouldn't have given our real names at City Hall," he said to Wickram hopelessly. "Every cop in town is probably looking for us. We could be in huge trouble." Now that he thought about it, shutting off his phone had been a good idea. They could probably track him through it! He sighed a ragged sigh. There was nothing to be done but wait. He dropped down in the grass beside Wickram.

The tall boy, who seemed to have returned to his usual placid state, said, "Did you notice, there was something on the statue's hat? Some weird blue thing."

"No, I missed that somehow."

"A blue thing and a lot of pigeon poop. Hey, Barn! I forgot to tell you; I got my audition at the music school! Nine a.m. on Wednesday morning."

Barnabas stared at him. "Wickram, tomorrow, in all likelihood, Glower is going to blow up the whole Tower District! There won't be any auditions or *anything* normal on Wednesday morning."

"Nah, I doubt it," Wickram said with a maddening smile. "You're going to stop him. I'm utter certain."

Barnabas was dumbfounded by this show of confidence. He didn't know what to do with the emotions he was feeling. There was something of gratitude in it, and something like the love he felt for his brother, Thelonius. But there was also a hideous certainty that he was going to let Wickram down — let everyone down. He turned away because he probably looked like he was about to cry. He rose up on his knees to peek over the tops of the bushes for whatever cavalry Deni was sending.

It came just a couple of minutes later. A cab pulled up to the curb, and the door opened. Barnabas got to his feet in surprise as Cal Kabaway stepped out onto the sidewalk, holding the door. "Come on, guys, get in," he shouted.

"This is flamtasmic!" Wickram enthused about his first ever taxi ride as they cruised down Bulwark Boulevard. His eyes darted back and forth between the passing city views and the little monitor on the back of the seat that was beaming commercials at them.

For his part, Barnabas was quietly fuming. He couldn't believe Deni had done this to him. "Where are we going, Calvin?" he asked, not bothering to hide his aggravation.

"My place. You and Wickram can spend the night." He sounded pretty enthused at the idea.

Barnabas, on the other hand, thought that of all the people he would choose to spend this last pre-disaster night with, Cal would be pretty low on the list — somewhere just above a deranged serial killer. He said, "Look, Calvin, it's really nice of you to offer to put us up, but we're running out of time! I need to figure out how to get to Mayor Tuppletaub. If I don't, things are going to get really bad tomorrow."

Cal smirked and said, "Well then, you're in luck. I happen to live in Delphic Tower, just a couple of floors below the Mayor's residence."

Barnabas just stared. It was kind of hard to believe. He knew the boy's family had money, but an apartment in Delphic Tower? Yet ten minutes later the cab was driving through the fancy avenues of the Tower District and pulling to a stop in driveway of one of the City's most exclusive residential buildings. While Cal paid the driver, Barnabas and Wickram climbed out onto the sidewalk. Wickram was rubber-necking skywards, in awe of the majestic building. The boy from the Valley looked embarrassingly out of place in this world of wealth, and Barnabas felt almost as awkward. Cal, on the other hand, was right at home as he approached the front doors and let the uniformed door man open it for him with a respectful nod. Barnabas and Wickram, caught up in Cal's force-field of privilege, followed, unquestioned.

Delphic Tower, Barnabas remembered reading, had been built in the 1940s. It had been modernized and renovated many times, but still carried its air of last-century opulence. Right from the start, the 50th floor had been set aside as the residence for whatever Mayor was in office at the time. Important as he was, the Mayor didn't occupy the top floor. There were three more stories of impossibly expensive penthouses above, owned over the years by some of the most celebrated (or feared) businessmen in the City.

At the back of foyer, Barnabas saw the most recent renovation to the building: a wall of thick (probably bulletproof) glass that could only be crossed at one heavily-secured, automated gate with a card reader beside it. Etched on the glass was the word "GateKeeper." In the cab, Barnabas had asked about the security system and Cal had shown them his key card, telling them they would sign in at the desk and then go in and out under his supervision. Barnabas had warned Wickram to use a false name. Soon they were riding the elevator up to the 48th floor.

Cal held the apartment door open as Barnabas and Wickram entered. He flicked on a bank of switches beside the door, and carefully staged lights came on everywhere. It was an enormous apartment, with walls more than three metres high and floor-to-ceiling, south-facing windows through which Barnabas could see the sun glowing low in the Western sky. The hardwood floors were dark brown — almost black, and contrasted the walls, which were the purest flat white. Accents of chrome glittered here and there. Barnabas was amazed at not just the palatial scale of the apartment, but by the fact that it was almost entirely empty. The only furniture was a huge U-shaped sofa unit in the centre of the sunken living room area, with a large coffee table in the middle that seemed to be a single slab of smoky glass. The sofa faced the biggest wall-mounted television he had ever seen. A small army of sleek speakers promised cinematic sound.

But there were no pictures on the walls, no books, no family photos, no evidence of home life of any kind. Cal closed the door, and an alarm system beeped discreetly. The sound of the door, of the alarm, of their footsteps echoed coldly in the cavernous space. Cal stowed his schoolbag in the hall closet and said, "Please leave your shoes here. There are slippers in that box if you want them."

"This is where you live?" Wickram asked, and Barnabas couldn't tell whether he was appalled or impressed.

"Yeah," said Cal. He seemed excited to have them there. "Let's take care of dinner and then I'll show you around."

Barnabas asked. "Where's the rest of your family?"

"Oh, it's just me and my father. He's usually away on business. I think he's in Argentina now. Come on." They followed him into the living room and they each sat on their own wing of the enormous couch. Cal reached into a cardboard box and pulled out a set of restaurant menus. They weren't the little photocopied kind that you find in your mailbox, either; they were real leather-bound menus. He handed them to Wickram and Barnabas and said, "Pick whatever you like. It's all really good food, and they deliver it pretty fast, considering it's fine-dining."

The prices made Barnabas' eyes go wide, but Wickram and Cal were already throwing out suggestions to each other for what was shaping up to be a huge and expensive feast. Cal pulled out his phone to place the order, talking to the restaurant in a loud, confident voice — the voice of wealth, Barnabas thought. Cal hung up and said, "Let me show you around."

They started at the windows, taking in the amazing view. The whole of the City was laid out in front of them, from the Manhammer Dome to

River's Edge park and everywhere in between. Barnabas thought he could maybe see the building where he lived, but he wasn't sure. He remembered that, in the whole of the Tower District, there were no windows facing the Valley — that is except the one set in the Mayor's Residence. He craned his neck upwards, but he couldn't see any of the 50th floor from where they stood.

Wickram had wandered away from them, and suddenly Cal was screaming, "No! Don't touch that!" in an urgent voice, like a frightened kid. Barnabas swivelled around and saw Wickram in an alcove just off the living room. He was standing behind a table covered in DJ equipment — multiple turntables, headphones, stacks of vinyl records, a jungle of cables running through meters and effects devices, and behind them, tall racks with more gear and a set of enormous speakers. It was like the system had been lifted straight out of a huge club and transplanted here. Wickram was standing stock still, frozen in shock as Cal ran up to him.

"Did you change anything? Any settings?" Cal asked in a panic.

"No, I dunno, I think… Uh, yeah, this knob was on three instead of five."

Cal changed it back, concentrating on the adjustment like his life depended on his precision. "Is that all? Are you sure?"

Wickram stepped away nervously, "Yeah, utter certain, sorry, sorry!"

Cal seemed to calm down a little. "As long as you're sure. I'm not allowed to mess with my father's DJ gear. And he remembers every setting."

Barnabas and Wickram exchanged a troubled look, and Barnabas asked, "Are there any other rules? Like, anything else we can't touch?"

Cal was walking back across the living room, wiping sweat off his forehead, and they followed him. "No, just that. Well, we can't go in his room, but he keeps it locked anyway." A minute later, Cal was his usual self again although Barnabas still felt deeply unnerved by the incident.

The next stop on the tour was the big kitchen with its black marble counters and large central island, four bar stools pulled up to it. If the huge steel fridge had been full, it could have fed an army for a day, but in fact, it contained only a couple of milk cartons and a gift-basket of withered fruit. It was Wickram, inquisitive and unembarrassed as a cat, who had opened it, along with every drawer and cupboard. All this effort revealed only a four-piece set of white dishes, some random, heavy cutlery, bags of plantain chips, and three or four unexceptional brands of cereal.

Even Cal's bedroom had a half-lived-in quality. There was a South American football poster on the wall and a couple of school books on the unmade bed, but that was really all. It was as if Cal and his father were afraid to commit to the place, like they might have to de-camp in a hurry.

The boys returned to the giant couch in the living room and watched videos of trampoline accidents on the giant screen until the food arrived. The delivery person was actually a waiter, crisply dressed in formal attire, and he didn't just hand them a bunch of paper bags at the door; he came in and laid out the whole meal elegantly on the kitchen island. Cal tipped him with a bunch of bills, and soon the boys were tearing into the food. It was maybe the best meal Barnabas had ever eaten. But it was Calvin who seemed the most grateful. "This is so amazing. You're actually the first friends I had over since we moved here. Even Deni hasn't been."

"Why not?" Barnabas asked. He realized, annoyingly, that he was starting to feel sorry for Cal. The big, confident guy who had won Deni's heart might be the loneliest kid Barnabas had ever met.

"I know why," Wickram said bluntly. "You don't want her to meet your dad."

Cal blushed. "Um, yeah, maybe."

Wickram nodded. "No, it's triple-clear. I wish my dad didn't know my girlfriend. I wish he wasn't practically in love with her."

"Hey, Cal," Barnabas interrupted, maybe partly to get them out of this depressing conversation. "This is great and everything, but I've got to get up the Mayor's apartment and talk to him. Any ideas how I can do that?"

"I don't think he's there. Deni says he's at a big campaign dinner tonight at the Festival Hotel. Wait, his publicist is probably live-Texxing." He tapped on a keyboard that was cunningly inset in the coffee table, and the Mayor's Texxit feed appeared up on the big screen. "We can keep track of him here, see when he's heading home."

"Okay, but when he does come home, do I just take the elevator up? Aren't there guards and everything?"

"And aren't you a wanted fugitive, Barn?" Wickram whispered in his ear.

Cal stood up. "Yeah, no, you can't just barge in. But I know a way." Barnabas followed him to the back of the apartment, the windowless north wall, where he put his hands on one of the smooth, white panels. "Help me with this; it's kind of sticky."

With no idea of what they were doing, Barnabas also laid his palms on the wall, and then the two of them lifted at the same time. The sleek, modern wall panel slid up and off its moorings, and they lowered it carefully to the ground. Behind it was an older wall of inlaid wood. And in this slice of the past, barely visible, was a secret door.

Cal explained, "I think this was the servant's entrance back in the day. Maids and delivery men could come and go unseen. The owners wouldn't have to share an elevator with them. I accidentally found it when I was bouncing a basketball around." He slipped a finger into a tiny recessed hole and, with a click, the door popped open. An eerie howl of wind emerged, along with a gust of greasy, metallic air. Barnabas stepped through the door into a huge air shaft with a network of metal stairs and walkways rising up and down through all 53 floors. It was like a fire-escape gone mad, and all hidden in the north face of the building. Filtered sunlight came into the airshaft through small, louvered vents in the back wall and lit the whole structure with a dismal blue glow. Theoretically, every apartment had such a hidden door. In this forgotten space, you could go anywhere in Delphic Tower.

Wickram stepped out to join him on the walkway. His voice, low with awe, was almost inaudible under the howling wind: "This is utter spectaulous. Skull-cracked level 8."

Barnabas was breathless with excitement. If Thelonius could only see this — it was the best infiltration *ever!* "Calvin, can you show me how to go the Mayor's residence?" he asked.

"Yeah, okay," Cal said, and Barnabas noticed he was still in the entrance to the apartment, gripping the door frame tightly.

"You all right?" Barnabas asked.

"Just … not so great with heights. Don't worry, I'll hang on tight."

They only had to climb two stories, but Cal's progress up the stairs was ridiculously slow, and Barnabas felt a dirty little feeling of superiority. He even leaned over the railings, ostentatiously enjoying the view while his host put one careful foot in front of the other. They finally reached the landing on the 50th floor.

Barnabas put his hand on the small doorknob, but hesitated, speaking over the wind into Cal's ear. "Do you think the door is alarmed?"

"I don't know. I kind of asked around, and no one seems to even know this part of the building is here. They covered it all up twenty years ago, and now everyone's forgotten." He paused. "But maybe."

"Get ready to run," Barnabas told his friends and pulled on the knob. No alarm rang. But instead of an entrance into the apartment, he found himself staring at a panel of unfinished wood, the back of some cabinet or bookcase. There were even some long-gone carpenter's measurements scrawled on it in faded pencil. He cursed in frustration, but then noticed that the wood didn't go all the way to the floor. Getting down on his hands and knees, he saw that there was a space at the bottom that he could just fit through. On the other side was Mayor Tuppletaub's apartment! He could see antique chairs, a Persian rug, a door on the far side of the room.

Wickram got down on all fours behind him. "You going in?"

"No, even if they don't know to alarm this door, there are probably motion detectors inside. Better to wait until the Mayor's home." They stood, and Barnabas closed the door.

"Okay?" Cal asked, clinging tightly to a railing with his eyes closed. "Ready to go back?"

They spent the evening on the couch watching action movies and keeping an eye on the Mayor's Texxit-feed. Cal spilled two packages of plantain chips into a big bowl and opened warm cans of strong cider from a case he found at the back of the hall closet. The three of them, soon pleasantly tipsy, laughed a lot and talked about girls. From his pocket, Wickram pulled out the little plastic figurine of the fertility goddess he had taken from Deni's apartment and walked it down the couch arm like a fashion model.

"Give me that!" Cal said, jumping to his feet. "Gimme! Gimme!" He grabbed the figurine and ran to the front door, where he began to dig in Barnabas' bag.

"Hey, get out of there!" Barnabas shouted, surprised to hear his words a little slurry from the cider. But Cal ignored him and returned triumphantly, holding the *diaboriku*. He stood the fertility figurine up on the coffee table and pushed the big rubber buttons on the device. A giant, faceless woman suddenly towered up over them, roaring, swinging her mammoth hips, shaking her mountainous breasts. Cal and Barnabas howled with laughter, and then laughed even louder when they saw Wickram cowering in the corner of the couch at the sight of this pendulous goddess.

Cal handed Barnabas the *diaboriku*. "You do one," he said. "Do Wickram's guitar." Barnabas was about to admit that he had never actually figured out how to make the device work. Then he could have asked Cal for a lesson, but he was too embarrassed. So, instead he turned on his phone and showed them the movie he had taken of Graviddy's performance at the circus. This inspired Wickram to stand up on the couch and declaim bad love poetry. During this impromptu show, Barnabas noticed there were five messages from his mother, so he turned off the phone again and tried not to think about it.

According to his Texxit feed, the Mayor was still partying at midnight. Cal and Wickram had fallen asleep on their respective wings of the couch, but Barnabas forced himself to stay conscious, keeping a drooping eye on the feed. Dreams began to overlay reality... The Texxit messages were being projected across the clouds, and he peered through the small window from his seat on an airplane. His history teacher handed him back his mid-term test, but there was secret note inside with the Mayor's location, only the words on the page were quivering gibberish, and he couldn't make any sense of them. Then Barnabas was asleep, too. Outside, the beautiful city, aglow with a million lights, didn't even realize that this might be its last night of peace.

CHAPTER 31

Barnabas had about five seconds to enjoy the warm, pink feeling of a good night's sleep before his eyes snapped open.

"What time is it?!" he called into the room.

"Sleep time," Cal grunted. Wickram just snored.

Barnabas sprang to his feet and shook Wickram. "No, come on! We fell asleep; the Mayor could be anywhere now!"

Without getting up, Cal reached for the inset keyboard on the coffee table, swiping and tapping. The picture on the big TV screen changed to a CCTV cam at the front door of the building.

"That's the Mayor's car out front," Cal muttered sleepily. "There's his driver, waiting, having a smoke."

The clock on the display read 7:15 am. Barnabas asked, "How long until he leaves, you think?"

"Anytime, I guess."

"Wickram, we have to hurry," Barnabas said, and five minutes later, the three of them were standing by the hidden door at the back of the apartment, Wickram with his guitar, Barnabas with his backpack. He patted down his pocket to make sure his cell phone was there as Cal handed them a couple of muffins. Wickram shoved the whole into his mouth and made muted noises of appreciation as he chewed the enormous bolus.

"You going to school, Cal?" Barnabas asked.

"I don't know. Deni texted me — asked if you needed our help."

Barnabas tried to imagine the coming hours, but he had no idea what they held. "Just go; I can always text you between classes if I need you."

"So, you're just going upstairs to give the Mayor some message?"

"Yeah. I guess I'll just tell him what I know, and then he'll do what he has to do."

"You remember that I still don't know what you're talking about?"

Barnabas stuck his finger in the little hole in the door and released the catch. The door popped open, and they stepped onto the secret walkway. Over the howl of the wind, Cal said a bit shyly, "Thanks for coming over. It was fun."

"Thanks for having us," Wickram said with sleepy affability, sticking his tongue out to collect a muffin crumb from his upper lip.

Barnabas said, "Thanks for everything. We should do a games night some time."

Cal grinned "That sounds great."

"Come on, Wickram," Barnabas said, and started climbing the clattering, metal stairs.

The howl of wind in the stairwell was worse today. Maybe that happened when the wind was coming from the Valley side. As they climbed, Barnabas ate his muffin and wondered how the fate of thousands had come to depend on someone as insignificant as him. Barnabas Bopwright was no hero. He wasn't a legendary jazz musician like his dad, or an infamous teenage Innervader like his brother had been. He wasn't a top student like Deni, and he didn't live his life tossed on the high seas of operatic emotion like Wickram and Tragidenko. He was just a quiet guy who got through life's struggles by keeping his head down and not being noticed. He didn't have the best grades in the school, he didn't have the worst. He wasn't the most popular, nor was he friendless. He was an average student, an average son, an average young citizen of the City. But somehow, starting last Thursday through the utterly banal act of falling asleep on a subway car, he had been thrust into another life, one where he had been given a larger role to play. It was a life that he hadn't and wouldn't have chosen. Did he regret it? *Ask me again tomorrow,* he thought.

On the 50th floor landing, he turned to Wickram and said above the roar of the wind, "You stay here. I'll be back soon."

"What if you're not?"

Barnabas considered this, but the alternatives were too scary. He took off his backpack and put it down on the landing, saying, "Just... I will be. Don't worry." Wickram shrugged and sat down on the stairs.

Barnabas opened the secret door of the Mayor's residence and got down on the ground to peer through the small gap. There was no movement, no sound, but then suddenly a pair of feet in shiny, black dress shoes shot past, just inches away. Barnabas gasped and kept perfectly still. As the shoes headed for a doorway on the far side of the room, he could see more and more of the person wearing them. It was Mayor Arthur Tuppletaub.

The Mayor left the room, and Barnabas snapped into action, giving himself no time to chicken out. He put his hands through the gap and pulled himself into the room. He was in some kind of study or library although the room was more like a museum display than a working office. All the furnishings were expensive, dust-free, and meticulously placed. Other than the new computer on the desk, he might have been transported back to the middle of the last century. He saw that it was indeed a bookcase that was covering up the hidden servants' door. He had crawled through the space under the lowest shelf.

Barnabas slipped out into the corridor, just as the Mayor had. He looked left, and saw a large area that must have been the main foyer. Beyond it was another whole wing. The apartment was enormous. The Mayor, however, had gone to the right, and Barnabas followed, walking silently along the thick runner with its elaborate Arabian design. The pictures on the wall were mostly signed photos of the Mayor posing with various celebrities. On his right, across from a closed door, was an antique cabinet with a glass front. Inside was a full set of commemorative plates, one for each mayor of the City, starting with Lawrence Glorvanious. All wore serious expressions except the last one in the series: Arthur Tuppletaub with his big salesman's grin.

Barnabas heard noise at the end of the hall and he followed it, turning right again into the Mayor's sunlit bedroom. He saw a big unmade bed with a chrome base, another desk covered in important-looking papers, a huge wall of closets with their accordion doors all pulled open... and the skinny, panicked figure of the Mayor himself, darting back and forth from drawer to closet like a hummingbird, and shoving clothes willy-nilly into a huge suitcase on the bed. Arthur Tuppletaub looked up in that moment, saw Barnabas and shrieked, prompting Barnabas to let out his own startled shout.

"Who are you?! What are you doing here?!" the Mayor exclaimed, his voice high and tight, his thinning blond hair standing uncombed in little tufts on his oversized head. "I told the guards no one was to enter! Not even them!"

"I-I told them I was your nephew," Barnabas said, impressed by the impromptu lie.

Tuppletaub looked at him, but his eyes seemed to have trouble focussing. In fact, he seemed crazy. "No, you're not my nephew; I'm certain of that! But you do look familiar." He resumed his packing, lurching back across to the closet and returning to the suitcase with a tall pile of underwear.

"Mr. Mayor, please! I have to talk to you; it's urgent!"

"Not today, any day but today! You have to get out, GET OUT!" He waved both arms at Barnabas like a scarecrow in a tornado. Barnabas found himself nervously backing toward the door, but Tuppletaub yelled, "Wait! Are you strong? Carry that suitcase to the foyer." He indicated a matching suitcase by the bedroom door, already closed but with various items of clothing caught in the seal.

Barnabas walked over to the suitcase and was about to lift it when he remembered himself. "Mr. Mayor, please stop! STOP! I need to talk to you about George Glorvanious." And the Mayor did stop. His face went white, and he staggered over to sit on the bed as if his legs could no longer hold him up. Barnabas said, "You know, don't you? I told the Guild Council down in the Valley, then I told the lady at City Hall, uh, the Prime Prelate: he's going to blow up the whole Tower District!"

The Mayor's voice was more breath than substance. "I-I know, she phoned me. Some boy told her." He looked at Barnabas accusingly. "Of course, she thought it was nonsense." His hands, folded in his lap, were shaking.

Barnabas then looked at the open suitcase and at the closed one in front of him. "Wait… you're leaving? *You're running away?!* No! Nono-noNO! Mr. Mayor, you have to stop him!"

"How?! I don't know where he is! And even if I did, what am I supposed to do? Fly in the window and punch him in the nose? Hang him up in a big net in front of City Hall?!"

"Call the police! Evacuate the towers!"

"I can't!"

"WHY NOT?!!" Barnabas screamed and then wondered if the guards were about to burst in. He steadied himself and walked over to stand in front of Tuppletaub. "Why not?" he asked more quietly.

The Mayor closed his eyes. "Because it's my fault." He looked up at Barnabas and laughed, a very tired laugh. "Of course; I remember now. You're the boy who asked about the secret subways, aren't you? At that stupid, pretentious school. Why am I cursed with people like you? Like Glorvanious? I wish I didn't even know about the damned Valley!"

Barnabas was trying to stay calm, but inside he was growing desperate. He needed the Mayor to save them, and the man was falling apart in front of his very eyes, his chin dropping to his chest like he couldn't bear the weight of his own thoughts anymore. Barnabas knew he had to keep the man focussed. "Sir, the Prime Prelate said there's no problem because Glorvanious can't get past the GateKeeper system, but I wonder if —" He heard the Mayor murmur something. "What was that, Sir?"

The Mayor raised his head slowly. His eyes, empty of emotion, regarded Barnabas flatly. "I gave him the pass codes. All of them. For every tower."

And now it was Barnabas who sat down heavily on the Mayor's bed.

"Why?" Barnabas asked in shock, staring down at his feet.

"He came to me months ago. I could barely believe it was him. George Glorvanious — missing for seven years! He said he had information about my opponents in the election. Said he could assure me another four years in office with this information. For a price."

Barnabas understood, and it was like cutting into a beautiful, red apple and finding the insides blackened and rotting, swimming with worms, with corruption. He said, "Glorvanious didn't want money, right? Just the pass codes." The Mayor didn't bother answering. The corruption, it was everywhere: in the Guild Council, at City Hall, in Ms. Rolan-Gong's office as she appeased the rich donor parents. Barnabas felt profoundly betrayed by the whole adult world.

Numb with shock and disgust, he asked, "Didn't you wonder why he wanted to get past GateKeeper?"

The Mayor dropped his head again. "Well, he was gone all those years... I thought maybe he had become an art thief or something. I told myself, why should I care if he rips off some billionaire? I never dreamed he was planning... that he would ever..."

They sat in dejected silence for a long minute. Barnabas even had time to think how odd it was that he should be sitting in the Mayor's apartment, on the Mayor's bed, sharing a problem like they were in the same study group at school. He was vaguely aware of Tuppletaub getting up and closing his suitcase. Barnabas asked, "What are we going to do?"

The Mayor had snapped out of his stupor. Barnabas could see the determined set of his jaw and the gleam in his eyes. "Do? We will do what we have to. Bring that suitcase to the foyer," he commanded. Barnabas had no other plan, so he obeyed, following Tuppletaub, who was pulling the suitcase from the bed, down the long, carpeted hall. They returned to the bedroom, and Barnabas watched Tuppletaub straighten his tie and put on his suit jacket. The Mayor seemed calm and in charge now, which was an improvement , though Barnabas noted that the man's hand was still shaking as he ran a comb through his hair.

The Mayor told the boy, "I'm leaving now."

"What'll happen to me?"

"Don't worry. In 30 minutes when I'm on the road, I will phone my guards and tell them to please escort my nephew downstairs and give him taxi fare home."

"What will happen when the towers go down?"

The Mayor seemed to be speaking as much to himself as to Barnabas: "The election will have to be postponed, of course. The City will be in chaos, in need of a sure hand on the wheel. It will be the defining moment of my mayoralty. My legacy moment."

He looked at Barnabas one more time like he was just another random variable, then turned on his heel, and marched out purposefully without saying goodbye. A minute later, Barnabas heard the door of the apartment slam. He thought it odd that the man would leave a strange boy alone in his bedroom, but then he remembered that the bedroom would be blown up along with the rest of the building in just a few hours. Barnabas didn't know what to feel or perhaps how to. His mind seemed so quiet — no anger, no fear, just emptiness. He looked up at the long line of windows and recognized what they were: the one and only set that looked onto the Valley.

The view was breathtaking. The morning sunlight lit up all the places he had come to know in the past week. Right below him was the Tumbles, and the big warehouse with the steel roof was the Drop Shop. Just down the road from that was the factory complex of the Forming Guild. There was the train station where he had arrived, and the food depot. He spotted the Commons, where he had climbed the pole to call Deni, and beyond that saw the big dry bowl of Lake Lucid with the Guild Mansion standing at the far end. He followed the path of the water pipes to the Coursing works, and then, closer to the cliff, saw the great Cathedral that formed the entrance to Clouding's steam plant. And there, up on its own little mountain was the green oasis that surrounded Pastoral Park. The dense canopy was the mysterious woods where the witch lived. And beyond that, of course, the whimsical majesty of the Big Top.

The whole Valley community was incredibly compact from this vantage point, a little world with its own magic. Barnabas felt a tender affection for it and a pride that he was part of a select few in the City that knew of its existence. He thought of the other view he had seen from Calvin's apartment: the City, with all its vigour and verve, its deeply layered culture. And there Barnabas stood, between these worlds, knowing that soon all this carefully wrought balance would collapse. He was without a plan, without hope. He wondered if he shouldn't just go down with the Towers. Or maybe he could go back to City Hall and turn himself in, let the Prime Prelate send him to prison like the Guild Council wanted to send him Doomlock.

Then there was a noise. He froze, cocking his ear. He moved quickly to the door and peered down the hall. He saw a distant figure there, leaving the foyer and heading down into the other wing of the apartment. The man had his gun out. Despite the distance, despite the brevity of the glimpse, Barnabas recognized that blond bowl-cut, that stocky little physique in the blue suit: it was the Mayor's security man, the psychotic Mr. Klevver.

CHAPTER 32

Barnabas pulled himself back into the bedroom, his heart pounding as he tried to comprehend the situation. It hadn't been 30 minutes... the Mayor had betrayed him! He must have told Klevver there was an intruder inside. Suddenly Barnabas wasn't ready to go down with the Towers or go off politely to jail. There had to be a way to stop Glorvanious, but it wasn't going to happen if he was captured or, thinking of how Klevver had hung him upside-down over the stairwell at school, killed! He couldn't hear any movement, so he dared another look down the hallway. The coast was clear. Running as fast as he could, he dived into the study and pulled himself against the wall, to the right of the open door.

He listened for noises of Klevver's movement in the apartment, but a persistent howling made it hard to hear. He realized that the noise was coming from the secret stairwell, through the open door behind the bookcase. It was time to get out, but now he was too scared to move from his inadequate hiding place. Why hadn't he just run straight for his exit while he had the chance? Suddenly, crossing the big, open room and getting down on his hands and knees to crawl through the opening under the bookcase seemed impossible.

Somewhere down the hall, a door creaked, and another slammed. Klevver was checking the apartment, room by room. There wasn't much time. *Go,* Barnabas told himself. *Just go!*

Not far away—not nearly far enough away—something said, "Meow." Was there a cat here? Would the Mayor have really left his cat behind to die? But the next cat call had a post-script: "Meooooow. Here, mousey-mousey." Klevver, not exactly the pinnacle of wit, was literally playing cat and mouse with him.

"Just do it, just do it. Now, now…" Barnabas whispered to his frozen feet. He could feel the wind from the stairwell blowing across them. And then, abruptly, the hidden door behind the bookcase, his only escape, caught a sudden gust and slammed shut. The howling wind stopped, leaving a terrible, revealing silence in its wake. Barnabas wanted to scream. Klevver, he knew, had heard the slam. The crazy killer was coming. To the right of the door was a red leather armchair—a chunky geometric piece of deco. Without thinking twice, Barnabas dived across the study's open doorway and scrambled over the armchair, hiding himself behind its bulk. And just as he pulled himself down and out of sight, Mr. Klevver entered the room.

"Ooh," cooed Klevver. "Is there a little mouse in *here?* A bad little mouse hiding from the hungry cat?" Klevver held the gun in both hands, his arms straight, pointing it around the room like a searchlight. "Meeeeeeoowwwww!" he offered casually, horribly.

Barnabas watched as Klevver's eyes fell on a closet door, just a little ajar, and the man crept quietly toward it, making no sound at all on the thick carpet. But that carpet, Barnabas knew, would mask his own movement just as well. With Klevver's back to him, Barnabas crawled out from behind the armchair, around its square girth, and scrambled out into the hall. Now what? Obviously, he couldn't just leave through the front door of the apartment; the Mayor's guards were waiting on the other side. Or were they? What if they had left with their boss? Barnabas couldn't be sure. The only certainty was to get back to the study and leave the way he had entered.

Barnabas knew Klevver would be finished his search of the study any second. Shaking with fear, he surveyed his surroundings, hoping for an idea. Down the corridor, halfway to the Mayor's bedroom, a door stood open that had been closed the first time he came this way. Barnabas peeked inside and saw he was in some kind of storage room, mostly for linens. Across from it, in the hall, stood the big cabinet of commemorative mayoral plates. He had an idea. He slipped into the linen-room, pulling the phone from his pocket, and thumbed open the alarm app. He set it for one minute and chose the loudest song in his library for the wake-up signal. Then he tossed the phone onto the highest shelf in the deepest corner of the room and ran back into the hall, hiding himself on the far side of the antique cabinet.

No minute in human history had ever passed so slowly. And yet when the alarm went off, Barnabas almost screamed, like he hadn't been expecting it.

"I DON' WANNA BEA ANOTHA BROK'NHEARTED BABY F'YOU!" wailed pop diva, Agranda Lattay from inside the linen-room, and Barnabas wished he could feel more empathy for her romantic problems. *Sorry, Agranda, I'm busy surviving at the moment.*

He strained to hear movement over the song, but Klevver, if he was there, was moving silently as a panther. Barnabas fought the urge to peek around the cabinet... And then, there he was, close enough to touch, following his outstretched gun into the linen-room.

"Oh, little mouse, you squeaky sneak," Klevver said in a sing-song as he vanished into the room. "Gonna bite into your flesh and hear you shriek!"

Barnabas moved. *Now! Now! Now! Now!* He slammed the door of the linen-room and then, dashing back to the side of the cabinet, pulled the top of it away from the wall with all his strength. For a second it didn't move, and Barnabas roared like he was summoning a demon from deep inside himself — a creature of strength and daring that was probably taller and braver than him, and had ears that didn't stick out so much. And then the cabinet began to move, tipping slowly off balance and picking up speed. The glass doors flew open as it fell and, with a crash of priceless antique porcelain, the cabinet hit the door of the linen-room, pinning it closed.

"YES!" Barnabas screamed.

And inside the room, Klevver howled back, "NO!" and began throwing himself against the door, which shook on its frame with each blow.

Barnabas scrambled over the tilted back of the fallen cabinet and ran for the study. He hoped against hope that Klevver was well and truly trapped, at least for a while, but he feared the psychotic strength the man might muster.

He ran across the floor and dived, sliding head first under the bookcase and pushing at the closed door behind it. The door rattled a little in its frame, but the latch held. He knew that, up above him, there was a little hole with a hidden lever like the one in Cal's apartment, but with the bookcase pushed right against the door, he couldn't reach it. Putting his mouth close to the wall, he yelled, "Wickram! Open the door. Do you hear me?!" He pounded on the wood, and then again, harder. Nothing.

A gunshot. Another. He had never known before just how loud a gun was in real life. He imagined Klevver breaking free, flying into the study in a rage and seeing him, butt and legs extended back into the room from under the bookcase, twitching like a trout on the dock. Barnabas pulled himself back out and turned around, this time putting his feet against the hidden door. Holding the edge of the bookcase for traction, he brought his legs back, almost to his chest, and gave the door a solid two-footed kick. He resisted the urge to look over his shoulder to see if Klevver was coming. What did it matter? If he couldn't open the stubborn door, it was all over, anyway.

Another volley of gunfire from the hall. The sound of splintering wood. Barnabas could hear himself screaming, "Come on! Come on!" as he kicked harder and harder, coiling his legs up and smashing at the door again and again. And then, with a crack, the latch broke, and the hidden door flew open. Without so much as a backward glance, Barnabas pulled himself through the gap and scrambled to his feet on the metal landing. He threw the door closed and leaned against it, his heart pounding so loudly, his ears buzzed.

But Klevver didn't come. Barnabas imagined him in the study, cursing and turning over the furniture in a rage. But Klevver, he prayed, didn't know about the hidden door. After a full minute of panting tension, Barnabas let go of the broken door. It stayed mostly closed, and he thought, *that will have to do.* He picked up his backpack and looked all around. Like lava in a volcano, anger began to rise in him, and he was seized with a desire to throttle Wickram for not being there.

He found the boy from the Valley down a couple of flights, playing his guitar with great concentration, the wind loud enough to mask the sound of the music until Barnabas was almost on top of him. Words of hurt, outrage, and desperation clogged Barnabas' throat, grinding against each other until the dam finally burst. "Where were you?!!" he screamed, and burst into tears.

Wickram sat there staring, his mouth working for several seconds before he managed to say, "Sorry?"

Barnabas glared at him, wild-eyed with fury and humiliation, and then started to run. Faster and faster, his clanging footfalls ringing like cathedral bells, he let his adrenaline propel him down four dozen floors, round and round the stairwell at a crazy pace. *Slow down, slow down,* he begged himself, thinking how ironic it would be to die in a tumble down the dusty metal stairs. Despite Barnabas' head-start, Wickram soon caught up with him, and they thundered downward together.

When the boys reached the tenth floor, out of breath, dizzy, feet sore and thighs aching, Barnabas looked up and saw Glower's handiwork. Wrapped around the huge upright girders that supported the whole north side of the building were white plastic bags, filled with something dense but flexible, like heavy clay. Explosives, Barnabas realized, supplied to Glower by Carminn.

Wickram was doubled-over beside him, panting. "Oh man, do we really have to run down a giant staircase every single day?!" Then he straightened up and saw the explosives. "Uh-oh. That doesn't look good."

The white bags were connected by a dense network of red wires. Barnabas descended the stairs slowly now as if in a trance, following the wires from the ninth floor to the eighth, passing more bags of explosives along the way. The wires finally came together in some kind of switching box on the seventh floor. And leading from this box, disappearing through the wall into the front part of the building, was a blue wire. Where did it lead? To some kind of trigger? One of the little blue pyramids he had seen in the demonstration at the Drop Shop?

Barnabas' horror was palpable. Somehow, until he had seen this actual evidence of Glower's plan, he had been able to preserve some small portion of comforting doubt. Maybe he needed to believe that if he failed, the result wouldn't be quite so bad. But now he could see what Glower had been doing with his secret codes all these months: rigging explosives and triggers in Delphic Tower, and probably in every other building in the Tower district. Here was the doubt-breaker; it was all sickeningly real.

In a fit of red rage, Barnabas grabbed the blue wire and tore it loose from the front of the switching box. Only when he had done this, did he remember all the bomb-defusing scenes in movies, where one wrong wire, cut in the wrong order caused the premature detonation. He let out a howl like an animal in a trap and stared upwards in complete animal terror at a million tonnes of concrete and metal over his head. But there was no explosion, only the sad moaning of the wind.

Barnabas' limbs suddenly failed him. He dropped to all fours and threw up his little breakfast, but the heaving didn't stop even when there was nothing left in his stomach. It went on and on until he felt emptied down to the bottom of his soul. He became aware of Wickram's feet beside him, and when he could, he let his friend help him to his feet.

"You gonna be okay?" Wickram asked, still holding his hand in a firm, warm grip.

Barnabas nodded, and said, "Yeah, let's just get this done."

Still a little shaky on his feet, he followed Wickram down to the ground floor. There, they found a door in the north wall. Beside it was a sign with old-fashioned, curvy hand-lettering: "Tradesmen — remember to lock the door behind you when exiting." Barnabas tried the doorknob, and although it turned, the door was stuck. They applied their shoulders to it, pushing it open against a heap of debris that the years had piled up behind it.

They found themselves outside, under the overhang of a covered walkway that ran behind the building. Leaving their footprints in 50 years of accumulated dust, they hurried along it until they came to another door, again unopened for decades. It opened into a wide alleyway, and Barnabas saw they were back in the known world. They walked past Delphic Tower's loading dock and then exited the alleyway, stepping onto the sidewalk.

"Ha!" Barnabas said.

"What?"

"We just left the building without signing out. We defeated Gate-Keeper." A little rush of pride flowed through him. He figured this must have been what Thelonius felt like when he returned from those Innervader missions in the middle of the night.

From where he was standing on the sidewalk, Barnabas could see four — no, five — of the towers of the Tower District. He found it all too easy to imagine the explosions that would blow out hundreds of windows, the smoke and flames that would billow forth, the chorus of screams from within as the towers toppled backwards over the cliff, disappearing into the abyss, dragging a century of pride down with them.

But he couldn't dwell on that now. He had one more thing to check. Telling Wickram to stay put, Barnabas ran down the sidewalk and turned up Delphic Tower's main driveway. Surveying the face of the building, he counted his way up to the seventh floor and looked along the line beneath the balconies until he saw it: the blue pyramid that would receive the detonation signal. If only he had known this yesterday, he could have told the Prime Prelate to look for the pyramids on every tower! But maybe it would have made no difference. He was just a kid with a story, and they all believed GateKeeper was infallible.

The doorman stepped out the front door and yelled, "Can I help you, kid?"

With palpable disgust, Barnabas called back, "Even if you could, you probably wouldn't." He returned to the sidewalk and headed west, saying to Wickram, "Follow me."

The next tower on the block was The Neverlander, and he could see its façade without even entering the grounds. He squinted at the ornate wall with its pattern of gold and silver tiles, and there, this time just below a sixth floor balcony, he saw it.

"Look!" he said to Wickram. "Little blue pyramid."

Next door, at Greatest Hiltz, the pyramid was nestled amid a forest of satellite dishes. Barnabas ended his investigations there. He had seen more than enough to be sure that the whole Tower District was wired and ready to blow. Across the road was a park, cleaner and better tended than any downtown. Little kids in expensive play wear cavorted on the slides and swings while their nannies chatted with each other. Barnabas and Wickram crossed the road and sat at a picnic bench in a shady corner of the park.

"So, the conversation with Mayor Tuppletaub didn't go as planned?" Wickram asked.

"He's halfway to the mountains by now. He's planning to return after the disaster and organize the clean up."

"Then we'll have to find Glower ourselves. Where do you think he is?"

Barnabas shook his head. "I don't know. He could be anywhere!" Barnabas thought of the view from Cal's window and sighed. *Anywhere* was a big place.

Wickram grabbed his shoulders and shook him, like he was trying to make the information fall out on the table. "You've been spying on the slizzy lizard for days. Didn't you hear anything useful?"

Barnabas chewed his lip. Was there a clue? Something he'd forgotten? He thought of Glower meeting Galt-Stomper in the subway, but they never mentioned the towers. What about when he first went to the Drop Shop with Wickram and Beaney? He had run into the workshop, but saw nothing that would help them now. If there was anything, it must have been the night when he and Graviddy took their ride in the dark on the beautiful white horse, the night he learned the terrible plan.

He spoke out loud, trying to pull free a loose strand of memory: "It was raining. Glower was showing Carminn the triggering system. The little blue pyramids and the orange cube."

"You mean the blue pyramids that we just saw on the fronts of the buildings?"

"Exactly. They're triggers. They receive the signal, and the orange cube sends it." Barnabas struggled to remember. The park seemed to disappear around him; he was once again in the workshop at the back of the Drop Shop, crouching behind the tool cupboard. Rain clattered on the galvanized metal roof, and he had to strain to make out their words. "Glower said... he said the pyramids and the cube needed to be *in line of sight!*"

"Well," Wickram replied as if the answer was obvious, "There's only one place with line of sight to the fronts of all the towers."

"Where?!" Barnabas asked, returning abruptly to the sunny park.

"The Manhammer Audio Dome, of course."

CHAPTER 33

Outside Trupstock Station, Barnabas grabbed one of the free commuter newspapers from a box and turned to the sports section.

"There's a baseball game at 1:30 at the Dome. Glower told Carminn he was going to blow up the towers at 2:30. We have to get tickets to the game."

Wickram started bouncing up and down with great enthusiasm, apparently more excited about seeing the stadium than worried about the disaster. "Then let's go!" he said.

"But the Crosshairs are playing the Juggernauts, and it might be sold out — even though it's an afternoon game. Besides, I can't afford tickets." He led them down into the subway. He could think of only one option, but he didn't like it.

It was only a short ride and a short walk to the building. The elevator opened onto the loud reception area of K97, Hit-Digit Radio. It wasn't so much loud in volume (though the station was being broadcast through ceiling-mounted speakers) as in the decor. The walls and furniture were a riot of aggressive colour choices, and laid over this disorienting mess were oversized photographs of grinning on-air personalities, plus promotional posters for the latest Top 40 chart sensations. Something about the atmosphere seemed kind of fake and desperate like someone had ordered a kit labelled "Instant Top-40 Station."

"Hi," Barnabas said to the receptionist, whose bottle-red hair and defiant black roots was as eye-popping as the decor. "I'm here to see my step-dad, Björn Olafsson."

"Oh yeah!" she said enthusiastically. "You're DJ Björn Free's kid! We met at the barbecue last summer; I'm Sunshine. He's still on the air…" She checked the time. "…for another 13 minutes, but you and your friend can watch from the control room if you want."

Barnabas tried to sound relaxed: "Uh, actually, is Raheem here?"

"Oh, yeah, he's in his office. Hold on." She made a call. Over the speakers, Barnabas could hear his step-father doing song introductions in his radio voice ("That was Doombot with 'Heartache Frequency…'"). Barnabas had watched the show before from the control room and he was kind of spooked by the way Björn could sound like he was smiling, while he looked as morose as a basset hound. The receptionist turned back to them. "Okay, Raheem's waiting for you in his office."

She buzzed them in, and Barnabas led Wickram down the hall, explaining that Raheem McLeod was the Station Manager. Wickram was hardly paying attention, looking wide-eyed at posters and framed gold records that decorated the walls.

"Hey, hey, it's my man Barnabas!" Raheem said, coming around his desk to greet him with a firm handshake and a big, bright smile. He was dressed in black as usual: a black leather vest over his black t-shirt, skinny black jeans over black cowboy boots. The only break in the colour scheme was the increasing count of white hairs in his dreadlocks. "And who's this?"

"This is Wickram," Barnabas explained with his own bright smile. "He's visiting from out of town, and I remembered that the station has some seats for the Crosshairs in one of the corporate boxes. Do you have anything left for this afternoon? Wickram loves baseball."

Wickram raised a fist and shouted, "Touchdown!"

"Yeah, yeah, I think I can swing it." Raheem said. He looked up at the big clock on the wall. "You know, Björn's off the air at 10:00. I'll let him know you're here and —"

"No, uh, we're in a rush. If you could just…" He was trying maybe too hard to keep his cool demeanour. "Just give me the tickets. I'll see Björn tonight at home, right?"

Raheem titled his head with good-humoured suspicion. "Hey, aren't you supposed to be in school now, little Mr. Bopwright?"

Barnabas threw up his arms in mock surrender and rolled his eyes. "You caught me! Look, Wickram's only here for the day and —"

"No, no, I got it. I never saw you." He chuckled warm and low. "Go wait in reception, and I'll be out in a minute with the tickets." He turned to Wickram. "You good on that guitar?"

Wickram said, "Yeah."

"You sing, too?" The tall boy nodded.

"We should get you to do a little live station ID. Can you play any Rumknuckle? 'Rain Check for an Angel' maybe?"

"I know a bunch of Bigmouth Grouper songs!"

Raheem shook his head, making his dreads swing. "Nah, no one listens to them anymore. Has to be something new."

Barnabas was watching the clock with growing concern. "Sorry, Raheem, no time for that today. The tickets?"

Back in reception, Barnabas made them sit on the couch in the corner so that Björn wouldn't notice them if he walked down the hall. It was 10:06 now. Barnabas' foot tapped the floor nervously.

"Oh, they're over there in the corner," he heard Sunshine say and got to his feet. But it wasn't Raheem who came into view; no, Raheem had sold them out. It was his step-father.

"Oh," was all Barnabas managed to say. The look on Björn's face was one he hadn't seen before, a little knot in his features that might be holding back any crazy emotion. Barnabas wasn't sure what was going to happen next. He tried to take a step backwards, but the couch was there, blocking his escape. What happened, in fact, was Björn hurried across the distance between and pulled Barnabas into a big bear hug.

"Oh my God, we were so worried about you," his step-father breathed into his hair. He pushed Barnabas back, holding him at arm's length and looking him up and down with such intensity that Barnabas blushed. "Are you all right? Your mother is frantic. She went to Deni's last night, but you weren't there."

"I'm sorry. I'm fine. This week is just... crazy."

Still gripping one of Barnabas' shoulders, Björn sat down with him on the couch. He noticed Wickram for the first time. "You're Barnabas' friend from out of town? Would you mind excusing us a minute. I need to talk to my son."

Barnabas almost did the automatic correction, "step-son," but managed to hold his tongue as Wickram went to sit at the other end of the reception lounge.

Björn's eyes were deep set and surrounded by a topographical map of premature wrinkles. But from this rugged valley, the eyes glittered, urgently blue. He said, "You have to come home with me now, Barnabas. You can skip another day of school if you need to, but your mother and I need you to be home."

"Björn, listen —"

"No, I know you got into trouble last week with the Mayor and Ms. Rolan-Gong, but you have to trust us. We won't let anything bad happen to you."

"No, listen. I-I can't come home now. There's something I need to do and it has to be today."

"You can take your friend to a baseball game some other time."

"No, it's not that. And it's not about school. It's... I can't tell you what it is, but it's important!" He felt like a fish caught on a hook, twisting elaborately and to no avail.

They were looking each other in the eye, tossed on the same sea of emotion, but unable to grab hold of each other. Björn was silent, and Barnabas could see him trying to think his way through this situation. "Barnabas, I'm sorry, I know I'm not your father, but you're forcing my hand. I want to be your friend, but I can't just let you go away now. I care too much to do that."

Barnabas frustration was sliding into anger. "Look, Björn, do I get in trouble? Am I bad kid? No! I never give you anything to worry about, so now I'm just asking —"

"You have been gone for almost a week! And then it turns out you're not even where you claimed to be. You had your friend lying to the school for you, covering up heaven knows what. How do I know you're not in terrible trouble, on the brink of something you won't be able to come back from? How can you expect me to trust you now?"

Barnabas turned away from the intensity of those eyes. He wished he could tell his step-father everything, not be so alone in this terrible situation. But every time he had sought help from an adult, he had been betrayed. The only sure path — and it was anything but sure — was to go it alone. Him and Wickram.

He took a deep breath to calm himself, willing himself to appear more

mature than his years. "Björn. I know it looks like I'm in trouble. I'm...
not. At least, I'm not doing anything wrong. I'm trying to do some good.
And it's almost over. I just need this afternoon. Then it will all be okay." *Or
not*, he thought. "Please, please, I need you to trust me." He watched the
struggle in his step-father's face. "You know me, Björn. You know I respect
you and I-I'm really happy that it's you Mom ended up with." As calmly as
he could, he said, "And now, you have to trust me with my mission."

There were tears forming in the corners of Björn's eyes. He sighed and
looked away. "And this important mission, it involves going to a baseball
game?" There was an edge of weary sarcasm in the question that made
them both smile a little.

"Yeah. Well, sort of."

His step-father pulled the tickets from his jacket pocket and handed
them over, along with two twenty-dollar bills. "Don't tell your mother
about any of this. Or else I'll have to move to Deni's with you."

"Was she totally losing it when she didn't find me there last night?"

"At first, but Deni's moms were having this fundraiser. Your mother
ended up making some a bunch of contacts for her charity." That made
them both laugh, and the relief Barnabas felt, the trust his step-father was
giving him, made everything that lay ahead seem suddenly possible. Björn
gave Barnabas' shoulder a squeeze. "Be careful. Please."

As Barnabas and Wickram were about to leave, Raheem came running
out carrying a pair of binoculars. "Sorry, man. I had to tell him. He's been
worried about you. Anyway, you're going to the game? Excellent, you can
borrow these. Our corporate box seats are cool, but they're a million miles
from the field."

CHAPTER 34

Gum Hill was a geological oddity. It stood alone, an isolated relative of the family of hills to the east of the City, jutting up a hundred metres above the surrounding neighbourhoods with nearly vertical walls. Frank Gumm, the man who founded the mill on the river that first put the City on the map had laid claim to this remarkable hill and built his mansion on its flat plateau.

At the turn of the Twentieth Century, the fortunes of the Gumm family had slid from the heights, and the City acquired the prime real estate , though the transaction was presented to the public as a bequest. The private mansion had been torn to the ground and Gumhill Stadium raised in its stead. Lawrence Glorvanious had presided over the opening, and included in his speech was the promise that the name would endure through the ages as a memorial to the family that had been so generous. This unimpeachable promise had been faithfully kept for 110 years when Manhammer Audio had made an irresistible offer to a cash-strapped City Council. At first, some outraged citizens, led by a few angry columnists, refused to use the new name, declaring that the City had sold the stadium off without public consultation and far below its worth. But the forces of apathy and advertising soon won the day, and now, other than a few historical fetishists, everyone called in the Manhammer Audio Dome.

But whatever it was called, approaching the stadium was one of the great rides in the City. The parking lots and Gumhill subway station (that name had endured, a bone tossed to heritage groups) were located at the base of the hill, and ticket-holders and tour groups were then transported up to the plateau in spacious, glassed-sided cable-cars that afforded magnificent views of the City. As the boys rode up, Barnabas saw that Wickram's eyes were shining. He looked like a religious zealot who was finally making the pilgrimage to the most holy of shrines.

Wickram sighed elaborately. "I can't believe we're here! The Manhammer Audio Dome is where Grubbyboy recorded his infamous live album 'Criminy and Crood,' and Agranda Lattay had her nuclear wardrobe malfunction."

They were very early for the game, but Barnabas didn't want to take a chance of missing Glower's arrival. When they got off the cable-car, he left Wickram sitting in the grass playing his guitar while he circled the huge building. When 35,000 people converged on this spot, how would he find the man? Was Glower already here? Barnabas peered at every person he past who might even conceivably be the madman in disguise.

The north section of the building was the only bit that remained of the original stadium. The Manhammer Corporation had rebuilt the rest, and the new construction with its big white dome looked to Barnabas like a pillow that was attempting to smother the old red brick building. But the old wing was the section with line of sight to the Tower District, so if Glower was inside, that's where he would be. Barnabas trained the borrowed binoculars on its windows. But what if Glower looked down and spotted him? Maybe he was already hurriedly changing his plans. Barnabas frowned and thought, *Yeah, because I'm such a massive threat.*

Circling back around the building, he found Wickram jamming with a three-piece band that was setting up to play classic rock and R&B for the crowds. Wickram broke away, high-fiving the musicians and returning to join Barnabas in the grass. "Hey, Barn! One of the hot-dog guys has already opened up. Aren't you starving?"

Barnabas got them two dogs with everything and two drinks. Although he continued to squint suspiciously at everything around him, he couldn't ignore the fact that the day was distractingly nice. The sun was shining, and everyone seemed to be in a great mood. The first big wave of people — the ones who wanted to be inside the minute the doors opened — were already arriving. They were playing hooky from work and school and otherwise trying to make this an afternoon to remember. If he hadn't known what was at stake, Barnabas would have been caught up in the celebratory mood. It was one of those perfect days when life was a big ripe fruit, ready to be picked and enjoyed. But didn't people always say that about the time leading up to disasters? "It was such a beautiful day; we had no idea what was in store…"

"You'll have to check in your guitar at the Security Office," the Ticket-taker at the VIP entrance told Wickram. Barnabas had already gone through, but now the Ticket-taker locked the turnstile so Wickram couldn't follow.

"What? Why?" the Wickram protested.

"It counts as an oversized bag. It's a security risk. You could be bringing in contraband inside it."

Wickram turned the guitar upside down over his head, sound hole down, and shook it. "See? Nothing."

"I don't make the rules," said the Ticket-taker, exquisitely bored.

Barnabas felt opportunity ticking away. He returned to the turnstile, talking to the man's back. "Look, we're in a rush. We don't have time to find your Security Office and —"

The lights overhead began to flicker. There was an announcement in progress ("Get your tickets for next week's Taco Tuesday extravaganza. The first 1,500 people to arrive win a…") and it cut off in the middle, replaced by digital shrieking.

"What the hell?" the Ticket-taker said as if it were all a plot to make his life harder. While he answered an incoming call on his head-set, Barnabas motioned to Wickram, who jumped the turnstile; the two boys ran up the concrete ramp. They soon reached a lobby, a big hexagonal space, ringed by concession stands.

"That was no way to treat VIPs," Wickram sniffed. "Hey, can you buy me a baseball bonnet?"

"You mean cap. I don't have enough money; those hot dogs were stupidly expensive." He checked the crumpled bills in his pocket. "I can maybe do popcorn. And don't let the phrase 'VIP entrance' go to your head. People who come in this way just think they're important. The real VIPs have an even VIPer entrance. Forget that and keep your eyes open for Glower."

The lights were continuing to flicker, and it was making all the employees nervous. Power to every system seemed to be coming and going randomly. Elevators were taking turns going out of service, various machines in the concession stands could no longer dispense their syrups and condiments. Barnabas stood in the middle of the lobby watching it all happen. "It has to be Glower," he said. "It's too much of a coincidence."

"Ladies and gentlemen," came a cheerful announcement. "The Manhammer Audio Dome apologizes for the current technical difficulties. Work crews have been dispatched, and we expect to have the problems resolved shortly."

Wickram said, "Maybe we should start searching or something."

Barnabas, his frustration and helplessness growing, didn't mean to shout: "Search where?! Every room, public and private in the entire stadium?! Probably just as well to stand here until Glower happens to walk by!"

"Okay, don't go all skull-cracked. Let's go up to our seats and see what we can see."

"Sure, why not?" Barnabas said in frustration. "If we can't stop the disaster, we might as well watch the game."

They checked their tickets in the disorienting glow of the intermittent light and headed down the corridor with the corresponding section number. The PA crackled and whined, and all the different sound cues for revving up the crowd — clapping songs, bugle calls, snippets of rock anthems — began to play back to back.

"What's Glower up to?" Barnabas said. "He's messing with the whole building!" The crazy sound show came to an end with a loud digital squawk.

They came upon a sizable crowd waiting impatiently in front of a bank of three elevators. One elevator stood open, and a dozen people were stuffed inside, stubbornly holding their ground as a security guard tried to make them exit.

"Please, the elevators are not safe to ride during these power fluctuations. Any of you that are able to take the ramps —"

"You expect us to give up our place? We've waited 10 minutes already!" shouted a man inside, firmly gripping the hand of his 8 year old, for whom he had bought every conceivable piece of team merchandise. "We're VIPs!" the man told the frustrated guard.

At that moment, an electrician in an orange vest and orange hard hat pushed his way through the crowd to the front. The guard, relieved to have some good news, said, "Here we go, folks. Shouldn't be long now." The electrician unlocked a panel on the wall and began to flip switches inside.

The angry man in the elevator yelled at him. "Do you know what I paid to be here? Fix this thing — and make it fast!"

The electrician pushed a button, and the elevator door closed, almost cutting off the man's nose. Then the elevator closest to the electrician opened. He slipped quickly inside, turning to face outward for the first time.

Wickram, standing at the back of the crowd, yelled, "Barn! It's him! Glower!"

Barnabas, too short to see, shouted, "Don't let him get away." The boys pushed roughly through the impatient crowd, who pushed back, annoyed. By the time they reached the front, the door had closed, and the floor numbers above it were climbing.

"No!" Barnabas screamed.

"Just take the ramp to your seat, kid," one of the security guards said. "You're not some old fatso. No, sir, sorry, wasn't referring to you."

A bell sounded and the third elevator opened. The crowd gasped and someone said screamed, "It's Agranda Lattay!" Everyone outside started snapping pictures of the pop star and calling her name. Agranda Lattay looked surprised for a second, but then she smiled an automatic smile and began cycling through various poses Barnabas had seen in a hundred pics of her online.

"What the hell?!" yelled a sharp-dressed woman at the singer's side. "We're supposed to be backstage at field level. What kind of amateur monkeys are running this place?!!"

The elevator's third occupant, the man she was yelling at, wore a Manhammer Audio jacket and a nametag that read "Oolie." Oolie began stabbing at the elevator controls to no effect. "I'm sorry, ma'am. The system is all... I'll have us going in just a..."

Barnabas looked up at Wickram and said, "We're getting on." As the crowd screamed for autographs, the security guards were trying to push their way to the front to protect the pop star. But Barnabas and Wickram had a shorter distance to traverse and they got inside first, just as the doors closed.

As the elevator began to ascend, Oolie took his frustration out on them: "This is not a public elevator!" He turned to the two women and all but crumbled like burnt toast in front of them. "Ms. Lattay! I'm so, so, so sorry."

Wickram raised his hands reassuringly. "Whoa, whoa, don't worry, buddy. Me and Barn are from K97, Hit-Digit Radio. We're here to make sure everything's going just the way Agranda needs. And maybe do a little interview?"

The star smiled and said, "That's really sweet of you. I'm just going to sing the national anthem, and then maybe we can sit down and —"

The sharp-dressed woman shook her head. "I'm Ms. Lattay's Road Manager. We have to be at the airport by three. Sorry. Maybe we can do a phoner from the car."

Barnabas saw that Wickram hadn't even heard this. He was just staring, star-struck at the singer, who looked to Barnabas like a video come to life, but also unnervingly human.

Just then the lights flickered ominously, and Oolie started going, "Oh no, oh no, oh no," like he was about to burst into tears. The elevator lurched to a halt and Agranda tipped over on her high heels, landing in Wickram's arms.

Her manager checked the time on her phone, cursing fluently and screaming at the man from Manhammer to get them moving.

"Thanks," Agranda said to Wickram as the red emergency lights came on. "I see you're a guitarist. I'm learning, too."

"Well, if we're stuck here, I could give you a lesson."

"No!" Barnabas said. "Wickram, we *can't* get stuck here." To Oolie he said, "Is that one of those emergency trap doors up on the ceiling?"

The man was sweating so hard, it looked like he had got caught in the rain. He said, "I think so, but…" He began to quote from some manual: "In case of emergency, we're to stay put and wait for assistance." His shaking hand could barely hold his phone. "No one's answering!" he cried.

Agranda's Road Manager screamed, "Entertainment Hourly is here to film my client!" She turned to Barnabas. "If you can get out and get us some actual help…"

Barnabas said, "Wickram, can you reach the ceiling? Push up on that panel. Yes! Okay, we're going that way."

He took the guitar while Wickram pulled himself up, legs flailing in the air ("Oops, watch your hairdo, Agranda. It looks beautiful, by the way."). Once he was through the little square door and on top of the elevator, Barnabas passed him the guitar and then reached up to grab his arms. "I need a boost," he said to no one in particular, and it was the surprisingly strong Road Manager, who all but lifted him to the ceiling.

"Hurry," she told him. "Don't let them start the game without Agranda!"

The air in the elevator shaft smelled of diesel and dust. Barnabas pointed to the ladder on the wall, and Wickram stepped carefully off the elevator and began to climb.

"We'll, uh, get some help," Barnabas called down into the car, and then followed Wickram up the ladder. They climbed until they reached a pair of closed elevator doors. Stencilled on the wall beside them was the word "Field." There was a big red button and Wickram pushed it. The doors opened.

The boys stepped out into noisy behind-the-scenes chaos. They were in a wide hall, big enough to drive a truck, and all through it, people were shouting into cell phones. The words "delays," "costs," and "unacceptable" featured prominently in the little curse-laden soliloquies. A few baseball players were going through their stretching routines while reporters interviewed them. One end of the hall was a big open portal onto the playing field of the Manhammer Audio Dome. The impatient crowd beyond sounded like the buzzing of a hive of large, angry bees. A sweating man in a dark suit with a considerable gut hanging over his trousers rounded on the boys and screamed furiously: "What the hell are you kids doing here?! This is an emergency! We're 15 minutes late! I'm having you arrested!"

Wickram pointed into the elevator shaft, pulling his hair in desperation. "Hurry! Agranda Lattay's trapped! They're running out of air!"

This caused the man and several other concerned types to peer down into the shaft and begin arguing with each other. Barnabas and Wickram ran towards the field entrance. The crowd noise was like a palpable force. Despite the technical problems, thousands were already in their seats and more than ready for the game to start. Barnabas checked out the Super-Screen and saw that it read: "Sorry for the delay."

"This is… amazing," Wickram breathed. And under better circumstances, Barnabas would have agreed.

He began scanning stadium with the binoculars. He found himself murmuring, praying to fate and Father Glory and Mother Mercy and his dad and Björn and everyone: "Just let me find him, let me find him before it's too late."

And then his prayers were answered. If Glower hadn't been wearing the orange hard hat, Barnabas would have missed him, but there he was, directly across the field beside one of the team mascots. Glower looked around quickly, then unlocked a door at the base of the outfield fence and slipped inside.

"Wickram, we can't lose him!" Barnabas shouted and took off straight across the field.

He heard his friend calling, "Barn, wait!" but there was no more time to wait. It had all come down to *now*. Overhead, the dome was open, the sun shining brilliantly. It was a perfect day for a game. Wickram quickly caught up with him, and together they powered across the field. The restless crowd had begun to clap, and Barnabas realized the applause was for them.

In the centre of the field stood a microphone, and as they passed, Wickram said, "Wait a second, Barn." Barnabas skidded to a halt in confusion and looked back at his friend. In the distance, five, maybe six security guys were leaving the back-stage corridor and heading across the field toward them.

"Wickram!" he shouted. "We can't stay here."

Wickram stood still, eyes wide, staring out at the thousands of faces staring his way. "Barn, you go. Let me distract them."

"What are you talking about?!" The men were getting closer.

Wickram smiled at him, like everything was just fine. "Run, dummy!" he said. "Glower's getting away." So Barnabas ran. And as he ran, he heard his friend's voice fill the stadium. "Uh, hi, ladies and gentlemen. Due to circumstances beyond comprehension, Agranda Lattay has been delayed, so, uh, here's the national anthem." As he ran across the grass, Barnabas turned his head sideways, and there, on the SuperScreen, 20 metres tall, Wickram was lowering the microphone and bringing his guitar into position before it. As cool as ice cream, he gave his instrument a quick tuning and then launched into a short, instrumental version of the anthem.

Panting heavily, Barnabas reached the far wall just as Wickram played his final notes. Something hit the mic with a stadium-filling thud. He turned and saw the mic stand on the ground, the security men pulling Wickram away. With his one free hand, the tall boy from the Valley gave the crowd a friendly wave. They cheered back, and then booed as the security men took away his guitar and roughly pulled his arms behind his back. Barnabas looked up at the SuperScreen, where a car ad was now playing.

There wasn't much time; three guards were running his way. He tried the door, but it was locked. Obviously. Why hadn't he expected that? He began pounding on the door's metal surface, shouting, "Hey! Hello?! Please open up! It's an emergency!"

The guards were getting closer, shouting inaudibly. He thought about running, but where would he go? Around the perimeter of the stadium until they cut him off? There was a camera above the door, watching him dispassionately. He waved at it with both arms, screaming, "Please! He's going to blow up the towers if you don't let me in! Hurry!" To his astonishment, the door buzzed and gave a brief click.

A tinny voice emerged from the little speaker beside it: "Enter now." Barnabas tried the door and found it was unlocked. He dived inside. As he pulled it shut, he saw the security guards were almost upon him. The door closed with a satisfying clunk. A second later, the men on the outside were shaking the handle, banging their fists savagely. Barnabas stared down, expecting them to unlock it any second. He thought maybe he should be running, but he just stood there holding his breath. It didn't take long before he was sure: they didn't have the key.

There was another speaker on the wall, and from it the same voice spoke: "Turn to your left and take the first staircase. I'm waiting for you on the fourth floor, third door to your right." So Barnabas began to walk , though the cold, metallic taste of fear was now filling his mouth. He knew that voice. It was George Glower.

CHAPTER 35

Only as he climbed the stairs did Barnabas realize he had no plan. He had never had one beyond finding Glower and "stopping him." The dangerous absurdity of this non-strategy had somehow not occurred to him until this moment. He felt sick with adrenaline, his heart pounding, and every instinct telling him to run in the other direction. But if Glower was on schedule, there were only 40 minutes left to derail his plan. *Derail his plan?* Barnabas almost laughed, almost puked — Glower had been setting this plot in motion for months, maybe for years. He was meticulous and driven. Barnabas, on the other hand... had no plan.

At least, as he marched to his death, Barnabas was able to appreciate his surroundings. The honey-coloured varnish on the mouldings was flaking away, the plaster ceiling showed water stains, but the old wing of the stadium had 100 times more personality than the concrete and plastic of the new. He loved the fading old team emblems in the scuffed hardwood and the brass signs on the doors that read "Photostat" and "Radio Room." The long halls were completely deserted. It seemed to be just him and Glower.

Barnabas climbed to the fourth floor. He counted three doors on the right side of the hall until he was standing in front of one whose sign read "Archives and Memorabilia." This was probably his last chance to run away. He had already done all he could, right? He'd told multiple authorities, including *the Mayor of the freaking City*, and they had not stepped up.

What more did anyone expect of him? He was just a kid! Then Barnabas thought of Wickram being dragged away by the guards. That crazy boy had accompanied him through the bowels of the earth and let himself get arrested so that Barnabas could get right here to this very spot. Didn't he owe it to Wickram to try? He wondered whether to knock on the door or not. *Not*, he decided, and opened it wide.

A musty smell of old newsprint hit his nose, and he sneezed twice and then three times. He rubbed his watery eyes and found himself staring at George Glower, who was on his feet, bent over a laptop that was sitting on an old wooden table in front of the large double windows. "I'll be with you in a minute," he said without concern. "Close the door."

The room was full of trophies from decades past, stacked haphazardly by the dozens on old bookshelves and around Glower on the big work table. Some were tall and ornate, but most were modest, bearing inscriptions like "Most Valuable Fielder" and "Chimney Cigarettes Player of the Season." There were framed newspaper pages on the wall, the stock yellowed, the bold headlines muted by the dusty glass: "The Championship Is Ours!" and "Hail the Conquering Heroes!" Fading plastic toys of smiling mascots peered out from behind filing cabinets, and to the left of the door, a wooden statue of Lawrence Glorvanious stood, half the size of a real man. It took a few seconds for Barnabas to recognize it as an exact duplicate of the giant statue in front of the City Hall. The Great Mayor was leaning on his shovel, the city he had dreamed into existence spread out around his feet. Perhaps it was a model the artist had carved before preparing the full-size version.

"We are ever grateful," said Glower, quoting the inscription on the base.

Barnabas looked up; Glower was facing him, pointing a gun his way. Barnabas had never encountered an actual gun before today, but now he'd been seen two of them in the space of a few hours. This one was worse. This one, held by Glower with deadly calm, was pointed at him.

"You keep appearing," Glower said. "Over and over this past week. At Crumhorn station, outside the school, in the Drop Shop, surprisingly. And yet you're too young to be anyone's agent. Who are you?"

Barnabas' had to clear his throat painfully before he could get his voice to work. "I-I'm Barnabas Bopwright." Through the windows behind Glower, Barnabas could see the whole of the Tower District.

"And you've been following me?" the man asked.

"Not at first. It was just a coincidence at first. I ended up in the Valley by accident."

"But now you're on a mission to stop me. I've been watching you since you entered the stadium." Glower nodded toward the shifting quilt of surveillance camera feeds on the laptop's screen. "You and the circus man's son, here to prevent my moment of triumph."

"I guess," Barnabas answered — there wasn't any point in denying it. He thought, *Maybe I'm about to die.*

"There isn't much time; you might as well watch," Glower said, and reached out a hand. "Phone."

"I-I lost it," Barnabas said, cursing himself for leaving it behind at the Mayor's apartment, even as Glower frisked him and checked in his bag. This regret made no sense, of course; Glower would have taken the phone anyway. But it somehow proved to Barnabas just how unequal he was to the task. *No plan, no plan.*

"Sit down against the wall beside that pipe," Glower said, still showing no signs of anger or panic or eye-twitching madness. Barnabas did as he was told, removing his backpack and placing it on the floor beside him. He was beside the model statue, looking up at the Great Mayor's confident chin. Glower pulled a length of plastic cable tie from his pocket and secured Barnabas' right wrist tightly to the pipe.

Barnabas remembered Wickram's faith in him, and he had to admit that he himself had nurtured ludicrous fantasies of the fame and glory to come when he saved the City. Even five minutes ago, in his heart of hearts, he had imagined that some gap of chance would materialize, and he would wedge himself into that crack to tear apart this evil plot. *Barnabas Bopwright, the littlest saviour!* But instead, here he sat with a front row seat to the worst disaster the City had ever faced. He had no weapon, no means of communication. He had and *was* nothing. Shame suffused his heart.

Glower locked the door before returning to the work table. Lines of code, white on black, had replaced the security feed on his laptop. The man was typing in little bursts each time a prompt appeared. Barnabas thought he had already been forgotten, but Glower suddenly said, "Bopwright? Is your father Harold Bopwright?"

Barnabas, startled by this question, stuttered, "Uh, yeah. Do you know his music?"

"Music? No. He painted my apartment once. I found the results adequate but his procedures sloppy."

Barnabas didn't reply. He knew his dad had done house painting when gigs were scarce. Instead, he asked, "What's with the all the electrical stuff? Why are you hacking the stadium? I mean, if you just need line of sight to operate the triggers…"

"First of all, I needed to control the movement of security in the stadium. But most importantly, I will be broadcasting the destruction of the towers live to the SuperScreen. I want 35,000 witnesses who will scream and then pour out of the building, spreading terror in their wake. I want the citizens paralyzed with fear. I want them to question their privilege and to feel that life is not the free ride they supposed it to be." Glower said all this without bravado or glee; it was simply a set of facts, meticulously worked out.

Barnabas pulled against the plastic tie that held him to the pipe; he only hurt his wrist. He kicked at the pipe, but it was firmly attached to the wall. Glower picked up the gun and spun around, pointing it at him.

"Stop that, boy," he said.

"You're a dick," Barnabas answered, staring down the gun, determined to not let his fear show.

But this petty insult didn't seem to upset Glower. He just put the gun down on the table and turned back to his work. He opened a wooden box, the very one Barnabas had seen in the back room at the Drop Shop. From it, Glower removed the orange cube and placed it on the table in front of him.

"Why do you have to do this?" Barnabas asked, and the question was no ploy, no time-wasting stratagem. He just suddenly really, really needed to understand. "People are going to die, Mr. Glower! Why doesn't that bother you?"

Glower powered up the orange cube, and it beeped three times and then two times more. A line of lights flashed in sequence across its surface.

Barnabas thought the man hadn't heard him, but then he answered: "Why *should* it bother me? It won't really bother anyone except insofar as they fear they will be next. Self-interest is the only principle that governs people's actions. Beyond that, any appearance of concern is a lie." The answer hit Barnabas like a slap. It couldn't be true! People cared about more than themselves, didn't they?

Glower emptied a box of "Go, Team!" buttons onto the floor and placed the box upside down under the window. He put the orange cube on it, so it was now above the level of the window sill, ready to send its message of death to the blue pyramids in each tower. As he worked with slow precision, he said, "Now I have a question for you, Bopwright. Before you left the Valley, you must have sought help. Who did you tell about my plan?"

Barnabas didn't answer. He felt like he was being tricked, like anything he said would help the man to justify his actions. Glower picked up an old glass paperweight from the desk and threw it at Barnabas, who cried out and batted it away painfully with his forearm.

Glower asked again, his voice as calm as before: "Who did you tell?"

"The Guild Council!" Barnabas shouted back, rubbing his arm.

"And they sent you packing, right? I'm surprised they didn't stick you in Doomlock and throw away the key. You're dangerous to them. If they know about my plan, they become responsible for stopping me." He reached across the desk and unlatched the big windows, turning their cranks to open them outwards. The noises of the City entered the room, the familiar hubbub of everyone just going about their business, ignorant of the danger they faced. Barnabas could also hear the closer buzz of the stadium crowd. Someone must have hit a runner home because a cheer rose up like a single joyous roar of a great animal. Blissfully ignorant.

The sound seemed to give Glower a jolt of excitement. He turned and looked at Barnabas. "The Guild Council knew that people were going to die. Why were they not bothered?" He raised an eyebrow and then sneered, an odd, frightening expression which showed too much tooth. "So then you got back to the City somehow. You're a resourceful boy, apparently. Who did you tell once you were here?"

"I'm not playing this game," Barnabas said tightly. Despite his anger, he could hear the fear in his voice, and he felt humiliated by it.

Glower abruptly lost his cool. Face darkened in fury, he picked up a large trophy with the golden figure of a batter on top and raised his arm to throw it at Barnabas, who cowered and covered his face with his free arm. "Stop! Okay! I told these old people at City Hall, the ones who know about the Valley. Then I told the Mayor."

Glower laughed and put the trophy down. It was a terrible laugh because it was so damn normal — as if Barnabas had shared a great anecdote. "Wonderful! And tell me, son of the sloppy painter, did the upcoming deaths of all those innocents in the towers bother any of these illustrious people?"

"I don't know," Barnabas answered, and then more quietly, "No, I guess not."

Eyes glittering, Glower leaned down toward him as if he really needed him to understand. "That's what people are like, Bopwright, don't you see? I wanted to save them; I offered to be their mayor and give them a better future. But they spat in my face. They're not worth saving, and the sooner you learn that, my boy, the less disappointment you'll encounter." They stared at each other for a few long seconds before Glower turned and begin tapping on his keyboard. "Running out of time," he muttered. "Can't waste it talking."

The man was starting to sweat and mumble under his breath. The calm, methodical shell of the engineer was crumbling, revealing the madman underneath. His fingers, a flying blur above the keyboard, froze, and he started saying, "Damn damn damn," low and intense. He pulled pieces of paper from his pocket, scattering them on the table and floor before finally finding the one he wanted. He typed again, reading from the scrap. His screen changed from lines of code to a view of the statue of Lawrence Glorvanious in Civic Square, in front of City Hall. It was, apparently, a video feed, the camera mounted somewhere up high on a building across the street. Barnabas could see people — tourists, kissing couples — walking past the statue. A flock of pigeons swooped by in front of the camera. *What does the statue have to do with anything?* he wondered with growing dread.

As if in answer, Glower said, "Family reunion," and a strange giggle bubbled out of him. Glower typed and hit "enter" with a little flourish. The stadium crowd suddenly reacted, a kind of surprised swell.

"What was that?" Barnabas heard himself ask.

"I put the image of the statue up on the SuperScreen instead of the usual meaningless garbage."

And so we're really starting, Barnabas thought. With the hijacking of the SuperScreen, the authorities would know something serious was going on.

Barnabas felt a cold wave of fear. "What are you going to do?" Glower ignored him. He swivelled his chair and gripped the orange cube. It was then that Barnabas remembered what Wickram had said… about seeing something blue on the statue's hat. He now felt certain it had been a blue pyramid.

"Wait…" Barnabas said, but in that moment Glower pushed a single key, and the cube beeped: once, twice, three times. On the screen, there was a flash of light, and the huge statue of Lawrence Glorvanious exploded, scattering shards of dust and debris across the plaza. There was no microphone, so he could hear no sound of the explosion, but behind him, beyond the walls and through the open window, the crowd cried out as one — the great animal roaring in terror.

Barnabas grew cold with shock. It was as if all the blood in his body had retreated to some dark cave deep inside. Through the window he could just see a little column of smoke rising in the distance. "Oh my God oh my God," he breathed.

Glower sprung to his feet and slammed his hand down on the table. "Boom!" He turned and strode in Barnabas' direction, and the boy curled himself into a ball. But it wasn't him the man was after. Glower bent over and screamed into the face of the half-sized statue, the wooden miniature version of the bronze that was no longer there. "How do you like *that*, Great-Grandfather?! Did you think you were immortal? Boom! You've gone up in flames. Nothing is forever, Lawrence. Make all your pretty plans as perfect as you can; nothing is forever. Nothing is safe."

He lurched back to the desk. His hands were shaking now, and huge moons of sweat stained his shirt under the arms and across the back. Glower reached into his bag and pulled out a video camera. He set it up on a mini tripod in front of the open window and then ran a cable to his laptop. Another video window opened on the screen, and he adjusted the zoom and focus until he had a clear image of the whole Tower District. He typed on the keyboard, and Barnabas knew from the rising roar of the crowd that the image had appeared on the SuperScreen.

Authoritative voices were shouting outside now, sirens screaming in the distance.

Barnabas noticed for the first time a clock on the wall — an old institutional analog clock, still dutifully counting out the hours and minutes decades after it had been installed. It was 2:25.

His mouth was dry. It felt like it was made of some substance other than mouth like a roast forgotten in the oven. But he had to speak: "Mr. Glower... Glorvanious... Please listen." The man was checking connections, making sure everything was ready for the final act of the show. He seemed to be paying no attention, but Barnabas continued nonetheless. "I know... the people in charge didn't care, but they're not everyone. All the people at Pastoral Park, they helped me escape, they got me and Wickram out of the Valley so I could save the City. The Lurkers underground helped us get back here. And my step-dad! He believed in me even though he had no reason to."

Glower ignored him, shifting the camera's tripod a bit, double-checking the view on his laptop, but Barnabas pressed on: "I get it... people hurt you. They were jerks. I know about that, I know about the jerks winning and the good people being ignored. There used to be this kid at school named Henry, and... Well, that's not important. The point is, there are all kinds of people out there trying to just have a good life — despite the jerks. Maybe they're even the majority. And you're just hurting them if you —"

Glower snapped his head around. "Those are the people I hate the most. Come on! Use that brain; I see it's a good one. Those are exactly the idiots who could have had me as their Mayor. I was their salvation! I was the last chance those brainless sheep had to follow the right shepherd. But now, they're lost. Better to slaughter them and start again."

With a wide sweep of his arms, he cleared the trophies of the past off the table, and they came crashing to the floor, one of them bouncing smartly into Barnabas leg. He cried out in pain as Glower threw back his head and sang the City anthem in a brusque, coarse baritone:

Hail to the future that has sprung from the land!
Hail to the roads built by spirit and hand!
A world where our children can prosper and play,
In this fair, golden city rising skyward today!!

From outside the open window, someone shouted, "Who's there? This is the police, show yourself!"

Barnabas didn't hesitate, he screamed in a raw, frenzied voice: "He's up here! Stop him, he's here!!"

Glower dived across the room and with a great backhand sweep struck Barnabas across the face, shouting, "Shut up, George!" Barnabas head smacked against the wall with a nauseating thump, and he saw stars. Through the tears in his eyes, he looked up into Glower's face, twisted into a mask of fury, the teeth showing, sweat pouring from his brow. He brandished the gun in one shaking hand and said, "I won't give you another chance, boy."

Outside, the police announced through a megaphone, "Come to the window with your hands raised. We need to see your hands. You have 30 seconds to comply."

Glower leaned across the table and stuck his head out, "Too late! Go to hell!" He pulled himself back in and turned to Barnabas. "I don't blame you for trying. I don't. Someday you'll understand that I was right." He put his hands on the orange cube and said, "Delphic Tower first. Are you home, Tuppletaub? I hope so."

He pushed a button and the machine beeped. Barnabas curled himself again into a ball, burying his head in his backpack. Moaning in terror, he braced himself for the explosion, wondering if he would hear it this far away.

"What?" Glower said. "What what what?" He was furious; apparently Delphic Tower was still standing. Barnabas opened his eyes and felt relief wash over him. Of course it was still standing — he had torn out all the wires that connected the trigger to the explosives! But the other buildings were still wired and set to blow. In a second, Glower would recover and try those. Something... he had to do something.

The police outside spoke again: "Approach the window with your hands visible. This is your last warning." Glower began to swear, a long stream of curses.

Barnabas realized that he might as easily end up being shot by the police as by Glower. He sat up in alarm and his bag tipped over. Something rolled out, and he kicked out his leg to stop it. Wide-eyed and with a shaking hand, he reached out to take hold of the *diaboriku*.

This singular object, which had tried so hard to escape him, now sat contentedly in his palm, oblivious to his distress and to the imminent danger. Barnabas suddenly knew exactly what he could do with it, if only he knew how! But just yesterday he had refused Cal's offer to teach him. He cursed his arrogance and began punching at the buttons in a furious panic. Again and again, nothing happened. He stifled the cry of fear and frustration growing in him. He wanted to hurl the stupid toy out the open window and scream, "Damn you, Thelonius! This is all your fault!"

He knew he had to calm down and focus. He took a deep breath and let it out slowly. He tried the buttons methodically, realizing that he was just repeating things he'd already tried. Was there some other variable he was missing? That was part of the trap of being human; we get into a pattern and then we get stuck. Our lives are like a bobsled run, and mostly we don't even understand that we are trapped in those narrow parameters. We think, oh, I'm so clever, banking slightly to the left today instead of slightly to the right. But what if we could escape the course altogether? Steer our sled free down a virgin mountain, cutting any trail we wished?

He remembered watching Cal operate the device. His friend hadn't made more than three or four movements; and yet surely, these were movements Barnabas himself had tried. But what if he held down the big red button while he hit the others? Something about this idea agreed with the ergonomics of the machine. And if this was the case, there were only a few permutations to try. The first sequence did nothing, ditto the second, but with the third, the machine buzzed in his hand, and its lights came on. Barnabas felt like his chest would explode with excitement. He had done it; the *diaboriku* was activating.

* * *

George couldn't understand what had gone wrong. Why was Delphic Tower still standing? In his mind, he reviewed each connection he had made, looking for any possible error. He had an almost perfect memory for events, for actions and attributes. He could tell you whether he had twisted a certain set of wires to the right of the left; he could tell you how many buttons were on the security guard's shirt when he had entered the building with the passcode the Mayor had provided. He knew the name of the painter who, nine years ago, had left latex spatter on his light switches, whose son, improbably, now sat witness to this moment.

Focus, focus. Delphic Tower should now have been a smouldering pile of wreckage, and it was not. The logical next step would be to bring down another of the towers. If that also failed, he would have to question the transmitter box in front of him. But the plan had called for Delphic first! He couldn't let it go. He willed his mind to be flexible, but it was not! *The plan is the plan… and the man behind the plan has to stand on his own two hands and demand his own brand of grandstand…* He smacked himself in the head. *Stop it!* Something… his mind was not behaving. *Focus, focus!*

"Approach the window with your hands visible," spoke the idiotic megaphone outside. George had a childish desire to hurl trophies and mascot toys out the window at them. But no, there wasn't much time. They would soon find their way in and everything would be lost. All right then: another tower! He checked that the video feed from his camera was still being broadcast on the SuperScreen. Seventy thousand eyes were watching! He could almost feel their viscous weight pressing on him.

See me! He said to them in his mind. *See what I have done. I am the Mayor you might have had. Could STILL have. Fall to your knees and beg for my leadership!*

A huge shadow rose above him, darkening the table and all his gear. He grabbed his gun and turned to confront whatever threat had suddenly entered the room. What he faced was terrible, incomprehensible, and yet somehow inevitable: rising higher and higher until his undulating grey locks brushed the ceiling like the tentacles of an octopus… was Lawrence Glorvanious! He had returned from the dead to demand an explanation! The right hand that stretched toward George from the torn sleeve of the Mayor's stained, time-worn wool suit was raw and bloody, the chipped nails like claws. The hand was clutching spasmodically at the air, closer and closer, like it wanted to choke the life from him.

"You are a worm!" the Great Mayor cried. "I sweated and fought and dreamed a city into existence! I am grace and glory, and the people still speak my name in awe! And who are you?!"

George tried to speak, but his voice emerged as a hoarse, meaningless rasp.

"You are nothing! A failure… a *shopkeeper!* I will destroy you rather than suffer you to live another moment."

George shot the gun, once, twice, three times into the advancing figure, who was water and steam and earth, power and rectitude. But the giant only roared, fire erupting from its nose and ears.

"I tried!" George screamed in a childish voice that humiliated him. "Please! Give me another chance! I will succeed, I will bring the family name to greatness again —"

"You have destroyed the great name of Glorvanious!" the ghost bellowed. George's back was pressed against the table, and now he scrambled up on it to get away. Emerging from the left sleeve of the ghost's coat, where his hand should have been, was a ceremonial shovel of shining gold, the blade sharpened to a lethal edge. The ghost-mayor swung it at George, who backed up until he suddenly hit the emptiness of the tall, open windows. He slipped backwards into the warm afternoon, a single hand and the heel of one shoe the only things holding him in place. The brilliant sunlight hit his eyes, blinding him.

The Monster Glorvanious spat out its final curse: "Better you had never been born!" And George lost his grip, tumbling backward out the window, head-first toward the pavement, and death opened its generous arms to greet him.

Part VI:

Ugly Little Bunnies

CHAPTER 36

The next minutes were a whirl of confusion and terror. Barnabas was curled on the floor, shivering uncontrollably when the door was broken down by helmeted police in black uniforms and opaque face plates that effectively erased their humanity. They poured into the tiny room, filling it with chaos and noise, and Barnabas pulled his hands over his ears and moaned to shut them out. They were yelling at him, barking questions he couldn't even come close to answering. Not that the questions were difficult when he thought back on them later — *Who was that man? How did you get here? Are there any more terrorists?* — but at the time, his brain was unable to take anymore. Circuit overload; system shutdown.

But then the woman in the Aqua Guard uniform was there, and somehow she made the police leave him alone. She knelt down, speaking calmly as she cut the tie holding his wrist. She squeezed his shoulder and promised she would get him out of the stadium and away from the madness in just a few minutes. He looked into her freckled face and calm green eyes and decided to trust her, or at least recognized she was the best option he had. She led him out into the corridor and found a chair for him so he could sit quietly, away from the centre of the action. There was another faceless figure in black standing a few metres to his left. The Aqua guard told Barnabas that the policeman would keep him safe, but Barnabas had the feeling the man was there to make sure he didn't run away.

Slowly, Barnabas came back to himself and his shivering stopped. He looked down and saw he was still clutching the *diaboriku* in his right hand. As soon as he became aware of it, he realized how much his hand hurt from gripping the toy so tightly. He put it in his lap and shook out his hand. In his head, over and over, he kept seeing Glower disappear backward through the open window. He could still hear the echo of his own scream — "Nooooo!" — and the terrible thud on the pavement below. He felt a tear running down his face and wiped it away quickly, embarrassed that the man with no face might see.

He tried to make sense of what had happened in the memorabilia room. The *diaboriku* had projected the giant, monstrous hologram based on the wooden statue of Lawrence Glorvanious, just like Barnabas planned; but when Glower began shooting, Barnabas dropped the toy and squeezed himself into the corner. The projection vanished then, but Glower continued to behave like the monster was there in the room. Not only that, he was answering it as if it were speaking. But it wasn't speaking! How could it? The *diaboriku* was just making the same tinny mechanical monster noises it had made in the school.

The Aqua woman returned and squatted in front of him. She introduced herself: "Lieutenant Blenbooly, Aqua Guard Frontier Deployment. How are you doing, Barnabas?"

"Okay," he said reflexively, but his voice was weak and shaky.

"You ready to go?"

"My backpack..." he murmured and she went to collect it. As they walked down the stairs together, he stuck close to her, feeling at least some comfort in the proximity of her strong, Valley-tall body. The police in their black armour were everywhere, and they were incredibly riled up, running and shouting more than seemed necessary. He and Blenbooly were challenged at every conceivable checkpoint, but each time she calmly produced a stamped sheet of paper on heavy stock, and as soon as each authority figure read it, they were allowed pass. Barnabas didn't even have it in him to ask what this amazing document said.

They emerged through the door onto the playing field. The crowd was being herded out in some well-rehearsed emergency procedure, and the stadium was already half empty. Blenbooly led him along the periphery of the field and then knocked at a metal door. It was opened by another Aqua guard, to whom she spoke quietly. When the man stepped aside, Barnabas saw Wickram standing there, looking perfectly cheerful, finishing off the last bites of another hot dog.

The tall boy ran out to greet him. "Hey, Barn! Did you see me on the big screen? Did you hear me play?"

Barnabas looked at the happy face, stained with mustard, and felt his own smile reboot. It was at that moment, he finally believed the danger was over. "Yeah! You were amazing."

"I utterly was. Ha! And now I'm not the skinniest bit scared for tomorrow's audition, you know?"

Lieutenant Blenbooly said, "Boys, this is Sergeant Trallergott. We all have to leave. Now." They were led through various secret passages deep in the stadium, down a big freight elevator and into a big garage at the base of Gumhill. There, they climbed into an unmarked, aqua-coloured SUV, and soon they were driving down an eerily deserted Grand Avenue, roadblocks shunting the usual traffic to a few brutally congested streets. Emergency vehicles blazed past from time to time with sirens screaming, and Barnabas asked, "But nothing happened, right? Other than the statue?"

Blenbooly smiled at him. "Nope. Thanks to you."

This somehow didn't make him feel any better, and he turned away to stare out the window. His beloved City looked different to him. All the great structures he had thought of as mighty and eternal now looked so fragile. And worse than that, what had been the best city in the world to him now seemed tainted by generations of secrets and lies.

The SUV took them to Admiral Crumhorn Station, where the boys were escorted into a windowless room. The two Aqua guards were joined by several City officials, who made Barnabas and Wickram relate everything they knew about Glower and his plan. When Barnabas told them about the explosives in the other towers, there was a great flurry of anxious discussion and urgent phone calls.

The interview went on for another two hours, and Barnabas felt like his mouth was just running on auto-pilot. He didn't even realize how hungry and dehydrated he was until Wickram, impressively confident given their situation, said, "Hey, if you're going to keep drilling Barn like this, you could at least get him a sandwich and a drink!" They did so.

There was a scary moment at the end. The City officials didn't want to release the boys even when Blenbooly showed her magic document, but after some impressive threats about the wrath of higher-ups, the boys were allowed to leave with the two Aquas. It was only when they were climbing back into the SUV that Barnabas considered how odd it was that the people he had been running from two days earlier were now his trusted allies. Not that he had much choice; there were no more daring escapes left in him. Blenbooly told him to call Deni and ask if he and Wickram could stay the night there. It seemed like a good idea, but later he wondered how she knew the details of his personal life.

When Deni opened the door and saw him, her face became strained with concern. It made him wonder just how bad he looked. Without a word, she pulled him inside the apartment and hugged him. She looked over his shoulder at Wickram and the Aqua guards standing in the hall and asked, "Are you, um, all coming in?"

"Just Wickram, ma'am," said Trallergott, and Wickram pushed past the hugging pair.

"Hey, Deni," he murmured. "I'm going to do a reconnaissance of the fridge."

Barnabas disengaged himself from Deni's arms and said to the guards, "Uh, thanks?"

"Our pleasure," Blenbooly said. "We'll be in touch soon," and she and Trallergott headed for the elevators.

Deni led him to the living room couch. "I'm not even going ask who those guys were. My moms are on their way home. The whole City's closing down for the day and everyone is freaking out. You were there, right? Like, in the middle of everything?"

"Yeah," was all he could say. "Mind if I lie down a bit?" Then he laughed quietly. "Every time I show up here, I just want to sleep."

Deni gave him a rueful smile. "Well, forgive me for being so dull."

"I could use a little dull in my life right about now," he mumbled, stretching out on the couch, and that was the last thing he remembered for a while.

His sleep was deep and dreamless, and coming out of it was unpleasantly vertiginous. Someone was shaking his shoulder and calling his name. "Barnabas, wake up, dear." He blinked and saw that it was Morgan, one of Deni's moms, the one who had made Deni into a Brownbag Bopwright fanatic. She was handing him a phone. "Deni told me she wants you boys to stay here tonight, but in that case, you need to talk to your poor mother right now! You've been putting her through hell, you know."

He looked up at Deni, who shrugged, which he knew meant, *Don't blame me.* Someone had put a blanket over him while he slept and it fell off his shoulders as he sat up and took the phone.

"Hello, Mom?"

"Bar...?" She only got one-third of his name out before she started sobbing. This reaction was so startling that he felt himself tear up too.

"Mom, don't! I'm fine." He didn't know what else to say, and just listened to her cry for a minute, feeling like he was a terrible son. From the direction of the bedroom, he could hear Wickram playing his guitar. The melancholy melody did nothing to make Barnabas feel better.

His mother pulled herself together enough to say, "I know, I'm ridiculous! But have you been listening to the news? They say that madman Glorvanious was going to blow up the whole Tower District!"

"I know. I mean, I heard that too."

"And... and... I just didn't know where you were! And whether he was taking care of you. I mean really watching out for you at a time like this."

"No, I'm great. There's no... Wait. Whether *who* was taking care of me?"

"Oh, Barnabas, I'm not a fool! I know you've been with your father for the last four days."

"What?! I wasn't with my father!" He looked over at Deni, who raised both hands, palms up, which meant, *I never told her, I swear on my Kurly Kuties collectibles.* Somehow, his mom and Deni had jumped to the same crazy conclusion. Was this a demonstration of the hold Brownbag Bopwright had on the imaginations of people who loved him?

His mother said, "I'm not blaming you, Barnie-lamb. Well, a little. You could have told me. Did you think I wouldn't have let you go?"

He found himself going along with her story like it had really happened. It almost felt like he wasn't lying. "Well, I did miss school, so yeah, you might not have let me..."

"I'm not the monster you think I am, Barnabas!" She shouted unexpectedly. "I want you to have a relationship with your father!"

"Mom! Did I *say* you were a —"

"Just please, promise me..." and she started crying again. "...you won't go live with him. I know how he makes everything feel like magic, but Barnabas, he can't offer you the stability we can. I know we had to move and money's been tight, but we're trying, really trying to give you a good life. And Björn, it means so much to him to be... like a father to you."

Despite how bad he felt for her, the conversation had steered so deep into the unbearable zone, he was close to ripping his own ears off just to escape. Exasperated, he cried, "Okay! I won't go away with him forever. I promise."

"When will we see you? I mean, this is practically kidnapping, Barnabas! You can tell him that for me."

"I'm not even with him tonight, okay? I'm back at Deni's, right? Morgan was the one who called you! And I'll see you tomorrow — right after school."

This seemed to placate her. Barnabas hung up with a huge sigh of relief. Deni's mom took the phone and left the room, chatting earnestly with Barnabas' mom about Glorvanious and mental health and security.

"Just tell me one thing, and then I'll leave you alone," Deni said, and Barnabas nodded. "If it weren't for you, would the towers be gone now?"

Barnabas considered his answer before speaking. He was getting confused about what constituted a secret and what didn't. He told her, "It wasn't just me. There was a whole bunch of people. Including you and Cal. So yeah, if it wasn't for us ..." They both sat in silence, feeling the weight of this fact settle on their shoulders.

The two parents and three kids prepared a big meal together. Their camaraderie in the kitchen and around the dinner table served to dispel some of the tension that was filtering in from the City outside. After dinner, Wickram performed the pieces he was going to play at his audition, and they all told him how beautiful it sounded. Nonetheless, Barnabas could clearly feel his friend's tension. He realized just how badly Wickram wanted this plan to work out.

Deni and her moms turned on the news at 10 and Barnabas watched a bit of it from a distance, standing in the doorway of the guest bedroom so he could escape if it got too freaky. The bomb squads had evacuated all the towers and were now removing the explosives. Other important City buildings and monuments were being checked and many would be closed for a few days. Mayor Tuppletaub appeared on screen, asking for calm heads in this time of tribulation. He assured all his citizens that they were safe, and that his administration was launching an investigation into the apparent failure of the GateKeeper System in the Tower District. He said that, for now, the election would proceed as planned, but if any delays were necessary, an announcement would be made as early as possible.

These words of reassurance (which made Barnabas feel literally ill) were followed by a profile on the life of George Glorvanious, which included various theories about where he had been for the past seven years. Already an urban myth was emerging that he'd been holed up all these years in the memorabilia room in the Manhammer Audio Dome, a crazy hermit, slowly crafting his revenge.

Barnabas stared at the man's face on the screen, and he could still hear the cold, logical voice in his head: "Self-interest is the only principle that governs people's actions. Beyond that, any appearance of concern is a lie."

This terrible summation of the human race filled him with hopelessness. He said good night to Deni and her moms and went into the bedroom, where Wickram was already in the bed, reading a big coffee-table book about jazz musicians from the 40s. Barnabas stripped to his t-shirt and briefs and climbed into bed, murmuring goodnight to his friend, pulling the blankets over his head. He begged his brain to turn off, to shake itself loose from Glower's dark words and embrace oblivion, but he was scared that despite his fatigue he wouldn't be able to sleep.

That was when Wickram said, "Hey, Barn. I wanted to say… thanks. Everything was going to hell in my life before you showed up last week. And now look: the City's safe and maybe I'm gonna move here."

"It wasn't just me," Barnabas said, almost in a whisper. He pulled his head free of the blankets, rolled over, and saw Wickram looking down at him, backlit by the bedside light.

"Oh, I know that. If I hadn't come along with you, this whole enterprise would have been fiz in a slizpot." He smiled gleefully. "Just think how proud they're gonna be of us back in Pastoral Park."

Barnabas thought of the circus people, who had risked so much to help. He thought of Cal and Deni, and the tall, crazy boy next to him. Then he thought of Glower, a man with no friends, no company but his dreams of revenge, and he thought how rich with friends he himself was in comparison. Barnabas felt his heart grow lighter. He returned Wickram's smile, and the effort was enough to finally send him tumbling backward into slumber.

CHAPTER 37

The next morning, Barnabas sat in a plastic chair outside a room marked "Ensemble B" in the Dieter Wieder Academy of Music. The whole building seemed thick with music that seeped through the walls, the ceiling, the floor, like a glorious soup of voices, horns, drums, and strings. Wickram had been inside the room for more than 15 minutes, and though there had been a lot of playing at the beginning, Barnabas hadn't heard the sound of guitar for a while. He was as nervous now as Wickram had been when they arrived.

He went back down the hall to talk to the Secretary in the office, who seemed to have picked out a blouse too small for her. "Will the audition take much longer?" he asked her, trying to keep his eyes on her face.

Without stopping her typing, she said, "Your friend's still in there? That's a good sign!"

"Yeah? I hope so."

The Secretary looked around to make sure they were alone, and they bent their heads closer as if by mutual agreement. She said, "So, that little guy who set up the audition — Falstep? Right? — Do you know him pretty well? Is he a serious guy or a player? You can be honest."

Barnabas didn't know what to say. "He's actually pretty funny…"

"That's not what I meant."

"Well, he doesn't live in the City," he told her. "But if I see him, I'll tell him you say hi."

She cleared her throat and he saw her face had gone a little red. "Right, thanks. So, um, you're the contact when we have news for..." She checked the name on her screen. "...for Wickram?"

"Yeah. I put my name and number on the form."

"Perfect. Oh, look: they're done."

Barnabas turned to see Wickram leave the room, accompanied by an older man with long, unkempt grey hair who closed the door behind them. Wickram was crouching a bit to bring his head level with the man's, and they remained in serious conference for a minute before the grey-haired man shook Wickram's hand and returned to the room.

When Barnabas approached him, Wickram was standing stock still, holding his guitar by the neck like a dead chicken someone had just handed him. The expression on his face kind of frightened Barnabas, who asked, "Are you okay?"

Wickram seemed to register his presence only then. He looked down and said, "Let's get out of here." Without a word of explanation, he turned and ran down the hall toward the stairs. Barnabas grabbed his backpack and raced after Wickram, who had already vanished into the stairwell. By the time Barnabas reached the front doors of the school, Wickram was at the far end of the patchy lawn, standing on a bench, hugging his instrument.

Breathless from the run, Barnabas looked up at his friend and said with trepidation, "What happened?!"

Wickram looked down at him, wide-eyed and said, "I'm in!"

"Really?"

Wickram jumped down and hugged Barnabas awkwardly with the guitar in between them. "It's not official," he said. "They have to inform me when they tell everyone else in next year's class, but Mr. Gileppsy — he's the head of composition — told me to go ahead and move to the City!"

Wickram threw his hands in the air, and that seemed to be the signal for both of them to begin jumping around like the ground had become a trampoline. Wickram started strumming big happy chords on the guitar, and Barnabas led them to a nearby park, where he bought them celebratory ice creams from a snack truck. Soon they were sitting in the grass, just basking in the joy of the moment. Barnabas had a strange thought: what if all the struggle they had gone through wasn't about Glower and his madness, or about the politicians, afraid of their own responsibilities?

For a few minutes at least, he decided to believe that the last few days had all been about giving Wickram this gift of a new life. He wondered if it was possible to live your life that way, saying "screw you" to the darkness and embracing the good parts instead.

"What now?" Wickram asked, looking up at banks of big white clouds crossing the sky from east to west like invading castles.

"Now you call your aunt."

"Huh? Oh, yeah, right." He looked a little nervous. "She doesn't even know me, Barn. Do you think she'll be glad to hear the news?"

He handed Wickram the phone Deni's parents had lent him and said, "Only one way to find out."

Wickram was uncharacteristically awkward talking to Sanjani's sister. As soon as he could, he handed the phone back to Barnabas, so she could give him directions. Thirty-five minutes later, they arrived in front of an old apartment building that probably dated back to the middle of the last century. It had a kind of faded elegance that Barnabas found appealing. The wallpaper and chairs in the lobby were tattered and worn, but they hadn't lost their dignity.

They took the elevator to the twelfth floor and walked down the dim corridor to a heavy door that swung open enthusiastically before they could knock. The woman looked so much Sanjani that Wickram gasped. On closer inspection, Barnabas could see she was younger, shorter, plumper. There was also something different about her eyes — a kind of unspoiled clarity that in Sanjani's eyes was misted over with wariness. When you looked at Sanjani, you wished you could make her laugh more. Not so with Kareena. Her smile was electric, and her first reaction on seeing the nephew she had never met was to laugh with abandon.

"My goodness! Oh my! So tall! That is excellent. This family has needed some height for many generations." She stood aside and ushered them in with a big, exuberant wave.

The apartment was more modern than Barnabas had expected — full of colour and shining chrome. He kind of thought it too would be frozen in the past the way the lobby was. Kareena, meanwhile, was busy hugging Wickram like he was an oversized stuffed toy she had just won at the carnival midway. Over her head, Wickram shot Barnabas a slightly panicked smile. Kareena brought them glasses of cola and a plate of chips, and they sat down in the living room to talk. She was absolutely delighted that

Wickram would be coming to live with her, and hearing this, he seemed to relax a bit.

"I have some leftover spaghetti for lunch; I hope that's okay with you. If I had known you were coming, I would have prepared something special. Something Indian! Does your mother ever make *aloo gobi* for you? That was her favourite."

"No, I've never eaten Indian food."

Kareena put a hand to her chest as if in shock. "What is my big sister thinking? That is part of your heritage, young man! I will stuff you full of paneer, hot pickles and vindaloos when you live here."

They talked about Sanjani, about Tragidenko and the circus. Kareena didn't seem to know about the Valley, and just thought that the circus was in some distant town and that Sanjani didn't want her to visit. For the first time, the smile died on her face and Barnabas saw the pain of the divided family.

Wickram looked around. "So, this is the same place Mom grew up, right? Wow. When did your mother — my grandmother, I guess — die?"

"Oh, Mommy died so long ago! Fifteen years I guess it is. That's her in the silver frame there." Kareena shook her head as if she was annoyed at the woman. "She looks so serious in that picture, but she wasn't like that at all! You could never convince her to smile for pictures. We begged her; even tickled her."

"And… her husband? When did he go?"

Barnabas thought this was an odd way for Wickram to speak of his grandfather, and he noticed how stiff he had become.

Kareena looked surprised, then embarrassed. She lowered her head, straightening magazines on the coffee table in front of her. "Well, he's not gone, Wickram dear. He's still with us — thank God, right?" She looked over at a closed door.

Wickram froze. "He's here? In this apartment? Now?!"

"Yes, of course. I take care of him; he has no one else."

Wickram jumped to his feet. "I-I can't stay here. Sorry. Barn, come on." He turned and almost ran to the door.

"Wickram, please!" Kareena shouted, jumping to her feet. "Where are you going?!"

Barnabas saw that scary, angry face appear, the one Wickram could whip out like a concealed weapon when provoked. He shouted, "That man is a monster! He hurt my mom, and I… I don't know what I'll do if I have to meet him. Do you really expect me to live here after the way he treated her? I don't know why you would take care of him!"

Kareena stood very still. Her eyes were wet, but her mouth was tight with anger. "My nephew, I don't know what my sister told you, so I cannot comment on it. Yes, there were bad times here, especially for her. Things happened that should not have happened. But just remember, your mother left — and left me here alone to care for our parents. You don't know me, and you don't have the right to judge me for my decisions."

Wickram was standing with one tense hand on the doorknob of the apartment. Barnabas could see that he was listening, but he didn't move or speak. Kareena went to him and reached out her own hand, which, after a moment, he took.

"Come," she said. "Come and meet your grandfather. You're named for him, you know. He is Vikram. Come, nephew, trust me." She turned and looked at Barnabas. "You, too."

She knocked twice on the closed door at the side of the room and then opened it, motioning them to follow. The room was dark and hot and smelled unpleasantly sour. There was a hissing sound and Barnabas saw, in the dimness, that it came from an oxygen tank. Kareena crossed the room and opened the drapes.

"Bapu, I'm going to open the window and let in some nice fresh air. It is warm out today." Light filled the room and Barnabas saw the shrunken figure in the bed, the oxygen mask on his face. His grey hair was in disarray, and his eyes were unfocussed and cloudy.

Wickram moved cautiously to the bedside as if drawn against his will. Kareena walked to the other side of the bed and said, "Bapu, this tall boy is Wickram. He is Sanjani's son."

Barnabas saw comprehension sweep across the old man's face, and he slowly raised a withered hand toward his grandson. Wickram flinched back a little, but he had nothing to fear from that hand; the old man didn't even have the strength to lift it more than halfway before it dropped to the bed again. Wickram said nothing. He just stared — without anger, without sympathy, just confusion. He turned and rushed out of the room.

Kareena smiled at her father. "You'll see him later, Bapu. He's a good boy. A talented musician like Uncle Abhi. I'll be back in a minute to take you to the bathroom, okay?"

Barnabas looked around the room. The man in bed, broken and helpless, seemed barely human, but this was the room of a real person, filled with mementos of a full life. Hanging prominently on the wall was what must have been his wedding picture, he and his new bride looking young and startled. It was a traditional Indian wedding. Hindu? Barnabas tried to remember what he had learned in his Cultural Panorama class. Kareena touched him on the elbow, and they left the room together.

Wickram was quiet until lunch, but then Kareena managed to cajole and joke him out of his funk. They talked about family memories, and Wickram told her more about his parents and their life together. The boys gave each other covert glances as Kareena brought up the matter of the "monster Glorvanious," and how the world was just not a safe place anymore. Then she had a lot of questions about Falstep, with whom, Barnabas could see, she was a little smitten. He thought of the secretary at the music school and wondered if the clown could reveal to him his secret power over women.

At around 2 o'clock, there was a knock at the door. Kareena, surprised, rose and answered. Behind it stood Lieutenant Blenbooly and Sergeant Trallergott in their Aqua uniforms. "Yes?" Kareena said with evident wariness.

"Ma'am," said Blenbooly. "We're here for Barnabas and Wickram. They need to come with us."

Kareena looked at the boys, and then turned back to say curtly: "I'm sorry, who exactly are you? I don't recognize your uniforms. Do you have some kind of identification?"

Wickram jumped to his feet and came to the door. "Wait, don't worry, Aunt Kareena, I'll talk to them. Hi, where are you taking us?"

Blenbooly said, "Please, don't be alarmed. We're instructed to escort you back across the Frontier to Pastoral Park. And I'm afraid we're on a deadline."

Barnabas stood up but didn't go to the door. "And what about me? Why do I have to come with you?"

"The President of the Guild Council has asked to speak with you. Then you will spend the night in Pastoral Park and return to the City on the morning train. I've been told to assure you that your presence is entirely voluntary , though it would be appreciated."

Kareena, alarmed, put her arm through Wickram's. "I don't understand! My nephew doesn't have to go anywhere with you!"

But Wickram turned and hugged her. "It's okay, these folks are from home. Thanks for lunch, Aunt Kareena. I'm... I'm really happy I'll be living here with you next year."

"Oh, Pickle," she said, wiping away a tear. "I just met you and you're already leaving." She pulled away, but held onto his arms. Looking up into his face, she said, "Tell my sister I love her and that I hope she knows I am still waiting for her. Every day."

Barnabas and Wickram left with the Blenbooly and Trallergott. The City was more or less back to normal today, but there were still streets blocked off and armed soldiers standing guard in front of buildings. They rode the same vehicle they had the day before, and again to Admiral Crumhorn station, but this time, instead of being ushered into an interrogation room, they headed for the secret subway station behind the regular one, and boarded a train to the Valley.

CHAPTER 38

"Hang on tight!" Wickram shouted over the wind.

Barnabas didn't need to be told. They were in the open back of an Aqua Guard transport truck that was racing away from the Valley train station at high speed. It took hardly anytime before the truck was bumping up the steep winding road to Pastoral Park, and Barnabas realized that the Valley wasn't actually all that large — not when you traversed it in a truck instead of a mule cart. They screeched to a halt in the parking lot, sending up a shower of gravel. Wickram immediately leaped over the edge of the truck bed and began running toward Maestro Tragidenko, who was standing in front of the main entrance of the Big Top. The Maestro threw his arms open, and his son fell right into them, accepting a surprisingly long hug.

Barnabas was about to climb down and join them when Blenbooly stepped out the passenger door and said, "No, stay there, please. We're taking you right to the Guild Council building." Barnabas was about to object, but then, to his immense relief, the immense form of Dimitri Tragidenko crossed the parking lot and climbed up into the back of the truck with him.

"I am accompanying the young man," he told Blenbooly, who appeared on the verge of objecting to this plan. But Tragidenko had already seated himself and clicked the seat-belt in place. "He is my guest in the Valley, yes? And his parents — even if they do not know this — are counting on me to keep him safe. We can go now," he announced as if he was in charge of the operation. Barnabas hid his smile.

They hardly spoke as the truck drove with the same, terrifying speed along the road around Lake Lucid, perhaps because of the howling wind in the their ears, perhaps because the Maestro still made Barnabas kind of nervous. At one point, Tragidenko squinted up at the cloudy sky and shouted, "It will rain later. Hopefully we are back by then, already dining deliciously at Pastoral Park."

Barnabas and Tragidenko entered the Hall of Deliberations. Barnabas had expected the full Council to be in attendance around the horseshoe table, but inside he found only Council President Borborik, sitting in his seat behind the raised front desk, and to his right, a Councilwoman Barnabas remembered from the meeting. A clerk instructed Tragidenko to take a seat on the benches at the back of the hall, while Barnabas was ushered forward.

"Welcome back, young Bopwright," said the President as he approached. "This is Councillor Ix-Navim of Forming Guild. She is Deputy President of the Council and Chief Liaison to the City. We requested your presence here so we might ask you some questions and discuss the future. Your future." This sounded ominous, and Barnabas sat down in a chair that had been placed in front of them.

From the back of the room, Tragidenko called out in his best Ringmaster's voice: "And I will be back here. Watching."

Ix-Navim pushed her glasses up on her nose and studied a sheaf of papers that lay in front of her on the desk. "This is the statement you gave yesterday following the incident at the Manhammer Audio Dome as well as various police reports." She looked up at Barnabas, and they sat staring at each other for an uncomfortably long moment before she continued: "First of all, on behalf of the Guild Council and the denizens of the Valley, we must thank you for your bravery." Barnabas looked at President Borborik, who nodded gravely.

Barnabas felt himself blushing. "Um, I'm just really glad it worked out. Can I ask something? Did you ever catch Carminn?"

"The former Speaker of Clouding Guild remains a fugitive," said the President.

"May she rot," Tragidenko commented from the back of the room.

Borborik looked pained. "Dimitri, if you could please allow us to —"

"Sorry, esteemed Mr. President, grave apologies. I did not realize I had spoken aloud."

Barnabas asked, "Aren't you afraid that she'll just try to do the same as Glower?"

"No. Her followers have been arrested, her steam elevator deactivated. Glower would not have been able to accomplish as much as he did without his knowledge of the City and his association with the Mayor. Carminn has no such knowledge or connection. We will find her eventually and bring her to justice."

This unresolved threat lodged itself in Barnabas' chest as another little ache he would carry for many years. It would wake him at night, along with the feeling that his apartment building was falling, falling into the abyss.

Borborik cleared his throat and said, "In retrospect, we feel that Council might have been reacting with too much caution when you brought us your concerns. Understandably, we were caught off guard by the severity of your news."

Caution, Barnabas thought. He came to close to saying: *You tried to throw me in jail instead of stopping Glower. I guess you could call that "caution."* But he kept his mouth shut.

Ix-Navim pushed the papers aside and said, "You have our eternal gratitude, and we offer you free passage out of the Valley tomorrow. Our trust is not generally so easily earned, but you have demonstrated exceptional character for one so young."

Just then, the doors of the Council chamber opened again, and they all turned to watch an old woman with a cane enter and walk slowly down the centre aisle. An Aqua hovered just behind, ready to catch her should she fall, but there was nothing in the purposeful gait that suggested anything less than steadiness and resolution. The old woman was Summer Coomlaudy, the Prime Prelate.

Barnabas, startled to see someone from the City here, just stared with mouth open as she circled round the front desk and took a seat to the other side of President Borborik. The President and Councillor Ix-Navim were standing and continued to do so until the old woman was seated.

Without acknowledging the Councillors, Summer Coomlaudy looked down at Barnabas and said, "Mr. Bopwright, I had not thought we would meet again, much less here in the Valley, but these have been days of exceptional circumstance." He wasn't sure if he was supposed to answer, so he only nodded. She continued, "We believe you have a bright future, and if you allow us, we wish to help you fulfill it."

Barnabas sat up straighter in his chair. "What do you mean?" Pause. "Ma'am?"

She smiled, but there was something in the smile that Barnabas wasn't sure he trusted. "The system of secrecy put in place by Lawrence Glorvanious and his associates all those years ago has been a great success." She looked over at her Valley colleagues. "Wouldn't you agree?"

Ix-Navim, with a reverential air, said, "It has brought prosperity to the City and allowed the Valley to fulfill its holy role undisturbed."

"Just so," said the Prime Prelate. "Obviously, we believe this system must be maintained for the good of all."

"Ahhhrrrmm-hemmm," said Tragidenko, and Barnabas turned to look at him.

President Borborik said, "Maestro, is something wrong?"

"No, no! Just clearing my throat," he said politely, but there was something less than friendly in the way he returned the President's stare.

"As I was saying," Coomlaudy continued, "In order to maintain the balance, we need to have a very small number of bright and capable people in charge of relations between the two realms. You have met most of them in recent days — our triumvirate in the City and my two esteemed colleagues here."

"What does this have to do with me?" Barnabas asked warily, feeling like he was talking to a telemarketer.

Borborik turned on a warm smile that didn't make Barnabas feel any warmer than Coomlaudy's had. "It has everything to do with you!" he said. "We hope that you will consider a life path that would someday put you in our unique company."

The Prime Prelate said, "We are talking about amazing educational and career opportunities. There are specific courses in civics and city planning at some fine institutions that we would like you to consider in a few years. And we can guarantee you admission to these elite programs, help you with tuition. We know that your parents might not be in a position to afford such schools."

How do you know that? he wanted to ask. He felt he should be smiling, grateful, but there was something strange about the offer. What did these people know about him and his abilities? Why would they be making promises like this to a high school freshman?

"That's... very generous," he said cautiously. "I don't really know what I want to do after high school." He thought of the posters on his wall — the film director, the mountain climber.

"We see how competitive your world has become," said President Borborik. "You probably won't get a better offer than this!" It felt vaguely like a put-down. Did they know about his less-than-stellar grades, just as they seemed to know his family's finances?

Summer Coomlaudy leaned forward, her smile fading, her eyes pinning him to the back of his chair like an insect she was mounting for her collection. "Of course, this opportunity would require a lot from you, primarily your ability to keep a *secret*." She paused and let the word sink in. "And that secrecy would have to begin now. Do you understand?"

Three sets of staring eyes bore into him. "Oh," he mumbled, "Yeah, of course. I wasn't going to tell anyone about... the Valley or... Glower or... whatever." Summer Coomlaudy leaned back in her seat as if relieved by his words.

President Borborik nodded gravely. "I'm glad to hear that. Because you need to understand the weight of responsibility your knowledge places on you, Young Bopwright. Telling anyone — *anyone* — what you have seen would not do *anyone* any good. Including yourself."

Ix-Navim nodded. "Exactly. Think of your bright future."

"Aaaaaa-hrrrmmmm-hemmrrr," Tragidenko growled, and Barnabas, Borborik and Ix-Navim all jumped.

The Prime Prelate banged a hand on the desk in front of her. "Who is that man, Borborik? What is he even doing here?"

The President barked, "What is it now, Dimitri?!"

Tragidenko rose and walked to the front, his heavy footsteps echoing in the empty hall. The size of his personality seemed to cause the Councillors to shrink as he approached , though Coomlaudy just glared at him. "Oh, nothing," he said. "I must have dropped off into a lovely little slumber. Your words... they startled me back to reality." He was standing behind Barnabas' chair now, and the boy felt a big warm hand fall on his shoulder. "So, perhaps you are done thanking this brave boy for his work of valour, and I might take him back to Pastoral Park. A feast is awaiting us, and you know how it disappoints the chefs if their culinary marvels dry out in the oven, yes?"

There was a long pause. Borborik looked down at Barnabas and said, "Just as long as the boy understands everything we have said here."

"Sure," Barnabas answered. And then, "Thank you. I'll think about it. All of it."

Summer Coomlaudy made a single percussive tap with one lacquered nail and said, "We'll keep in touch." Barnabas got to his feet and followed Tragidenko toward the door.

Just before they exited, the President called out, "Maestro! While we recognize the circumstances that led you and the people of Pastoral Park to break so many laws in the past days, we can't help but feel that this would be a good time to make some adjustments. We would like to implement a yearly review of the circus and the role it plays in the Valley. We cannot forever be guided by the decisions of the past, can we, my friend?"

Tragidenko raised himself up like a the dominant lion of the pride considering a challenger. He exhaled loudly through his nose and said, "No — my friend — we cannot."

They sat across from each other in the truck on the way back to Pastoral Park, and Barnabas found himself watching Tragidenko's face. The man's arms were folded across his chest, and he seemed to be looking out over some vista in his mind, considering the past or the future. He was not, it seemed, pleased by the view. After a while, Tragidenko noticed him looking and smiled warmly, patting the seat beside him. Barnabas unbuckled his seat belt and joined him.

"I hate this noisy transport," the man said to him, shouting a bit over the wind and the roar of the engine. "Give me instead the musical clip-clop of our dear mules, with the occasional aromatic *plop* behind for counterpoint, yes?"

"I guess this is faster."

Tragidenko sighed, "Yes, faster. So, what do you think of what our esteemed Councillors told you?"

"It was a pretty generous offer, the tuition and all. I mean, my mom will be over the moon although I'm not sure how I'm supposed to explain it to her."

"Secrets… I am thinking they are ugly little bunnies. They spend all their time just making more ugly little secrets."

"But sometimes they're necessary, right? President Borborik and, uh, Councillor Ix-Navim were right, weren't they? The system has been a really great success, and part of that is keeping the Valley secret from the people in the City."

"Yes, but how long before another Carminn or Glower wishes to change the balance? If not for the secret, would their plan have had a chance? Those bunnies, I am thinking, have grown uglier with time."

Barnabas felt an uncomfortable flutter in his chest. "Are you saying that I *shouldn't* keep the secret?"

"Look out there. Lake Lucid; it used to be so beautiful. I suppose if no one speaks of what was lost, the next generation can live in blissful ignorance. Is such a secret, then, a kindness? Or is it a blindfold?" Tragidenko threw his hands in the air. "Who am I tell the boy who saved the City what he should do, what he should not do? Bah! I have my own problems, Barnabas. You will have to do what your heart tells you."

"My heart is confused."

Tragidenko smiled. "I understand. But perhaps you just need more practice in listening to it. To really listen to your heart, it is like learning to juggle. It takes many hours of quiet persistence and the belief that the result will be worth the effort."

Barnabas thought about this, and he sort of got what the man meant. But instead of asking for clarification, he said, "President Borborik is pretty mad at the circus. Do you think you'll be okay?"

Tragidenko sighed. "What can you do but prepare for the next show and hope there's an opening night?" A mischievous look crossed his face and he leaned closer to Barnabas, almost whispering in his ear. "Sometimes… sometimes I think what it would be like if a tiny group of us — Sanjani, Falstep, some tumblers, an aerialist or two — just hit the road. A caravan of three or four wagons, travelling the forgotten highways of the world, visiting all the hidden places where there is a still a breath of humanity, a taste for the old magic. And we would pull into a parking lot and jump out, shouting "Tragidenko's Travelling Troupe! Here to bring you the ancient, revered arts of the circus, the wonders forged not by factories and committees, but by the human body, the human imagination. Lay aside your worries, ladies and gentlemen, and experience an hour or two… of grace!"

The light of this vision gleamed in his eyes for several more seconds, and Barnabas held his breath as if he could see the show, clearly see the wonder of it as it unfolded from the wagons, turning some mundane field or parking lot into a province of marvels. But then Tragidenko sighed again and looked out across the landscape, and the vision was gone.

The truck began to climb the hill to Pastoral Park.

CHAPTER 39

Barnabas and Tragidenko scrambled down from the truck in front of the Big Top. Lieutenant Blenbooly rolled down her window and said, "Barnabas, you have a 7:00 am train tomorrow, so I'll be picking you up here in the parking lot at 6:15. Be ready."

"Okay," Barnabas said and turned his back on her, walking with Tragidenko around the Big Top. Just a couple of hours ago, he would have said "Yes, ma'am" and been a bit more polite. But now, he was starting to feel weird about all the so-called authorities that were telling him what to do — that maybe wanted to tell him for the next decade of his life. Or maybe forever.

As they rounded the great tent, Barnabas saw Wickram running their way, his face in its "Angry-Wickram" mode.

"When were you thinking of telling me about Mom?!" he yelled at his father.

Tragidenko immediately got defensive. "Barnabas and I were in a rush! They were waiting for us at the Guild Hall! The President himself!"

"And that was more important than your wife's concussion?!"

They were standing nose to nose now. Tragidenko threw his hands in the air. "This was not news, my son! She has been in bed two days; the doctor says she will be fine!" He poked a finger into Wickram's chest. "While you were playing around in the City, it was I sitting by her poor side, spooning into her excellent broths made by my own hands for her betterment!"

Barnabas interrupted them, concerned. "What happened to Sanjani?"

Wickram said, "It was Carminn. She was there at the bridge after we crossed. They fought, and Mom's head got split open!"

Barnabas was speechless. He couldn't imagine slim, small Sanjani tangling with the powerful form of Carminn.

"Come on, Barn," Wickram said. The anger had fallen from his face, leaving only his worry. "She wants to see you."

Sanjani, her head bandaged artfully, sat up carefully in her bed. Wickram immediately pushed an extra pillow behind her back. "Pickle, stop acting like I'm about to die. I'll be fine in a day or two; Doctor Starbrott said so."

"I was so dumb!" Wickram whined miserably. "I should have realized Carminn was coming after us."

"We were all improvising that day. Who knew the old woman wouldn't let me cross the bridge with you? Who knew Carminn was around? Now hush!" She smiled warmly at them. "In the end, we all did our part. Look at my brave boys! You saved the City. I knew you would." She put one hand on Wickram's shoulder and the other on Barnabas' hand.

Barnabas said, "Did you hear we met your sister? She's really nice."

"Wickram told me! It's a strange world... I haven't seen Kareena in almost 20 years, but you just talked to her this afternoon." Her eyes filled with tears, and she brushed them away impatiently, forcing her smile back in place. "Pickle, I'm so glad you're going to be living with her while you go to school."

Wickram pulled away from his mother's touch. "If I go to school," he said, sulking.

Sanjani glared at him. "Oh for heaven's sake, Wickram! Are you planning to lock me in the house and stand guard outside in case Carminn returns? Of course you're going!"

Soon, he and Barnabas were walking down the street away from the house, and Wickram said, "I told her about her father, but she didn't want to talk about it. Do you think she'll be okay, Barn?"

"I don't think she was lying, if that's what you're asking. She's fine, Wickram."

"Cause I really want to go." The words had come out in a breathy rush. "To the music school. To the City." He looked around at the narrow streets of Pastoral Park. "Have you noticed just how krumping *small* this place is? I sort of never realized before."

They turned into the central square just as the sun slipped below the low ceiling of dark cloud that had been hiding it all afternoon. It would soon set, but for that little period, the world was tinted in reds and golds. And in that magical light, Barnabas saw that the Dining Hall had been decorated in spectacular fashion. Ranged across the ledge of the roof was a reproduction in cardboard of the buildings of the Tower District. Across the front of the building hung bright red letters that proclaimed, "Bravo to Barnabas and Wickram!!"

Barnabas hardly had time to register his embarrassment when he and Wickram were surrounded by well-wishers. Barnabas found himself shaking a lot of hands and trying to answer a thousand questions at once. They were swept into the dining hall, where they ended up, thankfully, sitting with circus kids, who treated them with some welcome sarcasm.

"Excuse me, Mr. Bopwright," said Huro. "Is it true you cured cancer with only an old onion and some scraps of twine?"

Buro shoved a dinner roll in front of Barnabas. "Could you sign my bread, please?"

At that moment, Garlip arrived and elbowed Buro out of the way to take the seat beside Barnabas. He felt a rush of pleasure as she smiled at him, and he asked, "Are you responsible for the decorations outside?"

"Yeah, been working on it since first thing Sunday morning."

Both of them blushed simultaneously, but Wickram leaned over and said, "Good thing you succeeded, Barn. Would have been kind of embarrassing otherwise." He looked around and said, "Where's Graviddy?"

Thumbbutter said, "Her rehearsal is running late. She'll be here soon."

"Rehearsal? This is a special occasion!" He looked hurt, and Barnabas remembered her promise of a special greeting for Wickram if they returned victorious.

But at that moment, Falstep showed up with a little entourage of clowns. He shoved a bunch of flowers at Barnabas. "Congrats!"

Barnabas leaned back warily. "Are these going to squirt me with water or something?"

"No!" the clown said, offended. "But they are a hat!" He plopped the arrangement gracelessly on Barnabas' head, and sure enough, the colourful blooms were built around a little cap. "You have to wear that all evening or you will offend the entire clown community," Falstep said with great solemnity.

The clown turned to Wickram. "So, all my efforts weren't wasted? You got into the school?"

Wickram leaned back in his chair, the soul of cool. "You bet."

Falstep snapped his fingers in the air like a Flamenco dancer. "You owe it all to me and my superior charm."

Barnabas said, "You're not kidding! Every woman we met wants to marry you."

Falstep adjusted his hat rakishly. "I'm not the marrying type, but let's just say, if I moved to the City, I wouldn't be hurting for company. Troops, move out!" he barked at clowns, and they followed him across the room to their usual table, all except Beaney.

"How was the City, Barnabas?" he asked with a grin.

"A little tense," Barnabas replied, and then saw who was standing behind the boy. He gave a happy cry: "Galt-Stomper!"

Glower and Greta's little assistant stuck out a shy hand and said, "Nice to meet you again, sir."

"Stomper didn't have anywhere to go after the Drop Shop closed," Beany enthused, "So we invited him to join the circus."

Galt-Stomper looked worried. "They say I have to learn to juggle, sir. I don't know if I can!"

Barnabas remembered Tragidenko's words to him. "It takes many hours of quiet persistence, Galt-Stomper. And the belief that the result will be worth the effort."

Dinner was served and the festive mood continued, aided by the bottle of elderberry wine that Thumbutter had snuck in and was secretly adding to her friends' juice glasses. Wickram alone refused her offer. "I just don't feel like it, okay?" he said.

People kept coming around to talk to Barnabas, and he was feeling kind of guilty. He couldn't help thinking that before he came to the Valley, the circus had been in a more secure position than they were now.

Just before dessert was served, the door of the Dining Hall flew open, and everyone turned to see Graviddy enter like a queen. Unlike the rest of the community, she was dressed in performance clothes — a shining white tunic with ruffled gold lapels, glittering pants and black boots. Her hair seemed to flow behind her as if caught by the wind as she crossed the room, straight to where Wickram was standing, and planted a long, passionate kiss on his startled mouth.

There were scattered cheers and Barnabas caught Tragidenko looking less than thrilled. When the kiss finally ended, Graviddy turned to the spectators and shouted, "Hail to the saviours of the City!" The toast was echoed back over raised glasses. Graviddy took the startled Wickram by the hand and led him back out the doors and into the dimming twilight. Barnabas thought his friend looked as scared as he was excited.

The doors had already swung closed when Tragidenko jumped to his feet and shouted, "You children! Come back!" but it was truly too late, and Whistlewort pulled him down into his seat and pushed a big glass of beer in front of him.

"They're not children anymore, Dimitri. Drink up," he said.

Despite how nice the party was, Barnabas was relieved when Huro, Buro, Garlip and Thumbutter escorted him out of the dining hall. The gang collected kerosene lanterns and headed out into the gathering night, eventually making their way to the forest. As they wound through the dark paths, the lanterns threw up looming shadows all around them.

Garlip said, "Do you feel the air? I think it's going to rain."

Thumbutter, clearing their path with a big branch said, "Stop worrying!"

They sat down by the river, not far from the stone bridge, and Barnabas told them the long version of their adventure, including the dark details of the end of George Glorvanious. They sat close together and grew quiet, feeling the weight of the tale, but enjoying the comfort of each other's company in the enclosing darkness of the forest.

It wasn't long before Wickram and Graviddy joined them, pressed tightly together, surrounded by their own warm aura. Barnabas felt a little jealous, both by the way Graviddy had taken all his friend's attention away, and because he was the immature kid again, the way he was around Deni and Cal. But then Garlip slipped her arm around his waist, and the situation seemed more promising.

"You know what we should do?" Thumbutter said, slurring her words a bit — she had managed to get more of the smuggled wine into her at dinner than any of them. "We should cross the bridge!"

Huro said, "Yeah, Barnabas, you and Wickram have already met the crazy witch, right? You can introduce us!"

Wickram said, "Hey! Quiet, she's probably listening!"

"But she's your friend now, right?" Buro asked.

Barnabas said, "I'm not sure I would call her our *friend*."

Wickram shook his head. "No way. I'm more scared of her than I was before. She was sharpening knives to go bear hunting when we met her."

Barnabas said, "I think she was just trapping rabbits, Wick…"

"Oh, that's what she *told* us, but I didn't believe it, man."

They fell silent, squinting into the darkness beyond the river, trying to figure out if they were being watched.

Garlip said, "Wouldn't it be flamtasmic if we did a set like this forest for one of the shows? The whole back wall could be giant tree, and the performers would swing from branches, fly out between leaves."

"A lot of sight-line problems," Huro said, and Buro added, "And really tricky to light."

"Well, tricky if we just use kerosene and reflectors," Graviddy said. "But if we used electric lights…"

Thumbutter sputtered wetly. "That can't happen, Graviddy! No electricity, remember? It's one of the principles this place is founded on." She sounded offended by the idea.

Graviddy tossed her hair. "But why does it have to be? Maybe it's time for a change. In a few years, we'll be the ones making the decisions around here."

The discussion devolved into a fight between Graviddy and Thumbutter, with Huro and Buro taking up both sides of the argument at different points. Wickram didn't get involved. Barnabas watched as he released his arms from around Graviddy and wrapped them around his own knees. Maybe it was sinking in that since he was leaving Pastoral Park, it wasn't his place to have an opinion.

Garlip, who had also remained a neutral spectator to the fight whispered in Barnabas' ear, "Want to go for a walk?" That was, in fact, exactly what he wanted. And it was sweet and thrilling to kiss her and feel her close against him among the trees, and though his body ached for more, there wasn't any clear path forward. Besides, it was enough for now. It was great, in fact. He knew that if they were up in the City, he would be giving her his phone number now. It frustrated him that there was literally no point in doing that.

Soon it was time to go, and the group left the forest together. Graviddy started singing a beautiful song that had been the theme of a show many years earlier. The melody was somehow both sad and joyous, and the others joined her in flawless three-part harmony. The words were about falling backwards with your eyes closed, trusting that your friends would be there to catch you. Barnabas smiled, but then suddenly the image of Glower's final moments filled his mind — backlit in the window of the Memorabilia Room, teetering above the fatal drop, falling backwards into nothing.

As they reached the village, the rain began, at first lightly, but then falling with gusto, making them scream with laughter and break into a run. At the crossroads, Huro, Buro, and the girls ran toward the dorm, shouting "Good night!" and "See you in the morning!" It was only when he and Wickram reached the house that Barnabas understood this wasn't true. He wouldn't see them in the morning. He wondered if he'd ever see them again.

CHAPTER 40

I t was morning. Everything was quiet in Pastoral Park, save for the gentle patter of rain on the roof. Barnabas, not quite asleep in his bedroll on Wickram's floor, was waiting for his alarm to go off. He wished he could just hang there, in this moment of peace, between all the craziness of the past seven days, and the uncertainty of the rest of his life. The alarm sound on the borrowed phone turned out to be a troop of monkeys, screeching in communal warning, which Barnabas hurriedly silenced. Wickram snorted and thrashed, but never woke from his deep slumber. Barnabas got up quietly and dressed. As he picked up his t-shirt from the floor, the rank smell of the sweaty garment hit his nose, and he decided on an alternate plan of action.

To his surprise, Sanjani was sitting at the kitchen table with a blanket wrapped around her, reading a book and sipping from a steaming mug. She smiled as Barnabas descended the stairs and said, "If I'm not mistaken, you're wearing my son's favourite piece of clothing."

Barnabas smoothed his hands across the oversized Bigmouth Grouper t-shirt. "Yeah, you'll have to tell him to come to the City or he'll never see it again."

"Excellent. Now he must decide whether to fuss like a hen over me or get his precious shirt back."

Barnabas sat at the table opposite her. "And go to music school."

"That too."

"Are you supposed to be out of bed?" he asked, a little concerned himself.

"Yes, yes, I'm fine." She stood and folded the blanket over the back of her chair. She was dressed as if she were ready to get back to work, clearly determined not to appear sick, but Barnabas noticed that she still moved a little cautiously. She asked, "Can I get you some bread and cheese? I have very good quince jam."

"Yes, thank you."

She brought the food to the table along with another mug of tea, and they ate together in silence. "The rain stopped," Barnabas said after a while.

"Yes. My garden got a good watering overnight." Sanjani put a hand on his. "I will miss you, young man."

"Me too. All of you. I hope I can come back some day."

"Perhaps you will, or perhaps we will all meet around my sister's table in a year. Or who knows? The brave and the desperate throw themselves into the sea of fate but don't always end up where they thought they would."

"Am I brave or desperate?" Barnabas asked her, and he meant it as a joke, but suddenly he wondered.

"Oh, young Mr. Bopwright, you are exceedingly brave."

He was about to make some lame joke to diffuse his embarrassment when someone knocked on the door.

Sanjani said, "Would you mind getting that?"

It was Lieutenant Blenbooly. Barnabas felt a little surge of annoyance. "I thought we were going to meet in the parking lot."

"Couldn't take the chance," she answered like he might be planning to hide out and remain in the Valley. He felt like telling her something rude in the colourful slang he had learned from Wickram.

Sanjani said, "Do you want me to call Wickram so you can say good-bye? Or Dimitri?"

Barnabas smiled. "I doubt you could wake Wickram up."

She laughed. "Dimitri is the same. I'll just tell your friend to come and collect his shirt soon."

Blenbooly was alone this morning, so Barnabas got to ride up front with her; good thing too, since the rain started again as soon as they were on the road. The food depot and train station were already hopping by the time they got there. Blenbooly escorted him through the crowd and put him on the 7 a.m. train, standing guard over him while the train stood in the station. Again, he felt annoyed by her lack of trust, but then he wondered if maybe he *should* try to escape; maybe he'd be happier living down in the Valley. Then the doors closed, and he was left with no option but return to his life.

At the Frontier, he showed the guards his transit documents and then crossed from one side of Admiral Crumhorn Station to the other. And that was that; he was out of the Valley, back from the secret into the mundane. As soon as he entered into the familiar crush of the morning rush hour, his borrowed phone found the network and alerted him to a new TxtChat message. It was from his brother, Thelonius and it had been sent about 15 minutes earlier.

TheLoneliest> Hey kid. u survive terror attack of ghost glorvanious?

He texted back:

Barnabustamove> yeh there's cops everywhere. like a war movie

He wondered if the enhanced police presence — they were positioned throughout the station, with their black riot gear and big guns — made the crowds feel safer. They certainly didn't make him feel safer; but then, he had more information than the rest of the citizenry.

Barnabustamove> getting on subway. VidChat 2night? @ 6:00?

It was still raining when he exited the subway, and he arrived at the school building a little damp. There was another hour before classes started, and the halls were eerily deserted. He could hear a choir practice happening in some classroom, but he saw no one and wandered the empty halls like a ghost haunting his own life.

Even when the school filled with students and teachers, he continued to feel like he wasn't really there. Everyone asked him if he was feeling better. One classmate asked if he had really been sick or it was something more interesting — like a short stay in a psychiatric ward. He laughed, but on the other hand, he did feel a little crazy. Had it all really happened? He felt like if he couldn't talk about the events of the week, he would start to doubt them himself. During lunch break, he looked in the bathroom mirror at the Bigmouth Grouper t-shirt for confirming evidence.

Deni and Cal stuck close to his side whenever they could, but kept the conversation trivial, and Barnabas suspected they had discussed this strategy in advance. He imagined her saying, "He's been through a lot! Don't bug him!'"

He was with Deni at lunch when his phone rang. "Hi, Mom. Yes, of course I'm coming home after school. Yes, straight home, I promise! What?

No, that's great. I'm looking forward to it. Yeah? She's right here, hold on." He put his hand over the microphone and said, "Deni, she's doing her big family dinner extravaganza thing tonight. She told me to ask you over."

"I have an Italian lesson after school, but I can be there by 6:45. Is that okay?"

He thought about asking his mom if Cal could come, too, but then a funny, troubling thought dropped from his brain into his chest, where it vibrated alarmingly. He decided not to invite Cal.

The reunion with his Mom after school was equal parts tears, scolding, and motherly manipulation, but Barnabas had grown wise enough during his time away to recognize it all as love. He was then ordered to his room to begin catching up on missed homework, while she and Björn took over the kitchen where they proceeded to make a shocking amount of noise and mess.

Two hours later, right on schedule, a VidChat alert chimed, and Thelonius appeared on the laptop screen. It was 6:00 a.m. in Japan, and Thelonius was getting ready for work. He was freshly shaven, wet hair combed back, blowing into a hot container of ramen he had just microwaved, stirring up clouds of steam with his chopsticks.

"I can't imagine what it's like there after yesterday," he said, and slurped down some noodles. "Is everyone curled up in a ball like they're about to be blown up?

"They can't stop talking about it, but they're more excited than scared, I think."

"Ha! Nothing stops the City."

Barnabas flopped back on his bed and began tossing the *diaboriku* from hand to hand. *Juggling 101*, he thought. He said, "So when are you coming home?"

"Well, my mom is visiting here in January, so maybe I'll try and see you guys at Christmas. I miss Carol, which you probably find hard to believe."

"Christmas? Flamtasmic!"

"Flam-*whatnow?*"

Barnabas smirked. "Just something we say. You've been away too long; you're out of the loop. What about Dad? Maybe he can come by at Christmas, too."

Something grew hard in Thelonius' eyes. "Don't get your hopes up. He'll probably be playing in the house band on some Caribbean cruise."

"But if we ask him now…"

"Take it from me, kid, don't let Brownbag too deep in your heart. He has a habit of breaking them."

A grey ache of loss and disappointment ground the conversation to a halt. The cameras on their laptops transmitted only the unseen image of their averted eyes.

Thelonius, his voice growing softer, finally asked, "So you figure out how to use the diaboriku yet?"

"Of course. It's easy," Barnabas replied, offended.

"Well, show it off to your friends while you have the chance. They're going to release them in the West next fall. Monsters everywhere!"

Monsters everywhere. Barnabas was instantly transported back to the Memorabilia Room, locked in with the madman, gasping in claustrophobic fear. And there was Glower, teetering on the window ledge, facing off against the monsters of his past. There… and then gone.

Thelonius gave him a funny look. "You okay, Beaner?"

Barnabas tossed the *diaboriku* back onto the bed and returned to his desk. "Yeah, I'm golden. I'm cinnamon toast. And don't call me 'Beaner.' Hey, guess what? I'm an Innervader now!"

"Shut up! Really?"

"Better than you were."

"Impossible. That would defy the laws of physics. Where did you infiltrate? Who were you with?"

Secrets, secrets. "I can't tell you. But it was utter sweet."

The door swung open, and his mom said, "Barnabas, I need you to go vacuum the living room rug."

"Mom! Try knocking first!"

From the laptop, Thelonius said, "Yeah, Carol, he might have been doing something embarrassing!"

"Thelonius, honey! How *are* you? Barnabas, vacuum! I'm going to talk to your brother for a minute."

"But we were already talking!"

"Go!"

Deni rang the doorbell right at 6:45, and Carol, back in the kitchen, dropped what she was doing and shouted, "I'll get it!"

She almost collided with Barnabas in the hall, and he said, "It's my friend, I'll answer the door."

His mother pushed ahead of him in the narrow hall. "Deni hasn't been here in forever; do you mind if I play hostess in my own home?!"

Barnabas came to huffy halt as his mother swung into the tiny foyer. He muttered, "You're just trying to impress her because you want her parents as contacts."

As his mom took her jacket and school bag, Deni looked around with a big smile. "The new place looks great, Carol. I was here back when everything was still in boxes."

His mom looked terribly pleased, but demurred, "Oh, it's so small. There's no room for any *visionary design*, you know? Not like your beautiful apartment." Barnabas rolled his eyes.

As dinner progressed, Barnabas grew more and more uncomfortable. He kept spacing out as he picked at his food, catching only dribs and drabs of the conversation so that it sounded like a patchwork quilt of trivia, politics, and hyperbole.

"To get into a really great program, your résumé is as important as your marks."

"Oh, I remember that day! You and Barnabas were so cute in your dinosaur costumes!"

"This morning, some of the parents were screaming at Ms. Rolan-Gong about security. Literally screaming."

Barnabas became aware of Björn keeping an eye on him, watching for signs of… something. His mother was just as obviously *not* watching him, which was actually another kind of attention. Barnabas knew what was up: after a week when their son had supposedly run away to his father, testing their limits as kids will do, they were trying too hard to act like nothing was up. His step-father, of course, knew from their encounter at the radio station that *something* was up , though he didn't know exactly what. But Björn could keep a secret. *Secret, secret,* everyone keeping *secrets,* high and low and in-between. A gummy despair filled his chest. He tuned back into the conversation and heard Björn talking:

"I interviewed the Acting Chief of Emergency Response this morning. They had over 900 police and firefighters at key spots in the City. It was a huge mobilization."

Carol touched her breast. "So much bravery!" she said, letting out a sigh of admiration. "The Mayor should have a parade for those people!"

Barnabas' mouth dropped open. *Where's my parade?* he almost shouted.

The towers hadn't fallen, Glower hadn't succeeded, and it was because of him! Then he felt stupid. He didn't save the City to become famous. And they congratulated him down in the Valley, right? But not in his own City. Not in his own family. He saw Deni looking at him, and she, too knew more than she was saying. She knew, at least, that if there was a parade, Barnabas should be somewhere near the front. *Secrets, secrets,* like fracture lines dividing the four people at the table, dividing City and Valley, dividing the powerful people in the know and the ordinary citizens who were kept in the dark.

"Can I be excused for a minute?" Barnabas said and got up without waiting for an answer. He hurried to his room and closed the door behind him, leaning against it while he tried to calm down. The greatest city in the world owed its success to secrets, he reminded himself. And just think about the future the Guild Council and the Prime Prelate had offered him! What a gift to his hard-working parents, who struggled everyday for him. But… but… what if their future wasn't the future he wanted? And what if Maestro Tragidenko was right about the ugly bunnies — multiplying everyday, trampling all over the truth.

He crossed to the window and looked out. Night had fallen and the City stood around him, a great organism of steel and flesh, its lights outshining the stars above. He knew the City — its people, its streets, its history. He knew it as well as he knew his own reflection in the windowpane, which was overlaid, ghostly, on the view. But he hadn't known everything, had he? Not before this week. He looked down at the crowds, pushing along under the streetlamps, and thought about their ignorance. He wondered how it served them. He considered all that had been chosen for them by men named Glorvanious, and by the people who maintained that legacy. Would the people of the City had made the same choices?

He, unlike those crowds, had a choice.

But who am I to choose? Barnabas Bopwright, age 15 asked himself. And the answer came to him: *I'm the one who was given the choice.* And maybe, in the end, that kind of randomness was all history came down to.

There was a knock on the door, and Deni said, "Can I come in?" He snapped on the lights guiltily like he had been doing something wrong, and opened the door. Deni entered, peering around curiously. "Your room looks good! Oh, and your mom says we should come out for dessert in 15 minutes. I think they're lighting it on fire."

"Oh, God. We should probably escape now while we still can."

"That's a new poster, right?" She walked over to examine the lone climber atop the snowy peak. "Dramatic. What does it mean to you?"

"Ugh, that is such a teacher question. I guess something about rugged individualism — conquering your mountain alone."

"Yeah, but he's not alone."

"What do you mean?"

"Duh, there's a photographer there with him. They climbed the mountain together."

This had never occurred to Barnabas. He stared at the poster, and it was suddenly a whole different story than he had thought. He shrugged. "Maybe I'm not a rugged individualist after all."

She laughed. "What are you, then?"

A sudden certainty, like a bold ray of sunshine, pierced the fog of his doubt. "I'm Barnabas, the Bunny Killer."

"What?!"

He was excited now. "What time do you have to be home?"

He saw Deni register his excitement. "I don't know. Late. It doesn't matter. Why?"

"I've got a story to tell you."

He could see she was trying to control herself — not let her imagination get the better of her. Still, she was a little breathless as she asked, "Good story?"

"Oh yeah," he said. "The best you ever heard."

The End

About the Author

photo: Emil D. Cohen

J. Marshall Freeman is a writer, musician, and cartoonist. He is a graduate of the University of Toronto, and a member of the Toronto Writers' Co-operative.

His previous novel, *Days of Becoming*, was in the realm of fanfiction, written under the name Talktooloose. The book can be found at: archiveofourown.org/users/Talktooloose

Upcoming work includes the young adult novel, *Copper in the Blood*, the novel, *The Release Party*, and the children's books, *Rhubarb's Double Life* and *Holly, Solly, and Blue*.

To read and view more of his work and to sign up for his email news list, please visit jmarshallfreeman.com.